RANDOM HOUSE

LARGE PRINT

ALSO BY IRIS JOHANSEN
Available from
Random House Large Print

Quicksand
Pandora's Daughter
Stalemate
Killer Dreams
On the Run
Countdown
Blind Alley
Firestorm
Fatal Tide
No One to Trust
Body of Lies
Final Target
The Delaney Christmas Carol
Dead Aim

DARK SUMMER

IRIS JOHANSEN

RANDOM HOUSE
LARGE PRINT

Copyright © 2008 by Iris Johansen Publishing LLP

Published in the United States of America by Random House Large Print in association with St. Martin's Press, New York.
Distributed by Random House, Inc., New York.

Cover Design by Jerry Todd

The Library of Congress has established a Cataloging-in-Publication record for this title.

ISBN: 978-0-7393-2755-5

www.randomhouse.com/largeprint

FIRST LARGE PRINT EDITION

10 9 8 7 6 5 4 3 2 1

This Large Print edition published in accord with the standards of the N.A.V.H.

DARK SUMMER

CHAPTER 1

Santa Marina Island

1:30 A.M.

"You're not going to find anyone, you crazy dog." Jude Marrok climbed over another pile of rubble, trying to keep up with the black Lab. "And I'm not going to keep on chasing after you. I'll give you fifteen more minutes. After that, I'm calling the helicopter."

Ned didn't even look back as he sniffed desperately at the remains of houses toppled by the earthquake. He was making soft, whimpering noises as he searched the ruins for life.

Marrok muttered a curse beneath his breath. Dammit, he should have taken the dog down to the main rescue area after they'd been dropped by the helicopter in the foothills. This side of the mountain had already been searched by the canine rescue teams.

When the volcano on this small Caribbean island had caused a 7.5 earthquake six days ago, it had devastated the two villages on both slopes of the mountain. The rescue teams had worked tirelessly on both villages, but after no one was found, they had abandoned this smaller village to concentrate on the one on the far side of the mountain. His dog, Ned, had refused to go to the other side of the mountain and insisted on going to the now-deserted village, and Marrok had gone along with him. Most of the time the Lab's instincts were pretty good, and it wasn't that unusual for him to find survivors after other rescue teams had abandoned hope. But they'd been searching for two hours, and Ned had not found any signs of life.

And the blasted dog wouldn't give up. The longer he searched, the more frantic he was becoming. He was whimpering now, and if he started barking, it could bring the soldiers who were guarding the ruins from vandals and looters. That couldn't happen. Jude hadn't had time to get papers when he decided to bring Ned to the disaster site. He'd put the usual Red Cross halter jacket on Ned, but the military would demand more proof.

Oh, what the hell. He'd worry about being thrown in the local hoosegow if it happened. After all, he'd brought Ned here to put a stop to the depression he'd noticed in him for the last few weeks, and he'd stay the course. The dog's depression used to be present only after he'd gone to a site and found nothing but the dead, but lately he always seemed to be waiting for any opportunity to make the attempt at rescue.

Ned had stopped at a heap of timber and turned his head to stare at him with pleading dark eyes.

"Okay, I'll take a look." He began to pull aside the debris. "But don't get your hopes up, buddy." He worked for fifteen minutes, and all the while Ned just sat gazing anxiously at him. "I told you. You know how many times it turns out that—" He stopped. "Shit."

Ned was whimpering, pressing close to his knees.

"Dead." The villager he'd uncovered was lying crumpled, his skull crushed. Poor bastard. "I told you. Now let's go to the other side of the mountain where we have a chance of finding—"

Ned lifted his head and howled.

"No." Marrok fell to his knees and put his

arms around the Lab. "Shhh, I know it hurts. Me, too. But you have to be quiet, Ned. We're not supposed to be here." Ned was whimpering again, but at least he wasn't howling any longer. He buried his nose against Marrok's chest. "We'll keep looking. You'll find someone alive. I promise." He hoped he was telling the truth. It was breaking his heart to see Ned grieving. He stroked the dog's head. "Come on. We'll go and join the rescue teams on the other side of the mountain. You can show those other dogs how smart you are."

And Marrok would be walking a tightrope and have to lie himself blue in the face if he was challenged by anyone. Well, it wasn't as if that would be unfamiliar territory. He had become an expert at both over the years. Ned was worth any amount of trouble he had to face. He got to his feet. "Let's go," he said gently. "No reason for staying here. We can't help him." He put a marker on the spot for body retrieval. "It will be better if we—"

Ned was no longer beside him. He was running across the rubble, his lean midnight-black body taut with eagerness. He had caught another scent, Marrok realized, and he was following it with reckless speed. It seemed the dog wasn't ready to obey him, he thought rue-

fully. It wasn't surprising since their relationship was that of close friends rather than master and canine. They had long ago passed that
point. "Okay, we'll go your way for a while."
He took off after Ned. "But you'd better be
right this time. I can't spend all night comforting you." But he knew he'd do precisely that.
You didn't question when a friend was in need.
He'd almost caught up with Ned, and the Lab
was staring at him hopefully. "Let's make a
deal." He started to bend to shift the debris.
"If we don't find anyone this time, you give it
up and do it my—"

A whistle of sound streaked by his cheek.

Ned cried out and fell to the ground, blood
pouring from his side.

A bullet, dammit.

Marrok fell sideways, grabbed Ned's collar,
and rolled with him behind the ruin of the
house.

Another bullet splintered the timber next
to Marrok as he pulled out his gun. It had
come from the direction of the trees to the
south of the site. Not the military. They
would have questioned him before shooting at
him. That Red Cross on Ned's halter would
have required it. His gaze searched the trees as
he moved to the side.

Another bullet.

One shooter and determined to make the kill.

Danner? Maybe. God, he'd hoped he'd sidetracked them in Morocco, but they must have uncovered his trail. The solution was the same as always. Kill the shooter. Disappear. It would take time for them to send someone else on his trail. But he couldn't leave Ned. The Lab was hurt and bleeding. He couldn't take time to go after the shooter. Not now. He had to stop Ned's bleeding and get him help.

He dodged two bullets while he dragged Ned farther behind the timbers. He sprayed a barrage of bullets at the trees before starting work to stop the bleeding. There wasn't much, thank God. Ned lay still, only whimpering occasionally. Marrok didn't think the wound was terminal, but he couldn't tell in the darkness. Anger exploded through him.

Come after me, you son of a bitch. Let me have my chance at you.

Shoot my dog? I'll tear your heart out.

But he could hear voices coming from the direction of the rescue site on the other side of the mountain. Someone had heard the shots, dammit. He wasn't going to get his opportunity to make the kill. The shooter wouldn't risk going after him and exposing himself to awkward questions. Danner didn't like questions.

He stroked Ned's head. "It's going to be okay. We'll get you fixed up. There's almost always a vet on these mercy missions." He glanced at the trees from where the bullet had come. It was only a postponement. The shooter wouldn't give up. He'd stick around and wait for another opportunity to take them out. Danner disliked failure almost as much as he did questions. "And then I promise I'll make sure that bastard never has another go at you."

Shit.

Kingston lowered his Remington, slid down the trunk of the palm tree, and sprinted back into the woods. He'd go back and cover his tracks later. He wasn't worried about the locals hunting him down. Marrok was the threat. Kingston had read every word of the report Danner had given him on the man who called himself Jude Marrok, and some of it was very impressive.

His phone vibrated in his jacket pocket. He pulled it out and checked the ID. Danner.

Dammit, he was tempted to ignore it. He didn't want to have to give explanations right now. But he couldn't ignore a man who wielded as much power as Raymond Danner.

He punched the button.

"I'm a little busy. I'll call you back."

"Did you get him?" Raymond Danner asked.

"I shot the dog."

"Dead?"

"I'm not sure. Marrok got in my way at the last minute."

Silence. "You shot Marrok?"

"No," he said quickly. "I was trying to lure him into a trap, but then the soldiers—"

Danner began to curse. "My God, can't you do anything right? I even told you where Marrok and the dog would be tonight. All you had to do was go in and get them."

"I was waiting on the other side of the mountain where all the other rescue teams were working. He didn't go where you said he was going. I had to reposition." He quickly added, "But I'll stake out the area and watch for the helicopter. There are military units all over this mountain, so he may not be able to get the copter back into the area. If the dog's not dead, he'll have to get help for it. Don't worry, Marrok won't get away from me."

"I'm not worried. I'm pissed. That damn

savage Marrok was a SEAL and has wriggled his way out of a dozen traps. You had a chance if you took him by surprise. I want the job done before Marrok leaves that disaster site." Danner hung up.

Kingston pressed the disconnect. He could feel his heart pounding. He'd seen Danner angry before and the results weren't pretty. He liked to make examples that stayed in the memories of the men around him.

Move. Avoid those soldiers.

Find Marrok.

Find the dog.

"Wake up, Devon." Nick was shaking her. "I just got a call from Captain Ramirez. They're bringing in a wounded dog to the first-aid tent."

Devon Brady shook her head to clear it of sleep. Lord, she felt groggy. She'd worked with her dog, Gracie, searching for survivors until almost midnight. She glanced at the clock. It was after two. "I thought I was the last one to break for the night. Whose dog was hurt? Jerry? His shepherd has a history of hip injuries."

"No." Nick Gilroy handed her the shirt and khakis, which were draped over the chair in her mobile quarters. "It's a Lab. Captain Ramirez said he was shot."

"Shot?" Her lips tightened as she started to dress. "Did the soldiers do it? Some gun-happy kid who thought he saw a wolf?"

"The captain swears it wasn't one of his men. They heard gunfire and went to investigate." Nick found her shoes under the bed and handed them to her. "The dog was wounded, and the man who was with him didn't give them a chance to ask questions. He said he wanted his dog taken care of, or he'd make a stink with the newspapers and accuse them of shooting a rescue dog."

Lab. She put on her shoes. The only Lab on the rescue team belonged to Phil Dormhaus. Phil was a quiet, intellectual type, and she couldn't imagine him threatening or making a stink about anything. He was a man who did his job, then took his dog home. But what did she know? she thought wearily. The dogs weren't the only rescue casualties at a disaster like this. The owners of the search and rescue dogs could take only so much death, so much sorrow before they started to break, too. This had been a rough mission, and it still wasn't over. Maybe Phil had been so grief-stricken at the wounding of his dog that he had slipped over the edge. "If the soldiers didn't shoot the Lab, it must have been done by one of the civilians here on the island. Tell the captain that whoever did it has to be found and thrown into jail. We're all volunteers who came here to help them. I won't have our dogs endangered."

"I'll tell him. My pleasure." Nick smiled. "Do you need any help with the Lab?"

"I don't know." She looked back at him as she opened the door of the trailer. Sometimes she forgot that Nick wasn't a young man any longer. He was in his sixties but still strong and agile. She'd taken over his veterinary practice several years ago. Nick had planned on retiring but instead had stayed on and become her right hand. They had worked together for so many years that they took each other for granted. Yet tonight she could see the signs of wear and tear this mission had imprinted on him; his gray hair was tousled and on end, and his face was lined with weariness. "After you talk to the captain, go back to bed. Take Gracie with you. She needs the rest more than I do, and she'll sleep better if she has someone with her." She glanced at her greyhound, Gracie, who was beginning to get to her feet. "No, stay with Nick, baby. I'll be right back." She started down the steps. "I'll call you if I need you, Nick."

He nodded as he yawned. "I know you will. You wouldn't let a dog be given less care than he deserves even if neither of us got any sleep."

"We can say no," she said quietly. "Most of the time a dog won't do that. You know they give until they can't give any longer." She closed the door behind her and strode toward the first-aid tent across the camp. There were only a handful of people on the site at this hour. A mechanic working on the crane. A woman clerk sitting at a desk in the makeshift morgue going through records. A few soldiers standing outside the first-aid tent. The twenty-four-hour-a-day drive and bustle had ended, and the mood was quiet, somber. The canine rescue part of the operation was winding down, and they only had one more day of work before they went home. The handlers and dogs were sleeping, trying to rest their bodies as well as their dogs so they could function efficiently in the morning for one more push, one more effort. She hoped Gracie would get a good sleep. The greyhound was always restless on a search and rescue, and she liked to be in the same room as Devon. But the dog knew Nick and Devon had no choice. She had to help Phil's Lab and probably Phil himself. He'd need someone to talk to and comfort if the Lab was badly hurt.

As she drew nearer to the tent, she could see a man in a black shirt standing over the examining table. Phil?

No. Phil had narrow shoulders and brown hair. This man was tall, lean, with broad shoulders, and sleek black hair cut close to his head. His back was to her, but she was sure she had never seen him before. Nor had she seen the black Lab lying on the table. Her gaze instantly zeroed in on the hurt animal, her attention focusing on the wounded dog. The owner must have taken off the dog's bloodstained halter with the Red Cross on the side because it was lying on the floor beside the table. That would help. She wouldn't have to struggle to get a pain-crazed dog quiet enough to—

"You're the vet?" The dog's owner had turned as she entered the tent. "My dog's hurt. The bullet is still in him. You need to get it out."

"I will." She came forward. "I'm Devon Brady. Who are you?"

"Jude Marrok. I stopped the bleeding, and

I don't think he's badly hurt. But I want that bullet out. I can't move him with it in him."

Marrok definitely wasn't the devastated owner she'd expected to see when she walked into the tent. His voice was crisp, cool, and his tone demanding. To hell with him. "I told you I'd take it out. But not until I take some X-rays and see where it is and if it clipped an organ."

"It hasn't." He pointed to the wound. "Close. But it missed it. It would have done more damage if the bullet had been a higher caliber. I think you'll find it's a 7.62 millimeter. It was meant for distance accuracy. From the sound of it, I'd say it came from a Remington M-24."

"Sound?"

"Like an M-16, but duller. It's used as a sniper weapon."

"I doubt it was that kind of weapon." She was examining the wound. The dog was amazingly docile. He was fully awake, but he only gave a low whimper. "I'm sure the villagers aren't equipped with that kind of firepower. It's probably a hunting rifle."

"It's a Remington," he said flatly. "I've heard that sound too many times to make a mistake. Now get that bullet out of him."

"Stop giving me orders." She tried to keep

the edge from her voice. She wheeled the portable X-ray unit toward the table. "I'm tired, and I'm giving up my few hours of sleep before I have to be up and starting the search again. This is our last day here, and we don't have much time left. They don't think we have a chance of finding anyone else, and we have orders to fly out this evening." She covered the dog with the protector cover. He seemed fully aware, but he still didn't move. Amazing. "I'm doing this willingly because most dogs are worth more than their masters. You included." She pressed the button. "So sit down and shut up."

He stared at her for a moment. "Sorry." He took a step closer to the table. "I won't give you orders, but you may need me to help with Ned. No one knows him better than I do. He'll do what I tell him."

"His name is Ned?" She pushed the X-ray machine out of the way and moved to the examining table. She gently stroked the Lab's black head. "Hello, Ned," she said softly. "I'm Devon, and I'm going to help you. I'll try not to hurt you, but if I do, I'll take it away as quick as I can."

The Lab made a sound deep in his throat and pushed his head against her hand. His brown eyes gazed up at her with trust and a sort of fearless understanding. Surprise rippled through her. She wasn't sure she'd ever seen a dog with an expression quite that . . . knowing.

"What a good boy." She felt a sudden surge of anger. And some idiot villager had tried to kill this animal, who'd only tried to help. What kind of world was this? "Don't worry, the soldiers will find out who shot him. Most of the time the villagers are grateful. I don't know why one of them went crazy."

"It wasn't a local." Marrok was watching her expression. "But you look like you'd like to go hunting for the bastard who shot Ned."

"I would." Her lips tightened. "And if Captain Ramirez starts giving me excuses about not finding him, I will. He can't get away with shooting my dogs."

"Your dogs?"

"I'm the vet on-site. All these rescue dogs may not belong to me, but their health is my responsibility." She went across the tent to her computer to view the X-ray. "And why the hell haven't I seen you and Ned on the mountain? You don't belong to any of the U.S. rescue groups that I flew in with."

"I don't belong to a group. Ned and I are sort of . . . freelance."

"Freelance? No way. Do you think I'm stupid? You have to have government permission even to enter the area. They wouldn't approve anyone not sponsored and approved by a government."

"We were here. We were doing a job." He met her eyes. "Now why don't you do your job? Take that bullet out of Ned."

He was right. The barely contained violence that glimmered beneath Marrok's cool exterior might be antagonizing her and filling her with suspicion, but she could deal with it later. She wasn't about to put him through a third degree until she finished taking care of the dog. Her gaze shifted to the X-ray on the computer. "You appear to have guessed right. The bullet isn't lodged in a vital organ."

"No guess. I told you that no one knows Ned like I do. Anesthesia?"

"Of course."

"I don't like anesthesia." He lifted his hand to ward off the words he knew she was going to say. "I'm not suggesting you cut into him without it. He'll need it for the initial pain. But I want you to use PropoFlo and work fast. He'll come out of it quicker, and he'll be himself again. That's important in Ned's case."

"It's sometimes better for them to have a

heavier sedation. They don't try to struggle after they wake and break the stitches."

"He won't struggle. I'll explain it to him."

Her brows lifted. "You may believe he's very intelligent, but it's instinct that makes—"

"He won't struggle." He met her gaze. "I promise you. I'll be right here when he wakes to quiet him if he does."

She shrugged. She preferred to use PropoFlo anyway whenever possible. Ned's calm temperament seemed to make him a good candidate. "I'll take care of him if there's a problem. You don't have to be here."

"Yes, I do." He turned to the dog and began to murmur to him. It wasn't English, Devon realized with surprise. She studied him. Even though Marrok was olive-complexioned and his hair and eyes were also dark, she had been sure he was American. High cheekbones, wide mouth . . . Italian? Spanish? No, neither one. But the dog seemed to understand. He was staring intently at Marrok's face, and when the words stopped, he closed his eyes with a little sigh.

Marrok turned back to her. "Get started. We have to get this over. I have something I have to do."

"It will take as long as it takes." She went

to the medicine supply chest. "If you're going to stay, scrub up and—"

"Wait. There's something you should know."

"Medical history?"

"No, Ned thought he found a survivor just before he was shot. I didn't get a chance to search the ruins of that house, so I don't know if he was right. I flagged the site."

She shook her head. "That entire village was searched thoroughly before we pulled out a few days ago."

Marrok shrugged. "Ned isn't always right, but he comes close. It's your call."

She hesitated. "Did you tell Captain Ramirez?"

He nodded. "Like you, he didn't believe there was a chance of a survivor after all the search activity you put into that village."

"There's always a chance." She frowned. "I'll call Ramirez and tell him that we need to get an excavation crew up there right away. I'll go myself after I finish with your Ned."

An indecipherable expression flitted across his face. "It would be better if you stayed here. It might not be safe for you up there."

"Of course I'm going. It's what I do." She looked up at him. "Do you think—" She forgot what she had been about to say as her eyes met Marrok's. His intensity was overwhelming and almost hypnotizing. For an instant she actually felt shaken. Safe? She suddenly had the feeling that nothing connected with this man would ever be termed safe.

Get a grip. Whether Marrok was safe or not wasn't important. He was just a man with a dog that was hurt and needed her.

She glanced away from him. "It's what I do," she repeated. She took out her phone and started to dial Ramirez. "Put on some gloves. I may need you to hold Ned in the correct position during the surgery."

CHAPTER 2

"**He should wake up any** minute now." Devon turned away and stripped off her gloves. "Ned should be fine. But you should keep him confined for two weeks. He mustn't get excited and tear out those stitches."

"I won't cage him. Ned won't tear them out. I'll have a talk with him." His hands were stroking the dog's head with exquisite gentleness. "He's smart and knows what's good for him."

She found herself staring at the hands caressing the dog. Beautiful, graceful hands, and the tenderness of the movement was mesmerizing. The first impression of barely contained violence was completely at odds with this Marrok. She tore her gaze away. "Until he sees a cat cross his path. You may be proud of your dog, but you shouldn't risk him because you have a false sense of his intelligence."

"Not false." He glanced up at her. "And he likes cats. I haven't found an animal or human being he doesn't like . . . except one. That's why he's such a terrific rescue dog. He never stops trying." Ned was waking up, opening his eyes. "Take it easy, buddy," Marrok said softly. "It's all over. Now all you have to do is heal."

Ned whimpered and closed his eyes again.

Marrok was still stroking the dog. "You did a good job, Dr. Brady. Quick, neat, and thorough. Thank you."

"It's my job."

"It's more than your job."

She shrugged. "I love animals. But so do all the handlers on the team."

He smiled. "I don't doubt their affection, but yours strikes deeper, doesn't it? Why else would you have become a vet? How many dogs do you own?"

"Five."

"And other animals?"

"What difference does it make?"

"I'm curious."

"Four cats. Three parrots. A pig. A donkey."

"I take it that they're not all house pets?"

"I have a place in the country outside Denver. It's a few acres, big enough."

"Why so many?"

"Some of them are strays. Some of them were abused. Some of them were left because their owners didn't want to pay their bill and told me to find them other homes."

"And you took them in."

"When I couldn't find them a good home."

"Who takes care of them when you're trekking over the world on these rescue missions? Your husband?"

"I have a housekeeper." It was about time she asked a few questions herself. "Don't you want to fill out a report on the shooting? Captain Ramirez will send someone to take a statement."

"I think I'll pass."

"I'd want to wring that bastard's neck," she said curtly. "And it's your duty to do it. If only to keep it from happening to someone else's dog."

"I don't have the time. I promise you that no other dog will be victimized by the shooter."

"How do you know? If they don't find him, you can't expect—" She stopped, her gaze narrowing. "You know who shot Ned?"

"I don't have a name. I know I can find him." He sat down in a camp chair. "Go on. I know you want to go check out that house that I flagged. I'll stay with Ned. Believe me, I've been through enough illnesses with him to qualify as an expert."

She hesitated. "I should be the one to stay with him. I never leave a patient on the first night." She added deliberately, "And I don't leave strangers with access to a medicine chest full of narcotics."

He shook his head. "There's a guard outside the tent."

"That's to keep thieves from coming in, not people from going out."

He smiled faintly. "Good point."

"And there were soldiers all over the mountain, and you managed to find your way to those ruins. You're lucky you weren't shot for looting."

He lifted his brows. "You think Ned and I were searching for loot, not survivors?"

"It's a possibility. What could appear more innocent than a rescue dog and his handler?" She added, "Even though they were scouring through ruins that the main team had already abandoned."

"Ned thought you were wrong. He thought there was still life in those ruins."

"It seems impossible. We were so careful."

"Could be. He turned up blank on the first try."

"Blank?"

"He made a mistake. He found a dead man. He was overanxious and wanted desperately to find someone alive. I don't think it was a case of his senses being off. His success ratio is in the 90 percent range."

"He's that good?"

"Exceptional. Some dogs are good, a few have the passion. From the moment I took him on his first rescue mission, he instinctively knew what to do and how to do it. I've never known any dog to have such a heady sense of joy as when he found someone alive in the rubble." His lips twisted. "Or such abject despair if we found them dead. He never got used to it. Every time it was new joy or fresh pain for him." His glance shifted back to Ned. "But sometimes the dead were too much for him. And then I tried to keep him at home. It's been a long time since I brought Ned to a disaster site."

"Why this one?"

"He was grieving," Marrok said simply. "He needed it."

"So you brought him to this island in the back of beyond because he needed to save a life?"

"It's not a bad reason, is it?"

She slowly shook her head. "Not to me. But most search and rescue dogs don't grieve when they're away from the disaster."

"Ned is different." He studied her face. "You look tired. Why don't you get someone else to go up and check out that house?"

"I'll be fine." She wearily rubbed the back of her neck. "I'll get my second wind on the way up."

His lips lifted in a slight smile. "I thought you'd do it yourself. You're not good at delegating, are you?"

"I'm already awake. Why rouse anyone else to trek up there on what is probably a wild-goose chase?"

"It may not be. What will you do if it isn't?"

"Jump up and down with joy. Then send up a flare for them to rush up a medical team." She looked at Ned. "I don't like to leave him. Are you sure you know what to do if there's a problem?"

"Ned is a powerhouse. He's strong, and his body heals faster than any animal you've ever treated. Now that the bullet is out, he'll begin to repair himself. You'll be amazed at how quickly he'll recover. I've told him what to do." He added solemnly, "And I promise not to rifle through your narcotics stash while you're off saving lives. Not that you won't warn that guard to keep an eye on me."

"You bet I will. You're going to have a lot of questions to answer when I get back." Though she couldn't believe Marrok was a petty thief. He was larger than life. She'd judge that he might find a way to embezzle a million, but he wouldn't be pilfering the medicine chest. As she headed for the entrance, she said over her shoulder, "If you need help, have the guard take you to my trailer. Nick Gilroy's a vet, too, and will know what to do."

He looked back at Ned. "I won't need help."

Devon paused a moment outside the tent to take a deep breath and look up at the mountain. Lord, she hoped Marrok was right about there being a survivor. It had been two days since the last person had been pulled out of the rubble, and the old woman had died on her way to the hospital in Caracas. Out of the two stricken village's population of 4500 people, they'd only been able to save 722. Dealing with disappointment as well as the grieving families of the lost ones had been agonizing for every rescue worker on site. She couldn't let herself be too hopeful. The odds against finding anyone alive weren't that—

To hell with it. She would hope until hope was gone.

She headed for the jeep.

Who was Nick Gilroy? Her friend? Her lover?

Marrok's gaze followed Devon Brady until she disappeared from view in the jeep. She was a woman who a man wanted to keep on looking at. Not pretty. Her mouth was too wide, her nose turned up a little, and she had a sprinkling of freckles over her cheeks. Yet together, the small imperfections gave her face interest and character. Though she was definitely not at her best tonight. Her short, brown-blond hair was tousled and her khakis and shirt rumpled. She was tall and thin, but her shoulders were squared even though he knew she was tired. There had been circles of weariness beneath her wide-set blue eyes, but you'd never know it from the way she carried herself. She walked with strength and purpose, and she'd treated Ned with the same strength and determination . . . and gentleness.

Oh, yes, there had been a world of gentleness when her hand had touched Ned. He valued gentleness. He had seen too much of roughness and brutality lately. Not that she wasn't a tough cookie. He had believed her when she said she'd go after the man who'd shot Ned herself. Toughness and gentleness . . . They were qualities he always demanded in the guardians.

Guardian?

Yes, he realized he'd been speculating about the possibility of using Devon Brady as a guardian since he'd first met her. **Use.** He grimaced as he thought how she would hate that word and concept.

Well, whether or not she would have to be used long term, he would have to use her to get over this bad patch with Ned. She was the right person in the right place, and he had little choice.

Get moving. She'd be busy on the search on the mountain for only a short while, then she'd be back. The excavators would have done the initial work by the time she got there. Whether or not she found anyone alive when she came back, she would still be suspicious and full of awkward questions. He took out his cell phone and dialed his pilot, Walt Franks.

Walt picked up on the second ring. "It's about time. Is Ned going to keep you up there all night?"

"Ned's been shot. Where are you?"

"Shot," Walt repeated. "How is he?"

"Okay. I had to have the vet here at the mountain take a bullet out of him, so I don't want to move him yet. Where did you set down?"

"But he's going to be okay?"

"Fine." Walt was crazy about the Lab, and Marrok should have known that he wouldn't get any information until Franks was assured Ned was not in danger. Well, he would have responded in the same way. "Two weeks, and he'll be bounding around like a puppy."

"That's good."

"Now, where are you?"

"I set the helicopter down in a glade on the other side of the island. Do you want me to come and get you?"

"No, you'd be spotted. The mountain is crawling with soldiers right now. The vet put a burr under them about a rescue dog being shot, and they're searching for the villager who did it."

"It was a villager?"

"No way. It was a Remington sniper weapon."

Walt was cursing. "Danner? He's found you?"

"That's my bet."

Walt was silent. "It's been four years, Marrok. How the hell did he do it?"

"Money. Manpower. Determination."

"I was hoping that we'd slipped under the radar."

"It was only a matter of time. Danner isn't going to give up until we find a way to take him out." He paused. "But first we have to take out his shooter here on the island. We can't risk leaving a trail for Danner to follow. If we can slide out from under here, we may have a little time for damage control."

"What do you want me to do?"

"Stay put. Be ready to pick me up when I call you and get me out of here."

"Anything else?"

"No. Yes. After you hang up from me, call Chad Lincoln with MI6 and get a report on Devon Brady. She's the vet taking care of Ned."

"You think she's connected with Danner?"

"No, that's not why I want it."

Walt was silent for a moment. "A guardian?"

"Maybe. At any rate, I'm going to have to leave Ned in her hands for a while. I can't risk moving him, and I can't stay here with him. I have to be sure I can trust her to take care of him."

"You wouldn't be considering her for a guardian if you didn't believe that already."

"I trust my instincts only so far. I have to be sure. I want that report before I leave the island."

"You'll have it. Do you know when you'll be ready to be picked up? What's the plan?"

"I don't have a plan. I'm just going hunting, then I'm going to kill the son of a bitch." He hung up.

But he couldn't leave now. Not until he was sure Devon Brady was on her way back down the mountain. He had to be certain that Ned was going to be under her personal care. He moved over to the entrance of the tent and stared up at the mountain.

She'd had time to get on the other side by now and had probably joined the excavators at the site where he'd planted his flag. She'd said if she found anyone alive, she'd send up a flare, and a medical team would tear up the mountain. All he had to do was wait.

Ned gave a soft bark behind him.

He looked over his shoulder and smiled. "Hi, back with me again? Don't move. Okay?"

Ned tried to get up and fell back with a little yip of pain.

"I told you. What a stubborn animal you are. You never listen."

Ned's tail thumped frantically on the table as he made another attempt.

"But this time you have to listen. You either do what I tell you, or you'll end up in a cage."

Ned froze, his eyes on Marrok's face.

"She wants to protect you from hurting yourself, and she doesn't understand that you don't need to be put in a cage. I told her you were smart enough not to do yourself damage." He grimaced. "And you promptly do something dumb. How can I help you if you—" He turned his head as he caught a brilliant flash out of the corner of his eye.

A flare lighting the darkness.

"Alive," he murmured. "Life, Ned. You found life up there. I told you that you'd do it." He turned and crossed back to the Lab. "They'll be bringing someone down soon. Because of you."

The dog was smiling. No one could convince Marrok that dogs didn't smile. He knew

Ned did. There was an expression of eagerness and joy on the Lab's face, and he was looking out at the fading splendor of the flare as if he understood what it meant. Maybe he did. Ned understood what Marrok said. It could be that he was aware of more subtle meanings. Ned was always learning, always changing.

"Now are you satisfied? You found your survivor."

Ned was still staring raptly at the sky as if he could actually see that person, the life he'd saved.

Marrok could feel his throat tighten. "Crazy dog," he said thickly. His hand stroked Ned's throat. "Okay, you were right. It was worth coming here. Even if you managed to set us up for Danner." He drew a deep breath. "But now we have to wriggle out from under. And you have to help. You have to do exactly what I tell you. I'm going to stay with you until she comes back, but when I see her jeep in view, I'm gone." He had to talk fast, be very clear. It would be better if he switched to the language Ned had known since he was a puppy. "Listen carefully; I'll be back, but until . . ."

* * *

"It's a child, Nick." Devon jumped out of the jeep, excitement soaring through her. "A little girl not more than five. Her parents were dead, but the little girl is alive. She was unconscious and buried deep under the rocks. She's dehydrated, but the medics think there's a good chance she'll live. They're airlifting her out to a hospital in Caracas."

"And we didn't find her." Nick was shaking his head as he came down the steps of the trailer. "My God, I thought we were safe leaving that side of the mountain."

"So did I," she said wearily. "Who could know? We shifted that rubble a dozen times. None of the dogs thought there was anyone there. She was buried so deep her scent must have been almost obliterated." But Marrok's dog, Ned, had known she was there. Astonishing . . .

Marrok.

She turned and started for the first-aid tent. "I'll be back after I check on the Lab. Go back to bed. I just wanted to let you know. Let everyone know. It's been too long since we found a survivor."

"That's for damn sure." Nick turned. "It's too late to go back to bed. I'll throw some clothes on and give Gracie her breakfast."

He was right. The first light of dawn was breaking over the mountain. Too late to sleep. They had to finish up the last search, then get packed up. She should be tired, but she felt wide-awake and zinging with energy.

They had found a child.

After days of despair, a miracle had happened. She was so grateful that the Lab had found the little girl that she was even feeling charitable toward Marrok. Not that she wouldn't still have him investigated. The presence of the rescue teams had to be carefully monitored; otherwise, it would pose a danger to both the dogs and handlers. She could tell Marrok had experience in the field, and he should realize that. She believed him when he said he hadn't been looting on that mountain, but whatever reason he'd had, he should have—

He wasn't there.

She stopped in shock in the entrance of the tent.

Ned still lay on the table. He raised his head and whined softly as he saw her.

"How are you doing?" She crossed the tent. He seemed to be fine. Fully awake and alert and didn't seem to be in pain. "And where is your friend, Marrok? I need to talk to him."

Ned gave a low growl deep in his throat as if trying to tell her and nudged his head against her arm. She melted immediately. What a sweetheart.

She stroked his head. "You must have a great nose," she whispered. "You found a little girl tonight. Did you know that?"

He made a sound that resembled a half yodel, half bark. She would swear he was trying to answer her. She had not known a dog that tried so hard to communicate since her German shepherd, Tess, had passed away years ago. "Is that supposed to be a yes? I think it is. I used to feel as if my Tess could read my mind. But that's a bond that—" She broke off as she saw a piece of paper lying half-under Ned's body. "What the hell?"

She saw that her name was scrawled at the top of the page in bold dark script as she eased the sheet of paper from beneath the Lab. It was only a few lines.

I can't stay with Ned. Take him home with you, and I promise I'll pick him up as soon as I finish my business here. I've had a talk with him, and he won't be any trouble. I'd offer you money, but I know that won't work

with you. You'll do it because you won't be able to leave him here hurt and with no one you regard as responsible enough to care for him.

Don't put him in a cage. Cages scare him and drive him crazy. Give him a chance to prove that it's not necessary. You won't regret it.

Marrok

Damn him.

Her hand closed around the paper, crushing it. She wished it was Marrok's throat. How irresponsible could you get? You didn't just leave your dog because it interfered with business. Particularly a dog like Ned. What business? She'd bet he'd skipped out before she had the opportunity to talk to the soldiers about his presence on the mountain.

She began to curse beneath her breath.

Ned tilted his head and gazed at her in hurt bewilderment.

"It's not you," she said. "You can't help it. You've just taken up with bad company. I could murder him."

"Anyone I know?" Nick asked from behind

her. "I haven't seen you this mad in a long time. Let's see, I think it was that politician in Nicaragua who wanted to quarantine all the rescue dogs."

"Marrok," she said curtly. "He's run out on Ned."

"And this is Ned?" He came forward and looked down at the Lab. "Beautiful fellow." He patted the dog's silky black head. "And he looks like he's in great shape for just having a bullet taken out of him. He's doing well?"

"Great so far. Marrok said he healed well." Her lips tightened. "He also said if I took that bullet out of him, he'd be well in no time. Dammit, it doesn't work that way. All kinds of things can go wrong. He can't just waltz off and leave him."

"He left a note?" His brows lifted as he saw the crushed paper in her hand. "I see he did. May I?" He took the note from her and un-folded it. "He seems to know you very well for such a short acquaintance. Very perceptive."

"For heaven's sake, I'm a vet. That doesn't take much perceptiveness to realize I'd care about an animal."

"Enough to fight to take him back to the States? It's going to be one big headache to battle the search and rescue home base and the U.S. animal immigration laws to get a dog with no documents into the country."

"I know that," she said through clenched teeth. "I'm going to be on the phone for hours trying to get clearance . . . if I decide to take Ned home."

"No 'if.' You've already decided. You haven't stopped stroking Ned all the time you've been ranting and raving."

"It's not his fault that his master is an ass." She scowled. "Ned is special. He found that little girl. How could Marrok just leave him? He doesn't know me from Adam."

"You're not hard to read. No one would believe you'd abuse the dog."

"But he couldn't be sure. I may just keep Ned. It would serve him right."

"Why not? You seem to be harboring a good portion of the animal population of Denver." Nick smiled. "Should I go get Gracie and see if they're going to be compatible?"

"Not now. I have to cage Ned, then take Gracie up the mountain for—"

Ned was howling mournfully. It was soft, almost a sigh of sound, but that only added to the pathos.

He had understood?

"Cage?" she repeated.

The howling rose. It was enough to break her heart.

"For Pete's sake, shut up. It's for your own good. I can't risk you—"

Ned tucked his nose beneath her arm.

"Good God, what a con artist." Nick chuckled. "Do you want help getting him in a cage?"

That was what she should do. The downside of her profession was making decisions she didn't want to make.

Cages scare him. Give him a chance.

He had found that little girl. He deserved his chance.

"No, we'll leave him out of the cage." She pushed the Lab away from her. "You stay here and start packing up our equipment and keep an eye on him."

Nick shook his head disapprovingly. "I can't believe you're going to leave him out. If he gets excited, he may hurt himself."

"Marrok said he wouldn't." Her lips lifted in a sardonic smile. "He had a talk with him and told him not to be any trouble."

"What?"

"I know. I know. But you'll be here if Ned decides to be a problem, and he's still under sedation. If I made the wrong decision, give him another shot to quiet him." She looked down at the Lab. He was gazing eagerly up at her . . . and smiling. "Are you satisfied with yourself? Got your own way, didn't you?"

He gave that half growl, half purr, and laid his head back down on the table.

"You're quite the manipulator. Maybe that's why Marrok dumped you." She turned and headed for the tent entrance. "I'll start the phone calls to Immigration while I'm on the mountain with Gracie. If you have any trouble here, phone me."

"I believe I can handle one dog," Nick said dryly. "Since I started my own clinic before you were born."

"Don't be so prickly. You know I'm not questioning your capability. But I'm the one who decided not to—"

"Get out of here," Nick said. "You're making it worse. Prickly? Old men are prickly. I don't intend to be an old man for the next thirty years or so."

"Longer than that." Her smile faded as she looked back at Ned. "I can't believe he left him. He seemed hard, but when he touched that dog, he was . . ." She hesitated, thinking about that moment.

"What?"

She tried to sort out the emotions she had sensed in Marrok. "Close. It was almost as if they were part of each other. Not dog and master. Not even friends. So close that . . ." She shrugged helplessly. "I don't know. I felt as if I could feel the bond between them. He was like a honed blade, hard and sharp and glittering, but with Ned he was gentle, incredibly gentle."

"Then he'll probably be back for his dog. You won't have him on your hands for long."

"If I decide to let him have Ned back." She said over her shoulder as she left the tent, "He hasn't proved that he's very responsible. Dammit, he got the dog shot, and heaven knows what Marrok was actually doing up on the mountain."

But they had found a little girl because Marrok had taken Ned to search those ruins, she thought as she moved toward her trailer to pick up Gracie. That miracle had happened.

So stop whining and accept the good with the bad. She'd take care of his dog and get him well and strong. After that she'd decide if Marrok was worthy of having her return Ned to him. She could have a battle on her hands. He didn't appear to be a man who would let anyone decide anything concerning him.

Yet she had a sudden memory of Marrok's hand on Ned. Strong, vital, full of power, able to crush, but possessing that incredible gentleness.

What did she know? They had been together only a short time. Perhaps that toughness was only a front. It could be that she was wrong. Maybe he really was a gentle man.

CHAPTER
3

Knife or gun?

Knife, Marrok decided as he knelt to examine the lay of the grass. A knife was quiet, and besides, it was more personal. He wanted to slice that bastard's heart out.

The grass was crushed beside the palm tree. This was where the shooter had stopped and climbed the tree to get the vantage point for his shot.

The shot that had taken Ned down.

Keep cool. Smother the anger. He was on the hunt, and every sense should be keen and unimpaired until he found the prey.

The phone in his pocket vibrated.

"Did I interrupt anything?" Walt Franks asked when he picked up. "Mayhem? Any removal of body parts?"

"Not yet. I haven't found him. And I haven't let him find me. I've been dodging the local military for most of the day. But it's getting dark now, and we'll be getting together soon. I'd bet he's in the foothills waiting to pounce. Why are you calling?"

"Dr. Devon Brady. You wanted a report to make sure that it wasn't a mistake entrusting your canine friend to her."

"Talk."

"Thirty-two. Parents dead. She was an army brat and traveled all over the world from post to post. Married when she was seventeen to a Lester Enright. Divorced four years later. No children. Her ex-husband is a detective with the Denver Police Department. She worked her way through school and managed to save enough by the time she was twenty-seven to buy a veterinary practice from a Dr. Nicholas Gilroy, who was supposedly retiring. But he's still working with her. Frankly, I don't know how she pays him. Most of her income seems to be going to local kill-free animal shelters and paying her way on volunteer Search and Rescue disaster missions. This is the third

one she's been on in the last eighteen months."
He paused. "Guardian material?"

Hell, yes. "That's not why I needed the info. I just wanted to make sure that Ned would be okay with her."

"But you're thinking," Walt murmured.

He was silent a moment. "I may have to find a place for her."

"Why?"

"Even after I clean up here, Danner will send someone else, and they'll find out she took Ned."

Walt gave a low whistle. "My God, you made her a target."

"I had no choice. I had to have Ned cared for by someone I could trust."

"They'll try to kill her?"

"Only after they spend a good deal of time trying to find out what she knows."

"And you didn't warn her?"

"Ned had to be cared for."

"And that justifies the possible torture and murder of an innocent woman?"

He didn't answer the question. "I'll try to find a way to keep her safe. Danner won't make a move until he knows whether Ned and I are dead. If I move fast, I may be able to—"

"Keep her from getting killed but completely disrupt her life? If I were her, I'd go after you with a hatchet."

And Marrok wouldn't blame her, he thought wearily. But that didn't change anything. He'd done what he thought necessary, and he'd do it again. Devon Brady had been in the wrong place at the wrong time, and there wasn't anything he could do about it. She had to go with the cards dealt her.

The cards he'd dealt her.

"Be ready. I'll call you as soon as I make the kill." He hung up.

The kill. He didn't even know the name of the man whose life he was going to end tonight. It didn't matter. It wasn't as if he'd never killed a stranger before. When he was a sniper in the SEALs, he'd learned it was better if you didn't know the target or think of him with any degree of emotion at all. But tonight he was full of emotion that he couldn't control. He was going to enjoy the hell out of killing the son of a bitch who had shot Ned.

He glanced at the west where the setting sun was splintering the sky with scarlet.

It was the end of the day. Devon had said that the team would be gone by evening. Soon she would be boarding a helicopter that would take her to the airport in Caracas where the canine rescue team would change to a jet to take them home. Ned would be with her. Even without the necessary dossier he'd had to get on her, he'd had no doubt that she'd find a way to keep Ned by her side. She had been wary with **him,** but she was all heart where Ned was concerned. He'd be safe with her.

He wished he could say the same about Devon Brady. There was no way she'd be safe. If he'd just had her treat Ned and taken him away, she might have had a chance. But he'd robbed her of all safety when he'd left Ned with her.

Stop standing here staring, he thought impatiently. What was done was done. Get on with the job at hand. Find the shooter. Make him talk before he killed him. He needed to know how he'd been found so that he could close the crack in the dam. Then he'd go get Ned and disappear again.

And try to convince Devon Brady to disappear, too.

"Be careful with him." Devon watched Nick and one of the orderlies lift Ned's stretcher onto the helicopter. "He may get nervous if we—"

"Shut up, Devon." Nick gave her a long-suffering look. "You're the one who's nervous.

The dog is fine." He glanced at Devon's dog, Gracie, who'd jumped into the helicopter and settled down beside Ned. "And it seems that Gracie is going to keep him company."

"So I see." Devon should have known Gracie would bond with Ned. The greyhound was one of the most empathetic dogs Devon had ever known. Loving, serious, always the mother of any new arrival in Devon's bevy of animals. She had been that way from the day Devon had taken her from a greyhound rescue unit. She'd had a broken leg, was half-starved and scared to death, but she'd immediately bounced back and became the loving Gracie she was now. "Okay, Gracie, but keep an eye on him. Nick called him a con artist."

She would swear that Ned gave her a glance of indignation as if he knew what she'd said.

But Gracie was contentedly laying her long elegant head on the stretcher and closing her eyes.

Devon shook her head. "Remember, I warned you." She jumped into the helicopter. The large aircraft was filled with dogs and their handlers, but there was a free seat beside Hilda Golding and her retriever, Socks.

Hilda was staring at Ned. "That's the Lab that found the little girl?"

Devon nodded. "I don't know how. Gracie went over that area a dozen times."

"So did Socks." Hilda scratched behind her retriever's ears. "He must have a great nose. How is the little girl doing?"

"Good. I got a call from Caracas an hour ago. Her name is Mercedes. Broken arm, concussion, but she's awake now. They've located her grandparents, who live on an island a short distance from here."

"That's wonderful." Hilda leaned her head back against the wall of the aircraft and closed her eyes. "Lord, this was a bad one. So many dead . . . Politicians trying to grab the relief supplies and sell them on the black market. That dog getting shot. I keep telling myself that I'm not bringing Socks on another mission, and then I get the call, and here I am."

Devon knew how she felt. "I always think about letting someone else do it. What would it hurt to skip one? But maybe it would be Gracie who'd find a little girl or an old man buried on a mountain or in a village. Maybe she'd be the only one to know." Her gaze shifted to Ned. "Like it was Ned this time."

The helicopter was beginning to lift off. Ned didn't move a muscle, and Gracie lifted her head to glance at him. Then, satisfied, settled down again. Ned was being amazingly docile, Devon thought. Nick had told her he'd had no problem with him all day.

He won't give you any trouble. I had a talk with him.

Bull. Marrok's dog had already caused her a world of trouble. She'd had to threaten and bribe, and now owed a staggering number of favors to bureaucrats and immigration officials.

"I guess you're right," Hilda said. "It's not as if someone else couldn't do the job. It's all about maybe me and Socks being the ones to make a difference, to save someone."

Ned lifted his head and looked at Devon with those brown eyes that gleamed with intelligence and query.

"All right, you were worth all the trouble," she said softly. "You knew what you were doing out there. You did a good job."

He laid his head down and closed his eyes.

The handlers might get discouraged and question their own motives and worth, but the dogs didn't have that problem. They knew the answer. Hilda had to puzzle it out, but it was simple and clear to them.

It was all about life.

* * *

Marrok jerked the knife out of the man's chest and wiped it on the grass.

It had taken too long. Two days, dammit. He'd expected to be able to take the shooter out on that first night, but the soldiers had been too active on the evening Devon Brady had left. Maybe Devon had put a spur to Ramirez to try to find the man who had shot Ned. At any rate, he'd had to bide his time and wait. Not good. He wasn't the only one who had gotten impatient. The shooter had turned hunter, and they had been playing cat and mouse in this forest since yesterday. When he'd finally zeroed in on him, Marrok hadn't time to be careful and take the shooter alive. Well, if he couldn't make him talk, he'd have to find out what he could.

He searched the body and found his wallet and cell phone.

His name was Albert Kingston. Age forty-two. An address in Dallas, Texas.

He stuffed the phone in his pocket. He'd retrieve the latest telephone calls in memory later. It was more important to get rid of the body. He'd kept Kingston busy on the run, and he wouldn't have had time to investigate what had happened to Ned. He had maybe a day before Danner sent someone else to the island to find out why he wasn't hearing anything from Kingston.

And to find Marrok and Ned.

That would give Marrok maybe two days tops to get to Devon Brady before Danner sent his vultures swooping. It would have to be enough.

No, it wouldn't. He had to make preparations. It was going to be a complicated extraction.

He reached for his phone to call Walt Franks to come and get him. After that, he'd phone Bridget Reardon and get her moving toward Devon's home outside Denver.

Janet McDonald was standing on the porch waiting for them when Nick and Devon drove the SUV through the gate and up to the rambling old farmhouse.

"She doesn't look very welcoming," Nick murmured. "Do you suppose we have a problem?"

"No more than usual." Devon waved at the housekeeper. She did not wave back. Janet seldom looked cheerful. She was a woman who'd lived a hard life, and her appearance reflected it. She was tall and strongly built, her red-gray hair cut short and her face generally without expression. "She probably missed us."

Nick gave a snort. "Yeah, sure. And pigs fly."

"People don't always show their feelings." Devon turned off the ignition. "Be quiet, Ned. Stop that racket you're making."

"What have you brought home this time?" Janet frowned as she came down the steps. "That's not Gracie I heard barking." She peered into the back of the SUV. "My God, another dog. I thought I was safe when you flew off to that island with Gracie. But, no, you bring me home another dog to take care of."

"Hush, Janet." Devon jumped out of the driver's seat and ran around to the back and opened the door. "His name is Ned, and he's hurt."

"They're all hurt or orphans or just plain crazy." She stood beside Devon. "Why was he barking?"

"I think he knew we were home. He's pretty smart."

"Pretty noisy." She reached out a hand and tentatively touched Ned's silky ears. He lifted his head and looked up at her and gave a crooning sound. "I can see how he'd get to a softy like you. What happened to him?"

"He was shot." She carefully lifted Ned out of the vehicle, carried him up the stairs to the porch, and put him on his feet. "I had to take a bullet out of him."

Janet scowled. "I hope you had whoever did it arrested."

"Didn't have the chance. But I imagine his owner may see to it. He wasn't pleased."

"He has an owner? Thank the Lord." She beamed down at the Lab. "No offense, pooch. But we have a few too many animals around here."

"If Devon decides to give him back," Nick said as he took out the suitcases. "She's not sure he's worthy of the dog."

"Not another one." Janet made a face. "If she's not sure, then we're probably stuck with him. It looks like Gracie's already adopted him."

Gracie was sitting beside Ned on the porch, every muscle of her lean, elegant body breathing maternal protectiveness.

"Where are the other dogs?" Devon asked. "Gracie needs to run and play and just be a dog again. She had a rough time on the island."

"They're down in the paddock teasing that donkey. Someday they're going to get kicked."

It was one of the pups' greatest joys to run back and forth on the other side of the fence trying to get a rise out of the donkey. "Casper will only threaten them. You know he likes the company. Go see Casper, Gracie."

The greyhound didn't move away from Ned.

"It's okay. We'll take care of him, Gracie."

"I'll take her down to the paddock." Nick whistled for Gracie, and she reluctantly got to her feet. "Come on, girl. You can play mother later. Devon thinks you need therapy."

"Devon is the one who needs therapy," Janet said dryly. "And you don't do anything to discourage her, Nick."

"No, I don't." Nick grinned. "She may be a little eccentric, but she keeps me young. She keeps you young, too, Janet. Admit it."

"I **am** young. I haven't turned sixty yet. I don't need to work my ass off taking care of critters to convince myself of that." Janet moved toward the door. "Supper will be ready in an hour. Feed the donkey, and bring up those dogs. I need a little help around here."

"Yes, ma'am." Nick disappeared around the corner of the house, with Gracie on his heels.

Janet was frowning down at Ned. "Shouldn't he be lying down? Why don't I take him in the kitchen and settle him on the dog bed? He won't get much chance when the other pups come up from the field."

"Ned can take care of himself." She tugged gently on his collar. "But that's a good idea. I'll give him some water and then I'll—"

"I said I'd do it." Janet strode into the house. "Come on, dog."

"Ned."

"Ned," Janet said, straight-faced. "Heaven forbid I be rude to the mutt."

She was joking. It was as much humor as Janet ever displayed. "Good. Ned is different. I think he's very sensitive."

"Then he'll probably be even crazier than the rest of them. I can't see why you keep bringing them home."

"They need help and give love," she said simply. "And when I give that help, it fills me with warmth. They touch my heart. I can't do anything else, Janet."

"I know you can't." She hesitated. "I've been getting a lot of hang-ups on the house phone since you've been gone. I think he's found out the new number."

Devon tensed. Oh Lord, she hoped not. "Not necessarily."

"Stop burying your head. It was the same the last time. It's him, all right." Janet's hands clenched into fists. "Men like him don't give up. They just keep on coming until you shoot the bastards. I should know. I was married to one for over twenty years."

"But you didn't shoot your husband."

"Only because you got me a fancy lawyer to have Chuck thrown into jail. Why can't you do the same with your husband?"

"He's not my husband. I told you I divorced Lester years ago," she said wearily. "And the situation is different."

"Yeah, he's a nutcase."

"A very smart nutcase. He's a police detective who knows how to work the system. I've only been able to get one restraining order on him since the divorce."

"Well, he'd better not come around here bothering you," Janet said fiercely. "I'll blow his nuts off."

"I don't think he'll be showing up on my doorstep. These days he limits himself to nuisance calls and making threats when he thinks I'm seeing other men."

"Fat chance of that," Janet said sourly. "You're so busy taking care of all those animals, you don't have time to do more than brush your teeth."

She smiled with an effort. "Well, I do manage a shower now and then. Don't worry, Janet. It may not be Lester. If it is, I'll handle it."

"**We'll** handle it," Janet said tersely. "Now you go lie down and get some rest. You look like you're ready to pass out. I'll call you when dinner is ready." She tapped Ned's collar. "Let's go. You don't need her. You got me."

Ned hesitated, studying Janet's face. Then he moved stiffly down the hall after her.

Maybe Ned was even more sensitive than Devon had thought. Perhaps he had been able to see beyond that brusque exterior. Janet did not have anything so clichéd as a heart of gold, but she was fair and hardworking, and though she would not admit it, she had a generous amount of the same maternal feeling as Gracie exhibited. Devon could not have asked for anyone more devoted or conscientious than Janet to take care of her animals.

Janet stuck her head outside the kitchen. "Scat."

"Right." Devon grinned and ran up the stairs to her room. She was tired, but it wasn't the kind of weariness that would be assuaged by an hour's nap. She'd take a shower and read her mail.

Should she disconnect the phone? The last thing she wanted was to have to deal with

Lester tonight. She'd hoped by putting the new number in Nick's name that it would make it harder for Lester to get it. It had been a feeble attempt but all she could think to do. But the police could find out anything if they wanted to do it.

And eventually Lester found out any information he needed. After the first restraining order, he'd convinced his superiors that she was the one who was bothering him. Cops always stuck together when it was one of their own in trouble.

Don't think about it. She couldn't be sure that Lester was starting the calls again. She'd face that ugliness when she was forced to do so. Right now she wanted to keep problems at a distance, but she'd created a bushel of them by taking Ned out of Santa Marina.

Lord, it was good to be home. This house was old and a little rickety but between her and Nick, they managed to keep it functioning. The secondhand furniture was shabby but comfortable, and the garden out back furnished them with vegetables and herbs. It was all she needed. All she wanted. A haven to come home to from the storms of everyday life.

"Want a cookie, Devon. Want a cookie, Devon. Stingy Devon. Give a gal a cookie."

Bronwyn, the most vocal of the parrots, was screeching at her from her perch in the sunroom.

"Shut up, Bronwyn. You'll get one after dinner." Devon closed her bedroom door behind her.

Peace.

She moved over to the rocking chair and dropped down on it. She'd take just a moment and close her eyes. She needed to unwind before she called Hugh Dalks, who was filling in for her at the clinic. It was hard to get out of the mind-set of search and rescue and into the more mundane job of veterinary medicine. She always felt remote when she came back, but that changed with the first patient.

No, it was the end of the office day, and Hugh would be going home. She didn't want to disturb him there. She dialed his cell number.

"I thought I'd hear from you soon," Hugh said when he picked up the phone. "I stopped hearing anything on CNN about the rescue mission. That usually means that you're going to be on your way home."

"I just got to the house. How are things at the clinic?"

"Wonderful. I haven't missed you at all. Why

don't you stay gone for a little while longer? By that time all your patients will be so enthralled by me that I'll be able to steal them away from you. I need to open a practice of my own."

"No deal."

"Then will you marry me and support me?"

"Hell no." She could almost see Hugh with his lean, angular face, horn-rimmed glasses, and quizzical grin. He had gotten out of school only two years before, but he'd worked at a county emergency clinic and the experience had made him one of the best veterinarians she knew. "You haven't missed me, but have any of my patients?"

"Well, Mrs. Johnson has been waiting for you to have her beagle spayed. She's very impatient. She won't trust me with her darling."

"Call her and tell her to bring Cuddles in tomorrow morning." She paused. "And save a little time to give an in-depth examination to a wounded Lab I brought home from Santa Marina. I don't think Nick or I will have time tomorrow. I'd bet there are a few more clients who just **might** prefer us."

"It's a possibility. Is this dog a stray or one of the rescue team dogs?"

"Neither. I just don't know where the owner is right now."

"I'll do the workup." Hugh paused. "It's good to have you back, Devon."

"Thanks, Hugh. It's good to be back."

"And I really would marry you and let you support me. We could let Nick run the practice, and I'd concentrate on opening a new world for you. Did I ever tell you that I minored in gigolo at college?"

She smiled. "And I'm sure you're very qualified. Good-bye, Hugh."

The smile still lingered as she hung up the phone. Everything was easing back into the same comfortable path as when she'd left. Tomorrow would be hectic and demanding and she would welcome it.

But right now she needed quiet time for herself. She didn't want any intrusive thoughts that might jar her.

Like Jude Marrok.

She rejected that thought immediately. She had seldom met a more disturbing man, and she did not want to be disturbed. She would be just as happy if she never saw him again.

Not likely. He would be back for Ned.

And then she would decide whether to turn him over to Marrok.

Conflict. Aggression. Battle. They all loomed on the horizon when Marrok showed up.

Not yet. Those might come with Marrok, but he wasn't here now. She didn't have to deal with anything more unsettling than the problem of staying awake until Janet called her for supper.

Take advantage of these moments.

The house phone rang.

She stiffened. No ID. Let Janet answer it? No, face it.

She picked up the receiver. "Hello."

"I hear you were batting around the Caribbean," Lester said softly. "How many men did you sleep with on that pretty island?"

Hang up? No, he'd just call back. Let him get the poison out, and he might give her peace tonight. "None. If you know I was on Santa Marina, you know that I was on a job."

"Yeah, everyone in towns says how noble you are, but we know different, don't we? You only go away because you want to fuck, and you know I'd kill you if I caught you with any man here. I'd kill you both."

Threats and obscenities. He never tired of them. "That's ridiculous. I was on a job."

"It's been a long time since I heard your voice, bitch. I've known the number since the second week after you changed it, but I wanted to make you think you'd fooled me.

Surprises are always more effective. I'm having a little trouble getting your cell number, but I'll persuade someone in the phone company office to give it to me soon." He paused. "The house phone is in Nick Gilroy's name. You have him wrapped around your finger, don't you? Do you sleep with him, too?"

"We're friends," she said between her teeth. For God's sake, let him hang up. She didn't know how much more she could stand.

"No, I think it might be Dalks. He's younger and I know your appetite. Do you do it at the clinic?"

"No. And I'm sure you know it." She couldn't take anymore. "I'm going to hang up."

"And you're hoping I won't call you back."

"Yes. I don't deserve this, Lester."

"You deserve anything I want to hand out to you." His tone was suddenly ugly. "Whore. No other man, Devon. You're coming back to me. You killed my child. Now you're going to give me another one."

"I didn't kill—" The pain was searing through her as it always did when he reached this point. "You know I—"

"No other man, bitch." He hung up.

She was cold, shaking. She shouldn't let him do this to her. God knows she was used to this ugliness. She should be stronger. But the threat wasn't only to her, it was to the people close to her. This time he'd mentioned both Nick and Dalks.

It didn't mean that Lester would move on them, she told herself. It could be a tactic to make her more afraid and drive her back to him. But could she take the chance? Lester was getting uglier with every contact. If he didn't hurt Nick or Hugh Dalks physically, he could find ways to make trouble for them. In the years since she'd left him, she'd known him do everything from planting drugs in the car of her date to giving anonymous tips that another male friend was a child molester. All ugly, all permanently scarring. It mustn't happen again. Not to Nick, who deserved peace and some measure of contentment. Not to Hugh Dalks, who was just starting out and might face ruin at Lester's hands.

No, tomorrow she'd find a way to change her phone number again and start to plan on how best to keep Lester from hurting these people she cared about. Would she have to go away again?

Dammit, this was her **home.**

I can make another home. So stop whining and do what has to be done.

* * *

"Devon Brady," Danner repeated softly. "You're sure, Rachoff?"

"Yes, she has the dog," Rachoff said. "She caused all kinds of upset trying to arrange to get him off the island. You're not supposed to take any livestock back to the States without quarantine but she pulled some strings and got permission to take him back with the rest of the search and rescue team."

"That sounds like a considerable hassle. Now why would she want to go to the bother?" He thought he could guess. He'd thought it was bizarre that Marrok had suddenly taken it into his head to go on a rescue mission.

Devon Brady.

Was she one of them? Had he used the disaster mission to make contact with her? Marrok had always made the effort to keep the identity and whereabouts of the guardians secret. He wouldn't risk contacting her in her usual environment. He'd transferred the dog into her care. Was that what he'd meant to do anyway?

"What do you want me to do?" Rachoff

asked. "There's no sign of Kingston. Do you want me to stick around and see if I can locate him?"

"Hell no. I wouldn't have sent you if I hadn't thought Marrok had gotten to Kingston. If you did locate him, he'd probably be six feet underground." And good riddance to the bastard. He'd had his chance and blown it. "Get back to the States. Marrok won't let the dog stay with the Brady woman now. We have to move fast and get to that Lab before he does."

"I've never understood why that dog is so important to—"

"I don't pay you to ask questions," Danner said curtly. "Where does she live?"

"Bayside, Colorado. A small town outside Denver. Do you think that's where she'll take the dog?"

"I don't know. We may get lucky. She may not have been able to make alternate arrangements so quickly. If we move fast, we may be able to scoop her up. I'll send a team to meet you in Denver. Get moving."

"The dog is alive. So is Marrok." Danner turned to Paul Caswell. "It's not going to be an easy retrieval. Dammit, we came so close this time."

"At least Marrok is on the radar screen again. We may be able to track him." Caswell shrugged. "It's been a long time since we got this close."

"You're very cool," Danner said sarcastically. "So slick. Why shouldn't you be? Marrok isn't trying to kill you."

"That doesn't mean I don't intend to get him." He rose to his feet. "Our reasons may differ, but our goal is the same. I'll arrange for air transport and check out what the situation is in Denver."

Danner's hands clenched into fists as he watched Caswell leave the room. What the hell. He couldn't blame Caswell for not having the same passion as Danner for getting Marrok. Four years ago, when they'd almost gathered him in, Danner had been angry and disappointed but he hadn't had this feeling of desperate urgency. The years had done that to him. He'd had all that power dangling before him and not been able to reach out and grab it. It had gone on too long, and Danner wanted it ended.

Caswell might not mind waiting, but Danner couldn't wait. He **wouldn't** wait.

This time they had to get Marrok.

* * *

"Does it have to be tonight, Bridget?" Fraser whispered. "It would be easier for you if you had the chance to let him get to know you."

"I know that," Bridget said. She didn't like the hurry any more than Fraser. She didn't like any of this business. Creeping around stealing someone's animal in the middle of the night was a good way to get shot. "Marrok says it has to be as soon as possible. He wants the donkey and all the other animals out of here. I told him it would be difficult as hell."

"Why can't you just go get Ned?"

That's exactly what she'd asked Marrok. "He said for us to get the donkey first. Marrok will get Ned himself. You know it never does any good to argue with him. He'd only say we work for him and to do what he tells us."

"That doesn't often stop you," Fraser said dryly. "I wouldn't talk back to him, but you never have a problem."

She shrugged. "This time he's right. He hired me three years ago to help him with Danner, and that means doing things that aren't always in the rule book. Just have the trailer ready." She moved toward the fenced enclosure the donkey occupied. His name was Casper, she'd found out by asking around the small town. He'd been injured, and the owner had wanted to put him down, but Devon Brady had healed him, then taken him under her wing. Bridget approved the action, but she didn't look forward to dealing with a donkey. Even the most placid could be temperamental at times and their hooves and teeth could do serious damage.

And it was going to be hard to make Casper understand, blast it. Particularly when she didn't have the time to prepare him. That's what she'd tried to tell Marrok but all he'd said was that the donkey would be the most difficult and had to be taken first. He was right, but that—

A chill suddenly struck her. Her head lifted, and her gaze shifted to the east.

"What is it?" Fraser asked, his gaze on her face.

"I don't know." She was shivering. "I . . . don't like . . ." Her gaze moved around the peaceful paddocks. Not here. Not now. "Are you supposed to stay here after I leave?"

He nodded. "Marrok told me to keep an eye on the place and let him know if there's trouble."

"Be careful."

"Why?"

"I don't know."

"Dammit, I hate it when you do that, Bridget," he said in disgust.

"Tough." She couldn't blame him. But it was just as frustrating for her. No, not frustrating, terrifying. Keep it under control. It could be a false alarm. "I'm giving you all I can. It's not right away. Maybe not at all. Now let me concentrate on this donkey."

"Who's stopping you?" He was uneasily following her gaze toward the east. "You're the one who decided to scare the pants off me."

"Sorry." She didn't want to frighten Fraser. She couldn't be sure. She wasn't right all the time. Forget it and get to the job at hand. "Okay, Casper," she said softly as she opened the gate. "We're going to go very slow. Just listen, and we'll see what we can do together."

Casper turned to look at her.

Not a warm response. She could sense only wariness and the gathering of strength.

"We have to help Devon." She was slowly walking toward him. "She needs us to go away for a while. Nothing is going to happen to you. I promise you."

Distrust.

"I know. You haven't had much reason to trust people. But it's started to turn around. There are people coming here that might hurt you. If she knew, Devon would want you to go." She reached out and touched the center of his head with her forefinger. Careful. Casper might look the picture of a friendly figure from a children's book, but those teeth were scissor-strong, and one bite could take off a finger.

He didn't move under her touch.

How much time did she have?

Not long.

But she had to take the time. If he brayed, he might wake the household. If she tried to put a halter on him, he might lead her all over the pasture before he let her catch him. He had to follow her willingly.

She gently rubbed the sweet spot on his muzzle. "It's okay. You don't want to be here right now. Nothing is going to happen to you. I wouldn't let it. I'm going to be with you all the way . . ."

CHAPTER 4

Home.

The sun was shining with hazy brilliance through the filmy white drapes at the window as Devon opened her eyes.

Something wasn't right, she realized drowsily.

Gracie wasn't on her usual place beside her bed.

That's right, after Gracie had come back from the paddock she'd eaten her evening meal, then settled down beside Ned in the kitchen. It was the first time she'd not spent the night in Devon's room since Devon had brought her home. She must be really concerned about the Lab.

Devon swung her legs to the floor and got out of bed. She'd shower, dress, and check Ned's stitches. Then she had to go to the clinic and ease back into the regular routine.

Sometimes routines were blessedly comforting. When she had been younger, she had been full of the love for adventure and change. That was before she had learned that adventures could be tragic, and changes weren't always happy. She was more cautious now.

That wasn't what Nick called it. He said she was turning into a stick-in-the-mud. He was always urging her to go away, set sail on a cruise, get away from the grind.

Get away from Lester, he really meant. He never mentioned Lester's name, but he'd been with her long enough to know what she was going through.

Maybe Nick would get his way, she thought sadly. She'd almost made up her mind that she'd have to leave this situation behind her.

Her cell phone rang. No ID.

Let it not be Lester.

"Devon Brady."

"Jude Marrok. I have to see you."

She stiffened. "The hell you do. Do you realize what you put me through getting that dog out of Santa Marina?"

"Yes, but I also knew you might be the only one who could."

"It would have served you right if I'd left him there."

"That wasn't going to happen." He repeated, "I have to see you. Can you meet me at your clinic in town?"

"No, I have work to do there."

"It's eight now. I'm in St. Louis waiting to change planes. I'll be there as soon as I can. Don't leave Ned. Take him to your office."

"Don't give me orders, Marrok."

"Do what I say. I'm doing what's best for you."

He hung up before she could answer.

Damn him. Marrok had been as curt and cool as he had been on the island. She still wasn't sure she should turn the Lab over to him. And she certainly wouldn't rush to be at her office to clear her calendar by the time he got there.

She took a leisurely shower, washed and dried her hair, and entered the kitchen a few minutes before nine. "Good morning, Janet. How did you sleep?"

"You know I always sleep good." Janet was turning the bacon. "No tossing and turning for me. You just have to set your mind to it."

Gracie got up from her place beside Ned and bounded toward Devon.

"It's about time you paid some attention to me," Devon murmured. She rubbed the greyhound's ears. "How's your friend?"

"That Lab's been begging me for bacon," Janet said. "Sitting there all pretty and expecting me to throw him a bite. He's teaching Gracie bad habits."

Devon stifled a smile. "And you didn't give in, of course."

"I threw him a few pieces. I wouldn't have done it, but protein is good to heal wounds. Right?"

"Absolutely." She knelt beside the Lab and examined the wound. She gave a low whistle. "But he may not need any help. This wound is doing incredibly well." Marrok had said that Ned healed well, but she hadn't expected the mending to have progressed to this degree. She patted Ned's head. "You're doing good, fella. Keep it up."

"If you're done with that coddling, you might sit down and eat your breakfast while it's hot, so I haven't wasted my time." Janet placed the eggs and bacon on the china plate. "Wash your hands first."

"I'm aware of the hygiene factor." Devon washed her hands at the sink. "Where's Nick?"

"He went down to feed Casper and the cats. Though those cats should be earning their keep being mousers in that barn. I saw a rat the last time I went down there."

"They were raised as house cats." She sat down at the table and started eating. "They'd be here with us if they weren't afraid of the dogs."

"They just like having their own kingdom in that barn, with all of us waiting on them." Janet poured her a cup of coffee. "You spoil them."

"Maybe." She was looking at Ned. He was bright-eyed and moving with only a little stiffness. "Your friend, Marrok, wants you back. What about it?"

Ned's tail thumped hard on the floor.

"Is that a yes? I'm not so sure. I certainly won't turn you over to him until I'm sure you're well on the way to healing."

"He looks good to me," Nick said from the kitchen door. "Better than good."

"I'll take him in and have him checked over just to make sure. Are you going with me?"

"No." He grimaced. "I have to get in the truck and see if I can find Casper."

She stared at him in bewilderment. "What?"

"I must have left the gate ajar when I went into the paddock to feed him last night. It was half-open when I went down this morning." He held up his hand. "Don't worry. No one is going to take Casper. Everyone knows he belongs to you. If I can't find him, I'll leave word with all the farmers in the neighborhood to let me know when they see him."

"I'm not worried about him being stolen. Casper's not too bright. He has a tendency to charge if he gets nervous. Maybe I should go with you."

"He'll be fine. I think I can handle that donkey. He'll recognize me as the bringer of good vittles." Nick took the keys to the truck from the cookie jar on the counter. "I'll call you when I locate him. Otherwise, I'll see you at the clinic later."

"Okay." She was frowning as she watched him go down the steps. It was odd that Casper had gotten loose. Nick was always very careful about locks. But he was right; the donkey would probably be fine.

"I never left the gate open," Janet said flatly. "Not once."

"And Nick usually doesn't either." She finished her coffee and got to her feet. "Come on,

Ned. Let's go to the clinic and check you out. We'll have my friend Dr. Dalks take a look at you, then I'll let you sit with the receptionist and charm all the patients. You'll like Terry. She's a pushover for Labs."

"Devon Brady left the house ten minutes ago," Fraser said when he picked up Marrok's call. "Nick Gilroy left before her. I think he's looking for the donkey."

"Did she take Ned with her?"

"Yes, he looked pretty spry."

"He should. It's been two days," Marrok said. "Are you still at the farm?"

"Yes." Fraser was silent. "Bridget says she thinks . . . she was nervous last night."

His hand tightened on the phone. "Any sign?"

"No, but I've been keeping my eyes peeled. I'm going to take another look around after I hang up. Bridget isn't often wrong."

No, she wasn't, Marrok thought. In her own way her instincts were as sharp and accurate as Ned's. Bridget would appreciate the comparison. She liked animals better than she liked most people.

Devon had said something like that the

night he'd met her. She would probably get along very well with Bridget.

If he could keep her alive long enough to meet her.

"Don't take any chances, Fraser. Your job is to report, not engage. Call me when you finish checking the area."

"I will. I'll see them before they see me." He hung up.

Dammit, he had at least an hour before he reached Denver, and it would be another hour before he could make it to the small town of Bayside.

He didn't have Bridget's gift, but he had a bad feeling. He wanted to be off this plane and able to move.

It was a busy morning at the clinic, and Devon was drawn into the usual hubbub of sick animals and concerned owners as soon as she walked in the door. She immediately turned Ned over to Hugh Dalks for his exam and didn't have a chance to pop her head into his examining room until the morning was almost over. "How's he doing?"

"You say that he was just operated on day before yesterday?" Hugh shook his head. "I'd never guess it. The tissue is almost completely healed. The stitches are almost unnecessary. I'm tempted to take them out."

"He must have good genes," she said lightly.

"Extraordinary genes." He was rubbing Ned's belly. "Did you know he has an ID microchip in his neck?"

"It doesn't surprise me. That's not so unusual. He's a valuable dog."

"Since you said his owner had disappeared, I thought you might want me to decode it and try to find the address. It wasn't easy. First, I tried the Vera chip RFD reader. Nothing. Then I tried the Avid remote. Still nothing."

"Weird, those are the two most frequently used microchip ID companies."

"Yeah, that's what I thought. Then I tried that old Sentar reader that Nick used years ago when they first started to microchip animals. It gave me the code number, but when I typed it into the computer the screen went blank, then it flipped as if it was going to another Web site."

"And?"

"Some kind of text came up, but it was all screwy."

"Screwy?"

"It's as if the chip was for another dog. Even the name is different. Not Ned. It's Paco."

"It must have been a tech error when they entered the information."

"I'll say. They've got everything wrong. Name. Date of birth, and the rest of the text isn't even in English."

"Really? Do you still have it up on the computer?"

"Sure, I thought you might want to see it." He went to the shelf and pressed the button. "There it is."

Devon frowned as she stared at the text message. It was long, and Hugh was right, it was completely bewildering. It had to be in another language, but she couldn't identify which one.

She had a memory of Marrok's words soothing Ned. She hadn't been able to decide what language he'd been speaking either. "Print it out for me before you blow it away, will you?"

"Okay, but I don't know why you'd want it. As I said, it's screwy." He lifted the Lab down from the table. "We'll have to make him a new one if you decide to keep him."

She nodded absently. "Yes, we'll do that." She looked down at Ned. "Well, are you ready to go out to the reception desk to meet and greet?"

Ned trotted toward the door.

"Smart," Hugh said. "If you don't want him, I might be persuaded to take him."

It seemed Ned was very much in demand. "You like him?"

"What's not to like? He's smart, and I have an idea he's a man's dog. Might to might."

"That's a chauvinist thing to say. Women aren't mighty?"

"Am I in trouble?"

"Maybe."

"Come on, Devon," Hugh coaxed. "Give him to me. You don't want a rickety old dog like that."

"Old? You're crazy."

Hugh chuckled. "Yep. But it's not me, it's that microchip." He headed for the door. "Completely nuts. The only part of the chip I could read was the line for the birth date at the beginning—5/13/82."

Her eyes widened. "What?"

"I know. Told you so." He left the examining room.

Devon shook her head. Hugh was right. The tech that had made up that chip must have been stoned. The life of a big dog like Ned was only in the teens. The chip would have put him close to thirty years old.

"Come on, Grandpa," she told Ned. "Your audience awaits. I saw a cute husky pup out there you can impress."

There wasn't anyone in the woods.

Fraser breathed a sigh of relief. He wasn't great in the forest like Marrok, but he would surely have been able to catch a sound, a glimpse, if someone had been here. He'd done his duty and now he could go back to the farmhouse, where he felt more comfortable. Bridget was wrong, and he shouldn't have let her spook him.

Though she never meant to do that, and he'd a hell of a lot rather she spoke up than keep those creepy feelings to herself. She'd saved his neck a couple times in the last three years he'd been working for Marrok. It still wigged him out, but he accepted it better now than—

A tearing pain in his shoulder.

A bullet. My God, he'd barely heard it. A silencer . . .

Run.

He could see the two men bursting through the bushes ahead of him.

Turn around and run.

They mustn't catch him.

Marrok had said that was the worse thing that could happen to him.

Another slicing pain in his back.

Keep running.

Find a place to hide.

Or get to the farmyard where someone would see him.

They were behind him, running fast.

And he was slowing, stumbling . . .

Faster . . .

The blood was flowing, spurting . . .

Don't let them—

"She's not at the farm," Rachoff said, when Caswell answered. "She got into a van with the dog just as we got here. You said to try to be discreet, so I had a man follow her and report back to me. She went to a veterinary clinic in one of those strip shopping centers and hasn't come out. Shall we wait here until she comes back?"

Caswell thought about it. "It would probably be safer than taking a chance in a public place."

"It would be my choice." He hesitated. "But we had to put down someone who was snooping around the woods. One of Marrok's people?"

"Any ID?"

"Nothing connected with Marrok."

But if Marrok had men already at the farm to protect the Brady woman, then they'd have to move faster than anticipated.

"Forget about being safe. Go get her."

Fraser wasn't answering his phone.

Not good. Marrok had tried to reach him twice on the plane when he hadn't checked back in with him. He'd called a third time once he'd reached the ground.

Marrok strode out of the airport and jumped into the rental car.

He got the call from Bridget when he was pulling out of the parking lot.

"Something's wrong." Bridget's voice was shaking. "Something bad."

"Take it easy. Do you know what it is?"

"Something's . . . gone."

Shit.

"Look, hold on, Bridget. I'll take care of it."

"Too late. It's already started. Fraser . . ."

"We don't know that yet. And if it is, we have to keep it from getting worse. I'm on my way to Devon Brady's office right now. I'm pulling her out."

"And I'm going to that farm to find Fraser."

"No," he said sharply. He didn't want Bridget blundering into Danner's hands if he'd already made his move.

"Don't tell me no," she said fiercely. "I worked with Fraser for three years. He's been as close to a friend as I've had here. I owe it to him."

"You don't owe it to him to get yourself killed."

"I'm going."

"Okay." Try to get something positive out of this since he couldn't convince her. "But take a team and try to get the housekeeper and Nicholas Gilroy out of there before you go looking for Fraser. Will you do that for me?"

Silence. "Yes."

She'd agreed too easily, Marrok thought. Because in her heart, she believed it was too late for Fraser. "Good. Keep in touch."

"Marrok."

"Yes."

"Hurry. Devon Brady's office, the clinic. It's not safe there either." She hung up the phone.

Marrok muttered a curse as he punched in the number Walt had given him for Nick Gilroy.

"Gilroy, you've never met me. My name is Jude Marrok."

"No, but I've heard about you. Devon is very irritated with the way you—"

"Where are you? Have you gone back to the farm yet?"

"How did you know that I—"

"Are you at the farm?"

"No, I'm filling up my gas tank at the BP station."

"Good. Stay there."

"Can't do it. I have to find that damn don—"

"You'll not find the donkey. Stay where you are. Don't go back to the farm. Devon is going to meet you. She'll call you when she's on her way." He hung up.

He doubted if Gilroy would obey him, but he'd probably call Devon, and that might delay his going back to the farm. Bridget would move fast, but he needed all the time he could muster.

He phoned Devon Brady. "Get my dog out of that office. Close up and send everyone home."

"I beg your pardon." Devon's voice was icy.

"Lock the doors. I'll be there in five or ten minutes, but you can't take a chance I'll be in time. Get out of there."

"I've no intention of doing anything you order me to do. I have appointments that—"

"Then get Ned out of there. He's the draw that will make them come after you."

"Who are you talking about? Who's coming—"

"Stop asking questions and get my dog away from there. I don't want him shot again." His voice lowered, and every word came out charged with intensity. "And I don't want anyone else shot either. I'm not crazy, and I'm not joking."

"Shot?"

"That's what's going to happen. I hoped we'd have more time, but I think they're on their way. They have their orders, and they won't care who they have to kill to get what they want."

"Dammit, who's supposed to be on the way? The man who shot Ned?"

"No, I took him out of the equation. Look, you don't have time to ask me questions. Lock the doors. Where's your car?"

She hesitated. "It's parked in the back parking lot behind the clinic."

"What kind of car?"

"Toyota SUV."

"Good. Put Ned in the back and tell him to play dead. I've seen that's one trick he knows to perfection. Cover him up with a blanket. Then get the hell away from the office."

"This is nuts." She was silent a moment. "You mean it."

"I mean it. Get moving." He hung up the phone. He'd done all he could do. It was up to Devon now. He had only one more call to make.

Crazy. Devon slowly pressed the disconnect. She should ignore the call and go on with her day.

But Marrok's voice had been dead serious.

And she believed he thought he was telling the truth even if it was completely bizarre.

Get moving.

Whatever was going to happen, he thought there was urgency.

Ignore it?

She got to her feet and moved toward the reception room. She didn't ignore warnings if she thought they held even a grain of truth. She had seen too many tragedies, too many villagers caught in mudslides and rushing floodwater and other disasters when they'd ignored warnings that might have saved them.

The reception room was empty of clients, and Terry was sitting cross-legged on the floor, patting Ned's belly. Red-haired, pretty, and voluptuous, she always reminded Devon of a model or showgirl. But her receptionist was smart as a whip and amazingly efficient. Terry glanced up with a guilty grin. "Okay, so this isn't my job. I was just massaging him. I thought it might help."

"Yeah, sure." Evidently Terry was clearly bewitched by Ned. "Do we have any more appointments today?"

"There's one at four." Terry got to her feet. "But that's for Dr. Dalks."

"I think we're going to call it a day." She clipped a leash to Ned's collar. "Call the client and postpone. Then lock up and go home, Terry."

"Really?" Terry smiled eagerly as she picked up the phone and started to look up the number. "Right away. You're not going to get an argument from me. I've got a hot date tonight, and I need to get a pedicure."

"I doubt if he'll be looking at your toes, Terry."

"You can never tell. Maybe he has a foot fetish."

Devon started for the back of the clinic and stopped. What the hell. She turned and locked the front door herself. "Go out the back door. We don't want any drop-ins delaying you."

"Good idea," Terry said absently as she started to dial the phone.

Devon stopped at the examining room where Hugh Dalks was filling out reports on the way to the back door. "Go home, Hugh. I'm declaring an official holiday."

"What?"

"You heard me." She opened the back door. "It's my first day back, and we're breaking early."

"Are you sure you're feeling okay? That doesn't sound like the workaholic I know and love."

"I'm fine. Get out of here. I want this place cleared in five minutes." She closed the door, and her gaze darted around the back parking lot. Nothing suspicious. God, she was turning paranoid. This was only a precaution, dammit. She unlocked the SUV, and Ned jumped into the back.

"Lie down." Okay, go for broke. She might as well go the whole nine yards. "Play dead, Ned."

Ned rolled over and closed his eyes.

He knows that trick to perfection.

Why had Marrok felt he needed to know that particular trick? She tossed the plush football blanket she kept for transporting sick animals over him. "This is crazy. I hope your friend Marrok isn't leading me down a blind alley." She got into the SUV and backed out of the parking space. "Because I don't like him interfering with my—"

Her driver's side window shattered, and a bullet plowed into the leather of the passenger seat!

What . . .

A man was running out the back door of the clinic toward her car. "Stop, bitch." He lifted the gun in his hand. "Gotcha."

A hot streaking pain seared the side of her neck.

Shot, she realized incredulously. She'd been shot.

She instinctively pressed the accelerator, but the man had reached her car and was running beside it, pressing the muzzle against the glass.

She was going to die.

There was no way he could miss from this distance. His face was only inches from the glass. Hard face. Ugly face.

Yet suddenly there was no face. His skull was half-blown away, and he dropped to the ground.

"Let me in." Marrok was standing at the

passenger door. His tone was so demanding, she automatically pressed the button.

He jumped in the SUV. "Now get the hell out of here."

She was staring dazedly at the man crumpled on the ground. "You killed him."

"Damn straight. I blew the bastard's head off. Would you rather I let him do that to you? He probably wasn't alone. Get this car moving!"

She stomped on the accelerator, and the car lurched forward. She didn't look back until she was almost out of the shopping center at the exit to the street.

This couldn't have happened. The sun was shining brightly, and she saw a mother and her two kids going into the ice-cream shop across the street. Everything was normal and as it should be.

Except someone had just tried to kill her and had died horribly in the attempt.

And there was another man running out the back door of the clinic and up the hill toward the street.

A navy blue SUV was parked directly in front of the clinic and the front door of the clinic was wide-open. She had locked that door herself. That door must have been forced only a few minutes after she had left.

Fear iced through her.

Hugh and Terry!

She stomped on the brakes. "No, I have to go back. Hugh and Terry are—"

"I called 911 after I talked to you. They should be here any minute. But it could be too late for you if don't leave now. You're the one they're looking for. Get out of here while we have the chance."

"What is—"

"Move!"

She pressed the accelerator, and the SUV took off. She heard the sirens in the distance. Relief poured through her. "You did call the police."

"I told you I did. I don't lie . . . unless it's necessary."

"How comforting."

"Your neck's bleeding."

She'd almost forgotten the wound. She touched it. "I think it's okay." She looked back. They were a block away, and the clinic was no longer in view. "I let you panic me. I have to go back and see if I can—"

"Are you nuts?" he asked harshly. "You should have been panicked. You almost bought it back there." He looked in the rear of the SUV. "Ned's in the back?"

"Yes." She was starting to think again. "You came out of nowhere. I didn't even see you until you—"

"I came in a Saturn rental car that's still in the middle of the lot. I jumped out of it when I saw what needed to be done."

Murder. He meant murder needed to be done. He'd taken a life. "You killed him."

"Of course I did," he said impatiently.

So casual. What was this all about? What was she getting herself into by letting him control this terrible situation? She suddenly pulled over to the side of the street. "I'm going back to the office. Those men must have been scared off by the police sirens by now. I have to talk to the police and explain what—"

"No," Marrok said flatly. "You're off the radar right now. I don't want them to get a fix on you again."

"Once more the mysterious 'they.'" She moistened her lips. "You only killed that man to save my life. You should come back with me and clear yourself."

"No way."

She unlocked the doors. "Then get out. Take your dog. I'm going back."

He shook his head. "I can't let you do that."

She looked at him in disbelief. "You don't have anything to say about it. I'm going to go back and make sure Hugh and Terry are—" She inhaled sharply as she saw the flicker of emotion on his face. "You don't think—You think those men killed them."

"I don't think they had a chance once Danner's men got into the office. They were probably dead within seconds."

"That's insane." But it was insane for someone to try to kill her, too. So how could she say that? "They're my friends," she said shakily as she started to pull out from the curb. "I can't go anywhere when there's a chance I can help—"

She felt a prick of pain on her upper arm.

"Don't be frightened," Marrok said curtly. "I can't let you run back there. It's only a shot. It will put you out for a little while until I can work a way out of this mess."

A shot.

Dimness . . .

Drowsiness . . .

Nothing . . .

CHAPTER
5

He called Bridget ten minutes later as he was heading for the highway. "They hit the clinic. They came up empty, so they're probably heading back out to the farm. They'd figure that's where Devon would run."

"I didn't think they were still here at the farm. They were in the woods, but I don't feel anything now . . . Ned's okay?"

"Fine." He looked back at the Lab, who was now curled up and lying beside Devon Brady with his head on her arm. "And so is Devon. She's got a wound on her neck, but I think it's only a scratch. At least, she'll be fine when she wakes up. Did you send someone to pick up Gilroy?"

"Yes. Now there's only the last bit to do at the farm." She paused. "If they think your Devon's here, they'll try to stop us. How much time do I have?"

"Probably fifteen minutes tops."

"If they come after us, I'm not going to hold back, Marrok."

"I'm not asking you to. I just want you all out of there in one piece." His hands tightened on the steering wheel. "I'm taking Devon and Ned to the Nevada ranch. When you finish up, I want you there, too."

"I'll be there . . . after I find Fraser." She paused. "There's no sign of him yet."

"Bridget."

"I have to make sure, Marrok." She hung up.

And risk getting her throat cut while she searched for him, Marrok thought in frustration. Well, he could do nothing now. He had to trust that she'd be all right.

He dialed Walt Franks to tell him to find a place for the helicopter to pick them up somewhere between here and Denver.

"I put the pig in the van earlier. You round up the other animals," Bridget said to Larry

Farland as she stuffed her phone in her jacket. "I'll take care of the housekeeper."

"Right. I saw three dogs down at the paddock." Larry motioned to two of the team to follow him and disappeared around the corner of the house.

Bridget whirled and went up the steps to the kitchen door. Get it over quick. She wished to hell she had a sedative or chloroform, but they'd moved too fast to get any supplies when Marrok had called. She'd just have to make it fast.

Janet McDonald was standing at the stove with her back to Bridget when she quietly opened the door.

"Is that you, Nick?" Janet's gaze never left the pot of stew she was stirring. "You might as well sit down and have some lunch. Though you don't deserve it. It was careless leaving that gate open. Did you find the donkey?"

"No, he didn't."

Janet stiffened, then looked over her shoulder. "What the devil are you doing here? Don't you kids believe in knocking?"

Though she was twenty-five, it wasn't the first time Bridget had been mistaken for a teenager. It didn't matter. Sometimes her small stature and baby-smooth skin came in handy. People usually trusted in the innocence of youth. She smiled gently. "I did knock. You must not have heard me."

The woman's eyes narrowed on her. "Nothing's wrong with my hearing. What do you want?"

Bridget could practically feel the other woman's tension. She had carefully kept any hint of aggression out of her demeanor, yet the housekeeper was sensing a threat. "I'd like you to go with me. Something's happened. Devon needs you."

"And you're a lying bitch. If Devon needed me, then she'd call and tell me so. Get out."

This was not going to be easy. Marrok had said to be careful. How to do it without hurting her?

"Is that her dog, Gracie?" Bridget asked as she came toward her. Gracie was a piece of cake. She wanted to love everybody. Her tail thumped wildly, and she ran toward Bridget. "Nice pooch."

"She's okay. No taste in people," Janet said. "I told you to leave. I'm not buying what you're selling."

"I'm sorry I intruded." She was standing next to the woman now. She was wishing again they'd had time to pick up an anesthetic. This was not going well. One more try. "I'm no threat to you. It's really best if you come with me."

"I'm the only one who knows what's best for me." The housekeeper stared her coldly in the eye. "You look all fresh-faced and butter could melt in your mouth. But my ex-husband used to bring home sweet-faced little foxes like you, and I know what's behind that smile. What are you up to?"

Dammit, Bridget didn't have time to try to persuade her. She started to turn away. "If you want me to go, then I'll—" She whirled back, with her hand arcing in a karate blow to the woman's neck.

But Janet blocked her hand and back-handed her across the face.

Dear God, she was fast.

Bridget dove for her legs to bring her down.

And felt hot stew splashing down her back as Janet knocked the pot on top of her.

Pain. Ignore it. Bring her down.

Forget being careful. She punched her in the stomach.

The housekeeper gasped and staggered back.

Bridget jumped up and brought down the side of her hand in the karate chop that had been blocked before.

The woman crumpled and fell to the floor.

Bridget was panting as she looked down at her. Good God, the woman was tough. The resistance had been a surprise.

A painful surprise. Her burned back was stinging from the hot liquid of the stew.

Forget it. No time. They had to get the woman bound and in the truck. She took the cord from her pocket and quickly tied Janet's hands behind her back. Gracie was sitting, looking at her in bewilderment. "It's okay. I know you're confused. You got all those good signals from me, then your friend is hurt." She put her hand on the dog's forehead. "It's what should be happening. Everything is fine, Gracie." She got to her feet. "Come on, we'll take you to Devon."

Larry was loading the dogs into the van when she opened the door. "Take Gracie up front. She's nervous."

"The housekeeper?"

"In the kitchen. Be careful with her. She's a tiger."

"So I see." Larry was looking at her soaked shirt and red arms. "Are you okay?"

She nodded. "Just get out of here. You have ten minutes."

"We'll be out of here in five."

"Good, I'll see you back at the motel where we're supposed to pick up Gilroy." She started for the woods. Then she had a thought and said over her shoulder, "The parrots. They have to be somewhere in the house. Be sure to get them."

"For God's sake, the van will look like Noah's ark." Larry sighed as he ran up the steps and into the house. "I'll go after them now."

Larry would be true to his word, Bridget thought, her eyes on the woods ahead. He was a good man and he'd see that the farm was deserted before Danner's men got there.

Fraser had been a good man, too.

She was already thinking past tense. Don't give up.

There was still a chance.

She could be wrong.

She wasn't wrong.

She found Fraser on the side of the path only a hundred yards from the tree line. His eyes were open and staring sightlessly up at the sky. There were five bullet wounds in his body, and the last had been the fatal one. It had pierced his heart.

* * *

A dog was whining somewhere . . .

Sad . . .

Why didn't someone stop it? Devon wondered. All it took was a loving stroke, a word . . .

Whining. Closer.

She would have to do it herself.

She forced herself to open her eyes.

Ned. His silky black head was lying on her bed, and his brown eyes were only a foot from her face. Wise eyes. Worried eyes. "It's okay," she whispered. She reached out a hand and rubbed the spot between his eyes. "What's wrong?"

"You didn't wake up soon enough for him."

Her gaze flew from Ned to the man sitting in the easy chair across the room, legs stretched out before him. Close-cut dark hair, high cheekbones, and an air of contained intensity.

Marrok.

Shock rippled through her.

She jerked upright on the couch as memory came flooding back to her. "My God, what the hell have you done?"

"Kidnapping?" He got to his feet, and she was once more aware of that catlike grace she'd noticed when she'd first met him. "I guess it could be termed that. I just did what I had to do to keep you alive."

Her gaze flew around the room. Cushiony beige tapestry furniture with punches of red. Wide floor-to-ceiling windows across one wall of the room. "Where am I?"

"Not in Kansas anymore, Dorothy. My ranch in Nevada."

"Nevada." She suddenly remembered the sharp pain in her arm. "You bastard. You gave me a shot to knock me out."

"It was either a shot or a more physical method to take you out of action. I figured you'd be angry no matter what I did, and the shot was more convenient for me."

Anger seared through her. "And that's what it's all about, isn't it? What's convenient for you and your dog."

He met her eyes. "Yes, that's what it's all about. I'm not going to hurt you. Believe me, I didn't want to involve you. It just happened."

Memories were bombarding her. A man's face exploding before her eyes through the splintered glass. "You killed a man."

"No, I killed a vermin." His glance fell to her neck. "Who almost killed you. I bandaged that cut on your neck, and it's nothing.

But another inch, and we would have had a problem."

Her hand instinctively reached up and touched the bandage. "Do you expect me to thank you? It's your fault that someone was trying to shoot me." Ned gave a low whine and pushed against her knee as she got to her feet. "Stop trying to soften me up, Ned." She pushed him away. "You've teamed up with the wrong person."

"He had no choice," he said wearily. "I was the only game in town for him. For all of them."

"I don't know what the hell you're talking about." She moved toward the door. "And I don't want to know. I'm going home."

"I can't let you do that," he said quietly. "There are guards outside. They won't hurt you, but they'll put you out again. I don't think you want that. You just want to know what's happening and get your life to go back to what it was." He shook his head. "It's too late for that. I'm the only game in town for you, too."

"You don't have anything to do with me." She opened the door. "And as soon as I get rid of you, I'll be—" She suddenly remembered the words she knew she had unconsciously tried to forget. She whirled on him. "Hugh and Terry. You said you didn't think they had a chance. It was a lie. That was just another part of the craziness you—" He wasn't answering, but his expression . . . Her stomach clenched with fear. "I don't believe you."

He was dialing his phone. "Will you believe Nick Gilroy?"

"Nick," she repeated. "Have you hurt Nick?"

"Ask him." He spoke into the phone. "Bridget, she needs to talk to Gilroy. Put him on." He handed Devon the phone. "They're on the road on their way here. He's calm and not afraid. You're the only one who can upset him. Your choice."

She slowly took the phone. "Nick?"

"Devon, thank God. I've been trying to phone you. I was afraid you were dead, too. The news report didn't mention your name, but I thought—"

"Dead, too?" She moistened her lips. "Nick, who's dead?"

Silence. "You don't know? I thought that was why you sent them to pick me up."

"Who's dead, Nick?"

"Hugh and Terry."

She inhaled sharply. "How?"

"The radio said that they were shot several times at close range. Possible burglary. There were narcotics stolen. The clinic was ransacked."

"In broad daylight?'

"Drug addicts aren't rational. You know several vet offices were victimized last year."

But no one had been murdered. No one had marched in and cold-bloodedly shot two people.

"But it wasn't burglary, was it, Devon?" he asked. "You wouldn't have sent someone to get me away from there if it had been a simple theft."

She didn't bother to tell him that she had not been the one to get him out of the area. She seemed to be webbed in lies, and there was no point in making Nick anxious when she didn't know his situation. "No, it wasn't a drug steal. You're sure they're dead, Nick?"

Silence. "What do you want from me? I didn't see them. I only know what I heard on the car radio on our way here. I was shocked as hell. I liked both of them."

So had she. "No suspects?"

"Three men were seen driving away in a dark blue sedan a few minutes before the police arrived. There was blood on the ground in the back lot, but they didn't find a body. The cops had received an anonymous 911 tip." He paused. "But they were too late."

Too late. Two lives ended in the space of a few minutes. "Terry was only twenty years old," she said dully. "She had a hot date tonight. She was going to go get a pedi—" She drew a deep, shaky breath. "I can't believe it, Nick."

"Neither can I. What's happening, Devon?"

What was happening was that the world was spinning around and upside down. "I'm not sure. I'm going to have to find out." She roused herself to ask, "You're okay, Nick? They're treating you well?"

"Sure." Then he added, puzzled, "Why wouldn't they?"

"No reason. I'll talk to you soon, Nick." She hung up the phone. She was so stunned that she couldn't think clearly. "He said he'd been trying to reach me."

"I turned off your phone."

"You shouldn't have done that. Good Lord, what am I saying? That's the smallest part of what you're guilty of. Two people are dead."

"I had nothing to do with killing them. I

tried to keep them alive." He paused. "But, yes, I was probably to blame."

"You admit it."

"I guessed wrong. I thought they'd attack the farm even if it meant waiting for you. They must have had orders to escalate. That meant going wherever you'd taken Ned."

Escalate. Such a slick word to mean what Marrok meant. "Why? For God's sake, why?" She lifted her hand to her head. "It's all—it's too bizarre, too ugly. It doesn't make sense."

"It makes sense." He stared at her a moment, then turned away. "You need some space. I'll go make a pot of coffee." He jerked his thumb at a door across the room. "Why don't you go into the bedroom and take a shower. I told Bridget to get you some clothes to wear."

"Who's Bridget?" Then she remembered he'd spoken to a Bridget on the phone before he'd let her talk to Nick. "She's your accomplice."

"You might say that. She works for me. But she wouldn't like the idea of being referred to as anyone's sidekick."

Her hands clenched into fists at her sides. "I'm not going to go anywhere, do anything, until you answer my questions. Why did you take Nick?"

"For his safety and because I didn't want him used against you."

"Then, if it was for his own good, he'll be free to go?"

Marrok shook his head. "I can't do that."

"Then you're the one using Nick against me. You know I can't make a move against you until I know he's safe."

"The thought did occur to me."

"Damn you."

"But it wasn't why I had him taken. I told you the reason."

"And I don't believe you."

"That's your privilege. I hope you will soon. The situation is getting pretty dicey." He looked up from scooping coffee into the coffeemaker, and said quietly, "Whatever it seems, I don't wish harm to you and the people you care about. I've worked hard to keep them safe."

"Two fine people dead," she coldly. "You haven't worked that hard."

His lips twisted. "Someday try walking in my shoes. You'll find all you can do is give it your best shot."

"Are you going to let Nick go?"

"Yes, eventually." He turned on the coffeemaker. "After you shower and have coffee and pull yourself together, we'll discuss it."

His tone was flat and his face without expression. He wasn't going to be moved. "Ten minutes." She whirled and turned toward the bedroom. "And then I'm holding you to your word."

He smiled faintly. "And yet you believe I've lied to you and will probably continue to do so."

She stared back at him in frustration. It was true, how could she believe him? Yet she had to have some explanation, something to hold on to even if she questioned it. "I'm not a fool. I hope I'll be able to tell if you're giving me a bunch of bull."

He nodded soberly. "I hope so, too, Devon."

Devon closed the bathroom door and leaned against it.

She was shaking. Lord, she hoped Marrok hadn't noticed. She didn't want to show him the weakness she was feeling. All the time he'd been talking to her, she'd been aware of the quiet strength that surrounded his every word, every action. Yet beneath that quietness she'd caught glimpses of recklessness and a hint of darkness. It was a strange combination and much more intimidating than swaggering or bombastic speeches. She had to be just as strong. She had never felt that urgency before, never doubted her ability to meet anyone toe to toe. Why should he be different?

Crazy. Everything connected to Marrok was crazy and horrible and with no basis in reality. But she had to make it real. Cut through the bewilderment and be coolly logical.

Kidnapping was not logical. Men killing two innocent people wasn't logical. A lovable dog like Ned being shot wasn't logical.

But if Marrok wasn't a complete psychopath, then there was logic in all those events. She just had to find it.

So stop shaking. Go take that shower, and try to go over every bit of information you've managed to gather since Marrok brought Ned into the first-aid tent.

She stripped off her clothes and reached out her hand to turn on the hot water.

Hugh. Terry.

Tears were suddenly pouring down her cheeks. She sat down on the edge of the tub and rocked back and forth in an agony of despair. The shock had ebbed and left her emotions as naked as her body. She couldn't be logical now. Not until she was able to push this sorrow and regret into the background. She had to grieve for her two friends who had died this day.

* * *

It was over an hour later when Devon came out of the bathroom into the adjoining bedroom.

She stopped abruptly as she saw the brown-haired woman sitting in the easy chair across the room.

"Sorry. I didn't mean to startle you. I'm Bridget Reardon. I have to talk to you." She looked at the towel draped around Devon. "Go on and get dressed. I can wait."

"I can't." She tightened the towel over her breasts. "You were with Nick. Is he here?"

She nodded. "We just got in. He's getting something to eat down in the bunkhouse. We only grabbed sandwiches on the road. Marrok had us rushing to get here. He knew you'd be worried until you saw him."

Relief surged through her. "He was right. And I still haven't seen Nick. I'd rather talk to him than you."

She smiled faintly. "Marrok said you were suspicious as hell."

"Why shouldn't I be?"

"No reason," she said bluntly. "You'd be stupid not to question everything we say or do.

I'm just telling you that, believe it or not, I'm not lying. I don't want to be here talking to you, but it's Marrok's orders. He thought you'd take it better from me." She shrugged. "I don't know why. I'm great with animals, but I'm not real good with people."

She stiffened. "Take what better?"

"Danner burned your place to the ground."

Her eyes widened in shock. "What?"

"See, I told you I wasn't good at this."

"You're right," she said numbly. "You're lousy."

"I'd want to know everything up front. I thought you would too."

"I do." Her knees felt weak, and she sank down on the bed. "You're not—It's the truth?"

"I told you that I wouldn't lie. I was still in the woods and watched the house catch fire. The barn was already burning."

"Janet. Oh, God, my housekeeper, Janet McDonald."

"We got her away a little while before they came. The animals too."

"Gracie?"

"All of them. We took the donkey and the cats the night before. They're all being well taken care of by our people."

Devon was half-relieved, half-bewildered. "You took Casper the night before. You were planning this?"

"Marrok was doing the planning. I just follow orders. He said that when Danner found you, there'd be no holds barred, and he wanted to protect those you cared about."

"No holds barred." Two good people had died, and the place she called home had been destroyed. "I'd say that's an apt description."

"It's knocked you for a loop." Bridget's gaze was on her face. "I know that most people consider the destruction of a home as traumatic, but we did manage to get everyone out. That should mean something."

"Of course it does." She dazedly shook her head. "Why would they do it?"

"Cover forensic evidence, set an example, punish you for helping Marrok. Take your pick," Bridget said. "If Danner captured you, he'd want you softened up, tortured. He probably thinks you know something."

A surge of anger tore through Devon. "Then he'd think wrong. I don't know anything except I'm being moved around like a chessman and you people are making me a damn victim." Her eyes suddenly filled with tears, but she would not cry. "I won't let you do that. There have already been too many victims to whatever game Marrok is playing." She suddenly went on the attack. "And you're just as bad if you meekly do what he tells you."

"Meekly?" She was suddenly smiling. "No, Marrok wouldn't ever ask me to be meek. He knows me too well."

"But you obey orders."

"Yes, we all obey his orders. He keeps us safe." She paused. "And we keep him safe. It's a mutually beneficial arrangement."

"From this Danner?"

"Yes, but if it weren't Danner, it would be someone else. Marrok's life is walking tightropes. He does it well."

"I don't care about Marrok and his tightrope."

"I know you don't. I wouldn't either. I'd feel raw and angry and violated." She rose to her feet. "I'm sorry your two friends were killed." Her lips tightened. "But you're not alone. We lost a man at your farm. A good man. He was reconnoitering the woods on your property trying to spot any of Danner's slimeballs. He was shot five times in the back."

"Marrok's tightrope evidently extends to

the people who work for him. Maybe you should get the hell away from him."

Bridget shook her head. "We can't do that."

"Why not?"

"Because working for Marrok is worth any risk."

"Money?"

"No." She lifted one shoulder in a half shrug. "I suppose it's because he makes us feel like knights from Camelot, the chosen to protect the castle."

She frowned. "I don't know what the hell you're talking about."

"I'm just trying to tell you that, whatever you may think, Marrok is worth it." Bridget nodded. "And I've probably said too much. I have a habit of doing that. I just don't want you to feel alone. Marrok won't give an inch when it comes to anything connected with Ned, and he can be damned enigmatic." She headed for the door. "Come down to the bunkhouse and see your Nick and Janet. We're trying to keep them cheerful, but your housekeeper isn't going to be easily pacified. I couldn't persuade her so I had to use other means."

"You hurt her?"

"No more than she hurt me." Bridget

opened the door. "I hope those clothes in the closet fit. I had to rely on Marrok's guess. But he's usually got a good eye."

"All these preparations down to the last detail," she said. "You were all planning on my coming here. None of this was spur-of-the-moment."

"Spur-of-the-moment can be fatal. We had plenty of time. Marrok knew you'd have to come the minute he left Ned with you. See you down at the bunkhouse." She looked back as she had an afterthought. "Your Gracie is having problems with the search and rescue missions. She's gentle and wants to do what you tell her, but it hurts her. She's not a natural."

Devon stared at her in astonishment. "How could you know that?"

Bridget shrugged. "I just do."

Devon stared at the door after it closed behind her. What a curious combination of toughness, belligerence, and sensitivity. She was clearly loyal to Marrok, yet Devon was having a hard time feeling antagonism for her. Her emotions were so mixed that she couldn't think straight.

He's worth it.

Camelot knights guarding the castle.

Well, she was no knight, and she felt as if she had been invaded and trampled by a ravaging army. It was time she stopped being a victim and turned and attacked.

She started getting dressed.

CHAPTER
6

"Is she awake yet?" Walt Franks asked, when Marrok picked up the phone.

"Awake and spitting mad," Marrok said. "She's giving me a break while she showers and changes. I sent Bridget in to break the bad news about the fire at her farm. It will be a shock, but she'll bounce back. After that, the attack will begin again. Have the police picked up any of Danner's men?"

"Not according to the news." He paused. "But one of the stations did add one bit of nastiness to the story. They're wondering why Devon can't be found, and did she have something to do with the murders."

It was what Marrok had expected. "There

was bound to be speculation. But the police haven't jumped on that bandwagon?"

"No, Devon Brady is too respected in the community. They wouldn't go in that direction unless there was cast-iron evidence. But the fire was pretty coincidental."

"Not at all. It's a good way to eliminate trace evidence. They probably would have done the same to the office if the police hadn't come so soon."

"The police are saying it could be the same perpetrators looking for more drugs at her home."

"They've got their teeth into a motive, and they're not going to let it go. It's just as well for us."

"But they're also suspecting that Devon was surprised at home and may have been kidnapped by the thieves to use to get more drugs." He paused. "And Devon's ex-husband is stepping in and taking interviews on CNN."

He went still. "What? Why?"

"Lester Enright is good-looking, well-spoken, and a cop. He's a gift to the media."

"And what is this 'gift' saying?"

"Why don't you turn on CNN and see for yourself?"

"I will." Marrok crossed the room and

turned on the TV. The appearance of Devon's ex-husband on the scene had come as a shock. He remembered Walt mentioning him when he'd done the check on Devon, but it had faded from his memory. Freudian? Maybe. His reaction to Walt's comment had been very basic, primal.

"It was a neat cleanup," Walt said. "It was a good idea sending in Bridget and the team."

"I sent in Bridget because I didn't want Devon to have to account for bodies if Danner decided that either Gilroy or Janet weren't necessary. But sometimes the police ignore the obvious. This time we hit—Hold on. I think I have the Enright interview on CNN." Walt was right, Enright was very personable. In his thirties, with sandy hair and blue eyes, his features had a regularity that was almost classical. And his expression was sincere, worried, and slightly stern. Perfect for the occasion, Marrok thought cynically. He turned up the volume as Enright spoke into the microphones.

"Of course, I'm scared. Terrified. My wife is missing. But I **will** find her."

"You mean ex-wife," the reporter reminded him.

Enright waved a dismissing hand. "Devon and I had our differences, but lately we've been working them out. I'm not going to let those dopeheads ruin it for us. After this is over, I'm taking her away, and we're going to start over." He stared directly into the camera. "I'm coming after you, scumbags. I'm coming after her. You'd better not touch a hair on her head."

Marrok turned off the volume. "Shades of Dirty Harry," he murmured. "I'm sure the female viewers are sending the ratings rocketing, but I'm finding I really don't like Detective Lester Enright." That was an understatement. He had felt an explosion of feeling that was purely primitive. "It makes me want to cram that melodramatic challenge up his ass."

"Whew," Walt said. "I wasn't expecting quite that response. I just thought you'd be interested."

"I'm interested. I want to know all there is to know about Enright. Phone Chad Lincoln in London and tell him that things are heating up, and I may need to call on him. And add Enright's in-depth dossier to Lincoln's list."

"Still, Devon Brady could get the cops off her trail now if you can convince her to phone Enright."

"Hell, no. Besides, I can't convince her to do anything that doesn't involve killing me at the moment."

"Did you tell her she'd have to stand in line?"

"I didn't have to tell her. She'd assume that was a given."

"What do you want me to do?"

Marrok had been racing to do damage control with Devon Brady, but there were other dangers to consider. "We have to find out how Danner knew when and where I surfaced. If he knew I was on Santa Marina, then he may know more. It's time Lincoln did his job. That's why I'm dealing with him."

"Do you want me to fly over there and talk to him in person?"

"No, stay here. I may need you." He paused. "In fact, give me a couple hours and come here. I might need a buffer."

Silence. "You've got to be kidding. You can't handle a small-town vet?"

"It's always a mistake to generalize. She's extraordinary. Take Devon Brady out of that small town, and she could probably run a multinational business."

"Or become a guardian?"

"Don't be late." He hung up the phone.

Yes, he could handle Devon Brady. He could lie and cheat and manipulate. He could even try seduction.

That's it; seduce her, he thought in disgust. It's what he'd been wanting to do since that night in the first-aid tent, and now he had a reason. He had admired her strength, her gentleness, the inner beauty beneath the toughness. But that wasn't all. There was something about her that touched him, stroked him, mentally and physically. It had been a long time since a woman had stirred him to that extent. And the flare of jealousy he had felt a few minutes ago toward Enright had been white-hot and brought that physical response to the surface.

Why not seduction? God knows he knew the tricks. He'd practiced all of the arts of persuasion and deception in hundreds of similar situations over the years. Someone gets in your way, you remove them. At first, it had given him a high to meet the challenge.

Not anymore.

He would never seduce a guardian. Damn, he was already thinking of her as a guardian, and it was probably the worst thing that could happen to her. Take away the life she loved, then risk it again. And what were his motives? He'd told himself it would be safer for her, but had he really only wanted to keep her close for the moment when he got so hot he wouldn't care if she was a guardian or not?

He hoped he'd evolved beyond that selfishness. It was a young man's impulsive lust, and he was no longer that man. He had grown away from reaching out and grabbing. He had left impulsiveness behind.

But not lust.

Lust was the strongest entity always seeking to come into its own through whatever means necessary, striking, letting itself simmer undiscovered, then emerging.

So push it back, he told himself wearily. Be honest. Don't try to manipulate her.

If he could make honesty work.

"I was about to come and knock. You were a long time," Marrok said as Devon came out of the bedroom. "I decided to make supper." He nodded at a chair at the kitchen table. "Sit down."

"I don't want to sit down. I want to go see Nick and Janet."

"You need food and another thirty minutes won't matter."

"It matters." But maybe she'd be better able to cope if she had something to eat. She was feeling drained. She sat down at the table. "But I'll eat."

"Good. Fried chicken and a salad. Is that okay?"

"Unless you've put a mickey into that, too," she said sarcastically. "Anything. I'm hungry."

He smiled. "And ready for battle. Is that why you were locked in that room for the last two hours?"

"I was ready for battle before. Then you sent your friend, Bridget, in to give me another knockout punch with news about the burning of my home. I could take that. Possessions have never been important to me. I just had to get over the effect of the first blow you dealt me."

"First blow?"

"Killing my friends," she said baldly.

"That would take some getting over."

"You're not denying it."

"No, I called you as soon as I had an idea there might be a direct threat." He poured coffee into her cup. "But if you're talking responsibility, then I probably killed them the minute I left Ned in your care. If you were the target, then Danner would have no compunction in killing anyone around you. Domino effect."

The name that Bridget had also mentioned. "Who is Danner?"

"Drink your coffee."

"Danner. Now."

"You're not ready yet. We've been hurling too much at you at one time. How can you believe me if you can't even absorb? For instance, you may be ready for battle, but your hand is shaking."

Damn him for noticing. Yes, put it on hold for a minute and do something normal, comforting. She took a bite of chicken before lifting the cup to her lips. She had to make an effort to keep it steady. "You're sure Janet and my animals are well?"

"Absolutely sure." He met her gaze across the table. "I did my best to remove as much of your life intact as I was capable. It's all I could do."

"Bridget said they were all down at the bunkhouse?"

He nodded. "I wanted to keep you apart from them until you could make your own adjustment to the situation. I'll take you there so that you can see I've been telling the truth. Say the word."

She shook her head. "It wouldn't prove anything. You've set it all up." She took another bite. "You've built this whole scenario, and I don't know what's truth or lies. I have to—I don't know what to think. You were responsible for everything that happened, and yet you saved Nick and Janet and my animals." She pushed the plate away and jumped to her feet. "I've got to get out of here. I can't just sit here drinking coffee and trying to eat this—I'm going to go down to that bunkhouse to see Janet and Nick, and I don't want you to go with me. Will your damn guards allow that?"

"No." He held up his hand. "Ned and I will trail behind you until you're ready to go back. We can be very unobtrusive. Let's go, buddy."

Ned got to his feet and ran over to Devon. He touched her hand with his nose and looked up at her.

Those brown eyes were shining, knowing, yearning to help.

"He senses you're hurting," Marrok said.

"I know that." Her hand stroked Ned's head. "I had a dog like Ned once. Her name was Tess, and she would always be there when I needed her most. She knew what I was feeling, what I was thinking. So much love . . ." The tears were welling to her eyes again, and she blinked them back. She didn't even know why she was crying. Tess, Hugh, Terry, the fire. Probably for all of them.

"Devon." Marrok took a step toward her.

"Don't you touch me." She whirled to the door. "I don't need comfort from you. I need answers. I'll be fine. Just keep those guards away from me or I'll deck them."

The night was cool and the stable yard deserted except for the two jeans-clad men leaning casually against the corral fence.

Not so casual. They straightened warily as she came down the porch steps.

"Okay." Marrok made a motion, and the wariness was suddenly gone from the guards' demeanor. "Brian Olivska, Dean Rodlake."

"Good to meet you, ma'am," Olivska said with a smile.

Rodlake murmured something equally polite.

"She's going down to the bunkhouse." Marrok gestured down the sloping yard. "Follow the lights, Devon."

She was already on her way. She could see the lights of the large, long, wooden structure some distance away. They cast a cozy, warm glow in the darkness. All the outbuildings seemed to be good-sized and in excellent repair. Three corrals, a barn, a stable. She couldn't determine the nature of the other buildings. All the livestock must have been put away for the night.

A bray broke the silence of the night.

Except for the donkey in the corral she was passing.

"Casper?"

He was at the fence, and she stopped and reached up a hand to stroke his muzzle. "Okay? How are you doing?"

Evidently fairly well. He wasn't nervous or edgy and seemed his usual self. She wouldn't have expected it. It had taken Casper two weeks to settle when she'd brought him to the farm. "You're suspiciously calm, boy. Did they give you some kind of sedative?"

"We gave him Bridget for an hour or two last night."

She turned to Marrok behind her. "What?"

"You might say Bridget has a way with animals. She's something of a Pied Piper." He nodded at the long building only yards away now. "There's the bunkhouse. I'll wait out here with Ned." He leaned against the fence. "When you're done, I'll be here."

She strode toward the bunkhouse door. "I don't want your company."

"Yes, you do. No one else will answer your questions."

"You haven't done so well in that department so far." She opened the door. "But by all means wait. I want another go at you."

He chuckled. "By all means."

She immediately dismissed Marrok from her thoughts as she saw Nick lolling in front of a stone fireplace a few yards away with a cup of coffee in his hand. Bridget was curled up on a nearby denim-covered couch, Gracie beside her. "Well, you look comfortable."

Nick jumped to his feet, a smile lighting his face. "Lord, it's good to see you." He was across the room in three strides. "I was suspecting something fishy when they wouldn't let us see you when we got in."

Gracie jumped down and darted over to Devon, yodeling with joy. Devon stroked her lovingly. "I'm glad to see you, too, baby."

"I told you that she'd come, Nick," Bridget said as she swung her legs to the floor. "After traveling all those hours with me in the van, you'd think you'd learn to trust me."

"You may be able to hypnotize critters, but I require a little more than they do." He gave Devon a hug, then looked down at her with concern. "How are you doing? I feel like I'm in shock."

"Me, too." Her voice was shaking. "And

every time I think about Hugh and Terry, it gets worse. At first, I couldn't believe it. But now it's becoming more real to me. Real is a hell of a lot more pain—"

"I'll leave you two alone." Bridget moved toward the door. "Fill her in on the animals, Nick."

"And Janet."

"By all means. I certainly can't do that. I haven't seen her since we got to the ranch." The door closed behind her.

Devon's gaze flew to Nick's face. "Is something wrong with Janet?"

"Physically, no. Mentally, she's pissed big-time at Bridget, who knocked her out back at the farm."

"She's afraid of her?"

"I said pissed. She's ready to take on everyone at the ranch. Including me, for accepting the comforts that have been extended to me." He picked up his cup from the table where he'd set it down. "Coffee? It's damn good."

"No." She sat down on the couch. "Where is she?"

"At the barn, feeding the cats. She wouldn't trust any of Marrok's people to do it. She said they'd probably poison them."

"What do you think?"

"I wouldn't be sitting here if I thought they were in any danger. You know that, Devon."

"Yes." She rubbed her temple. "It's just that I'm not sure about anything right now. I guess I need reassurance."

"You've got it. These people know animals and like them, maybe even love them. The dogs have been given their own person to take care of them, and they're being cosseted like royalty. Ditto, the pig. The parrots are in the back in A1 cages for the night. They were being allowed out of the cages before it was time to put on their covers. The cats were taken to the barn because that's what they're used to now." He smiled. "We're all being given what we like and are accustomed to. Humans and animals alike. I've an idea that's Marrok's modus operandi. I haven't seen any hint of an iron hand, but I've been stroked by the velvet glove." His smile faded. "How about you? You've been involved with the man himself."

"The iron hand is definitely there." She had a sudden memory of Marrok's hand that had so fascinated her when he was in the first-aid tent. Iron hand, velvet glove, stroking, exploring, the soft brush of the nap against flesh . . . She tore her thoughts away. "And I haven't noticed any attempt at masking it for me."

"What's happening, Devon?" Nick asked quietly. "What have we gotten mixed up in?"

"I don't know yet." She grimaced. "It has something to do with Ned and a man named Danner. I'll find out more, I promise. And you're not mixed up in this. It's my fault for bringing Ned home. If I can, I'll try to get Marrok to let you go. But he seemed to think that you'd be at risk if he did."

"Will you be able to talk him into letting you go?"

She shook her head. "He says I'm a definite target, and he's gone to a hell of a lot of trouble to get me here. I'll have to get away on my own."

"Then we stay. We don't go anywhere without you."

"Can't you see, that will keep me from trying to get away? It would be a stalemate."

"Then we've got a stalemate." He shifted his gaze to the blaze in the fireplace. "I'd have trouble functioning without you, Devon. When I sold the practice to you, I thought I was ready to retire. I would probably have died within a year like so many men who have nothing to live for after they give up their work. I didn't care. I was tired and wanted out of the fight. I'd lost my wife, Carol, and my little girl to that scum of a drunk driver. All my ideals and zest for living had been eaten away. Then when I was working with you the month I'd agreed on before I was due to leave, I found something. You wouldn't give up. You kept fighting. No matter what happened, you just went on. I found I wanted to stick around until you did something to disappoint me." He lifted his gaze to her face. "You never have."

She felt her throat tighten. "Nick . . ."

"Enough of this maudlin bullshit. I just wanted to let you know that Janet and I need you. We're not about to let anything happen to you."

"Janet would argue about that. She doesn't need anyone."

He shook his head. "You're blind. You helped Janet when she was down and out. You found a way to get that abusive husband of hers thrown into jail. You gave her a job. You gave her a place in life. You think she doesn't need you? We're family, Devon. An awkward, crippled, sometimes dysfunctional family, but it's been working for us. Right?"

She nodded jerkily. Nick had never talked to her like this, and she was unbearably touched. "Yes. And I may be the most crippled one of all."

"Because of that son of a bitch Enright?" He shook his head. "He didn't cripple you. He just made you grow in another direction. Not a good direction for you, but the rest of us reaped the benefit. You couldn't have a normal life with him on your heels so you channeled all that stored-up love and gave it to all of us. Me, Janet, the animals. Hell, the whole damn world. I've never met a more giving person. It's almost a compulsion with you. So don't talk to me about being a cripple. That's a bunch of crap."

"Are you trying to embarrass me? For Pete's sake, I just do my job." Her throat was tight with emotion. "Could we change the subject?"

He smiled. "Sure. I just wasn't going to let you get away with bad-mouthing the most important member of our family."

"And if I persuade Marrok to let my 'family' go, it might be the worst thing I could do. At least here he seems to offer some kind of protection."

"If you believe him."

"The big 'if.' " She tried to work her way through the maze of doubts. "I believe he did save my life at the clinic. It was close, very close. And he called 911 for the police when he thought there was a possibility there would be trouble. Even if he had nothing actually to do with Hugh's and Terry's deaths, he admits he's to blame for everything that happened because he let me take Ned home."

"He accepts responsibility for it? That's not a bad sign."

"Isn't it? Then it comes down to whether it's safer to trust him now or run the risk of some unsubstantiated future threat." She got to her feet. "And I can't make any decision until I know more. I'll let you know. You're comfortable here?"

"Janet and I are fine. There are several little private cubbyholes in this monstrosity of a bunkhouse. Bed, nightstand, reading lamp. What else could I want?"

"I'll try to get you moved up to the house."

"No hurry." He sat back down in the easy chair. "I'm kind of enjoying the company. Bridget is interesting. She has an astonishing ability with animals."

Devon smiled. "A dog whisperer?"

"Except it seems to extend to every species. She should never have been able to get Casper out of our corral. But she did. And he's settled in very well."

"So have you. Has she been whispering to you, too?"

He chuckled. "Maybe she has, and I didn't know." His smile faded. "Don't worry about us. We're not in any immediate danger. I'm a pretty good judge of character, and I'm not seeing any threat in these people."

"You haven't met Marrok yet."

"No, so he's in your court. As I said, you've never disappointed me, Devon."

"And I'll try not to." She opened the door. "I'll come tomorrow and tell you if—"

"So you've finally seen fit to come down and see us." Janet was coming toward her. "Took you long enough."

"I came as soon—How are you, Janet?"

"Well enough considering this mess you've gotten us into." Janet's eyes squinted as she studied Devon's face. "Your eyes are puffy. You been crying?"

"Yes."

"Sad, or they been hurting you?"

"Sad. My friends . . ."

"I know all that. What are we going to do about it?"

"I'm not sure yet. I think we're safe here right now."

"Safe? With that viper swishing around like she owns the place."

Viper? "Bridget?"

"I don't believe vipers swish," Nick said. "Try slither."

"It don't matter," Janet said. "If she comes around me, I'll crunch her head." She swung back to Devon. "What's this on your neck?" She reached out a surprisingly gentle finger and touched the bandage. "Who did it?"

"Not these people. I'm okay, Janet."

"See that you stay that way." Janet passed her as she entered the bunkhouse. "I'm working on a way to get us out of here. I'll tell you when I have a plan."

"That's good." She reached out and pressed Janet's arm. "I have to go back to the house now."

"You should stay down here where we can keep an eye on you," Janet said gruffly. "I was going to go up and take you out of there."

"I'll be fine." She tried to distract her. "How are the cats?"

"Pretty good," she said grudgingly. "They gave me salmon to feed them. It's too rich. It will probably make them sick. They're not used to it."

"They're adaptable." She paused. "That's a good trait."

"You mean you want me to be like Nick and cozy up with these people?"

"No, I just don't want friction. It will make it more difficult for me."

"I'll see what I can do." Janet turned away. "Until I can think of a way to get us out of here. You take care of yourself." She closed the door behind her.

Lord, Janet was going to be a problem. She didn't need this right now.

"Ready to go back to the house?"

She turned to see Marrok still standing by the corral fence where she'd left him. She didn't answer as she started back in the direction of the house.

Gracie ran forward to greet Ned, and they both took off ahead of them.

He fell into step with her. "How did you find Gilroy?"

"Not bad."

"No bruises, no psychological trauma?"

"You know that didn't happen. He feels safe." She made a face. "And he likes your coffee."

He smiled. "Then I'll make sure it's always available for him. I'm sorry I haven't been able to find a comparable security blanket for your housekeeper."

"Janet would throw it back in your face. She thinks Bridget is a viper."

"What do you think?"

"I think she could be dangerous, but not as a snake in the grass."

"You're right. But I'm surprised you picked up on that side of her. She doesn't usually come across as a threat."

And Devon had not felt threatened by her. But she had been aware of hidden depths, and the unknown was always intimidating. "I believe she must be very clever. And she's very loyal to you."

"Yes."

"She talked about you as if you were some kind of King Arthur setting knights out to battle. You must really have her snowed."

"I hope not. I've never tried to deceive Bridget."

"How long has she worked for you?"

"Three years. I was lucky to have found her."

"Found?"

He shrugged. "You don't really want to talk about Bridget, do you?"

Not really. But Bridget seemed to be an integral part of this place, and she had been postponing the questions that might not be answered. "Everything and everyone I don't know about is important right now."

"You're shivering. Are you cold?"

"No." She hadn't been aware that she was shaking. She had gained some measure of calmness and composure in her time with Nick, but the shadowy darkness was still clinging to her. "You don't look cold at all."

"I'm not. Heat and cold don't bother me. I suppose it's my genes." He turned and started back in the direction they had come. "My people are used to living outdoors."

She remembered the foreign words he'd spoken to Ned that night. She lifted her brows. "Oh, hobos?"

He chuckled. "You couldn't resist the jab. No, Apaches. I'm half-Apache, half-Spanish. I lived on a reservation until I was twenty." His smile disappeared. "Are you ready to talk now?"

"I'm ready to ask more questions. Unless you have more bad news to hurl at me."

"I never believe in dribbling bad news out. I thought you'd rather take it on the chin. Ask your questions."

"Who is Danner?

"A bastard, a son of a bitch, a murderer."

"What else?"

"A billionaire who dabbles in any research that will bring him megabucks."

She stared at him in disbelief. "Oh, for

God's sake, are you telling me that this is all about some damn secret scientific project? What is it? Germ warfare or something? I don't believe it. People like me don't get involved in stuff like that. It sounds like something out of a spy movie."

"You seem to be involved, don't you?" He looked away from her. "And no, it's not bacteria warfare. Danner wouldn't be interested in germ warfare. It's not profitable enough for him to risk working his deals."

"Then what is he dealing?"

"Promises. Many, many promises."

"Don't you do this to me," she said through clenched teeth. "Don't talk around it. I want black-and-white facts, dammit."

He shook his head. "You don't get everything. I'll give you what I can."

"Damn you. I deserve to know what you know. You **hurt** me."

"Yes."

But he wasn't going to give an inch past the line he'd drawn, she realized in frustration. She attacked from another angle. "Why was Ned shot?"

He was silent a moment. "Because he'd be easier to retrieve than if he was taken alive."

She frowned. "Retrieve?"

"I think Danner knew that Ned was carrying information that he wants to get his hands on."

"What? How?"

"Ned's microchip. He has info encoded on the message tapped by the microchip embedded in his neck. If Ned were dead, Danner could just steal the body and decode the message."

"Slimeball," she said curtly. "Using a dog to carry some dirty message in his body sucks. No one cares what happens to the dog."

"I care."

She knew he cared. She didn't know how he felt about anything else, but his love for the dog couldn't be questioned. "And you're not going to tell me what was on that message?"

He didn't answer.

She shrugged. "Well, it was for nothing anyway. Whoever encoded the message screwed up. It didn't make sense." But maybe part of the chip made sense. "I thought it was garble. Could it have been—"

"What the **hell** are you talking about?" He'd stopped and whirled her to face him. "What was for nothing?"

She stiffened warily. He was no longer contained, controlled. His face was taut, his eyes glittering with violence. "The chip. We decoded it."

He began to curse. "Why? You knew I was coming back for him. I promised you."

"Hugh did it without asking me. He thought we should know where you—" She flinched as his hands tightened on her arms. "Take your hands off me, or I'll knee you in the nuts."

He didn't release her but his grip loosened. "You decoded the entire info on the chip?"

"I suppose we did. I couldn't tell. I told you, it didn't make any sense." She stared him in the eye. "Or did it? What I thought was garble could have been a language I didn't recognize. Apache isn't exactly common. Are you the one that encoded that nasty little chip?"

"Yes. That's not important right now. How the **hell** did you do it? The chip shouldn't have been able to be triggered by any of the machines in your office."

"It didn't. Hugh couldn't do it at first. He tried Vera chip and Avid. Then he decided to use one of the old machines Nick had before I took over the practice. He said it was doing some funny stuff in the transfer, but it made contact."

"Dammit to hell. It would be one chance in a thousand you'd have that out-of-date RFD remote. Did you print out the information you got from the chip?"

"Yes, I was curious. But I decided that it was tech error, like Hugh said."

"Where's the printout?"

"In my purse."

"Good. Then the only record would be in the memory of the decoding machine in your office and the computer." He released her. "They may still be there. The police wouldn't have any reason to take them if they suspected a drug theft." He turned, his stride quickening as he headed for the house. "I have to get back to the clinic."

She had to half run to keep up. "Why?"

"I've got to get that computer." He was cursing again. "If Danner's men didn't take it with them. They might not have had instructions to do it. If they think you work for me, there wouldn't be any reason for you to try to decipher the microchip." He added harshly, "Dammit, it shouldn't have **happened**. Everything went wrong. I was counting on taking that sniper down the same day you left. That would have let me get to you a day earlier."

She tried to follow his thinking. "Before I

went back to the clinic. Before I had even a chance to decode the chip."

"Yes, but I didn't really think you'd try a decode. I just wanted to keep Danner from killing you."

"You did that." She added bitterly, "But you didn't keep them from killing Hugh and Terry, did you?" She added, "Taking down. You mean killing. Who did you kill, Marrok?"

"Kingston, the man who shot Ned. I knew if he was dead, it would buy me a little time." He slanted her a glance, and said deliberately, "But I would have killed him anyway. He tried to kill my dog, and he would have kept coming after us. I couldn't let him do that."

The answer was raw and honest and brutal. He was not trying to sugarcoat any of his actions. It was bizarre to listen to him talk about killing as if it was an ordinary occurrence, she thought. It was just another example of how her life had changed, twisted down this dark path. He dealt out death as casually as those murderers who had killed Hugh and Terry. "And your only regret is that killing him delayed you?"

"Yes." He met her eyes. "And kept me from being in the right place at the right time. Sometimes that can change everything."

"That night on the mountain on Santa Marina you were in the wrong place for me."

"Possibly. Probably. I can't do anything about that now. That's past history."

"Not for me."

"Sorry, I'm not known for my sensitivity. I've said all I can. Done all I can. Now we have to just go on." He took out his phone and dialed. "Walt, we're going back to Denver. We left something behind. Arrange it." He listened impatiently, "No, I can't send someone else. Dammit, this is my responsibility. I'm the one who sent Ned back with her." He hung up and dialed again. "Bridget, Ned's chip's been decoded. I know. I know. Danner may not have it and, if he does, it will take him time to do a translation. But we can't count on either one. Go to Carmel. Danner will probably hit there first." He hung up. "**Shit.**"

She was still in shock from the violence her words had unleashed in him. "Why are you this upset? Tell me what's happening."

"The sky is falling, that's what's happening. If you wanted to get back at me for using you, you couldn't have picked a better way. You lost two people you cared about? I'll be lucky if I don't lose a dozen."

And there could be no doubt of his desperation and agony at the thought of that possible loss. "No matter how bitter I am, I'd never want to cause anyone hurt because of something I'd done. You're going back to the clinic?"

He nodded. "I have to get that—"

"It's really that important to you?"

"It couldn't be more important."

"And it will mean more deaths if Danner gets that decoding?"

"If I can't find a way to prevent them."

She walked in silence for a moment. "I'm going with you."

"No."

"I'll do what I please," she said fiercely. "I don't care about your chip. Except that I don't want those killers to get anything they want. And I don't want anyone else to die."

He was silent a moment. "It's not your fault. I was angry."

"And desperate."

"Yes, it's been a long time since I've been this desperate."

"You kept talking about the domino effect before. Well, something I did evidently caused the dominos to start falling again. I'm not going to look back and find out that I caused anyone to die or be hurt."

"You can't help."

"It's my clinic. I can locate the equipment fast."

"You can tell me where it is."

"I know every inch of that place. I could find that computer blindfolded with my hands tied behind my back." She shook her head. "And I don't trust you. You're too damn violent. There's bound to be police guarding the crime scene. I haven't had great experiences with my ex-husband's pals on the force but I don't want you hurting a cop just doing his job to get that computer. I'm going to be there to make sure you don't."

"I won't kill the damn police—"

"I'm going," she said fiercely. "I won't be moved from pillar to post wherever you choose to put me. This is **my** life."

He didn't speak for a moment. "You'd be safer here at the ranch. There's a good chance Danner may have left men stationed at both your farm and office. He covers all his bases."

"Then you'll have to make sure I survive. Providing everything you've told me isn't crap."

"It's not crap," Marrok said.

"That's for me to find out. I do know that your damn research isn't worth a human life. Prove it to me. Tell me what's on that chip."

He shook his head. "Same answer. Is it worth a life? It depends on who you ask. But I didn't start this. I didn't take the first life."

"But you're willing to take the last."

"No question." They had come to the steps of the front porch. "Change your mind. I worked hard to keep you alive. I don't want to risk you again."

"I'm the only one who decides what risk I'm going to take." She turned to face him. "Now there's only one thing I want to know. Were you telling me the truth when you said that Danner would have killed Nick and Janet if you hadn't gotten them away?"

He nodded. "After questioning them first. You'd be his first choice, but what he really wants is information, and he doesn't care where or how he gets it."

"And he'll try to get at them again?"

"Yes."

She stared at him in helpless frustration. Should she believe him? He was the stranger who had totally disrupted her life. It wasn't safe to accept everything he said.

Yet there had been no doubt about how angry and desperate he was about the decoding. It was dangerous to ignore what he told her until she could get proof one way or another. She had to know more, and she couldn't do that by sitting here. "I'm going with you."

He shrugged. "Suit yourself. I warned you. Just stay out of my way." He started up the steps. "We'll go to the local airport and meet Walt Franks. We'll take the helicopter to San Francisco, then rent a private jet to Denver. Pack some of the clothes Bridget bought for you. Enough for a couple days."

"We're going to be gone that long?"

"Probably not. But I believe in preparing for any emergency. Things don't always work out the way we want them to."

"I believe you mentioned that. You didn't kill a man in time to save my friends." She passed him as they entered the house. "Who's going to take care of Ned?"

"He goes with us. You'd better take Gracie back to Nick."

"You always take Ned with you?"

"When I can. When it's good for him." He reached down and stroked Ned's head. "Usually it's safer. I don't trust him with everyone. Walt and Bridget." He looked up. "And you."

"Considering the consequences, I wish you'd not included me on the short list."

"You'd rather I'd left him to be found by Danner's man?"

No, she couldn't stand the thought of a helpless animal being slaughtered. It hurt her to even imagine it. "I'd rather you told me, warned me, and let me decide."

"There wasn't time. And I'm not used to letting anyone else decide anything about Ned." He headed for the library. "Get moving. Ten minutes."

CHAPTER 7

"Walt Franks, Devon Brady," Marrok introduced them briefly as he opened the door of the helicopter for Devon. "Are we ready to get under way, Walt?"

The pilot nodded. "I told you I'd be ready. I've already arranged for the rental of the private jet for us to change to in San Francisco." He smiled at Devon. "It's good to see you with your eyes open."

"You brought me here?" Her brows rose. "That makes you an accomplice, you know."

"I've been an accomplice to worse things than keeping a nice lady like you alive." He started the engines. "Buckle up. We're on our way."

Walt Franks wasn't what she expected. He was a man in his fifties or early sixties, with grizzled gray-black hair and squinty hazel eyes. His drawl sounded Southwestern, maybe Texan.

"You're not going to give Walt a guilt trip," Marrok said. "He told me a long time ago when he came to work for me that he was leaving both responsibility and guilt on my shoulders."

"No one can do that. Everyone has to shoulder their own share."

"Why?" Walt said. "Marrok causes the ruckus, I just come in and pull him out." He grinned at Marrok. "Just like I did in the jungles in Colombia when he was in the SEALs. He owes me big-time."

"You were in the service together?"

Walt nodded. "That's where we met. Little did I know it was going to lead to me wiping his nose for all these years."

"Walt."

Walt chuckled. "Do you hear that tone, Devon? That's his big chief shut-up-or-I'm-going-to-scalp-you voice."

"That's remarkably politically incorrect," Marrok said dryly. "And I was never anything as grand as a chief. The closest I ever got was being an apprentice to the shaman in the tribe. I didn't even do that well. I conducted most of my holy rites in the nearest bar." He shrugged. "What the hell. I was only a kid, and I could see that all the government officials at the reservation thought we were all stupid pieces of crap. Why not get drunk and for a moment feel like a man who could be respected?"

She couldn't imagine Marrok as that wild, reckless boy. He was so totally in control and contained now.

He glanced at her and smiled faintly. "You don't see it? It took a long time to move away from that wild kid. I made a lot of mistakes. I still make them. I spiral out of control every now and then. I just don't use liquor as a crutch."

"Violence instead of booze?"

His smile faded. "Violence, despair, regret. Do you ever lose control, Devon?"

"I'm a vet. I can't afford to lose control. I could cause hurt."

His gaze was suddenly narrowed on her face. "You were married."

"Yes." There was no doubt she had lost control with Les to her eternal regret. "I was seventeen, and I thought sex was love. He didn't make the same mistake. He knew exactly what he was after." Good God, what were they talking about? The intimate confidence had just tumbled out, prompted by Marrok's words. She tried to shift the subject away from herself. "But control is usually—"

"You don't sound too warm toward En-right," Marrok interrupted. "I thought you were reconciling."

She stared at him, shocked. "What? Where the hell did you get that idea?"

"The same place the rest of America got it. Enright told CNN that you'd settled your differences and were going to go away together once he rescued you from the bad guys." He tilted his head. "No?"

"No," she said flatly.

"I'm very relieved," Marrok said. "Since I'm the 'bad' guy in the equation. I wouldn't want to interfere with true love. Now why would he make a statement like that?"

She had an idea, and it was making her uneasy. "How should I know?" She tried to veer away from the subject. "Are you married?"

"No, I skipped that." He shrugged. "But I've done most things at least once."

That didn't surprise her. There was a world of experience mirrored in the lines of his face. What experiences, she wondered suddenly? There was a sensual curve to the setting of his lips, and his eyes were hard, glittering, and knowing . . .

Walt chuckled. "Yep, until you got bored. Though how you could get bored with that madam at that house in Bangkok, I can't fathom. You said you'd learned all she could teach you, but if it was me, I'd have stayed around and practiced."

"Walt, you have an extremely big mouth."

"And a memory to match." His eyes were twinkling as he lifted off. "That's probably why you keep me around. You're so closed up that you need someone who knows where you came from. Otherwise, you might forget."

"No, I wouldn't." Marrok looked out the window at the ground dropping away. "You've got my number. Everyone needs a friend to share experiences. Otherwise, you get hollow inside. I know about hollow."

"I know you do," Walt said. "And when I'm not around, you always have Ned."

Marrok nodded. "Who doesn't talk when he should be concentrating on flying."

Walt laughed. "I don't think Ned can fly a plane yet. Though it wouldn't surprise me. He's getting smarter and smarter." He reached back and patted Ned's head. "How about it, buddy, want a lesson?"

Ned lifted his head and gave a ruff.

"Don't promise what you can't deliver," Marrok said. "Ned will hold it against you."

The chemistry between the two men was interesting to watch, Devon thought. Walt Franks must have been at least twenty years older than Marrok, but his demeanor and personality seemed much younger. It was clear they were friends of long standing, and Franks was definitely not intimidated by Marrok.

"Have you figured us out yet?" Marrok was gazing at her again.

"I'm not wasting my time." She scratched the Lab behind his ear. "Ned is the only one who's worth the effort."

"Ouch." Walt made a face. "That stung. But I suppose I can't blame you since kidnapping was involved."

"How generous." She turned to Marrok. "How are we going to do this? The police **will** have a guard at the crime scene? Right?" She suppressed a shudder at the term. The place where she had spent so many satisfying hours had changed, became a place of tragedy and horror.

"Probably. And as I said Danner may have his man there on the watch, too."

"How do we do it?" she repeated.

"We reconnoiter. I take out the police

guard and we go in and get what we want." He held up his hand to stop the protest he knew was coming. "No, I promise I won't kill him."

"And Danner's man?"

"We hope he comes in after us and not wait for us outside. Privacy is always good." He looked her directly in the eye. "And I make no promises about his disposition, Devon. If you want to keep your hands clean, then don't come with me. Stay in the car with Walt and Ned."

Marrok might be wrong. Danner's man might not even be waiting for them. And, if he was, would she care if the murderers of Hugh and Terry were killed? The fierce surge of rage at the thought shocked her but brought an answer in itself. "I told you, I'm going with you."

A tall, heavyset man in a police uniform was standing in front of the door of the clinic.

Walt cruised by and parked down the street in the parking lot of a convenience store across from the shopping center. "Over to you, Marrok," he said as he started to get out of the car. He whistled for the Lab. "Come on, Ned. Let's stretch our legs."

"No, what are you thinking?" Marrok said. "Stay in the car. If any of Danner's men are here I don't want them to see Ned. And I want you at the parking area behind the clinic in fifteen minutes."

"Right." Walt hesitated. "I could take out the policeman for you. No trouble."

"Just take care of my dog." Marrok took Devon's elbow. "Come on. Let's do it." He spoke rapidly, concisely, as he propelled her across the street to the shopping center and down the side of the hill. "Move fast toward the back entrance while the cop is still out front. He'll probably be doing regular rounds soon. You go inside the clinic." He reached in his pocket and pulled out a small flashlight. "Take this. Don't turn on the lights, but don't use the flashlight until you need it. I'll make enough noise to bring the cop around back once we're ready for him. I get rid of him and join you inside." They had reached the back of the building, and he lowered his voice. "Find that computer as quick as you can. I hope to hell they didn't take it."

"The door is padlocked," she whispered. "How can we—"

"Quiet." He bent over the lock. A moment later he released the padlock and opened the door. "Go!"

She slipped inside and closed the door.

A second later she heard the sound of the lid of the garbage can by the back door being hurled against the side of the building.

Make enough noise to bring the police officer, he had said. That certainly was enough noise. He'd promised not to kill him. Could she trust him? She was tempted to open the door and look out.

No, it was too late. She had to trust his word. Find the computer and get out of here.

The computer they used for IDs was in the examining room where she'd last seen Hugh. A chill went through her as she remembered how he'd looked up from his paperwork and smiled at her right before she'd left.

Don't think about it. Get the computer.

She walked quickly down the hall. She didn't need to turn on a light. She knew every inch of the clinic. She opened the door. The laptop computer was usually on the shelf across from the examining table. Now was the time to flick on the light. There were no windows in the room so it shouldn't—

Dear God!

She shrank back against the wall, staring at the floor.

"Devon."

It was Marrok, standing in the doorway.

"I wasn't expecting—" Lord, she felt sick. The outline in yellow chalk on the floor had to be where Hugh's body had been found. And traces of something dark red . . . "I suppose I should have known. I've seen enough TV police shows. It surprised—"

"Shh." He was suddenly holding her in his arms. "I know. Take a deep breath. You'll be fine in a minute."

"I was just remembering that last thing I said to him. And then I saw—" She pushed him away. "I'm okay." She wasn't okay, but she couldn't lean on him. She had to stand on her own. "The laptop is on the shelf across the room." She averted her eyes from the yellow outline as she moved toward the shelf. "Hugh was always very neat about putting away—It's not here!"

"Shit. The RFD remote?"

"There were four of them. They're all gone."

"Make sure. Look around. Could they be anywhere else?"

She shook her head. "We kept them here."

"Keep looking. I'm going to go through the other rooms."

She looked on all the other shelves, then went to the medical chest across the room. It was sealed with yellow tape. That's right, they'd suspected drug theft.

She broke the tape and opened the door. Not many bottles or capsules left. No computer.

"Anything?" Marrok was back.

"No."

"I drew a blank, too. Let's get the hell out of here."

She followed him out of the room.

"Wait. I'll go ahead."

Because someone might be waiting outside? At the moment she was more afraid of staying here in the dark knowing that pitiful, horrible chalked outline was in the next room. Was there another outline on the floor in the reception room? Of course there was. And more blood . . .

He opened the door a crack and looked outside. "There's Walt. Let me go ahead. Run!"

"They've left the clinic." Caswell glanced up from the cell phone to look at Danner. "Sherwood wants to know what to do."

"What does he think he should do? Kill the bastards." Danner gazed down with angry frustration at the computer that had been delivered to him from Brady's clinic. "I've got the info from the microchip."

"Little good it's doing us. We can't even decode it."

"I'll get there. It may take time, but I'll find a way to do it. I just didn't realize that this damned code would be so hard to break, or I would have had a roomful of cryptologists waiting to work on it."

"You've always underestimated Marrok. You still think of him as that Indian kid you could bamboozle and manipulate. He's not that kid any longer."

"I never tried to manipulate him," Danner said. "I only did what I had to do. I was the only one who was capable enough to manage the project. That old man was pissing away everything I'd dreamed about since I was a boy. If Marrok hadn't exploded and taken away what was mine, I'd have given him the opportunity of a lifetime. He betrayed me." Danner's eyes were glittering with emotion. "I looked upon him as a son."

Caswell opened his lips to make a skeptical comment, then closed them. Danner probably believed what he was saying. A son? Danner might have felt a myriad of emotions toward that young Marrok, but Caswell would bet paternal feelings weren't among them. He'd always been amazed that Danner never felt hypocritical about any of his dealings. He believed that he could do no wrong, and anyone in conflict with him had to be misguided and, therefore, subject to punishment and destruction. "Marrok obviously didn't regard you in the same light."

"He betrayed me," Danner repeated. "He was a drunken piece of refuse, and I still made him my friend. I let him sit at my dinner table and taught him to be a human being instead of a savage."

"He must have had a little bit of potential of his own, or he wouldn't have been able to keep us from catching him all these years." He paused. "And you seemed to be very willing to eliminate your 'son' even before he broke away."

"Sometimes it's necessary to sacrifice for the higher goal. I would have tried to save him. He didn't understand that."

"It's difficult for a man to look upon himself as a sacrifice."

"That's why I had to be stronger and wiser. Like Abraham when he was told to kill his son."

Talk about a God complex. And Danner didn't even realize there was anything odd about the comparison.

"May I point out that Marrok may still be of use if we can't decode this?"

"Any code can be broken. And this one was concocted by a geeky kid."

"Geeky kids have found ways to break into secured sites at the Pentagon. And Marrok may have gone in and improved the code over the years."

"If we kill him, then we'll have plenty of time to work on it."

Caswell waited. Danner was a brilliant man, and most of the time he used that brilliance with a manipulative skill that was astonishing. It was only when the subject of Marrok came up that his emotions ruled him.

Danner was silent a moment. "I always intended to take Marrok alive if possible. I gave orders to that effect. The old man swore Marrok knew nothing, but I could never be sure. It would have been much more efficient to verify one way or the other."

And given Danner a chance at an elaborate and painful revenge on Marrok. Danner was a sadistic bastard, and his enjoyment of others' pain was always excused as necessary and right. "I realize that," Caswell said.

Danner made a decision. "Tell Sherwood he has the option to kill everyone but Marrok.

Leave it up to him. But I want Marrok alive."
He sadly shook his head. "I would have preferred to make it easy on him. We shared so
many good memories. Like a son . . ."

Devon darted after Marrok for the SUV.

Walt had the door open, and Marrok
pushed her into the car then followed her.
"Get out of here."

"Right." The car lurched forward as Walt
stomped on the accelerator. "Did we get what
we came for?"

"No." Marrok was gazing at the rearview
mirror. "Hurry."

"I'm going over the speed limit now." He
glanced at Devon. "You're pale. Okay?"

No; she could still see that grotesque outline on the floor. She'd probably remember it
for the rest of her life. And it had all been for
nothing. They hadn't been able to get that
damn computer. "It wasn't pleasant." She
turned to Marrok. "I didn't see the policeman.
Where is he?"

"Tucked neatly out of sight around the side
of the building." His eyes never left the mirror.
"He'll be out for another fifteen minutes or so.
I gave him a chop to the carotid artery. And,

yes, I'm sure that he'll wake up. Not that I expect you to believe me."

She did believe him. "Will that give us enough time to get to the plane before he raises an alarm?"

"No, but that won't be a problem. He couldn't identify—We're being followed, Walt. Lose him."

Devon's gaze flew to the rearview mirror. Two headlights were spearing the darkness. "How can you tell? Are you—"

"I'm sure."

"Then he won't be behind us long," Walt said. "Hold tight."

The warning was not in vain. In spite of the seat belt, Devon was tossed back and forth like a rag doll as Walt turned corners, went the wrong way up one-way streets.

"He's good," Walt murmured, glancing at the rearview mirror. "Fear not, friends. I will persevere."

"Wait." Marrok's gaze was on the overpass ahead. "Don't lose him. Lead him down the underpass to the access road."

"Why?"

"I need him." He unbuckled his seat belt. "Slow down as you take the down ramp. Then speed up and get Devon out of here. You should have no trouble."

"What about you?"

"I should have no trouble either." His hand was on the handle. "Swerve to the left so that it will close the door behind me."

"You're actually going to jump?" Devon asked. "Are you nuts?"

"Hopefully not. This shouldn't be too difficult." He was tensing, his gaze judging the speed and incline. "Like jumping off a log."

She couldn't believe it. His expression was intent, but there was also an element of excitement. He was enjoying himself. "Don't **do** this."

He shook his head. "I told you. I need him." He shoved the door open. "Now swerve!" He jumped, tumbling head over heels as he hit the ground.

The door was swinging shut as she saw Marrok roll behind the shrubs bordering the access road.

"Crazy," she whispered. "He probably broke some bones."

"I doubt it."

"What's he going to do?"

"Probably shoot out his tires." Walt's foot pressed the accelerator, and the car speeded up.

"There's our tail entering the down ramp. The gray Volvo. Come on, Marrok . . ."

A shot. The gray Volvo suddenly swerved violently as the left-front tire blew. The driver was fighting the wheel, trying to keep on the ramp. Another shot. The back tire blew. He swerved again and ran up on the grass bordering the access road.

"Got him," Walt said. "Now we get out of here per instructions."

"No, we should go back and pick Marrok up."

"He doesn't want company."

"Suppose there's more than one—"

"He'll take care of it," Walt said quietly. "He doesn't want us, Devon. He particularly doesn't want you and Ned there. Now I'm going to get back on the freeway, drive up to the next exit, get off, and wait for him to phone."

"He's only one man. How can—" She stopped. Why was she protesting? It wasn't as if she wanted to be any more involved in this horror than she already was.

But murder had been done and was still too close to her. There was no doubt in her mind that the car that had followed them had been driven by someone who meant them harm.

"Why couldn't Marrok have just let you get away from him?"

"I have no idea."

"Yes, you do."

"He probably wanted information." He drove into a service station and parked on the side of the lot. "I'll get us a cup of coffee. It may be a while. How do you take it?"

"Black."

"Me, too. I can't see how anyone can ruin a good cup of coffee by putting junk in it." He got out of the car. "You keep her company, Ned."

Ned stuck his head between the seats and laid it on her arm.

"Wait. Why should it take a while?"

"Sometimes information isn't that easy to pry out of the kind of hard-asses that Danner hires." He strolled away into the service station.

Torture?

She closed her eyes, feeling sick. Murder and torture and a nightmare of fear. Why had she insisted on coming tonight? For all she knew, Marrok was worse than the man who had been following them. Yes, she knew Danner was a monster. He had proved it by his actions. But she knew too little about Marrok. He had thrown her a few bits of information and she had let herself believe that he could be one of the good guys. What if there were no good guys in this equation? What did that make her?

"Here's your coffee."

She opened her eyes and took the cup Walt handed her. "Thank you."

"You're welcome. You look like you could use it." He got into the van. "Don't worry about him. He usually comes out on top."

"I'm not worried about him. I don't even know him. He's almost a stranger to me." But she was worried, she realized with panic. What kind of macabre intimacy had grown between them? It was like the bond that she had read about that was forged between kidnappers and their hostages. No, it wasn't like that. She had felt that sense of intimacy the night he'd brought Ned to her. Suspicion and intimacy mixed and twisted until they became one entity.

"Drink your coffee," Walt said gently. "It's going to be okay. See, Ned's not worried."

She took a sip of coffee. "How can you tell?"

"He'd be howling and fighting to get out of the van."

"He's done that before?"

"A couple times. And it turned out that

Marrok was not in the best shape. Dogs have great instincts."

"Yes." He didn't have to tell her about instincts. Tess had almost been able to read her mind, and she had always known if Devon was ill or sad. She had once been caught in a mudslide, and Tess had found her against all odds. Tess had dragged her out of the muck, and they had lain together all night, sharing warmth until the rescue crew found them.

"So Marrok is probably just fine." Walt turned on the radio. "How about some music? It's supposed to soothe the savage breast. I always used to think that quote was supposed to be beast. It made more sense to me." He raised a brow. "Am I talking too much?"

"No." She was barely hearing him. Her nerves were keyed to the breaking point as she waited for Marrok to call. "You're taking this very calmly. I can't do that. All this violence . . . is Marrok always like this?"

Walt didn't answer for a moment. "He's a violent man. He's had a hard life, and he has problems with restraint. He's much better than when we first met years ago. I think he has focus now, and that helps."

"Right now he's focusing on a man who's probably trying to kill him."

"True. But it'll be a piece of cake for him," Walt said. "Trust me."

He was bleeding like a stuck pig.

The bastard had nearly gotten his jugular, Marrok thought. He had only managed to deflect the knife at the last minute, and it had gone into his shoulder. He'd been good. Danner had upgraded the talent. He was better than Kingston had been on Santa Marina.

He tightened the garrote around the son of a bitch's neck and dragged him farther into the bushes beside the road. Don't strangle him. Don't kill him. Not yet.

All this would be for nothing if he let him die.

But he had to be quick. Someone might notice the Volvo on the side of the ramp.

Or this blood flowing from the wound might make him pass out.

He straddled him, his hand still twisting the garrote. "I'm going to loosen this for a minute, and you're going to talk to me." He was searching in his pockets as he spoke. He flipped open the wallet and glanced at the driver's license. "Sherwood."

"It's . . . a . . . mistake. I wasn't going to

hurt you." Sherwood's voice was a pleading croak. "Just the others. They told me to make sure you weren't hurt."

"Then you won't mind our having a little conversation, will you?"

"I don't know anything." Sherwood said, panicked. "Do you think Danner would tell me anything?"

"No, but you have names, telephone numbers, addresses. No man is an island. I can put them together. I like puzzles."

"I'll make a deal."

Marrok shook his head. "I've found that loose ends always come back to bite me. But I'll make it quick if you give me what I want."

Sherwood's lips curled. "The hell you will."

"Oh yes, I'm very good at this kind of thing. Did Danner tell you I was Apache? I grew up on stories of how my great-great-grandfather taught the white men pain. I was pretty bitter. I enjoyed it then." He tightened the garrote again. "The years haven't made me any more civilized."

He waited until Sherwood was gasping, then released the pressure again. "First, phone numbers you've been given to contact anyone in Danner's organization."

"Screw you," he hissed. "You're bleeding all

over me. All I have to do is wait until you pass out, then I'll gut you."

"I don't think you'll want to wait." Shit, he wished he had time to rig a bandage to stop the bleeding. He had to be quick, or Sherwood would be right. "Do you want to bet in three minutes you'll be begging me to let you tell me all you know? There are so many ways . . ."

Walt's phone rang. "Marrok." He pressed the connect. "You took longer than I thought. Devon was beginning to—" He listened. "I'll be right there." He hung up.

"It's done." He started the car and backed out of the parking space. "But evidently not as smoothly as I hoped. He was a bit curt."

"Is Marrok still where we dropped him?"

Walt shook his head. "He said he'd probably be a half mile down the access road. He didn't want to be seen if someone spotted the wrecked car." Walt entered the down ramp. "You may have to do a little first aid. Marrok said the bastard was a knife man and managed to prick him."

"He's been stabbed?"

"Marrok had to get in close, so he couldn't use a gun after be blew out the tires. He said

Sherwood was a street fighter and pulled a knife out of a shin holster."

"How bad is Marrok's wound?"

"We'll see. Couldn't be too bad if he can hike a half mile."

"We'll still have to get him to a doctor."

"That would be awkward. You'll have to talk to him." They had reached the exit ramp, and he started down it. "There's the Volvo. Keep an eye on the side of the road." He suddenly pulled over to the side. "Never mind. I see Marrok. He's coming out of that stand of brush."

She saw him, too. Even in the darkness she could see the stiffness in the way he was carrying himself. His dark hair was tousled, and he was moving toward them slowly. She hadn't realized until this moment what a springy, lithe gait he usually had.

Walt muttered a curse, put on the brake, and jumped out of the van. "You look like death warmed over." He put his shoulder beneath Marrok's arm. "Some prick."

"It's not serious. I just didn't have time to stop the bleeding until I finished." He was leaning hard against Walt. "It could have been worse. He was aiming for my jugular." He looked at Devon, who had gotten out of the car. "I don't suppose you have any sutures on you?"

"It's not something I generally carry around with me except on a disaster mission." Her lips tightened. "Perhaps I should start. My life's been one straight disaster since you dropped into it." Damn, he looked pale. "For heaven's sake, get in the back of the van and let me take a look at it."

"There's a first-aid kit on the plane." Walt helped Marrok into the back. "We should be there in ten minutes." He turned and trotted back to the driver's seat.

"Good." Marrok closed his eyes. "Then I think I'll take a little nap . . ."

"No, you won't." Devon crawled in after him. "Not until I'm sure you're not going into shock. You're not going to die on me, dammit."

"I wouldn't dare." He opened his eyes and gazed up at her. "I didn't cut an artery. It's going to be okay."

"Nothing is okay." She pushed Ned away from him to loosen the makeshift bandage. It was an ugly wound, but it was no longer bleeding, she realized with relief. She started to redo it. "But it would be worse if you died and left me in this mess by myself. I'm staggering around in the dark, and I need you to tell me how I can get myself out of it."

"I might have had an answer before tonight," he said wearily. "But everything is blowing up in my face." He suddenly shook his head. "God, I sound like a wimp. What the hell. I'll still get us out of this." Between clenched teeth he said, "Just get me sewn up, and I'll take care of the rest."

"I'll do what I can. You do know you should be seeing a doctor?"

"I like the way you stitch. Ned's wound was clean as a whistle when you finished. And look at him now, he's almost normal."

"You said he healed fast."

"So do I. We just need a little help from our friends."

"I'm not your friend."

"You could be." His eyes were burning, glittering with intensity. "And more . . ."

She couldn't look away. She felt breathless. "I think you have a fever."

"Probably. Maybe we both do."

Fever and a strange yet familiar languidness. Why the hell would she feel like this now? It was totally bizarre. "You're the one who's wounded." She steadied her hands to button his shirt. "And that means that Ned isn't as clever as Walt thinks he is. He swore that if you were in any danger Ned would put up a ruckus."

"But I wasn't in any danger. Not after I took away Sherwood's knife."

"You might have bled to death."

He shook his head. "It would have clotted eventually."

"So Ned's instincts still rule supreme," she said dryly.

He was silent a moment. "You haven't asked what I did to Sherwood."

"Walt didn't hesitate to tell me what you planned." She moistened her lips. "I don't have to ask if you followed through, do I?"

"No. I'm behind the eight ball, and I have to find a way to survive."

"By torture and killing?"

"Whatever."

"Doesn't it bother you at all?"

"Maybe. On some level. But I can't let it stop me." He paused. "Would it matter if I told you he admitted he had orders to kill?"

"I don't know." Her lips twisted. "You haven't seen fit to tell me enough about this so that I'd have enough information to judge. I don't think I could ever sanction torture or murder, no matter what the circumstances."

"You could. It would be difficult for you, but you could. We're all primitives. The anger would just have to be deep and blistering enough to tear away the last scruple." He closed his eyes again. "I'd hate to see it. There are few women like you. I like gentleness. Maybe because I have so little of it myself. You glow like a light . . ."

"Don't fall asleep, Marrok."

"I'm not. I'm just trying to make a decision, and I can't think straight when I'm looking at you. You disturb me." He was silent a moment, then called, "Walt."

"We're almost at the airport," Walt said over his shoulder. "I'll whisk you back to San Francisco in that kicky little jet to pick up the copter and we'll be at the ranch in no time."

"We're not going to the ranch yet. I want to go home."

Walt's brows rose. "That's a surprise."

"We won't stay long. I need to get something for this wound." He paused. "And Devon wants answers, and I'm going to give them to her."

Devon's eyes widened.

"Shocked?" Marrok was gazing at her again, his lips curved in a reckless smile. "There's no real reason not to bare my soul.

Everything is heading toward an explosion anyway, and it will probably blow every safeguard I've put into place to kingdom come. You're right. You have a right to know everything I know. It may help to protect you if Danner manages to kill me." He reached out and stroked Ned's head. "And Ned will need a guardian. A very special guardian."

"You're sounding very pessimistic."

"I can be a moody bastard on occasion. It's an emotion I can't afford. That's when I go home and recharge."

"Where is home?"

"Arizona. Only a short flight, and we won't be there for more than a few hours." He held her eyes. "But this time I'm asking, not whisking you off. Will you come with me?"

She hesitated.

"Come," he said softly.

Why not? She suddenly knew she wanted to see the land of Marrok's roots, the surroundings that had created him. "Why not?" She nodded slowly. "If it's only for a few hours."

CHAPTER 8

"I can't get in touch with Sherwood," Caswell said.

Danner swore beneath his breath. "Marrok took him down. Dammit, you should have hired someone better."

"Sherwood was very good. He could still be alive. I may still be able to reach him."

"Good? You don't send merely **good** against an expert like Marrok."

"Sherwood came highly—"

"Forget it," Danner said. "Sherwood bought it. Now we have to find another way to get Marrok."

"The decoding should—"

"I'm not counting on the decoding. It may

take too long. Now that Marrok knows we have the computer, he'll set to work making it useless for me. No, Marrok is the key. He's always been the key. Try another way. You always have to have more than one arrow to your bow." He shook his head with frustration. "Why am I telling you that? You've never learned to think outside the box." He gazed broodingly down at the computer for a few moments. "The woman was with him tonight?"

Caswell nodded.

"Then she's definitely working for him."

"So it would seem. But you saw the CNN story with her ex-husband. It seemed to be a little . . . odd."

Danner thought about it, going over that CNN interview in his mind. "Did Enright impress you as being intense, Caswell?"

"I didn't pay much attention."

"I did. Enright is very, very intense." And Danner had sensed something else in the detective that had struck an answering chord in him. "Was it the situation or is he a little unstable?"

Caswell waited.

"Either way we may be able to use him. If handled right, he may lead us to the Brady woman." Danner smiled. "And she may lead us to Marrok. I think we need to know a good deal more about Lester Enright."

"Here we are." Walt was rapidly descending. "When do you want to be picked up?"

"Four hours. No longer."

"Good God, it's barren here," Devon said. The small jet plane was landing in the middle of a stretch of flat plateau of red earth. The area was dotted with cactus and skimpy patches of grass and surrounded by low foothills leading to huge, sun-baked bluffs bordering a deep canyon. "And I don't see any houses."

"There aren't any." Marrok jumped out of the plane, turned, and helped her down. "We had a shack on the reservation down below, but I was never there. I always came up here and stayed with Paco when I wasn't at the local bar. Sometimes I'd bring up one of the girls I picked up in town, and we'd screw our brains out."

"Where?"

"There's a cave." He started down the path. "Paco lived there. Though he never approved of my using his cave for carnal purposes."

"Wait." She was looking back at the Lab, who was still in the cockpit. "Aren't we taking Ned?"

"No. He never wants to come with me to the cave. He starts grieving when he's around anything that reminds him of Paco." He frowned. "I've got to do something about that."

"And who is Paco?"

"He was the **Diyi**, the shaman of the tribe. I told you, I was his apprentice. He took me on when I was twelve. It was considered a great honor by the elders of the tribe." He grimaced. "Not that Paco let me do much. He told me that the great spells were for the great shaman, and I was not going to be a great shaman for a long, long time. Perhaps never, unless I learned to curb my temper. I was allowed only to putter with his minor magic and brews. That was enough for me. It was better than staying in that filthy shack with a father who was shooting up every chance he got. Of course, the bureaucrats who managed the reservation called Paco a bizarre old faker."

"Was he?"

"Probably. I always told him they were right about him, but he only laughed. He knew I was a cynical little bastard and didn't believe in his 'magic.' I do know he was great with herbs and healing potions. Every now and then I saw him do something that made me wonder." He shrugged. "But most of the time I was either drunk or breathing smoke. He kept shaking his head and telling me I could be a great and wise leader if only I'd tame my soul. I didn't want to be great or wise if it meant staying down in the dirt and bowing my head. That was what the council was doing, that was what my father did until he finally killed himself with heroin. Instead, I liked playing with Paco's potions and spells and making up a few of my own. It pleased my sense of the dramatic."

"Slow down." She was having to hurry to match his stride. "Two hours ago I was afraid you were going into shock, and now I can barely keep up with you. How far is it? Do you need any help?"

"No, I told you I healed well." He raised his face to the sky. "Particularly in the sun. It sinks in and makes me strong."

"Vitamin D doesn't heal wounds."

"Then maybe it's my imagination." He smiled. "Or maybe I'm remembering all the times Paco told me that nature was the only real healer."

"No magic potions for that?"

"A couple, but he preferred to try sun and water first." He stopped and pointed up the bluff. "The cave's up there. Let me go up first and make sure that it's not been taken over by scorpions and rattlesnakes."

"Be my guest."

She watched him as he climbed the slope. Every step was imbued with sensuality, strength, and grace, and his dark hair shone in the strong sunlight. He was truly a magnificent specimen, and it was no wonder he'd had no problem getting those town girls to come up here. When he had spoken before about his wild youth, she had not been able to imagine it. But now she had experienced the boldness and impatience beneath that quiet control. She had caught a glimpse of that reckless boy.

Boy? No, she would bet that even during his youth he was totally male, totally adult. If he was wild, it would be with the full knowledge of his actions and acceptance of the consequences.

"Come ahead." Marrok was waving to her. "Not a rattler in sight." He disappeared into the cave.

But were there ghosts? she wondered as she started up the incline. Perhaps the ghost of Paco and the life that Marrok had lived before.

If there were spirits, there was nothing threatening about them, she thought as she entered the cave. It was a small area, no more than ten by twelve. There was a mattress covered by a dusty blanket in the corner. A red plastic ice chest was shoved against the wall, and three camping lanterns were scattered about the cave. "I expected to see—I don't know. Didn't you say your shaman friend once lived up here?"

"And you don't see any signs of him." He opened the chest and pulled out a sealed bottle of water and handed it to her. "This is all stuff I brought up after he died. But there wasn't much more than this when he was alive. He believed in living simply. He had a chest for his clothes and one for his potions. I gave him a hand-operated generator to charge the cell phone I bought him, and he tucked it in the corner over there. Most of the time he'd let it go dead, and I still couldn't get in touch with him. Every now and then he'd charge it up to call me and tell me that I was wasting my time, and I needed to come back so that he could continue teaching me. I never paid any attention to him, but it was good to hear his voice." His gaze wandered around the cave. "When he died, I burned everything belonging to him. Including his body."

"What?"

"It was Paco's wish." He opened a bottle for himself. "I did it all by myself. He didn't want anyone else attending. I scattered his ashes to the four winds."

"Wasn't that illegal?"

"Ask me if I care. I certainly didn't at the time." He was searching through a compartment in the ice chest and brought out a small vial. "And I probably wouldn't now." He uncapped the vial. "Come here. I need your help."

"Why?" She crossed the cave to stand in front of him. "And what is that stuff?"

"A medicine created by Paco and refined by me." He handed her the vial. "Take a few drops and rub it into the wound. It helps accelerate the production of blood cells."

She frowned. "I will not. I'm not about to administer a medicine that hasn't been approved by the FDA."

"Then I'll have to do it myself. It will just be awkward."

"Don't do it. I gave you penicillin on the helicopter. That should be fine."

"But slow. Too slow. I have to get over this fast." He took a few drops on his forefinger and rubbed it into the wound. He flinched. "I'd rather you'd done it. It stings, and having you touch me would have been a distraction.

Oh, yes, definitely a distraction." He unbuttoned his shirt and took it off. "Come with me. If you refused me medication, you can at least give me company."

She stiffened. "I don't know what—"

"And you're jumping to conclusions." He added softly, "Seductive, interesting, erotic conclusions, but I know it's not the time. It may never be the time." He was heading for the cave entrance. "Certainly not on that dirty pallet. I just want sun on this wound. It seems to help the medicine to sink in. Or so Paco always told me."

"In spite of what you told me about not listening to him, you seem to be willing to follow his advice." She followed him out into the sunlight. "I can understand wanting to follow a dying man's wishes about the disposal of his remains. But you could have gotten into trouble."

He shrugged. "I was in trouble all the time anyway." He dropped down on a flat, smooth rock outside the cave entrance. "Sit down. The heat radiates and comes up out of this rock and eases every muscle in your body."

"Not scientific." But he was right, the heat was wonderfully soothing. "But good."

"Paco used to sit here in the afternoons." He took a drink of water and closed his eyes.

He looked lazy and totally sensual, half-naked, with the sun stroking the bronze smoothness of his bare skin. "Sometimes I'd sit with him. He wouldn't let me talk. He said those were the moments to repair the soul. Usually I was too restless to worry about my soul and took off after a few minutes. Later, I wished I'd spent more time with him."

"We always want to get those moments back after we lose someone." She lifted the bottle to her lips. "Marrok doesn't sound Apache. Did you take your mother's name?"

"Why would I do that?" He opened his lids and took another drink. "She cared nothing about me."

"You don't know that. Sometimes circumstances get in the way."

"And sometimes a baby gets in the way if a woman wants to be free. My father used to talk about her sometimes when he was stoned. Pale ivory skin, fine Castilian features and eyes dark as night. He wanted her back. Not me. I didn't need her. I didn't want her either."

"Your name?" she prompted.

"Now what would be a good name for a half-breed? Joseph Running Deer?"

"It's a beautiful name."

"But not mine." He took another drink.

"Though I was once called Joseph. I changed it when I came to live with Paco."

"A new start to a new life?"

"Maybe. Something like that. Paco didn't care what I called myself."

"How did Paco die?"

He looked out at the horizon. "Danner killed him."

Her gaze flew to his face.

"Not personally. He hires people for that kind of job. He had him beaten to death."

Shock jagged through her. "Good God."

"I didn't think there was much good about God that night. I found Paco down on the plateau, where they'd dumped him like a heap of garbage."

"How did you know it was Danner?"

"Paco wrote about it in his book of spells. He was expecting it to happen. He'd made preparations."

"Against Danner? Dammit, I want to know about this Danner. Details, not vague bullshit."

"From the beginning?" He took another drink of water. "Danner grew up poor and never got enough power or money. He was the son of a missionary who dragged him all over the world into jungles and third-world villages to preach the gospel. He hated the life, but he was exposed to all varieties of primitive herbal medicines and cures. From voodoo priests to jungle witch doctors. Some of the cures and potions seemed to work, and he thought he'd found a way to get away from a life he hated and onto the gravy train. He became a chemist and went back into the wilds and began to 'appropriate' the secrets of those primitive tribes. Two years later he sold an arthritis painkiller to a pharmaceutical company for a staggering amount of money. After that he was on his way. In the next twenty years several homeopathic cures and little-known herbal breakthroughs paved his way to billions."

"If he's so rich, why would he be doing this?"

"I told you, for Danner there's never enough." He paused. "And all his life he's been searching for the big bonanza. The drug that would make him king of all he surveyed."

"And what is that?"

"The panacea."

She frowned. "What?"

"In every culture there are tales of a mythical drug or potion that can cure any illness."

"Mythical is right."

"But what power would a man possess if he could be the one in control of a drug like that?

He could control life or death. Danner has always had a God complex. He wants to be worshipped and feared. The panacea would give him what he's been searching for all his life. To what lengths do you think he'd go to gain that power?"

"You're saying that's what's at the bottom of all this? Danner thinks he's found this panacea? Why?"

"Paco."

"That's crazy. You mean because he was a shaman, Danner thought he'd discovered a way to create this cure-all?"

"Not at first. I think word of Paco's supposed magic was probably like the rustle of the wind in a cornfield in the beginning. But Danner and his people were keeping their ears to the ground and asking questions. He believed in the potential for native healing. Why not? It had made him rich. He had feelers out all over the world for any sign of an authentic breakthrough of any sort. Our reservation was no exception. Danner began to hear stories about Paco and started to pay attention."

"What kind of stories?"

"There were occasions when Paco would visit someone terminally ill, give him an elixir, and he would get well."

"Then they obviously weren't as ill as everyone thought."

Marrok shook his head. "Oh, they were that sick. I used to go with him and sit there on the floor with Ned and watch Paco do his thing. He always insisted that I had to trail along and learn."

"You said occasions. It didn't happen all the time?"

"No. But enough times that he began to get a reputation. And that made him important enough to attract the big man to the reservation. Danner rented a house in town and began to come up here himself to talk to Paco. It was all done with great respect and courtesy." His lips twisted. "I even grew to like Danner. He treated me with the same respect as he did Paco. I was obviously not important to him, but he still spent a long time getting to know me. I didn't realize he was trying to pave the way to getting information about Paco's panacea if Paco couldn't be persuaded. Even after he found out how little Paco confided in me, he was still friendly, even fatherly toward me. Hell, he was a rich, important man who thought two no-account Indians were worth his time. I wasn't used to that."

"Did he find out anything from Paco?"

"Not then. But he was a patient man. He was willing to watch and wait and make sure all the talk about Paco wasn't bogus. He invested six years doing that."

She shook her head. "That's a long time. You must have seen through him by then."

"I wasn't there. I couldn't take the reservation life any longer and took off. I kicked around the world for a while and joined the SEALs. I came back occasionally to visit the old man, but he seemed the same and as contented as ever. I'd run into Danner now and then, and he'd greet me like a long-lost son." His lips tightened. "Now it's easy for me to read strangers. But Danner had worked himself into my good graces at a time when I was wild and needy and reaching out for any kind of understanding. He was very clever. He fooled Paco, too, until right before he died. But he must have gotten impatient and tipped his hand. One night I got a call from Paco, and he told me to come home. He said he thought Danner was going to kill him." He drew a deep breath. "He told me that even if he died, I wasn't to try to fight Danner. It would be useless. He said that I had to leave right away and protect the dogs. He said I had to promise. I thought he was out of his head."

She frowned. "What dogs? Ned?"

"Ned and three other dogs that Paco owned." He grimaced. "He didn't actually believe that he owned them. They were his friends. He didn't like people much. Dogs were a part of his life ever since I can remember. He said Danner would be after the dogs, and I had to make sure they were safe."

"Why would Danner be a threat to them?"

He ignored the question. "Paco was talking fast and hard by that time. I couldn't get a word in to find out anything. He said Danner was coming, and he couldn't talk much longer. He told me to look in his book of spells. He kept saying over and over that he'd had to do it, and there wasn't any other way to keep the truth safe. He'd already told Danner that he'd destroyed the formula when he'd realized the danger it would bring him. But he couldn't destroy the dogs, and he didn't know if he'd be able to hold out and keep from telling him. He might have to tell Danner about the dogs, that it was always the dogs . . ." His lips tightened. "He hung up, and he didn't answer when I tried to call him back. I took off and arrived here within six hours. It was too late. He was already dead. When I came up here to the cave, I found that it had been ransacked, his medicine chest stolen, and everything else in shambles."

"If you suspected he'd been murdered, why would you dispose of the body? You might have been able to tell from the autopsy what had—"

"Paco wouldn't have wanted his body chopped up and probed. He told me what to do with his remains. I did it."

"At the cost of letting Danner get off scot-free?"

"That was never in question. Danner would probably have been able to buy his way out of any court in the country. I knew that. He couldn't be allowed the chance." He added softly, "I wanted to be the one. I **had** to be the one to kill him. I loved that old man. When he died, it broke me into a million pieces."

She could see that he did. The passion vibrating in his voice was unmistakable. "But Danner's still alive."

"I had to obey Paco. God knows I never did much of that when I was growing up. But I'd made him a promise. Danner had to wait." His lips twisted. "Though I didn't think it would be this long."

"The dogs," she prompted.

"Ah, yes. There are four. Paco had acquired them through the years. He always seemed to have a dog running around him. Nika was a stray, Addie and Wiley he picked up from rescue shelters. Ned was a pup given to him by Hakan, the leader of the council, for casting a spell to cure his own dog. Addie is a golden retriever, Wiley, a German shepherd, Nika's a mixed breed, half-Weimaraner, half-boxer, and Ned. The last few times I visited him, they were constantly with him. He said they were helping him with a new spell and were much better apprentices than I'd ever been to him."

"What did he mean?"

"I didn't know at the time. I thought it was just another one of Paco's usual scathing sarcasms. He was always telling me I should stop wandering and come home where I belonged." He paused. "One night he had me sit by the fire while he chanted and made his smoke dreams. I didn't mind. It reminded me of the old days. The flames jumping, forming shadows on the walls of the cave, the acrid smell of the smoke, Paco staring into nowhere and making me believe that the world was full of possibilities . . ."

He was living that night again, Devon thought, gazing at his expression. Or maybe he was reliving the entire life he'd rejected.

He shook his head as if to clear it. "But the

dogs didn't seem to be any better apprentices than me. They just lay around and slept and licked their balls." He smiled. "At least I didn't do that."

"Where is this going?"

"Toward the end of the ceremony, he had me feed the dogs their dinner, and he put something from his pot into the dishes." He lifted his hand. "Nothing harmful. Paco wouldn't have done that."

"Then what was it?"

"That's what I asked Paco. He answered, **shii**. It didn't make sense to me but he—" His cell phone rang, and he glanced at the ID. "Walt." He pressed the button. "Trouble?" He listened for a moment. "Shit. No, tell him to meet us at the ranch. I'm on my way." He pressed the disconnect, stood up, shrugging into his shirt. "Come on." He pulled her to her feet. "Walt will be picking us up in fifteen minutes. I have to get back to the ranch."

"Why?"

"I have to smooth troubled waters." He was striding down the slope. "Dammit, trust Lincoln to show up now. Why the hell couldn't he have stayed on the other side of the water?"

She had to hurry to catch up with him. "Who is Lincoln?"

"Chad Lincoln, British Intelligence. I've had to use him from time to time when I needed help, but he wants control, and I have—"

"British Intelligence. Why not the FBI or some other U.S. agency?" She shook her head. "For that matter, why bring the government in anyway? If Danner is a criminal, it should be a civil—"

"Devon." Marrok wasn't looking at her. "I can't deal with explanations right now. You've found out as much as I have time to give you. I've got to think of a way to keep Lincoln from trying to take over. I'll answer questions as soon as I can."

"You bet you will." He had left her hanging, and she was frustrated and annoyed. She wanted to know more, dammit. "Okay, tell me one more thing. What did Paco give the dogs? This shįį . . . Dammit, I can't even pronounce it."

"Apache is a difficult language. Try shi'i'go. It's how Paco usually referred to it when he was talking about his potion."

"That's not much better." But at least she could get her tongue around it. "So what is it?"

"What does Paco's shi'i'go mean?" His gaze was searching the sky for the plane. "Summer."

CHAPTER
9

"Oh, no. You wait just one minute." Devon caught up with him and stood before him, blocking his way. "I'm not letting you hand out a damn teaser like that and just walk away."

"We have to meet Walt."

"Then you can talk to me while we're walking down to the plateau. You're not leaving me hanging like this."

He gazed down at her with impatience that suddenly turned to amusement. "What would you do if I did?"

"You don't want to know."

"Oh, but I do. I'm finding that you're a constant surprise to me."

She wanted to sock him. He was standing there, smiling, every muscle of his body radiating male power and an innate arrogance of which he was probably not even aware.

"I'm tired of having you dribble out information. Lay it out on the table. Talk to me, dammit."

He lifted his shoulders in a half shrug. "You're right, I'm not being fair. Maybe I was avoiding telling you about Ned and the others. It's not exactly the easiest thing to explain or make anyone believe."

"Nothing about this has been easy." She stared him in the eye and repeated, "**Shi'i'go.**"

"I told you, it means summer." He went around her and continued down the slope. "In everyone's life there's a changing cycle of spring, summer, fall, and winter. But what if we could just stop the cycle and live in summer?"

"I don't know what the hell you're talking about."

"What if our immune systems could be altered to make us strong enough to delay the deterioration of cells that eventually kill us?"

"And what could do that?"

"I've no idea. But Paco evidently knew. When I went to the hiding place in that far bluff where Paco always kept his book of spells,

I found out he'd been playing with a formula to make that happen. There was no formula in the book, but he wrote about experimenting, then destroying it."

"And he didn't tell you about it?"

"I told you before that Paco believed in sharing only his minor 'magic.' I think he wanted an audience, not an apprentice." He paused. "And maybe company to hold the loneliness at bay. We both needed that."

Loneliness. Yes, she could imagine the old man and the reckless young boy bound together in that strange companionship. "And he said he destroyed the formula? Why would he do that?"

"You've got to understand that old man. Paco didn't want money or power. He was just interested in the way things worked and the way he could change the way they worked. The **shi'i'go** was just another of his medicines to do with as he liked. If it was going to cause him trouble, then it wasn't worth bothering with. He could see already where **shi'i'go** could lead. Danner was hovering like a shark." His lips twisted. "And then he stopped hovering and attacked. He beat that old man to death trying to get the formula for the panacea. I don't think they meant him to die so soon. It would make sense that they'd keep him alive to try to reproduce the formula he'd destroyed. One of Danner's men must have been a little too enthusiastic and killed Paco before they could get all they needed out of him. That's why they tore the cave apart trying to find answers." He paused. "But Paco was forced to tell him about the dogs."

"What did the dogs have to do with this? He was giving the dogs this **shi'i'go**?"

"Yes. The smoke and magic that night was just a bit of sleight of hand to mask the administering of the potion. I found out later that he'd been giving it to them for years. I don't know how many. Perhaps he'd come to the point where he even wanted to share with me, and this was the only way he could force himself to do it."

"And he experimented on the dogs?"

"Don't say it as if it was a crime," he said sharply. The muscles of his body were suddenly corded and tense, as if ready for battle. "He would never hurt them. Paco liked dogs. He told me once he wondered what they would become if we helped them along a little. He didn't like people nearly as well. He used to say there were few great souls on earth, and so it was best the rest of us weren't around that long to spoil it."

"But you said he'd given people this medicine and healed them."

"I thought he had."

She stared at him in bewilderment.

"It was the dogs. The medicine he gave the patients was a placebo. I told you that he brought me and Ned along on several of the visits. He'd have me take Ned over to the bed and let the patient touch, even pet him if he was able. No one thought much about it. Everyone knows that dogs are taken to hospitals to visit all the time, and they make patients feel better. Purely psychological." He paused. "Or is it?"

"Of course, it is."

"But they're very empathetic, they want desperately to help, to share. If they possessed the power to heal, to share their own health, wouldn't they do it?"

"Hypothetical question. They don't have it."

He was silent a moment. "Ned does. So do Nika, Wiley, and Addie. Paco destroyed the formula and the panacea itself, but it still lived on in the dogs. The dogs **are** the **shi'i'go.**"

"I can't believe that."

"I told you it wouldn't be easy."

"You're damn right it's not. You're saying that Ned is some kind of superdog?"

"No, he's very normal." He paused. "Except that he's extremely healthy in every way. He heals with a speed that's remarkable. Something goes wrong within his body, and it manages to overcome and develop instant defenses against it."

Devon couldn't argue with that reality. She had seen it for herself after the shooting. "There are fast healers and slow healers in the normal course of recovery."

"Not like Ned." He shook his head. "Okay, let's go down another path. How old do you think Ned is?"

"Five or six."

"He was four when I started apprenticing with Paco. I was twelve years old. I'm thirty-four now. Do the math."

"You're kidding. That would make him twenty-six years old. Labs almost always die in their early or mid teens." Yet there had been that weird date on that microchip that she had dismissed as a bizarre error.

"Twenty-six and going strong. There's no telling how long Ned could live. There have been no signs of disease in any of the dogs over the years. They show a distinct increase in intelligence and understanding." He added, "And they appear to radiate . . . an aura . . . something . . . that transmits that same health and vitality they possess to those around them."

"How?"

He shook his head. "I don't know. I've been studying the dogs since I rescued them from Danner and I can't come up with an explanation yet. I've had blood tests and biopsies done, but they appear normal except for extreme good health. I've been thinking that maybe the panacea might have affected the gland centers. When you put a flea medicine on an animal, it radiates and repels. It could be that the oil glands are radiating whatever Paco gave them."

"But you can't tell."

"No." His lips thinned, and his dark eyes were suddenly glittering in his taut face. "And I have no intention of chopping those dogs up and putting them under microscopes to try to find out."

She shuddered. "That's what Danner wants to do?"

"Of course. Kill them, autopsy them, and find a way to reproduce the **shi'i'go.**" He looked straight ahead. "And he wouldn't be alone. They'd be standing in line to get their hands on Ned and the others. All those billions beckoning on the horizon. Even the animal-rights idealists would probably sanction killing them on the grounds that the scientists might discover some wonderful way to benefit humankind. After all, they're only dogs." He said fiercely, "But they're **my** dogs, and nothing is going to happen to them. Even if I hadn't promised Paco I'd protect them, I couldn't let them die. I'll keep trying to find what's going on with them. I'll give the world what they want or need from those dogs, but no one else is going to touch them."

"Wait a minute." She was trying to put all the pieces together. "If the microchip decoding isn't the formula for this **shi'i'go**, what is it?"

"The location of all four dogs. For safety's sake, I had to separate them and give them individual guardians. It cut down the danger of having Danner get complete control of the panacea even if he found one dog. I made sure no one knew all the locations but me. I wanted to keep the information always with me, not hidden away where I couldn't control it."

No, Marrok would always have to be the one in control, she thought. The dominant forcefulness he was exuding in this moment was almost tangible. "What if something happened to you?"

"If I was killed, I had to make sure there was a way for the person I chose to manage the care of the dogs to find them. Ned is very strong, always with me, so that I can watch over him, and, if a bullet didn't get him, he'd survive. He was the logical dog to carry the microchip."

"But if Danner didn't know about this microchip, why did he take my computer?"

"That's what I've been asking myself. Perhaps he didn't know; maybe they took the computer just on the chance of finding out more about you and what you knew. But I don't like the odds of that. And how did that shooter on Santa Marina know I was there?" He added softly, "You can bet I intend to find out."

Soft-voiced but everything else about him was hard and sleek and lethal. She recalled that moment in the first-aid tent when she'd realized that safety was out of the question where Marrok was concerned.

"The person you chose to oversee the care for the dogs would know about the microchip. It would be logical to start there. Who is it?"

"Bridget."

That didn't surprise her. "And?"

"I trust her." He waved a hand as she opened her lips. "As much as I trust anyone. I don't have blind faith in anyone these days. Even Bridget doesn't know the locations of all the dogs. I go so far and no farther. But Bridget could have betrayed me a hundred times in the last three years, and it didn't happen."

"I'm not sure I could trust her. She's a little too violent for my taste."

He shrugged. "But then so am I."

She had a sudden memory of something Marrok had told her. "You said once that Danner dealt in promises."

"If he had control of the **shi'i'go**, do you think he wouldn't sell it to the highest bidder? Health and longevity are commodities that are more valuable than nuclear bombs. Every person, every leader, is vulnerable to the ravages of ill health and death. Whether a dictator lives or dies affects events all over the world. **Shi'i'go** would be insurance and the ultimate source of power. Danner could at last be God. He was already negotiating under the table with leaders all over the world even before he killed Paco." He added harshly, "But he didn't get a chance to reap any benefits. I took the dogs away from him the night Paco died."

"He already had them?"

He nodded. "I scouted around and found out he was shipping them to one of his experimental labs in the desert to be killed and autopsied." His teeth bared in a tiger's smile. "They never got there. I shot out the tires on the truck and released the dogs. Then I blew up the truck and went after Danner's lab. It was my bad luck that he wasn't there."

He'd blown up the truck and a laboratory and killed how many men that night? She could see in his expression the ferocity he had felt that night of Paco's death. "And you took the dogs under your wing." The phrase was ludicrous when applied to Marrok. It would be like being tucked under the wing of an eagle with all its power and cruelty. "How many years ago was that?"

"Four." He was waving at Walt, who had just set down and was starting to taxi toward them. "Well, did I give you enough to think about?"

She nodded. "But some of it is pretty indigestible."

"Then let it settle. You wanted it all laid out for you, and I did that. I can't make you believe it." He walked toward the plane. "That's up to you."

* * *

Bridget called Marrok ten minutes after they took off. "Addie seems fine. I've set up an observation point outside the walls, and I've been watching her. She's playing with the other dogs and having a good old time. Actually, she's adjusted very well. I didn't think it was a good idea bringing her here, but I was wrong."

"You, wrong? Good God, an admission of that magnitude stuns the imagination."

"Shut up, Marrok. You know I like the idea of hired and assigned guardians for all the dogs. This was an experiment that could have gone wrong."

"I didn't have any doubts. Addie is safer behind those walls than she would be anywhere else. And she does have a guardian."

"Who you can't order around like you do the rest of us. That could be a problem."

"I haven't noticed you jumping when I crack the whip." He paused. "You said Addie seems okay. No sign of Danner?"

"I've scoured every inch of this place and the surrounding area, and it's clean."

"And?"

"Okay, I haven't sensed anything either.

But you know it doesn't happen all the time. It didn't with Fraser. Not in time."

"Bridget . . ."

"I know. I know." She changed the subject. "So what am I supposed to expect? Did you manage to do damage control, or does Danner have the decode?"

"He has it."

"**Damn.**"

"And it's only a matter of time until he gets a translation. I made sure that it was complicated enough so that he'd have to do it piece by piece. But Addie's location came first, and he won't wait until he gets the rest of the translation. Things are going to go to hell fast. Even Lincoln is on his way to the ranch."

"Lincoln? That's not good."

"I'll handle it. Get back to me if there's a problem." He hung up and turned to Walt. "No Danner yet. We may get lucky." He reached into his pocket and pulled out a small notebook and handed it to him. "Information I got from Sherwood. It's not much. Get to work and see what you can come up with." He glanced at Devon. "Bridget is with Addie. She thinks that everything is okay for now."

Devon tried to remember the description

of the dogs Marrok had given her. "Addie is the golden retriever."

"Yes." He added curtly, "As soon as I can arrange it, I'll try to get you and your people away from us and out on your own."

She stared at him in bewilderment. "I thought you were set on keeping us with you at the ranch."

"That was before I found out Danner had the computer, and the decoding will most certainly happen. We can't stay snug and safe waiting to get our chance at Danner any longer. I'll have to shift the dogs right away. We'll be on the move as soon as we hear he's started out. The ranch won't be safe. Nowhere will be safe once we come out in the open. I won't be able to protect you."

She looked away from him. "I've never asked you to protect me. I've just wanted you to leave me alone to live my life."

"And what about your friend, Gilroy, and Janet McDonald?"

"We're not helpless. As long as we know there's a threat, we can all take care of ourselves."

No, she wasn't helpless, he thought. She was tough and smart and able to handle most emergencies. She had seen death and horror on a dozen disaster sites. But she had never had to deal with a man like Danner. She had never had death come close enough to touch her as it was now. He had seen the shock she had felt in the clinic at just the sight of that macabre outline on the floor.

And, dammit, he didn't want to have to send her away. Why else had he told her about the **shi'i'go** when he'd known he might have to let her go? He wanted to have a reason to keep her close, to draw her nearer, to be the one to keep her safe. He couldn't remember the last time he'd felt this protective about anyone.

But he had felt protective of Paco. Not that it had done the old man any good, he thought bitterly. Marrok had never shown him how much he cared, and he'd gone away and let that bastard kill him. The only thing left was to revenge his death and keep his promise. It should be all that was important to him. Nothing had changed. Nothing was different. This feeling he was experiencing for Devon Brady would fade.

He glanced away from her. "I'm sure that you're entirely capable of running your own life. I'll get out of it as soon as I can find a way."

* * *

Dammit, what was Lincoln thinking, Bridget thought as she hung up the phone. He shouldn't be here. He'd promised to stay in London unless either Marrok or she sent up an SOS.

Why was she even wondering? She knew what he was thinking. Lincoln was smart and savvy and he wanted to be the one to call the shots. That couldn't be allowed. Marrok would have to handle him.

But, dammit, if Lincoln dug in his heels, the situation was so delicate that he might shatter it by his interference. She'd better handle it herself.

She quickly dialed her cell.

Lincoln picked up on the third ring. "Ah, Bridget. How good it is to hear from you. And it will be better still to see you. Are you at the ranch?"

"No." She added curtly, "And you shouldn't be going there either. Go back to jolly old England and stay there until you're invited."

"How rude. Actually, Marrok did tell me to stand by. I decided to regard that as an invitation."

"Stand by meant just that. You send a crew

in to take care of cleanup if we need it. You find ways to keep the media away from us. You prepare a place for the dogs if we need to send them out of the country."

"Which I've always insisted should be done sooner rather than later. I could do my job much more efficiently on my home turf."

"And have the opportunity and power to take over the project. I couldn't trust you that far, Lincoln."

"**You** couldn't? What about Marrok?"

"I meant we couldn't trust you."

"Did you, indeed? I wonder. Perhaps I should discuss your role in this with Marrok. There are things he should know about you. I've been doing some investigating of your very interesting past lately."

She was silent, considering the implications. "You're bluffing. There's nothing that you could find out about me that would be a weapon for you. And would Marrok believe you if you had? You're the one who recommended me to Marrok three years ago. If you start coming up with anything that might be suspicious, the suspicion would fall on you, too."

"How clever you are. But you'd be more clever if you'd come over to my side. Marrok is too volatile. He's been a wild card all his life, and he could turn on all of us if the mood took him."

"He won't turn on me."

"What touching faith."

"You don't know him. He's changed."

"I hope you're not wrong . . . for your sake." He paused. "But you'll keep my offer in mind?"

She was silent a moment. "Yes."

"Excellent. Then we'll forget this conversation took place until you're ready."

"No, we won't. You'll play the game straight with Marrok, and you'll walk the line while you're here."

"And if I don't? Will you turn our savage, Marrok, loose on me?"

"No, I'll handle you myself," she said coldly. "And you don't want that to happen, do you?"

"Bridget, I'm hardly intimidated by—"

"Do you, Lincoln?"

He chuckled. "It might be interesting to have you try. Are you as good as I hear?"

"Yes. And I've no tendency toward the volatility or wildness you're attributing to Marrok. I'd just set my focus and keep on going until it's over. I'd never stop, Lincoln."

He was silent a moment. "I don't really

wish to offend a possible ally. Perhaps I can modify my plans."

"Good choice." She hung up. Lincoln had been more forthcoming than she had thought he'd be. She had known he'd approach her at some point, but she had thought that he'd play his cards close to his chest during this emergency.

Had he been bluffing about investigating her? Not to worry. She had buried all the threads that might cause her problems, but she didn't want Lincoln trying to stir up trouble now. After three years of waiting, working, and watching, she was getting close to the goal. She didn't need Lincoln stepping in and getting in her way. She'd better tip Jordan that there might be trouble ahead. She dialed London.

Jordan Radkin picked up on the second ring. "Trouble?"

"I'm not sure. Lincoln says he knows about my lurid past. Does he?"

"Probably not." He chuckled. "I'm the only one who knows your terrible secrets, Bridget. Aren't you lucky?"

She ignored the question. Jordan could be an ass when he chose. She could see him sitting there, his glacial gray eyes glittering with sly humor. "You'd better make sure. Things are moving fast here. I don't want any interference."

He was silent. "What's happening?"

"I may know where all the dogs are by the end of the week. After that, I can start to move."

"With caution."

"As much as I can. Good-bye, Jordan." She hung up.

Jordan hadn't been absolutely sure about Lincoln's threat, but he would become sure. No one was more keen or probing than Jordan when he was on the hunt. She could leave it in his hands.

She settled herself more comfortably in the grassy knoll above the mansion where Addie was being sheltered. The golden retriever was living the good life, and Marrok was right, the security around this estate was top notch. Not because of Addie but because of the people who lived on this strip of land overlooking the Pacific. There had been rumors that the estate might someday be known as the second White House. Bridget had been forced to avoid two security guards earlier in the day, and she would have to keep a sharp eye out.

She lifted her binoculars to her eyes and focused on Addie romping in the grounds below her. Lord, she was beautiful, all golden power and sleekness. Screw, Lincoln. If she had to deal with him, she'd do it. The complications were growing by the minute, but this was her job now.

The dogs of summer had to be kept alive.

A tall, thin man was standing on the front porch, watching as the helicopter descended in the paddock a few yards from the stable yard.

"There he is," Walt murmured. "Trouble."

"Only for the first ten minutes," Marrok said grimly. "After that he'll either be cooperative, or he'll be gone."

Devon stared curiously at the man who was now coming down the steps to meet them.

Chad Lincoln looked to be in his early forties, and his expertly barbered gray hair, silk shirt, and finely tailored trousers came as a surprise. He was smiling and waving, and Devon was having a problem connecting that friendly, urbane, elegant appearance with the man who had caused Marrok to react with such grimness.

"He's British Intelligence?" she asked doubtfully. "He looks more like a dress designer."

Walt chuckled. "May I tell him that?"

"No," Marrok said. "Just keep out of it." He opened the door of the helicopter. "And, Devon, Lincoln is definitely not a dress designer. When he was younger, he was with the Royal Marines and since he took a job with MI6, he's proved himself to be exceptionally deadly in the field." He helped her down. "Besides being a self-serving son of a bitch."

"For allies, you're obviously not on the same wavelength. And what does he think about you?"

"Probably the same." He shook his head. "No, not the same. I respect him, and he regards me with contempt. He likes everything to be civilized, neat, and tidy, including his kills. He regards me as a mongrel half-breed and a savage. Since that's exactly what I am, I can't argue with him."

"You can and should. We're what we make of ourselves, not what we're born," Devon said.

"But, you see, it doesn't matter to me if I'm savage and a mongrel," Marrok said. "Maybe I even like the idea of having an excuse for not becoming civilized."

Her eyes were narrowed on his face. "And you use it. I can see how eager you are. You're anticipating this confrontation with Lincoln."

"How well you read me." He smiled reck-lessly. "Let's just say, I have a few bones to pick with Lincoln. I've been in a position on occa-sion where he's called the shots. I don't like being manipulated. I want to get my own back." His smile faded. "And the bastard can just keep his hands off my dogs."

"What does he have to do with the dogs?"

"Ask him," Marrok said as he called to Lin-coln, who was now only a few yards away. "Chad Lincoln, Devon Brady. Devon wants to know what you have to do with the dogs, Lin-coln."

"Not enough." Lincoln smiled at Devon. "Delighted to meet you, Dr. Brady. Though I knew it was in the cards when I was told to prepare a dossier on you when you were in Santa Marina. For once, it was a pleasure to run a check for Marrok. Usually, the people with whom he's involved are the scum of the earth."

"You had me investigated?" Devon asked, startled.

"I was entrusting Ned to you," Marrok said simply. "I didn't have the right to take a chance. These days I believe in my own judg-ment, but I've been fooled before."

He'd been fooled by Raymond Danner, she thought. And that error had led to the death of his friend Paco.

"You could have sent for me," Lincoln said. "I would have been there in a heartbeat and taken Ned off the island."

"I'm sure you would. And what would my chances be of ever seeing Ned again?"

"Fifty-fifty." Lincoln turned to Devon. "But you wouldn't have had to be involved. I'm sure you must be very bitter about the way your life has been torn up."

"Yes." But she wasn't going to allow herself to be used as a pawn for him to use against Marrok, and that was obviously what he had in mind. She asked again, "What do you have to do with the dogs?"

"I'm the safety net. Isn't that how you look on me, Marrok?"

"Yes. Though lately I've had my doubts about the 'safety' part."

"You should have considered the conse-quences when you came to see me," he said softly. "You couldn't expect us to sit and play your game when you take so many chances."

"I didn't. I knew you'd undercut me as soon as you felt secure about doing it." He looked him in the eye. "But that time's not now. You'll tip us into the quicksand. Do you want Danner to get control?"

"No, I intend to do that. MI6 is getting impatient." His glance shifted to Devon. "But I'm being rude. You want to know about my association with Marrok? He came to me four years ago with a wild tale and an even wilder proposition. He said he couldn't trust any U.S. government department to offer him protection for the dogs. Danner had too much power and influence in this country. We were to provide cleanup assistance, when requested, and refuge for the dogs when and if it became necessary. I almost laughed him out of my office." He paused. "And then he started to provide me with demonstrations of his dog, Ned's, rather remarkable ability. I'm not an easy man to convince, but eventually he did convince me."

"How?"

"A lengthy visit by Marrok and Ned to St. Cecelia's Hospital and several terminally ill patients. Seven out of nine were not terminally ill at the end of that visit."

She stared at him, shocked. Perhaps she shouldn't have been so stunned. Marrok had told her that the dogs could accomplish this wonder. But she realized now that she had not really believed him. The panacea, the effect on the dogs, Paco . . . it all seemed like a story from a book. Yet this cool affirmation from Lincoln jerked her from storybook to reality. She moistened her lips. "Seven out of nine?"

"Good percentage, isn't it? Good enough to convince my superiors that Marrok and his dogs of summer were worth the investment."

Marrok smiled sardonically. "But not without an immediate payback."

"Not quite immediate. And you couldn't expect us to fund you without receiving something in return."

"No, I didn't expect that." He turned back to Devon. "You've gotten practically no sleep in the past twenty-four hours. Why don't you go inside and try to catch a nap?"

"Are you trying to get rid of me?"

"Yes. I have to talk to Lincoln, and you don't need to hear it. As Lincoln said, you're bitter enough about being involved without getting in any deeper."

Bitter? Of course she was bitter. Yet she found she didn't like the idea of being sent away like an outsider.

But what else was she but an outsider? Her heart was touched by those dogs, but they weren't her problem. Marrok certainly wasn't her problem.

"You can't help, Devon." Marrok's gaze was on her face. "And once you get a little rest and get your balance back, you'll not want to help."

"I didn't say I wanted to help." She turned and started up the porch steps. "And I wouldn't be interested in anything the two of you are going to say to each other. I'll call and talk to Nick and let him know that everything is okay."

"And take a nap."

"If I feel like it." She closed the screen door behind her. She wouldn't look back at the two men. Close them out. She'd make her call, then lie down and block all this craziness from her mind. She was dialing Nick as she walked toward the bedroom.

"How are you?" she asked when he picked up.

"Fine. Did you get the computer?"

"No. Things didn't go well." That was an understatement. That moment when she'd stared down at that chalked outline on the floor of the clinic seemed a long time ago. "And they may get worse."

"For us?"

"I don't think so. Marrok has changed his mind. He doesn't want us here."

"And that's what you wanted. When?"

"Soon. Is Janet okay?"

"Sure. She's alternating between being belligerent and following her natural instincts and trying to run the place."

"Gracie?"

"Missing you. But she loves everyone. She's getting along just fine."

"Good. I'll be down to see you as soon as I get a little sleep. Bye, Nick."

"Devon, you sound . . . Why don't I come up there, and we'll talk?"

"Thanks. But I don't need a shoulder to lean on. I've just been hit in the face with something that's pretty strange. I have to decide whether to accept it." But she'd already accepted it, she realized. That moment of shock following Lincoln's almost casual statement had broken through the haze of bewilderment that had enveloped her. There might still be moments of disbelief and doubt. She would never be entirely certain until she was a witness herself. But she had accepted the possibility, and she couldn't turn her back on that knowledge. "I'll talk to you later, Nick." She hung up.

She moved slowly toward the bed. If she had accepted that there was such a panacea as **shi'i'go** and it had been somehow transferred to Ned and the other dogs, then it could change everything. The potential was enormous and a little scary.

Try walking in my shoes, Marrok had said. Yes, she could see how difficult and conflicted it would be for him. So many irons in the fire, so many ways he was being pulled. Responsibility for the panacea, revenge for the death of his friend, protectiveness toward the dogs, determination to keep Danner from gaining control. How would she have balanced all those elements not for a few days but years? Probably not the way Marrok had handled it. Marrok's instincts leaned toward reckless violence and she had always been reasonable and logical.

But she had not been behaving reasonably and logically since Marrok had entered her life. She had made impulsive decisions and been driven by emotion. She had not only wanted to keep others from being killed by Danner, she had wanted revenge for her friends who had been murdered. Marrok had remarked on her gentleness, but where was the gentleness in that? The answer was plain.

She was walking in Marrok's footsteps and discovering things about herself that she had never known.

CHAPTER
10

Nine twenty . . .

She had slept for hours, Devon realized drowsily. The room was dark except for the pale moonlight streaming through the window. She had been too on edge to go to sleep immediately, her mind had been in turmoil and her emotions stretched to the limit. Sheer exhaustion had finally prevailed.

And she felt better now, calmer, more able to manage this horror of a situation. God help her, she'd better be able to cope. She felt as if she'd been more of a sounding board than an active player. That had to stop.

She sat up in bed and swung her feet to the floor. Take a shower, dress, and grab a sandwich from the refrigerator. Then she'd be ready to deal with Marrok.

But Marrok didn't seem to be around to be dealt with. The house appeared to be empty. Where the hell was he? She'd try the bunkhouse. She wanted to see Nick and Janet anyway. After eating a ham sandwich and drinking a glass of milk, she went out on the porch.

"Sleeping beauty is awake at last." Lincoln was standing at the far end of the porch. "Rest well?"

"Yes." She said. "But I'm no beauty, and this is no fairy tale."

"I beg to differ. You're not my type, but beauty is in the eye of the beholder, and it's obvious that Marrok finds you very attractive." He tilted his head. "I can see how he'd be drawn to you. The rule of opposites."

"Where is Marrok?"

"He took off with Walt Franks several hours ago. I think he's checking up on his canine charges."

"Don't you know?"

"Marrok keeps me as much in the dark as possible. I believe the dogs may be scattered within a few hundred miles' radius but that's all." He smiled. "And Marrok is exceptionally good at making sure I remain in ignorance. I can't tell you how often I've tried to bug his helicopter or car. He's always found me out."

"No wonder he doesn't trust you."

"Trust doesn't enter into our relationship." He leaned against the porch railing. "You have to have a code to define the rules. Marrok has no code. He grew up as a savage, and that hasn't changed with the years."

"I think it has."

"But you don't know him as well as I do. He hasn't been anything but obstructive since the day he came into my office."

"Which means you didn't get your way," she guessed shrewdly.

"Very good." He chuckled. "But my way is the right way, the civilized way. Marrok should no more have control of those dogs than Danner. They have no background or experience to make the necessary judgments."

"And you do?"

"Modesty prevents me from—Yes, I could do it. Given the chance I could do the job. My superiors have total faith in me."

"And what would you do with Ned and the others?"

"We would be humane."

"Would you kill them? Experiment?"

"Only if it was necessary. The stakes are bigger than you could imagine. I realize such an admission could alienate you, but I want to be totally honest."

"Why?"

"Because I don't want you to get in my way," he said bluntly. "Stay out of it. Marrok sucked you into his ugly little world, and I can see he holds a certain fascination for you. You didn't like it when he sent you away."

"I don't like orders."

"If that's all, then I'll be very happy. But I believe it's more. Women do seem to be drawn by the primitive type. I have no idea why."

"This conversation is totally absurd."

"But it had to be said. I'd prefer you to realize that Marrok will be brought down. Either by me or Danner. There's no doubt about that."

"But in the meantime, you're still going to help him?"

"We have to hedge our bets. Marrok is clever. There's a remote possibility he could still come out on top." His smile faded. "And he's unpredictable. Just when you think he's cornered, he manages to slip away and strike like a snake. He proved that in Ethiopia."

"Ethiopia? What are you talking about?"

"All I asked of Marrok was that he do a simple job. After all, he owed it to us."

She remembered something Marrok had said. "Your pound of flesh?"

"What a gory phrase."

"No more gory than what you'd inflict on those dogs."

"I told you, I'd try to be humane."

"How hard would you try? As hard as Marrok?"

"I'm afraid not. One has to be objective, and Marrok is all emotion and no objectivity."

She had a sudden memory of Ned gazing up at her with eyes that were full of love and sadness and strange wisdom. She said curtly, "Screw your objectivity."

"That's what I would expect of a woman of your background. But in the end I'm sure you'll see the light. It's the only sensible method to secure a valuable commodity like—" He broke off, his head lifting. "I think I hear the chopper. I'm afraid our little discussion is at an end. But it was enlightening for both of us, wasn't it? It's always good to have an understanding."

"Yes, I do understand you, Lincoln."

He nodded. "Then I'll say good night. Tell

Marrok I'll see him in the morning. Since my job is to stand by, I'll stand by here and await developments."

"Why not tell him yourself?"

"It won't be news to him. We spoke while you were taking your nap. He wants me to go, but that's not an option now that there's a chance that Danner may take the dogs."

"And by staying here you're hoping to find the location of the other dogs."

"There's always that possibility. Or there's sometimes a break in the ranks, and I may get a little help." He turned away. "But I'm not going to get that help from you, am I?"

"Not one iota of help."

He sighed. "Too bad. But it's not unexpected. You damned animal lovers have been a great source of disappointment to me in this trying situation." The screen door closed behind him.

My God, what a conniving son of a bitch. She could see why Bridget had said Marrok was used to walking tightropes when even his supposed ally was waiting for his chance to slip in the knife. Even Lincoln's frankness had been aimed in only one direction. He had been testing the waters, observing her reactions, trying to find a weakness.

"Devon."

She turned to see Marrok crossing the paddock toward her. She felt a rush of relief. She hadn't known she had felt uneasy about his absence. It couldn't be because she was worried about him. It was just that he seemed to be the center of all this madness swirling about her, then he was suddenly gone. She started down the stairs. "I was just going down to the bunkhouse." She bent down to pet Ned, who had run to her. "Hello, boy, want to go down and see Gracie?"

"I'm sure he does. I'll go with you."

She straightened. "So that your guards won't have to stop me?"

He smiled. "I have to protect them. You threatened to deck them."

She had forgotten that threat. It seemed a long time ago. "I don't see them anywhere around."

"They're on watch. I told them to keep a low profile." He paused. "I saw Lincoln go into the house."

"Yes. He told me you'd probably gone to check up on the dogs. Are they okay?"

"Fine. I just had to hand out a warning that I'd be moving the dogs and see if their caretakers wanted to back out of the job."

"Did they?"

"No, they're crazy about the dogs. They wouldn't desert them." He paused. "I imagine Lincoln was talking about more than my trip. No matter what he promises, don't trust him, Devon."

"What do you think he promised me?"

"I don't know. To get you away from here, to put you in a witness protection program."

"He didn't promise me anything. He just talked about you and your total inability to take charge of the panacea." She looked straight ahead. "It seems you have no code and are completely uncivilized. You don't play by the rules."

"That's right."

"What happened in Ethiopia?"

"What did he tell you happened?"

"Nothing. He just mentioned it. But he was very pissed."

Marrok smiled with satisfaction. "Good."

"Are you going to tell me?"

"Why not? It will just give you another example of how Lincoln is right about me not playing the game properly. Two years ago, Lincoln sent me and Ned to Ethiopia on a nasty little job. It wasn't the first time, but this one was particularly ugly."

"Lincoln's pound of flesh?"

"That covers it. Even after MI6 came on board and agreed to shelter us, I knew that there would be a price. The prospect of taking over the panacea was too vague. They wanted immediate gratification. Ned was a valuable commodity and should be used to the hilt."

"How?"

"Sometimes the balance of power in a country rests on a particular person or event. In Ethiopia, MI6 was backing and promoting Zafur Car-mak to eventually take over the country. He was a bandit whose primary income came from stealing food supplies donated by various countries and charity organizations and selling them on the black market. Some of the other things he did made Idi Amin look like a saint. But MI6 thought they could control him, and that it would be the way to control the flow of terrorists using Ethiopia as a training ground."

"Dear God." She had seen photos of the starving children of Ethiopia. "What kind of a trade-off is that?"

"Not an unusual one." His lips hardened. "But this time Lincoln had the bright idea of bringing Ned and me in to lend a little assistance."

"Why?"

"Zafur was dying. He had AIDS. He wasn't going to last another two weeks. Lincoln and his team would have had to find and groom another scumbag to use. He flew us into the country and had us driven to Zafur's palace. Ned and I spent the night in his room."

"Ned cured him?"

"Zafur was on his feet and spitting out orders to his men when I left. It was dawn, and Lincoln's men drove me over those parched cracked plains to the helicopter. It was a mistake. In the daylight, you could see the hundreds of huddled families by the roadside. Skin and bones. Malnourished children with swollen bellies. Flies everywhere. I made the van stop once to let Ned and me out and we walked among them. I thought maybe it would help a little. But Lincoln's men hustled us back into the van after twenty minutes. That's not what we'd been brought in the country for, and they wanted to get us out." He leaned down and stroked Ned's silky, black head. "You wanted to stay, didn't you, boy? I did, too. I looked at those people, and I remembered Zafur and how Ned had been used to probably put him back in action so that he could steal more food. It made me angry. Very, very, angry."

"What did you do?"

"Nothing. I got on the plane and left the country."

She stared at him in disbelief.

He shrugged. "There was nothing to do then. It would have been an exercise in futility. I took Ned back to Bridget."

"That wouldn't have made Lincoln pissed at you."

He smiled. "I waited two weeks, then I went back to Ethiopia. I stalked Zafur like the hyena he was and killed the son of a bitch. What Ned and I had given, I took away. Poor Lincoln, I blew all his plans for Zafur to hell. He was a bit upset with me."

"What did he do?"

"Raved and ranted. I listened until he stopped sputtering, then I asked him to tell me which one of us was the real savage." He stopped as they reached the bunkhouse. "He's sent us out on other jobs since then, but he's been very careful at choosing them."

"And never stopped hating your guts."

"There was a certain amount of humiliation connected with the fiasco. Lincoln doesn't like to be humiliated." His gazed shifted to her face. "And I don't like the dogs or the **shi'i'go** to be misused. Ethiopia reinforced my skepticism at the idea that it was safe to trust anyone else with them."

She could see that an experience that devastating would cause Marrok's determination to harden irrevocably. "I can understand how it would be a deal breaker. I'm surprised you're still working with Lincoln."

"In spite of the fact that he thinks I'm too volatile, I don't do anything stupid that might hurt the guardians. When they need help, they're going to get it."

"The guardians. You were talking about needing a guardian for Ned in the car last night."

"I was a little woozy. I take care of Ned."

"These guardians take care of the other dogs?"

He nodded. "When I knew I'd have to separate the dogs, I had to pick three other people I could trust to take care of them. It wasn't an easy choice."

"Did they know about Danner?"

"Not in the beginning. I wanted the situation solid before I brought in a disturbing element."

She stared at him. "You bastard."

He nodded. "I searched hard until I found guardians with just the right mixture of gentleness and toughness. I didn't want to blow it. I knew it would be all right later."

"Because you knew they'd grow to love their dogs and would run the risk." She added, "Just the way you risked my life without explaining zilch."

"I had to protect the dogs. I gave my word."

"Good God, and who is going to protect the rest of the world from you, Marrok?"

"I don't know." He was silent a moment before he said awkwardly, "I wouldn't risk you again, Devon. I want . . . to take care of you."

"It's a little late." But his halting words were causing her to feel strange, vulnerable, a melting. "And I don't need anyone to take care of me."

"I don't care about your need. I want to do it."

"Marrok, that's the most incoherent . . . listen to yourself."

"I know. I'm a little off-balance." He reached out a hand and delicately stroked her throat. "I've done a lot of things that you'd have never done. Danner and Lincoln are both right about me. I've always been selfish and unstable and ready to explode at the first sign of things not going right." He said softly, "But it won't happen again with you."

She moistened her lips. "Wouldn't it?"

"I like to touch you. My fingertips are tingling . . ."

And her skin was tingling beneath his fingers. She couldn't breathe . . .

His fingers dropped to the hollow of her throat. "Your pulse is beating hard. I did that, didn't I?" He rubbed lazily, sensuously. "Come on, harder . . ."

Her heart was already beating so hard that she could scarcely take a breath. "What are you doing, Marrok?" she asked shakily.

"I'm not sure. Probably something I shouldn't." His head lowered, and his lips brushed her temple. "I told you, I've never been good at controlling myself."

And she had always been very good at that since leaving Lester, she thought hazily. Where had that control gone? The moment he had touched her, she had gone up in smoke. "I don't want this, Marrok."

"Yes, you do." His tongue was touching her ear. "Be honest with me. I'm being honest with you. I want to drag you into the field and screw you until we both go crazy. I'll make it good for you. Tell me to do it."

She was shuddering. His words, his touch, his breath on her temple . . .

"Just say yes," he whispered. "One word . . ."

Yes. Yes. Yes.

And she opened her lips to say that word.

Casper brayed in the paddock.

God in heaven, what was she doing? She drew a shaky breath and pushed him away. "This doesn't make any sense."

"No." He smiled recklessly. "Let's do it anyway."

She shook her head. "I don't do one-night stands." She took a step back. "I'm not one of those town girls you used to take up to Paco's cave. I'm boringly conventional."

He tilted his head and gazed at her. "Your cheeks are flushed, and you're still shaking. You're as hot for me as I am for you. I could probably persuade you."

"Maybe." She stared him in the eye. "But you said you wanted to take care of me, protect me. Is screwing me how you'd go about it?"

His smile faded. "Low blow. Can't I do both?"

For a moment she could almost see the reckless, hungry kid who wanted the whole world and tried to devour it. "No, you can't do either." She took a deep breath. "I'm try- ing to come out of this with as few scars as possible. Don't make another move on me, Marrok."

"No promises. I still think a roll in the hay would be therapeutic for both of us. Besides the fact that I get hot every time I look at you, and I need it like hell." He paused. "But I'll wait until the move is a little more welcome." He turned away. "I'll let you go back to the house alone. We're both still in the zone. I'm no good with restraint." He suddenly looked back at her. "It was the damn donkey, wasn't it? I almost had you until he cut loose."

"Yes, it was Casper."

He shook his head. "I never did like donkeys."

She was smothering a smile as she watched him walk away. She wanted to call him back, she realized with shock. Her body was still ready for him. Cripes, he'd barely touched her, and she had been ready to let him screw her. How long had it been since she'd felt like that? Her ex-husband, Les? No, that had been experimental teenage sex, then fighting his overwhelming obsession. This intense, roller-coaster sensuality bore no similarity to anything she'd felt before. The chemistry was different, hotter, explosive, bewildering, yet crystal clear at the same time.

And she'd be very wise to stand firm and far away from that chemistry.

There was a whining inside the bunkhouse.

Gracie.

She quietly opened the door and let the greyhound out.

Gracie leaped for her, making low, happy sounds, her entire narrow back end wagging ecstatically.

"Shh, Gracie," Devon whispered as she fell to her knees. "It's a little late. I don't know if anyone's awake in there." She hugged her. "I missed you, too."

Gracie gave a low howl and nestled closer.

"Yes, it's okay now." She stroked Gracie's sleek coat. "Calm down." She sat down cross-legged on the ground, and Gracie plopped down beside her. "Ned almost paid you a visit, but Marrok had to leave and took him with him. He'll be back. Things got a little . . . confusing." What wasn't different and confusing since Santa Marina? She had a sudden memory of something Bridget had said. "Are you confused, too? Bridget said the rescue missions bothered you. Was she right?" She wasn't expecting Gracie to respond, but it felt good to get it out. "I don't know whether to believe her, but I guess I've got to keep a closer eye on you. I don't want you hurting. It's okay if you don't like it. I'll still love you."

Gracie whined happily and rolled over on her back with her four feet straight up in the air. She always did that when she wanted her tummy scratched. Devon obliged, then tugged at her paw. "Come on. Let's go see if Nick and Janet are awake."

Damn, he'd acted as careless and raunchy as an eighteen-year-old, Marrok thought in disgust as he strode toward the house. Why be surprised? He was raunchy. But he wasn't careless, not any longer. He'd been through the fires and come out with a knowledge of what being careless could mean. But that moment with Devon had brought back all the dizzying sensuality of that younger Marrok.

Not good. He had to send her away, and sex would only make it more difficult.

And it didn't matter to him. He was hurting. He wanted to reach out and grab and play and hold on. She'd been right to step back because he sure as hell wasn't going to back off. Give him the chance, and he'd be right back, prowling around her like a tomcat. Dammit, she didn't deserve that from him. For once, why couldn't he forget what he wanted and think of Devon?

But she wanted it, too. And he could make her want it more. Go back. Take what he wanted and to hell with—

His cell phone rang. Bridget. He stabbed the button. "What's happening?"

Silence. "What's happening there? You sound as if you were in the thick of something. Did I interrupt?"

"I wish." He asked again, "What's going on? Trouble?"

"A little. Not Danner. But the security guards around this estate are keeping me running from place to place. I can't keep a good eye on Addie. Can you pull them off me?"

"If I can think of a way. The situation is delicate."

"Don't try, do it. You won't let me get rid of them myself, so it's up to you."

"Thanks a lot."

"You're the one who set Addie up here. Now deal with it."

"What a bossy bit of goods you are."

"That's what you need." Bridget chuckled. "I've decided that's why I was sent into your life. You've had things too much your own way, you strong-willed bastard. You had to have someone like me around to calm you down and help you grow up."

"I beg your pardon?" he asked with soft menace.

"See, you're even learning politeness," Bridget said slyly. "But you're short on obedience. I'll have to work on that. Now get those security guards off me before we have an incident." She hung up.

Marrok muttered a curse as he hung up, then a reluctant smile curved his lips. Bridget's occasional flashes of puckish humor didn't always come at the right time. She was always her own woman and totally independent, but she didn't often try to jab at him as she had tonight. Maybe it was a good thing that she no longer seemed to be brooding about Fraser's death.

But that didn't mean she wouldn't be after him tooth and nail if he didn't do what she asked. Bridget might think he was too strong-willed and lacking in diplomacy, but he'd been walking a fine line with Addie's guardian. Now he either had to think of a way to keep the status quo or establish a new base.

Whichever route he decided to take, it had better be quick.

* * *

"You were down there a long time. Almost three hours." Marrok was sitting in the rocking chair at the far end of the porch when Devon started up the steps. "I was wondering if you'd decided to cling to old friends in the middle of the storm."

Devon tensed. She had hoped she wouldn't have to face Marrok tonight. Talking to Nick and Janet had quieted and distracted her. She didn't want to be plunged back into the haze of sensuality that had shaken and disturbed her. "I'm not in the middle of a storm."

"No? I am." He made a face. "And I'm not talking about **shi'i'go.** I want this storm. I want to drown in it, burn in it." He saw the almost imperceptible change in her demeanor. "Yes, I'm being shallow and immature and selfish. Ask Bridget, she'd agree with me."

"As far as I know, Bridget isn't here to ask anything. Good night, Marrok."

"Stay. I didn't sit out here waiting to launch an attack on that front." He leaned back in the chair, and his face was once more in shadow. "I want to know about Lester Enright."

She stiffened and then vehemently shook her head. "Good night."

"For God's sake, talk to me. I was going to play it cool and let you keep your blasted privacy, but I can't do it. It's eating at me. You know everything there is to know about me. I need to know about Enright."

"Why?"

He was silent, then burst out, "It's bothering me, okay? Lincoln gave me the bare bones, but I need you to fill in the blanks."

"Lincoln told you about Lester in that dossier?"

"Not at first. I told Lincoln to go back to the well after I saw Enright on CNN."

"And that's why you wanted me to leave you alone with Lincoln? You wanted to question him about me?"

"Among other things."

"Why? It's none of your damn business."

He scowled. "I didn't like Enright."

"So you were trying to get something on him?"

"Maybe. And later when I mentioned him, I didn't think you liked him that much either. So tell me why you don't like him. Tell me why he lied."

"You tell me why I should confide in you about anything."

"Because Lincoln told me that you filed a restraining order against him a year after you divorced him in San Antonio, Texas. He said that the order was dropped when Enright went before the judge and swore you were having mental problems."

She smiled bitterly. "God knows that was the truth."

"No way."

"There are all kinds of mental problems, Marrok. I was in a deep depression."

"Why?"

She didn't answer.

"Dammit, let me help you."

"It's not your concern."

"Okay, you won't talk?" He leaned forward out of the shadow and she could see the recklessness in his expression. "I'll just go and cut the son of a bitch's balls off."

"Marrok."

"Sounds to me like a good idea. I don't really need to know anything more."

His dark eyes were glittering, his lips tight, and the muscles of his body were coiled and ready to spring. Devon had never seen him look more lethal. "Why are you reacting like this?"

"I'm jealous as hell. And for some reason it

makes me crazy that I wasn't there to protect you all those years ago."

"That is crazy."

"Why were you in a state of depression?"

He wasn't going to give up. "I'd lost a child the year before."

He didn't speak for a moment. "Enright's child?"

"Yes."

He was silent again. "That had to be right before your divorce."

"Yes."

"How did it happen?"

Oh what the hell. Just tell him and get it over with. "I'd found out I was having the child, and I was leaving him. I'd been trying to cope with his obsessive behavior, but I wasn't going to make my child suffer. I **wanted** that baby. He went into a rage and hit me. I ran out of the house and jumped into my car. He followed me and ran me off the road." She tried to steady her voice as the pain of that night came back to her. "I was four months pregnant. I lost the child."

"Bastard."

Her lips twisted. "He thought he was in the right. Lester always thought he was right, and everyone else was wrong. In his eyes I was the one who was at fault. I'd killed his baby, and I had to pay for it."

"Harassment?"

"Ugly phone calls, visits in the middle of the night, demands that I come back to him. He got it into his head that I owed him another child since I'd killed his. Lester can be very clever, very believable, even appealing. It's not surprising that the judge at the hearing thought I was the one who was unbalanced. I was very . . ." She searched for the right word to describe that nightmare period. "Fragile at that time. I left town after the court hearing, but he found me. He always finds me. But after I bought the practice from Nick, I stopped running. I wanted my life back. Lester showed up in Denver three years ago, but he's been more careful this time. He could see I wasn't that bewildered woman he'd victimized any longer. I can take the malicious phone calls as long as he leaves the people I care about alone. I learned to live with it."

"Why? The answer is so simple. You should have hired a hit man to deep-six the bastard." He shook his head. "No, you couldn't do that, could you? Don't worry. If I decide to step in, you'll never know."

"Marrok, Lester is my problem. I'll handle it."

"Enright is claiming that you're going back to him. What's he up to?"

"I don't know. I don't like it."

"Neither do I. So it's okay if I kill the son of a bitch?"

She sighed. "No, it's not. I'm tired of all this violence. If you want to go out and kill someone, I can't stop you. But not for me, Marrok. Never for me."

"Only for you," he said quietly.

She inhaled sharply. She couldn't breathe. She couldn't look away from him. "I've told you what you want to know. I'm going to bed now."

"Not yet."

"I'm not going to tell you anything more about Lester."

"I'm done with Enright. Well, not yet, but I won't involve you." He paused. "I have another problem I have to solve, and it suddenly occurred to me that I could solve another at the same time." He added harshly, "But, dammit, I don't want to solve it this way. I want my chance at you."

"I've no idea what you're talking about."

"Lust, death, security. You name it." His

hand tightened on the wooden arm of the chair. "I think I've found a safety net for you. It's not foolproof. I'd be hiding you in plain sight."

"Where?"

"Carmel. With Addie's guardian. Bridget just called complaining about the depth of security she's facing. Danner will try to strike there, but he'd have massive problems. You'd probably be safer there than anywhere else. You'll be out of it."

She felt a sudden hollowness. "How long would I have to be there?"

"Until it's over. Until Danner is dead. Until I have to move the dogs again."

"You're going to move them?"

"I'll have to do it. I could see it coming. Even without Danner to worry about, there's always Lincoln and whoever else in MI6 has a file. I'm lucky to have been given this many years."

"What about Nick and Janet?"

"I'll try to arrange a package deal." He paused. "It's up to you."

"It always was."

Out of it. He'd said she'd be free of the turmoil and danger that surrounded her and the people she cared about. The dogs of summer weren't her problem or responsibility. Marrok would care for them as he had done for so many years.

And she would not have to face the emotional havoc that was beginning to tear at her when she was with Marrok. Eventually, she could go back to the life she had led before. That was what she wanted, wasn't it? That was the path she should take for all their sakes.

"Well?"

"When would I have to go?"

"Day after tomorrow at the latest. I'm going to Carmel in the morning to set it up."

She thought about it. Why was she hesitating? "I can't make a decision without knowing the circumstances. I won't go anywhere blindly. I've had enough of that."

"Then come with me tomorrow."

She didn't speak for a moment. "I will." The commitment didn't bring her any sense of relief. She felt as if she had taken a step back rather than forward. "What time in the morning?"

"Seven."

She turned toward the door. "I'll meet you here."

"Wait."

She looked back over her shoulder. He'd leaned back into the shadow again, and she could no longer see his eyes. It should have been a relief, but she still was aware of everything about him. She could feel the tension, the watchfulness, the physical impact of his every move.

"I didn't want to offer you a way out," he said roughly. "I was hoping you'd say no. But then that's the kind of bastard I am."

And she'd been tempted to say no, she realized. Crazy. "Seven."

She shut the door and headed for her bedroom.

Ned was lying in front of her door. "What are you doing here? Go back to Marrok."

His tail thumped on the floor.

"Okay, come in with me. I'm a little lonely. Gracie is keeping Janet company these days. Maybe Janet's a little lonely, too."

Ned ran into the room and jumped in the easy chair. Devon knelt down and stroked him. He whined low in his throat and looked up at her. All that love and gentleness and willingness to share . . .

And he'd been shot once and would be a target as long as Danner was alive. And what about afterward? Who could be trusted not to take the easy way to get that panacea? Just kill the dog. So simple a solution.

Fury seared through her at the thought, and her arms closed around his lean body. "It's not right. It won't happen again," she whispered. "I won't let them hurt you, Ned."

CHAPTER
11

"Does it hurt?" Paco asked as he rubbed the salve into the open wounds on his back. "Cry out if you like, Joseph. It would be no shame. You're not twelve yet, and I've had men weep with the pain of this salve."

It did hurt. The sting was bringing the tears to his eyes. He bit his lip. "I told you, old man, my name's not Joseph. I won't take anything from that bastard."

"Well, you took something from him tonight. You took a hard beating. I thought you were unconscious when I found you in those rocks tonight," Paco said. "What did your father use on you?"

"His belt."

"Why?"

"I flushed his heroin down the toilet."

"That would do it. Now, what am I to call you? Should I make up a name? I'm good at that. My magic will bring you luck."

"I'll make up my own name." He shuddered as Paco's finger moved over the lacerated flesh. "And I don't need your magic. It's all phony anyway."

"Is it?" Paco asked. "You don't believe in magic?"

"No. It's all lies." He closed his eyes. "If you had any real powers, you'd be rich and bossing everyone around and not living on this stinking reservation."

"Is that what you'd do?"

His hands clenched into fists. "Yes. I'd climb so high no one would ever hurt me again. I'd make them all pay."

"So much bitterness. It's a good thing you're not a Diyi. You're like a wild animal, ready to destroy the world."

"Better than a liar, old man."

"If I don't have a magic, why will your back be healed by my salve tomorrow?"

"Herbs aren't magic either. I could probably scratch in the dirt and mix up a better salve."

"Could you? Perhaps I should let you try, you ungrateful whelp."

"I didn't ask you to help me. You're the one who made me come to this cave." His lids opened, and his gaze wandered to the fire a few feet away. The flames were casting shadows on the wall of the cave, and the smell of the wood and mesquite was acrid in his nostrils. "It's as dirty as my father's shack on the reservation."

"Caves are not supposed to be clean. The Great Spirit told me so. They are all part of the earth cycle, Joseph."

"My name's not Joseph. And all that earth bull is an excuse for being lazy."

Paco chuckled. "That's true. How smart of you to see through me."

"It's not hard. I don't know why the elders don't tell everyone what a faker you are."

"They have to believe in something. There's not much left." He capped the vial of salve. "And I'm a truly wondrous faker."

"You admit it?"

"Why not? You wouldn't believe anything else, Jos—What shall I call you?"

"Jude."

Paco's thick gray brows rose. "Jude? Why?"

"I like the Beatles."

Paco still looked puzzled.

" 'Hey, Jude,' " he said impatiently. "The song. Don't you know anything?"

"I must have missed that one. Are you taking a last name from the Beatles?"

"No. I found a name in one of those baby-name books at the drugstore in town. Marrok."

"It has a good sound. I heard your mother was Spanish, wasn't she? Is Marrok Spanish?"

"Why would I want to call myself something because of her?" he asked scornfully. "She didn't care anything about me."

"Not Spanish." Paco sat back on his heels. "French?"

Jude was silent and then said, "Marrok was a knight from King Arthur's court."

"A knight? Now that surprises me. It's a little tame."

Jude was immediately defensive. "Not one of those wimpy knights. Marrok was different."

"How different?"

"He was a werewolf."

"And you like werewolves?"

He shrugged. "Maybe."

Paco smiled. "But werewolves could be considered magical like me."

Jude shook his head. "It's not the same."

Paco was studying him. "Let's see. A werewolf is weak, without power, until he becomes the beast. Then he takes his victims by surprise and shreds and finally kills them. You must feel very weak when your father whips you like this."

"I'm not weak."

"But if you became a werewolf, you wouldn't be a victim any longer, would you?"

Jude got to his knees and reached for his shirt. "I'm going now."

"Yes, it's time." Paco said. "Come back tomorrow, and I'll put on some more salve."

"I don't need it."

"That's right, you told me that. Come back anyway. I might have use for a werewolf to test my potions."

"You're making fun of me."

"No, I wouldn't dare. You might tear me apart . . . Marrok."

"I might." He stood up. "And I might not, old man."

"My name is Paco. I may be old in your eyes, but I don't like to be reminded of it." He turned away. "And I'm not joking. A fierce cub like you might be a fine apprentice."

"Why? I don't believe in your magic. I won't lie and say I do."

"I know. But you amuse me. I can find something for you to do. Will your father let you come to me?"

"Yes."

Paco smiled. "Or you'll turn into a were-wolf and tear him apart?"

"Yes."

"Then I believe we must see that you stay away from him. I'll talk to the elders in the council."

The old man really meant it, Jude realized. Unless he was only playing with him. "Why are you doing this?"

"Not out of kindness. I'm not a kind man. Perhaps I want to see if I can convince you that I have true magic."

Jude shook his head.

"Or maybe I'm wondering if you'll turn on me and let loose all that bitterness and ferocity. I don't believe I've ever seen anyone with all that stored hatred. It will be interesting."

Jude stared at him. What could he say? Hope was beginning to unfold deep within him. "That's not all. What do you want from me? I'll pay my way. Do you need drugs? I'll go to Nakadano and get them for you."

Paco shook his head. "If I want smoke dreams, I'll make my own." He pulled the blanket closer around him. "Go away. I want to sleep now. I know you won't stay tonight. You'll want to go up to those rocks where I found you. You'll hide, you'll think, and you'll fume. Such a waste of time. Then you'll come back . . ."

"Maybe."

"No maybe. You'll come back, Jude Marrok . . ."

Paco.

Marrok opened his eyes and stared into the darkness. He hadn't dreamed about Paco for years. Not since he had come to terms with his death. Why now?

He got out of bed and moved toward the window and threw it open. The air was cool on his naked body, and he took a deep breath.

Jude Marrok doesn't sound like an Indian name, Devon had said.

Just a sentence, and all those memories from his childhood had tumbled back.

She was coming too close to him in many ways. Sex was basic, sex was safe. Memories were never safe. They twisted, they turned, and became something that could change and disturb.

Yet he wouldn't send her away. The lust was too intense. He was in a fever, and he could handle the rest.

Paco was gone. That bitter boy he'd been all those years ago had matured. Yet Devon had come into his life, and they were suddenly both here with him.

It was okay. He could handle it.

"Your Addie is living in one of those houses?" Devon was looking out the window of the helicopter down at the huge mansions below them. "She must be spoiled rotten."

"She's a golden retriever. It's hard to spoil a retriever."

"No, it's not. They just make it so appealing you don't mind doing it." Devon shook her head as the helicopter started to descend. "These are incredible estates and the views . . ."

"It's the Seventeen Mile Strip. Some of the priciest real estate on the coast." He pointed to a huge mansion on a hill overlooking the Pacific. "That's Addie's place."

Devon gave a low whistle. "That's some kennel."

"And guarded like Fort Knox. The owner is a billionaire, and everything he owns is treated like the Hope diamond."

"How did you persuade him to take on Addie? Is he a dog lover?"

"Yes. And he loves his wife even more. She's the one who took Addie for me." He paused. "Though I didn't tell her why I wanted her to do it."

Devon shook her head. "Marrok, you're impossible. You can't go around manipulating people to suit yourself. It's not right or fair."

"I know." He grimaced. "I thought it best. And it was good for her, too. But now I have to face the music if I want her to take you in."

"Another homeless stray?"

"Yeah. I guess you could call yourself that. Since I took your home away from you."

There was a note in his voice that caused her to look at him. "Danner took my home."

"Domino effect." He reached for his phone. "I've got to tell her we're coming in, or we'll have the security boys all over us."

"I'd appreciate that," Walt said dryly.

Marrok dialed the number and waited until it was answered. "We're right above you. Tell Security, okay?" He hung up. "Sarah sounded tense. We may have a problem."

"Sarah?" Devon asked.

"Sarah Logan, Addie's guardian." He pointed to a woman standing on a pad beside the house and looking up at the helicopter. "There she is."

Devon could only make out a tall, slim woman with sun-streaked brown hair blowing in the wind from the rotors. "Sarah Logan . . . I've heard that name . . ."

"I thought you might have. And it wasn't on the society pages," Marrok said. "Sarah and John live a very quiet life."

"No, it wasn't in the newspaper." The helicopter had landed, and she was getting a closer look at the woman striding toward them. It wasn't only Sarah Logan's name that was familiar. It was the way she carried herself; she moved with strength and litheness, and her gaze fixed on Marrok was direct and a little belligerent. "She doesn't look pleased to see you."

"Hold on to your hat," he murmured as he helped her from the copter. "We're about to see a few fireworks." He smiled. "Kind of you to come to meet us, Sarah. This is Devon Brady. She's a vet."

"Nothing's wrong with my dogs. I don't need her." She added coolly, "And I don't need you either, Marrok. Go away. You're not taking Addie."

"You always knew it was a temporary arrangement. You were only doing me a favor."

"She's doing fine with us. You're not taking her."

Suddenly it clicked for Devon. "Turkey. An earthquake disaster rescue mission. Years and years ago. It was only my second rescue mission. You were on one of the search and rescue teams from California." She frowned, trying to remember. "You had a golden retriever . . ."

"Monty," Marrok supplied.

"That's right," Devon said. "What a beautiful boy . . . But I never ran across you again on any other mission."

"I only went on one other rescue mission after that," Sarah said. "Monty was getting too old for the strain of the trips." She looked at Marrok. "Indonesia. That's where I met Marrok. He was there with Ned. We got to know each other very well." Her lips twisted. "We had a good deal in common. We both have Indian blood."

"I need to talk to you alone, Sarah," Marrok said.

"It's not going to do you any good. You're not taking Addie."

"That's not why I'm here. I may have to take her someday. But that's not going to happen right now."

Devon could see the tension ebb away from Sarah. "Then, dammit, why didn't you say so?"

"You didn't ask. You just jumped to conclusions."

"Well, then come back to the house." She turned to Devon. "I'm sorry. I was rude. But Marrok was his usual noncommittal self and was worrying the hell out of me."

"I can sympathize."

Sarah studied her, then nodded. "I can see how you would." She turned. "Come around to the back verandah, and we'll talk, Marrok."

"Alone," Marrok repeated. "We'll drop Devon off at the grounds, where she can meet Addie and the others."

"Why don't you want her?" Sarah narrowed her eyes on his face. "What are you up to?"

"We may have some negotiating to do.

Devon doesn't have to be involved." He added, "And you may start cursing me when I do a little explaining. Devon would get too much satisfaction from that."

"You may be right," Devon said.

Sarah nodded. "Okay, the dogs are right off the verandah. They have the run of the grounds." She led them around the house. "There they are."

Three dogs were tearing around the grounds, their tails pluming behind them. "Addie is the red golden." She slanted a glance at Marrok. "You can see she's well taken care of."

"I never doubted it."

Devon stiffened. "Dear God, that's not a dog running right behind her. It's a wolf."

Sarah nodded. "Maggie. But she gets along very well with the dogs."

The third dog was catching up to Addie and nipped at her tail, then turned and joyously streaked away.

"And what dog is that?" Devon asked.

"Monty." Sarah's gaze was fastened on the dog. "That's my Monty. Isn't he beautiful?"

"Monty?" She remembered Monty. The golden had been loving and a great rescue dog but even when she had seen him years ago he had been declining. "He looks . . . wonderful."

"Yes," Sarah said. "I put him out to pasture expecting to lose him at any time. But then he seemed to rally and slowly he began to get his energy back. I think it had something to do with Addie."

"You do?" Marrok said warily.

"Having a younger dog to play with seemed to give him a reason to keep on. He should have died a long time ago, but I'm not asking questions. I'm just accepting and hoping desperately for another day, another week. He's always been strong, and now he seems as strong as ever." She turned to Marrok, and said fiercely, "And I won't give Addie up. I won't take a chance on having Monty go into a depression or decline. At his age, every moment is precious."

"Yes, it is," Marrok said. "Go join in the fun, Ned."

The black Lab streaked away and the next moment was in the middle of the pack.

"Devon, we'll be back shortly." Marrok gestured to the verandah. "Let's talk, Sarah."

It was more than an hour before Devon saw Sarah Logan coming down the steps to the path leading to the grounds. Marrok was not with her.

"Did you send Marrok packing?" Devon asked. "I think I would."

Sarah dropped down on the grass beside Devon and crossed her legs. "I told him to let me talk to you. He has a habit of trying to handle everything himself." Her lips tightened. "Why the hell didn't he tell me about this damn **shi'i'go** before? Oh no, he let me worry that any minute Monty could take a turn for the worse, and I'd lose him. Secretive bastard."

"He was wrong," Devon said.

"You bet he was. Do you know one of the rules about me taking Addie was that I had to take her to one of the hospitals in the area to visit patients once a week? That was fine; I usually took my own dogs occasionally anyway. Except for Maggie. Wolves weren't welcome." She drew a deep breath. "I could murder him. He could have told me why."

"I agree. But he has Addie and the other dogs to worry about. I suppose he's gotten in the habit of not confiding."

"You're defending him." Sarah was studying her. "I'm surprised, considering all he's put you through."

"I guess I am." Her gaze went to the dogs lying on the grass, panting after their wild play. "Look at them. I love watching dogs. Even when they grow old, you can still see glimpses of youth in them."

"Summer."

Devon nodded. "Summer." She didn't look away from the dogs. "You don't have to take us in. It could put you in danger. I'll understand if you told Marrok that it was impossible."

"I didn't tell him it was impossible," she said. "I told him I'd welcome you and your friends into my home. No dog-killing son of a bitch is going to get Addie." She smiled fiercely. "Or anyone connected with her."

"But I'm not connected with her."

"I think you are." She shook her head. "I can almost see the bond between you and Ned. And the way you're looking at those dogs . . ."

"That's no proof. You're obviously just as much a dog lover as I am."

"Yes," Sarah said. "But occasionally one dog comes along that takes your heart and won't let go. Monty's always been that dog for me." She paused. "And no matter what Marrok did or does, I'll still be grateful to him for the rest of my life. He didn't have to let me have Addie.

But I think he could see how I was hurting for Monty on that last trip. I remember him sitting by the fire with Ned while we were talking one night at that last disaster site in Indonesia. He reached over to pet Monty. He was smiling, and his hands were so gentle . . ." She cleared her throat. "That was the only time I saw that side of him. He's definitely a rough diamond. But two weeks after we got back to the States, he came and brought Addie. He asked me to take care of her for a little while. He said she was a bit lively, but she had a good heart." She shook her head in wonder. "And I thought I was doing him a favor."

"You were. You became Addie's guardian."

"And he gave me back my Monty." Her eyes were glittering with tears. "That kind of outweighs everything else, doesn't it?"

Devon nodded. "You believe in this panacea?"

"I have to believe in it." Her gaze went back to Monty. "I'm living with it."

"What about Maggie? Is she showing any signs?"

"You saw her. The same strength, the same energy." She paused. "I asked Marrok if maybe this **shi'i'go** is transferable. If whatever those dogs are emitting is that powerful, couldn't they not only heal but become carriers?"

"What did he say?"

"He said he didn't know enough about it. He'd been too busy just keeping the dogs alive. But I'd like to think that Monty and Maggie could be dogs of summer."

"And what was the response of the patients at the hospital where you took Addie?"

"Most of them became much better. I didn't connect the healing to Addie. And two patients still died. So evidently it's not perfect." Sarah added, "But what is perfect? My old friend, Monty, is still alive and happy. That's good enough for me."

"It wouldn't be good enough for the people who are after the dogs."

"I know. I'm going to talk to John this evening and discuss a way to protect them legally. He's been involved with politics lately and has contacts in the White House. It would have to be handled very discreetly because if word got out, there would factions fighting all over the place."

"It could be too late. Marrok said that Danner was closing in."

"Then that's Marrok's fight. I'll do what I

can. He won't have to worry about Addie. I'm doubling the security on the grounds. Marrok said his Bridget was having trouble avoiding them now. By tonight, she'll be stumbling over a guard whenever she turns around. It will take an army to get through the security. Besides, it's handy to have a husband like John, who's so powerful. Anyone who gets in his way has big trouble." She added briskly, "And I'll tell Marrok to send for your two friends. We'll keep you safe."

"Thank you. I appreciate all the trouble you're going through."

"No problem. It all goes with the territory. I believe what Marrok is doing is right, and I've never been able to stop myself from diving in if I believed in a cause. That's why I became a search and rescue worker." She smiled. "And that's probably why you became a vet."

"Yes." The memory of that last trip on the helicopter out of Santa Marina came back to her when she and Hilda Golding were talking about why they kept going to disaster sites.

It was all about life.

And wasn't that what Sarah was talking about now? The panacea was life and worth any amount of risk or sacrifice to keep it safe.

That was what Sarah was going to do.

That was what Bridget was doing. Guarding Camelot from the invaders.

"You're frowning," Sarah said. "Is something wrong?"

She nodded. "I have to think about it."

Sarah got to her feet. "Well, whatever it is, we can fix it. Marrok told me to ask you to meet him at the helicopter with Ned. He said he'd fly you back to the ranch to get Nick Gilroy and your housekeeper. He thought you'd want to talk to them."

"He's right. They've been bounced around without consulting them too much already." Devon slowly stood up. "I'll go get Ned."

"Do that," Sarah's voice was absent as she headed for the house. "I've got to call John . . ."

Ned was up and playing again, this time with Addie. The black Lab and the golden retriever were a splendid flash of color against the green grass. They had both been Paco's dogs and had probably played together like this on that sunbaked earth in Arizona. Ned was obedient. If she called him, he would come to her.

She didn't call him.

Devon moved slowly toward the dogs. Monty and the wolf, Maggie, were standing still, watching her approach. There was no threat, just curiosity in their regard. Their coats were shimmering in the strong sunlight, and their eyes had the same wisdom she had seen in Ned's. Could Sarah's wish have come true? Had just the contact made them one with Marrok's dogs? Or maybe they had been special before, and she was just seeing the reflection she wanted to see. Each dog was unique and golden in its own way.

"Hello," she said softly. "I'm Devon. I won't hurt you."

Ned had seen her and was bounding across the grounds to meet her, barking joyously. Addie skidded to a stop, then turned and ran after him. The next moment, Devon was surrounded by the four animals. They were rubbing against her, making soft sounds deep in their throats. Circling and moving, trying to get closer. Full of love and trying to give it to her.

She stood there and lifted her face to the sun. She felt light as air, as if she could float off into that brilliant blue sky. Her heart was swelling, beating with the sounds and scents of nature. The smell of the grass, the rustle of the wind in the trees . . .

And with all the love and beauty of the dogs of summer surrounding her.

*   *   *

Bridget tensed, her gaze on Devon Brady standing with the dogs in the grounds below. Something was going on down there. Devon's head was raised as if to drink in the sun. It should have been a peaceful scene, but it wasn't. There was too much going on beneath the surface. Bridget could sense the waves of emotion vibrating from the other woman. She couldn't sort out what they were, but whatever Devon was feeling was incredibly intense.

And emotion that intense couldn't exist without a release that would be explosive.

"What's happening with you, Devon Brady?" she murmured.

Storm clouds.

The sun was shining, but storm clouds seemed to surround the woman with the dogs.

Bridget felt a chill.

It was nothing, she told herself. It wasn't like Fraser. Not yet. She didn't even know Devon Brady very well.

But she could see the darkening of those deadly storm clouds all around her.

*   *   *

"It's very kind of you to come out here to see me, Detective Enright," Danner said. "Particularly in this time of your great stress."

"I couldn't do anything else," Lester Enright said bluntly. "Not when your friend Caswell dangled such persuasive bait. He said you could get my wife back."

Danner studied him. Yes, he had judged Enright correctly from the reports Caswell had brought him. You could never be sure until you actually were brought face-to-face. He had been aware of the anger, the darkness, beneath that façade he showed the world, but he hadn't sensed the viciousness. Enright would do very well. Now all he had to do was set him up and push the right buttons. "I've noticed you persist in forgetting she divorced you."

"That was a mistake. We're getting back together. Now can you or can you not give me information as to my wife's whereabouts?"

"I was hoping we might cooperate toward reaching that goal."

"You don't know where she is?" Enright started to get to his feet. "Then you're wasting my time."

"Sit back down. I don't know where she is," Danner said. "But I know who she's with. And it's not some cokehead trying to force her to get him crack. I believe you suspected that, didn't you?"

"Did I?" Enright asked warily.

Set him up. "She's run from you before. Only this time she's found someone to keep her entertained. She took the opportunity the robbery at the clinic gave her and bolted."

Enright's face flushed with anger. "This is bullshit."

"I'm not attacking you. I want your help. Think about it. No bodies found at the farm. All of her animals mysteriously disappeared. I'm sure you considered the possibility."

He didn't answer for a moment. "I considered it."

Push the button. "And you want to know who the little whore is sleeping with now."

He didn't answer, but Danner could see the sudden tension of his body. "Marrok. Jude Marrok. Women seem to like him. He certainly has no trouble getting any of them into bed. Particularly not Devon Brady."

"Where is he?" Enright asked hoarsely.

"Well, you see that's the problem. I'm not sure. I don't care anything about your Devon, but I have a score to settle with Marrok. If I can lure your 'wife' into the open, I may be able to get Marrok. Interested?"

"If you can't find them, how can I?"

"I have the money to bribe, but you're a police detective. You have a badge. You can check phone lines, arrange traces, get information that's only available to law enforcement. And you've studied Devon Brady. No one knows her better. You may be able to tell me which way she'll jump."

"And what's in it for me?"

"Ah, the eternal question. Isn't finding Devon Brady enough?"

"Not this time." His lips curled. "She's played her games for the last time with me. She has to be punished."

"I sympathize." Danner leaned back in his chair. "Let me think. I believe I can accommodate you. How would you like to take a little vacation? Say for five or six months? I have a half interest in a drug distribution business in Nigeria and own a wonderful house there. You could be very comfortable. I'd provide you with the funds to ease your way."

"Is that all? I've checked up on you. You're a rich and powerful man. If you want something from me, you're going to pay through the nose. And I don't want to go to Nigeria."

"Yes, you do. Money is everything in those little African towns. For instance, I've been having problems with the local government about distribution of my drugs, and a little discreet bribery and the council just looks the other way."

"What kind of problems?"

"The main drug we distribute is one that's issued to newborn AIDS babies to pump up the immune system. The town council has been complaining that the drugs are diluted and so old that they've lost their potency, that we're buying on the black market."

"Is it true?"

He shrugged. "What difference does it make? Those babies would probably die anyway." He paused. "But I only told you about my solution to a sticky problem to open your eyes to the freedom men like us can have in the right circumstances."

Enright's eyes narrowed on Danner's face. "Freedom?"

Now close the deal. Push the bastard over the edge. "It's still a savage land," Danner said softly. "There are places there you could keep a woman and do anything you wanted with her. Rape, abuse, humiliation of any description. You wanted to punish Devon Brady? I'll give her to you. If you tire of her, you won't find it difficult to have her disappear from the face of the earth."

Enright was silent, but Danner could see the emotion flicker in his expression. He **had** him.

Enright moistened his lips. "You could be lying. How do I know that would be possible?"

"I spent a pleasant six months there several years ago. It was very entertaining . . . for me."

"And the woman?"

"It wasn't a woman. I took a young boy who had been stupid enough to be unfaithful to me. He was truly a beautiful young man when he arrived, but that didn't last long."

"Why are you telling me this?"

"It's quite safe, you could never prove it. And I want you to know how much alike we are. The moment I saw you on CNN, I knew that you'd like my house in Nigeria. It's perfect for you and your Devon Brady." He smiled. "I can see the offer excites you. Why not? It's what you've wanted all along, isn't it?"

Enright slowly nodded.

Danner waited, giving him the chance to come the rest of the way himself.

Enright leaned forward. "What do I have to do?"

CHAPTER
12

Devon's expression was calm, almost serene, Marrok thought as he watched her walk toward Sarah's helicopter pad. She was evidently content with Sarah's decision to accept her into her household. Why not? Sarah would be as protective as a mother hen, and this house was a dream dwelling.

"All set?" He opened the door of the helicopter. "You took longer than I thought. Were you catching up on old times with Sarah?"

"No, I didn't know her that well. She had to go to make a telephone call, and I spent a little time with the dogs." She got into the helicopter followed by Ned. "But I like Sarah very much."

"So do I." He climbed in and fastened his seat belt. "She's genuine and always tells you exactly what she thinks. Let's go, Walt."

"On our way," Walt said.

"Then I imagine she told you enough to burn your ears, Marrok," Devon said. "She wasn't pleased with you."

"That seems to be the consensus around here."

"You can't just go bulldozing your way through people's lives and expect them not to resent it."

He frowned. "I didn't bulldoze. I just wasn't totally honest. She had a choice." He paused. "Not like you."

"I had a choice. I could have left Ned. And you were honest . . . as far as it went. But dammit, it didn't go far enough."

"So I'm not perfect. I told you to walk in my shoes before you judged me."

"Yes, you did." She turned to look at him. "Which was the worst bullshit of all. I have no intention of either walking in your shoes or trailing after you."

"No, that won't be an option. You'll be out of it staying with Sarah."

"Out of it," she repeated. "There's no way

I could be out of it. It's too late for me." She reached down and stroked Ned's head. "Just like it's too late for you, boy."

Marrok gazed at her warily. "What are you talking about? If you stay with Sarah, you'll be safe."

"I imagine I would be."

He was silent, attempting to read her expression. "What are you trying to say?"

"I'm not trying, I'm saying it," she said coolly. "No deceptions, no beating around the bush. I'm not surprised you can't recognize it. Oh, yes, frankness is totally foreign to you."

"Devon."

"I'm not going to stay with Sarah. We're going to take Nick and Janet to her place and leave them. Then I'm going to go back to the ranch with you."

"What?"

"Oh, don't be worried. I'm not throwing myself at you like those town girls you told me about."

Walt made an indistinguishable sound somewhere between a gulp and a chuckle.

Marrok gave him an annoyed glance before turning back to Devon. "I didn't think you were. It's clear that's not what this is about.

Your attitude is less than warm. Why aren't you going to stay with Sarah? Did she say anything to offend you?"

"She said a lot but none of it was offensive. How could it be? We think alike."

"Then for God's sake, will you explain?"

She met his gaze. "I'm not leaving until this is over. Until the dogs are safe."

He muttered a curse. "Yes, you will. You'll go where you'll be safe. This isn't your battle, remember?"

"It wasn't to begin with, but it is now. I was sitting in the grass with Sarah and listening to her talk about Monty and how keeping him alive and well was worth the sacrifice, worth the battle. Because that's what love's all about, that's what life's about. And after she left me, it came to me that she might have been voicing what I've been feeling all my life." She gazed out the window. "I've been working since I was a teenager to keep animals well and happy, I've been fighting abuse, I've been working with rescue dogs to find and save men, women, and children. When I think about **shi'i'go**, it's as if it blends all of those parts of my life into one."

He stared at her in frustration. "My God, you've gone idealistic."

"Don't sound so horrified." She turned back to him. "Another concept that's foreign to you? I promise I won't let it get in your way."

"And I promise I won't let it kill you," he said grimly. "Because you're going back to Sarah's place."

"No," she said coolly. "Hell, no. I'm going to make sure that your dogs are kept alive."

"I don't need you."

"Who said I was going to work with you? I said I was going to do it. I'm not doing it for you. I'm not doing this so that you can get your revenge for Paco's death." She stared him straight in the eye. "I'm doing it for me. And I've always taken care of my own battles. So shut up, Marrok. I'm not going to discuss it again."

"The hell you won't."

She turned and gazed out the window again.

Marrok could almost feel the steel of the barrier she was raising against him, closing him out. For the first time since that night on Santa Marina, he could sense no vulnerability, no shock, no bewilderment. The woman he was seeing now was the woman who made soldiers snap to attention when she turned on them in fury. Tough, very tough. Combined with that streak of gentle idealism that was her core, it was going to be almost impossible to find a way to persuade her to abandon her path.

Impossible, hell. He had no choice. He had to do it or risk Danner's killing her.

"I'm not sure I like this." Nick hesitated before getting on the helicopter. "I think I should stay with you, Devon."

"And I think you and Janet should go to Sarah Logan and take care of the dogs there." She looked at Janet. "You'll be sure to give Gracie lots of attention? I think she's a little confused about what's going on."

"She's not the only one," Janet said dryly. "You spoil her." But her hand was gentle on Gracie's head. "Do you know she actually crawled into bed with me last night?"

"And what did you do?"

"I kicked her out. Oh, I let her stay for a little while, but you have to make those dogs toe the line."

"Then I'm glad you're going to take her with you to Sarah's. I wouldn't want Gracie to get into bad habits." She stroked Gracie's long nose. "And you'll be able to protect her

from those other dogs on Sarah's property."
She added for good measure. "And there's a
wolf in the mix, too."

"Wolf?" Janet's eyes widened. "What are
they thinking? You're darn right I'll keep an
eye on Gracie." She got into the helicopter.
"I'll have to whip that ritzy place into shape."

"I'm sure you will. Thank you, Janet."

"You're welcome." She leaned forward.
"But you're not fooling me, you know. You're
trying to distract me so I won't give you hell
for doing something stupid."

"It's not stupid. It's something I have to
do." She smiled. "And I do need you there. I'll
feel much better knowing that you're going to
be in charge."

Janet was silent before saying grudgingly,
"Well, Nick will help a little."

Nick chuckled. "I'm grateful for your condescension. I'll try to do my bit. It should reas-
sure you that Casper was kidnapped, and I
didn't lose him."

"But you couldn't remember whether you
left the gate open or not."

Nick sighed. "I assumed since the donkey
was gone that I might have—Oh, never mind."

Devon stepped back and motioned for

Walt to start the helicopter. "Marrok's people will take good care of the other animals, Janet. I'll try to call you both every night to make sure everything is okay."

"You do that," Janet said as she leaned back in her seat. Her gaze went to Marrok, who was standing on the porch watching them. "And you watch out for him, too. I don't like the look of him. He looks . . . foreign."

Devon smiled. "He's half-Spanish and half-Apache. One bloodline might be described as foreign, but the Apaches were here before Plymouth Rock."

"That's not what I mean. He doesn't look safe."

No, Marrok definitely wasn't safe, Devon thought. He was exotic and dangerous and unpredictable. "I can handle him."

"If you can't, call me," Janet said. "I'll take care of him."

"I'll sing out loud and clear." Devon stepped back away as Walt started the rotors. "Bye. Keep safe."

She couldn't make out their response through the noise as the helicopter lifted off.

She stood watching as the helicopter rose, then turned and headed west. She felt suddenly hollow, lonely. This had been the right thing to do, but it didn't change the fact that it was her family that was flying away from her.

"I can get Walt on the phone and bring him back. You can go with them," Marrok called from the porch. "Just say the word."

"You won't hear it." She turned and walked across the paddock toward the porch. "I haven't changed my mind. But there's nothing wrong with accepting that I care about those people and am sorry to see them go. You may have had trouble all your life expressing affection, but I don't. If I'd had a Paco in my life, he'd have known how I felt about him."

He was silent. "Yes, and he would have been a hell of a lot luckier than he was with me."

She felt an instant of compunction before dismissing it. She had to be totally honest with Marrok, or her decision to stay might be a disaster. "I don't think so. He seems to have been pretty happy with you. You understood each other." She smiled. "And I have a very tame nature. I can't see myself brewing potions over a fire and seeing visions in smoke."

"I can. I can see you doing anything you want to do."

There was a note in his voice that caused her to glance at his face. She looked away quickly. "What I **want** to do. That's the key word." She changed the subject. "Nick and Janet will be safe with Sarah. They don't need me there."

"**I** need you to be there."

"Too bad."

"One more time. Let me talk you out of staying."

"No."

"You're sure?"

"Marrok, drop it."

"It's dropped." His dark eyes were suddenly glittering, and his smile held the recklessness she was beginning to know so well. "I gave you your chance. I did everything I could. It's not my fault."

"What's not your fault? Danner's hurting me?"

"Anything. Everything." He opened the screen door. "Step into my parlor. I'll make you a cup of coffee."

She was studying him warily. "You seem very happy."

"Not happy. But being responsible and serious hasn't done me any good, so I'll revert to my natural character. That's always more fun."

"You don't give the impression of ever being either serious or responsible." She amended, "Except about the dogs."

"I was trying." He filled the carafe of the coffee. "But I think your Janet saw through me. She was staring daggers at me."

"She doesn't think you're safe."

"And did you defend me?"

"No. I said I could handle you,"

"Oh, you can," he said softly. "Any time, any way."

A wave of tingling heat went through her. Don't let it pass. Put him straight. "I didn't stay here to go to bed with you, Marrok."

"No, that will be a plus for both of us." He pressed the switch on the coffeemaker. "Because it will happen, Devon. I can't tell you how I'm looking forward to it. I'm regarding it as my reward for my noble attempt at being something I'm not." He got two cups from the cabinet. "Stop tensing. It will come when it comes. Just don't expect me to hold back. It's not my nature."

"I don't expect anything of you." She sat down at the table. "Except a place to stay and information that may help me. I haven't seen Lincoln today. Where is he?"

"He left midday. I'm sure he'll be back either today or tomorrow."

"What's he doing?"

"I've no idea. Probably trying to find a way to plant bugs all over the house."

"You believe that? How can you stand having him here?"

"If it wasn't Lincoln, it would be someone else. I had to have money to keep the dogs safe and undercover. I didn't have a dime and was on the run after Paco was killed." He poured coffee into the cups. "So I took the money, and I took the crap that went along with it."

"Until Ethiopia."

He shrugged. "It choked me. So I had to teach Lincoln a lesson." He sat down in the chair opposite her and lifted his cup to his lips. "It made him hate my guts, but he would have gotten to that point anyway. I held the power. Lincoln doesn't think anyone like me should be in control."

"He's wrong."

He raised his brows.

"You're the man who should be in control of **shi'i'go.** You love the dogs, you're smart, you have determination and passion. Even though you won't let the dogs be victimized, you're trying to guide them to benefit the sick. None of this is easy, but you're doing the very best you can. That says a lot." She lifted her cup to her lips. "I can't think of anyone else I'd choose to do the job."

"My, my. I didn't know you thought so well of me. What about my violent nature and my lack of Lincoln's precious civilized code?"

"Deplorable." She took another drink. "But it doesn't change my opinion. However, it might make me pause if I was working on the same team."

"But we are." He smiled. "As I told you, I'm the only game in town. At least where Danner's concerned."

"The hell you are. You haven't done so well in getting rid of him since Paco's death. Maybe you need a fresh viewpoint."

"I'm glad you didn't say fresh blood. That's exactly where you stepping in could lead."

"And it could throw Danner off-balance and get us close enough to get the bastard." Her hands clenched around the cup. "I don't want to wait and see if Danner comes looking for us. I want to go after him. Can't we do that? Where does he live?"

"He has a place on the coast near Portland, Oregon. He has more guards around him than the president. Do you think I wouldn't have tried to get to him?"

"Of course, you would." She frowned, thinking. "You said they'd come after Addie. Could we set a trap?"

"We could. Providing we could locate them before they flitted off. With that many guards around Sarah's place, they're not going to attack. They'll wait and see if they can gather us in."

"And who is the next dog they'll be targeting?"

"Wiley. His location was next on the list."

The German shepherd. "Is he secure?"

"Not as secure as Addie, but his guardian should be tough enough to protect him until I'm ready to move." He was silent a moment. "Okay, I wasn't going to wait for trouble. I'm not as complacent as you seem to think. I'm going to bring the other dogs here and bait the trap."

Her eyes widened. "All of them?"

"I'm going back and forth on Addie. But it would be irresistible for Danner if he could gather all the dogs up at one time."

"It would be risky."

"Do you think I don't know that?" he asked roughly. "I've kept those dogs separate for one reason and one reason only. Now I'm throwing safety down the toilet and risking everything I've fought for."

She frowned thoughtfully. "We'd have to be certain that we could keep the dogs from—"

"Listen to you," he said through his teeth. "You're not invited to this party, Devon."

"Then I'll throw one of my own. I'll go back to Denver and make sure I generate enough publicity to draw Danner. You did say he'd want to—"

"Dammit." His gaze searched her face. "You'd do it."

"Of course I would. Bait is bait. As a matter of fact, I'd rather not involve the dogs. I don't want to spend the rest of my life worrying about this mess. I want to know that the dogs are safe and we have a chance of finding a way of to—"

"You're not important enough to Danner to bring him down full force. He'd send someone to pick you up, then he'd torture you until you told everything you know."

"You really don't want that to happen. It would be very inconvenient to have me blabbing away, wouldn't it?"

"Inconvenient? Yes, you're damn right it would be inconvenient."

"So then you'd have to go after me and probably ruin all your plans. And you would go after me. Bridget once told me that she felt like a warrior protecting Camelot. But I think you have a little of that in you, too, Marrok." She stared him in the eye. "So why not avoid the entire problem and let me stay with you here at the ranch."

He started cursing again. "I don't like being put in—" He stopped and then started to laugh. "Damn you."

"I don't mind fighting alone. I've done it all my life. But it's more logical that if we combined efforts, we'd have a better chance."

"Heaven forbid I argue with logic. Though God knows how I'm going to—" His cell phone rang, and he glanced at the ID. "Bridget." He punched the button and listened. "Yes, I know Devon Brady wasn't on the helicopter. She decided that she'd be of more use to us here." He glanced at Devon. "She's very hardheaded." He listened again. "I had no choice. Why are you upset about it?" He was silent, frowning. "Do what you like. You will anyway." He hung up. "Bridget said she's coming here as soon as I send Larry Farland to replace her. She wants to see you. She's a little on edge about you not going to Sarah's."

"Why?"

"She said you should be somewhere safe. I agree."

"But her coming here isn't going to change my mind. You should tell her to stay where she is."

"You call and tell her."

"You have no authority over her?"

"Like a good soldier, she obeys me in emergency situations. She recognizes that there can be only one commander in those cases. Otherwise, she definitely puts in her two cents' worth."

"And you respect her opinion." Devon stared at him thoughtfully. "Bridget is . . . unusual. She seems to combine the talents of a dog whisperer with the training of a soldier. Where did you say you found her?"

"I didn't say. Ireland. A village outside Dublin. Lincoln gave me the tip I might find her useful, and I went to see her. She was training horses for a local politician. I spent two weeks there and in the end I persuaded her to come home with me. She was everything I needed. She'd been trained by MI6 and proved herself on several missions. She was magic with animals." He shrugged. "And I felt she was a woman to trust. Nothing she's done since has convinced me that I was wrong."

"She's wonderful with animals," Devon

said slowly. "It's almost eerie. Is it some psychic ability?"

He was silent a moment. "Probably. Though it took a long time for me to admit it to myself. I don't want to believe all that weird stuff. I thought at first it might be just a strong instinctive bonding. But Bridget sometimes senses other things."

"What?"

"Bad events coming. The presence of enemies. I don't know what else. Bridget doesn't talk much about it. It was over a year before she opened up to me at all. She's not happy about it."

"I can see why she wouldn't be. Does she have any family?"

"Her parents are dead. She was in an orphanage from the time she was ten until she went to work at sixteen. She said that we had that in common. But she never had a Paco." He smiled. "But he would have liked her. He didn't care for many women, but Bridget is special."

"Special to you, too?"

His gaze narrowed on her face. "Do you mean have I slept with her?"

"No, that's none of my business."

"But you're curious." He leaned back in his chair. "That's encouraging. No, I look on Bridget as a guardian. Lincoln may think I have no code, but I don't go to bed with guardians. It would interfere with the relationship and might impact their work. Did I want to?" He tilted his head. "For some reason I never even considered it. She was always my friend, not a potential lover. Which is strange because I'm definitely not a celibate man."

"That doesn't surprise me." She moistened her lips. "But it doesn't interest me."

"Yes, it does. Just as I'm curious about your marriage."

"I'm not going to satisfy your curiosity." She lifted her cup. "I've told you all I'm going to tell you about Lester. I didn't like your response last time."

"What if we don't talk about the fact that I'm going to kill the bastard someday? It's other details that I want right now. Oh, I don't care anything about the way you met, the things you had in common. I want to know why you felt you had to go to bed with him. What did he do?" He added softly, "How did he please you?"

Her chest was tightening, it was hard to

breathe. She tore her eyes away from him. "If Lincoln recommended Bridget, how are you sure that she's not working for him?"

He accepted the change of subject, thank God. "I can't be sure about anything. I'm careful. I'm always very, very careful."

"That's good." Devon set down her cup and stood up. "When will she be here?"

"A few hours. Where are you going?"

"Down to the barn to check on my animals."

"Are you running away?"

"Yes," she said bluntly. "You're not paying attention to what I want you to pay attention to."

"You're right, but there's a solution. Have sex with me so that I can concentrate on more serious things."

"I believe you're concentrating on more serious things right now. You just don't want me to concentrate on them."

"You're half-right. The other half is just a poor misguided half-breed who wants what he wants and can't help himself from trying to get it. You know savages are like that."

"No, I don't. I don't know what you're like. Just when I think I do, you change on me."

"Then you've changed opinions about me

being a suitable custodian for the **shi'i'go**?" he asked mockingly.

"No, whatever else you are, I'd trust that side of you to hell and back. That wouldn't change."

His smile faded. "I believe I'm touched."

"And I believe you're making fun of me." She headed for the door. "I'll come back when Bridget is here. I want to see her, too."

"Devon."

She stopped but didn't turn around.

"I'm not making fun of you," he said quietly.

She didn't want to turn and see his expression. She had already been moved to a dozen different emotional highs. It had to stop.

She opened the door and ran down the porch steps. Slow down. No one was pursuing her. Yes, she was running away. She could still see Marrok lolling in that chair, his legs stretched before him; insolence, sensuality, and tension fighting for dominance. There was always a struggle going on within Marrok. Recklessness against wariness. Gentleness against violence. From the moment she had met him she had been aware of that battle. She should have run from him then. He was nothing she wanted in a man.

And everything she wanted in a lover.

Shock jolted through her at the thought that had come out of nowhere. She tried to push it away, dismiss it. A few chemical responses didn't mean anything. She had been so cool, so sure that she could handle anything when she had made the decision to throw all her efforts behind destroying Danner and saving the dogs. She'd been filled with a glowing sense of right.

That feeling was still there. Of course, it was. She just mustn't be distracted by these emotions that Marrok was stirring.

Easy to say. He had no intention of letting her ignore the way she felt. Heat tingled through her as she remembered the curve of his lips, his eyes dark and intent on her face. He wanted to make love to her, and he wasn't going to stop until it happened.

No, not make love. What was between them was erotic, sensual, but it had no basis in anything deeper. She had to remember that.

Going to bed with Marrok could be a mistake.

Thinking that there was anything between them but sex could be a tragedy.

CHAPTER
13

Bridget arrived at sunset, and Marrok walked down to the helicopter to meet her.

"Where is she?" Bridget asked as she jumped out of the aircraft.

"Down at the barn." His brows rose. "You act as if you thought I was keeping her tied up in the basement. Where did you think she was?"

"I have no idea. I don't know why you let her stay. She shouldn't be here."

"I'm aware of that, Bridget. I couldn't convince her to go."

Bridget was studying him. "And you're not sorry she's staying. What are you up to, Marrok?"

"The oldest game of all. You know what a

self-indulgent bastard I am. Why not risk her neck if I can get a little pleasure out of the situation?"

"Don't give me that bull. I know you."

"Then you don't know me well enough." He turned to Walt, who was still in the helicopter. "Tell her, Walt. He's been with me a hell of a lot longer than you have."

"He's a real lowlife," Walt said. "Scum of the earth. Do you want me to stay here at the ranch or go back to the airport, scum of the earth?"

"Here," he said curtly as he turned back to Bridget. "You're welcome to try to talk her out of staying. But I'm done with it. Devon's so full of ivory-tower idealism, she thinks she can move the world single-handedly."

"So what? So do you." She strode toward the house. "Don't give me that crap about how cynical and wicked you are. You're no kid any longer. All that may have been true at one time, but I've seen you change just in the last three years. If you want to have sex with her, do it. But don't tell me it's because you're such a 'bad boy.'"

He chuckled. "But I am, you know."

"You have your moments. But you have other moments when I'd bet on you to be able to shift the earth to suit yourself." She turned to face him as they reached the porch. "If you're going to get Devon into bed, do it quick and send her to Sarah's. I don't know how much time she has."

His smile vanished. "What are you talking about?"

"I don't know. I never know, dammit. I just **feel.** What the hell good is that?"

His hand closed on her arm. "Stop rambling. Tell me."

"It's . . . I'm not sure. Something's going to happen to her . . . around her. I don't know which. But it's bad."

"What the hell do you mean?" His hand tightened bruisingly. "You can't just leave it like this. What—"

She tore her arm away. "Let go of me. I told you all I know. Maybe I'm wrong."

"You're damn right you're wrong. Nothing is going to happen to Devon."

"Then ignore what I said," she said fiercely. "Only you won't do that. Because as often as you tell everyone how skeptical you were about Paco's powers, you believed in him. And you believe in my particular brand of weirdness, too." She turned toward the barn. "And that's the reason you're going to get Devon away from here, away from you."

"She won't listen to me, dammit. You try."

"That's what I intend to do," she said over her shoulder. "Just don't do anything that will stand in my way."

Bridget could see Devon standing at the fence looking at Casper. Okay, get your thoughts in order and be ready to talk sense to her. But people like Devon might be sensible and go into battle anyway. It was a dicey situation. Even if Marrok didn't interfere intentionally, his very presence might blow her efforts. She had observed him with women before. There was no one more erotic or magnetic than Marrok when he was aroused, and she had never seen him like this. He was sending off signals as strong and basic as a forest animal. Most women would be fascinated, drawn irresistibly toward the challenge.

She could only hope that Devon would be in the minority.

Devon absently rubbed Casper between the ears as she watched Bridget walk toward her.

The woman was moving briskly, a hint of impatience in her stride. Devon had watched her walk from the helicopter with Marrok, and her stance had been even more tense while she was talking to him. It was clear she wasn't happy with him or the entire situation.

Well, neither was Devon.

Casper brayed and moved toward Bridget as she came nearer.

"I seem to be deserted," Devon said. "Marrok told me that you were a Pied Piper."

"Casper still cares about you. I'm just the new kid in town." Bridget said as she reached up and stroked the donkey. "And he's grateful you saved him from getting shot by that farmer."

"You do your research."

Bridget smiled. "Doubting Thomas. You remind me of Marrok. He calls it hocus-pocus but he doesn't scoff any longer. I had a hard time with him when I first met him. In his heart Marrok does believe in things that he can't hear, see, or touch. He won't admit it. He took too much punishment as a kid as an apprentice to Paco. The elders might have respected Paco but his peers, the children on the reservation, laughed at him."

"He seems to have survived just fine."

"No, the scars linger, and they've caused a hell of a lot of trouble. It's no wonder he became so volatile. A drug addict for a father, a mother who took off and left him when he was a baby."

"Did she divorce his father?"

"No, she died a few years after she left the reservation. It was a car accident, but she was drunk. It was just as well she deserted Marrok. From what I've been able to piece together, she was pretty erratic herself. Catrin Munoz was born in Spain and was traveling the world when she met Marrok's father in San Francisco. He'd just gotten out of the navy and probably had a good deal of the same sex appeal as Marrok. Catrin was experimenting with everything else, liquor, drugs, sex, and decided to include him in the package. He was just another fling to her."

"You know a lot about Marrok's background."

"Yes, you don't think I'd take any job without investigating what I was getting into."

Devon was silent a moment. "And you had Lincoln to help you research."

"You've been doing a little research yourself. Did Marrok tell you that?"

"Yes." She added, "I don't like Lincoln. I told Marrok that I found your connection . . . suspicious."

"Marrok finds it suspicious, too. But he still trusts me."

"I don't trust you. I don't know you."

"That's why I'm here. I have an idea we may need each other. If you trust me, it may make it easier."

"Marrok said you were upset I didn't go to Sarah's."

"That's putting it mildly."

"I couldn't leave. I have to—"

"Don't explain. I know why you want to stay. You want to save the world or at least this part of it. It's very commendable and very stupid. You're going to ruin everything."

"I'm not stupid and not a fanatic do-gooder. I have to do this." She smiled faintly. "You told me once you weren't good at being diplomatic. You're proving it right now."

"Oh, crap. How can I convince you that you should go to Sarah's until this is over?"

"You could tell me how I'd ruin everything. You can't do that. I'm intelligent, not overly impulsive. I've worked disaster sites for years, and I know karate and can handle a gun. I'm determined and persistent. I'd say I'm a damn valuable asset."

"And I'd say you could blow us out of the water." She frowned, trying to put it into words. "Look, I don't doubt that under ordinary circumstance you could be helpful. But sometimes there are certain people who become catalysts. Put them into the mix, and events change, people do what they ordinarily wouldn't do. You plan on their jumping one way, and they go another."

"Danner?"

"And Marrok. I could accept you tilting the odds in Danner's favor, but I can't risk you doing anything that might affect Marrok."

Devon frowned. "Isn't that the same thing?"

"No." She sighed. "I'm not getting to you." She hesitated, then said a rush, "Okay, what if I told you that you'd die if you jump into this?"

A chill went through Devon. "I'd say you were pretty desperate to stop me. Did you see this in your crystal ball?"

Bridget shook her head. "It doesn't work that way." She made a face. "And I didn't actually sense you'd die. Just that you were in danger of . . . something."

"I could be in danger of stubbing my toe." She shook her head. "Bridget, if you're trying to frighten someone, you shouldn't throw it out there, then start qualifying."

"I was trying to frighten you." She added simply, "Because I'm frightened, Devon."

And that grave simplicity scared Devon more than the words that had gone before. She moistened her lips. "I was in danger a hundred times on those search and rescue missions through the years. You can't stop because something might happen." She kept her voice cool and steady. "Particularly when the warning comes from someone who I don't know and has admitted that she just gets 'feelings.' You could be trying to influence me into doing what you want."

Bridget stared at her helplessly. "It's true, you know. I don't hit it every time, but this time I think . . ." She shook her head. "You won't do what I ask?"

"I won't go to Sarah's." She stared her in the eye. "What are you going to do about it?"

Bridget didn't speak for a moment. "I'm going to accept it and make the best of you." Her voice became brusque. "I don't want you near Marrok. Suppose you work with me."

"Why not? I think it's a good idea for me to be in a position to keep an eye on you." She paused. "As long as I'm doing something constructive, and you don't expect me to take orders."

"You'll have something to do that's constructive. You're a vet and good with dogs. Marrok tells me we may be bringing the other dogs here. It's risky, but if we—" She stopped, her gaze on the road where two headlights speared the darkness. "I think that's Lincoln. It's about time he showed up. Come on, let's go up and meet him."

"Why?"

"Because I need him to see me. We haven't been together in a long time. It's always good to do person-to-person reinforcement." She was already walking toward the house. "And I want to ask him where he's been."

"Will he answer?"

"Probably not. But if I ask it in the right way, he'll wonder if I already know."

Devon shook her head ruefully. The more she learned about Bridget, the more she felt she had to learn. This conversation had revealed her to be a combination of toughness and vulnerability. The toughness was undoubtedly real. The vulnerability could be feigned. There was no question she was clever enough to be playing both sides against the middle. Maybe she didn't want another player in the game if there was a greater chance of her being exposed.

And maybe she did believe that Devon was going to die. She had rushed to qualify, but that could have been a lie. What was the truth?

"I'll be fair with you." Bridget was studying her expression. "You're not going to have to be afraid of me. Unless you do something to hurt Marrok."

"I'm not afraid of you," Devon said. "And Marrok can take care of himself." She saw Marrok coming down the steps of the porch as a car pulled up before the house. "You were right, that's Lincoln behind the wheel." She said with mock wonder, "Gee, you must be psychic."

"And you must be a smart-ass," Bridget said. "It's nothing to joke about."

"I need to joke about it. You said the Grim Reaper was about to cut me down."

"That's not what I said. Well, maybe I did. But I told you I wasn't sure what—" Bridget grimaced. "And it didn't work anyway. I didn't do it right."

"You obviously don't exude the correct amount of menace. They didn't teach you well at MI6."

"They taught me well." She was watching Marrok turn on his heel and go back to the porch. "I believe Marrok is pissed off with our Mr. Lincoln. I'll have to take my turn at him." Her pace quickened as she left Devon and went toward Lincoln.

Devon had no desire to tag along behind Bridget. The woman had her own agenda, and

Devon would end up standing around and observing. She had done enough of that for the past few days. She wanted to initiate, not witness.

And she didn't want to go up the steps to the porch, where Marrok was standing. He had turned and was watching her.

The porch lights shone on his dark hair and highlighted his high cheekbones, but his eyes and the hollows of his face were in shadow. His stance was straight, unmoving, almost wary.

Her own response was instinctive, her body tensing. She hadn't been away long enough, dammit. She was right back where she was when she had left him. Well, she couldn't stand here like a doe caught in the headlights.

She slowly climbed the steps. "Bridget said she thought you'd quarreled with Lincoln. Is he staying?"

"So he tells me. Unless I decide to toss him out." He paused. "Are you staying?"

"Yes." She tried to smile. "Though Bridget pulled out all the stops trying to convince me to go to Sarah's. Even a psychic premonition about my impending doom."

"That doesn't amuse me."

"Me, either." She gazed at Bridget and Lincoln talking beside the car. "Particularly since I believe she meant it."

"Then go back to Sarah's."

She shook her head.

Marrok muttered an oath as he took a step closer. "Stop being stubborn. You can't help. Leave here."

She could feel the warmth of his body though he wasn't touching her. Dear God, she was starting to shake. "I'm not going to repeat myself. Back off, Marrok."

He went still, his gaze on her face. "Verbally or physically?" he asked softly. "I'll shut up. I don't want to talk anyway."

He was close enough now that his eyes were out of shadow, and she could see the glitter, the dark softness. And his mouth . . .

She should move away from him. She could feel heat tingle through her, and her body was readying.

She didn't move.

"Come on," he murmured. "I'll find us a place. Though it will have to be fast. I'm about to—"

"No." What was she saying? Yes. Yes. Don't say that word, or she'd be lost.

She saw his hands clench into fists at his sides. "Why? You want it. Is it because I'm a half-breed?"

Her eyes widened in shock. "Don't be stupid. And insulting. Where did that come from?"

"Twenty years ago." His lips twisted. "It just tumbled out. I thought I'd gotten over it. You never know what poison lingers, do you?"

"No." She felt a surge of sympathy so strong it was like a tidal wave. How many scars did Marrok have from that ugly childhood? She wanted to reach out, touch him, comfort him. "You probably got the best of both worlds by being a half-breed. They say mutts are the smartest, most loyal dogs. It's probably the same thing."

"Oh." He looked startled, then smiled slowly. "Only you would make that comparison. I know you're trying to kiss and make it better, but calling me a mutt is a strange way to go about it."

"I guess it is." Something had changed, she realized. The sexuality had not ebbed away, but there was now a tenderness, a gentleness, a humor, that had insinuated itself into the whirlwind of eroticism. "But it's true."

"And you're defending me the way you're

going to defend my dogs of summer. They're worth it. I'm not sure I am."

"If you expect me to say anything else to expand your ego, you're going to be disappointed."

"No, calling me a mutt is compliment enough." He shook his head. "But you've spoiled what might have been a promising start to seduction. You were close. If I'd pushed just a little harder . . ."

If he'd pushed harder, she would probably have been in his bed tonight, she thought. She was still hot and aching and empty.

"Me, too," he said softly and she knew he had read that unspoken response. "But I can't go on the attack now. I'd be wondering if you were still trying to heal my misspent youth."

Disappointment.

"Look at me." He was holding her eyes. "It's just the beginning. Once you think about it, you're going to run away. You'll change your mind. I just hope you change it back pretty damn quick. You may not be backing off because I'm a half-breed, but I'm still too wild for you. So I'll be ready to go crazy by the time we come together. But I can wait . . . if you can."

She couldn't look away from him. There was too much there, passion, humor, understanding. Emotions were swirling around her, around them.

Lincoln gave a low whistle, his gaze on something beyond Bridget's shoulder. "Well, what do you know . . . ?"

Bridget looked over her shoulder.

No.

She stiffened and swung around to face Marrok and Devon. The electric tension between them was palpable. You could almost see it, smell it, warm your hands at the heat. They weren't touching, but they didn't need to touch. The bond was there, waiting only for the final melding. She had never seen Marrok and Devon together, and it came as a shock. It was too strong, too primitive, too earthy.

Lincoln was chuckling. "What do you bet he kicks his faithful Ned out of his room tonight?"

"Maybe." Didn't Lincoln see anything but the obvious? she wondered. If he didn't, she wasn't going to call his attention to what was coming through to her.

"Or maybe our savage won't wait to get her into bed. Bed may be too civilized for him."

Malice. Let Lincoln be as malicious as he wished. It might keep him focused on the sexual side of the scene before them. Because she was seeing something much more dangerous between Marrok and Devon, tentative, fragile, but more frightening than any sexual bond.

Shit.

"Hello, Marrok." Bridget bounded up the porch steps. "I guess Devon told you I struck out?"

Devon shook her head to clear it. The atmosphere had been so intense between Marrok and her that it was hard to be jarred out of it by the intrusion.

Marrok didn't look at Bridget. "I expected it. I'll handle it from now on."

"No, we've got it worked out," Bridget said. "She'll work with me. She thinks I need to be watched." She called to Lincoln, who was coming up the steps, "Your fault. She believes I'm your mole."

"Why would she think that?" Lincoln asked. "We're all friends, working together." He turned to Devon. "But I applaud the decision. You're safer with Bridget than Marrok.

Though you'd be much better off going home and getting away from both of them." He shrugged. "And it would do no good to tell you that I'm your best bet of all." He moved toward the door. "So I think I'll go inside and make a few calls to London. Good night all."

Lincoln had the right idea, Devon thought wearily. Just walk away and avoid all this tension. "And I'm going to bed." She turned away. She was tired of the guarded interplay among all of them. She wanted her life clear and simple again.

She almost laughed at the thought. The moments before Bridget had run up the steps and interrupted them had been neither clear nor simple. It had been like being caught in a tropic windstorm, hot, dizzying, robbing her of breath, and bending her, leading her. She should be grateful that Bridget had broken the spell.

She wasn't grateful. She wanted it back. She wanted **him** back.

Crazy. All the more reason to get away from here and rebuild her defenses.

She opened the screen door. "Come to think of it, I have to call Nick. I'll see you in the morning."

She didn't wait for a reply but escaped into the house. **Escape** was the right word. She had been so calm and clear when she'd faced Marrok earlier. Even when she'd left him and gone down to the barn, she hadn't felt this ragged. It was those last moments that had been so hard. She'd had to fight both the desire to let him take her to bed and the intense sympathy that had made her want to hold him, soothe him, make everything all right in his world.

But she didn't even know how to cope with his world. He had grown up wild and undisciplined, and she had always had order in her life.

Forget it. Go to sleep. Wake up to a fresh morning with fresh perspectives. Nothing had happened that had changed anything.

She just had to keep it that way.

"It's not going to work, Bridget," Marrok said quietly.

"I don't know what you mean."

"Devon. Why are you set on keeping her away from me? What difference does it make to you?"

She didn't try to pretend she didn't know

what he meant. "She could be an Achilles' heel. If anything happens to her, I don't want her near you."

His brows rose. "It's really none of your business."

"It's my business to take care of the dogs," she said. "Anything that affects my ability to do that will have to be addressed." She started down the steps. "I thought it would be okay if you screwed her. It would be over, then we could go on. But it's not going to be okay. It's not going to be over . . ." She looked back over her shoulder. "It might get worse. So I'll try to keep you apart as long as I can."

"Do you know how ridiculous you sound?" he asked sarcastically.

"Hell, yes." She strode away from him toward the bunkhouse. Ridiculous as trying to stop a raging forest fire with a garden hose. Marrok wouldn't let her get in his way for long. She couldn't blame him. She'd bitterly resent interference in her affairs if the situation were reversed.

But something had to be done. She had to have help. God, she hated admitting to anyone that she couldn't handle the job.

Bite the bullet.

She reached for her phone and dialed London. It rang three times before Jordan Radkin answered. "It's the middle of the night here, Bridget. It had better be important."

"Dammit, do you think I like calling you?" She drew a deep breath. "Something's changed. It could get out of control. We may have to bring Danner in sooner."

CHAPTER
14

"We've got it!" Paul Caswell threw the computer slip down before Danner. "Not everything. That bastard changed the code three times during the message. But we've got a start. The location of the golden retriever. Addie."

"If he hasn't moved her by now," Danner said bitterly. "We should have had that translation yesterday."

"He hasn't moved her," Caswell said. "I sent a man to the house as soon as I got the first line of address." He paused. "But it will be difficult to get at the retriever. She's staying at John and Sarah Logan's place on the Seventeen Mile Strip."

"Logan." He started to curse. Dammit, he knew that name well. "Difficult? It will take weeks to find a way to take the dog away from him. I can't afford to stir up a hornets' nest with Logan. He's even got the ear of the president. Keep watch on the retriever and go after the other dogs. If they try to move the retriever, go after her. And I want that second location by tonight."

"We're doing the best we can," Caswell said. "And in a few hours we'll know everything that's going on at Logan's place. We might be able to find a weak link."

He needed a weak link, Danner thought. Marrok had been running rings around his men since Santa Marina. He'd thought Enright would be the answer, but the bastard was moving as slow as those translators trying to locate the dogs. But it was going to end. He had to find a way to bring Marrok to his knees. The thought of Marrok humbled gave him a flash of enormous pleasure. Perhaps he'd make Marrok watch as he slaughtered the dogs one after the other. That would make him realize how futile it was to oppose him.

And he'd kill Marrok, and that would be the final triumph.

His cell phone rang, and he glanced at the ID. London. He stiffened and hope surged through him. He punched the button. "It's about time. What have you got for me?"

"Get up." Bridget opened Devon's bedroom door and stuck her head in. "We're going to get Wiley and bring him here."

"It's still dark." Devon drowsily lifted her head and looked at the digital clock on the bedside table—5:37. "Is there an emergency?"

"No, but we may be running out of time."

"I thought only Marrok knew where all the dogs were located?"

"I knew about Addie, and he gave me Wiley's location when he thought we might have to move them. He still hasn't told me where Nika's being cared for. Trusting bastard, isn't he?" She added, "There's toast and coffee on the kitchen table. I'll be back to get you in thirty minutes."

The door closed behind her.

Devon shook her head to clear it and sat up. Bridget had obviously been sincere about having Devon work with her. So get going and do your share. She swung her legs to the floor.

Thirty minutes.

She was waiting on the porch twenty minutes later, watching Bridget walk toward her from the helicopter.

"You're early," Bridget said when she reached her. "But Walt's ready to go."

"So am I," Marrok said from behind Devon.

Bridget stiffened as she and Devon turned to see him come out of the house.

"Though I wasn't invited," he said. "I wouldn't have even known about your excursion if Walt hadn't decided he had to check in with me."

"You said you wanted the dogs brought here," Bridget said. "I'm bringing Wiley to you. Don't you trust me?"

"Sometimes. Most of the time. But I have no right to trust anyone right now. You're behaving a little erratically lately."

"Bullshit."

He smiled. "Perhaps. But I still think that I'll be the one to take Devon to pick up Wiley. You stay here and hold down the fort with Lincoln. Maybe you can renew old ties."

"I told you that you shouldn't be with her. It's not safe."

"Did it occur to you that if something's

going to happen to Devon, that I'd want to be there to stop it?"

"It occurred to me. I hope the best for her. But my job is to keep you safe."

"No. Where did you get that idea? Your job is to keep the dogs safe."

She gestured impatiently. "Same thing."

Devon was tired of listening to them wrangle. "I'm not a piece of meat you're fighting over. Back off. Both of you."

Marrok chuckled. "A very nice piece of meat." His gaze shifted back to Bridget. "You heard her, back off." He nudged Devon gently forward. "Let's go, Devon. Walt's waiting."

Devon hesitated. She didn't want to spend any extra time with Marrok. She had been avoiding it, and now she'd been tossed back into his company. Oh, what the hell. It wasn't as if she was afraid of being with him.

He said quietly, "You set the pace, Devon."

"That's right, I do." She ran down the steps and set out for the helicopter. "That goes without saying. So long, Bridget."

Bridget didn't answer. When Devon glanced back at her, she was frowning as she stared at both of them walking away from her.

"She doesn't like being thwarted," Marrok murmured. "I don't blame her. Neither do I."

"I could tell," she said dryly. "Just don't use me in your games."

"It never used to be a game. This is the first time Bridget and I have had a real conflict. She's behaving out of character."

"She's certainly being overprotective of you. You'd think I was some kind of Typhoid Mary."

"Did she scare you?"

"Of course not." She wasn't telling the truth. The determination that Bridget had shown in trying to keep her away from Marrok had been disturbing. It was more chilling than the first time Bridget had told her about the danger surrounding her. It was somehow more real to her since Bridget was feeling strong enough about the premonition to act on it. "I don't believe in fortune-tellers."

"I didn't either until I met Bridget. It's strange, all the time I spent with Paco, I fought against believing in his so-called magic. I played his game, but I took everything with a grain of salt. Yet Bridget was different. Maybe because it couldn't be more clear that she didn't want it to be true."

"That's not very comforting," she said dryly.

"Bridget didn't actually say you were going

to die." His lips tightened. "And it's not going to happen. I intend to make sure it doesn't."

"I can take care of myself. I don't need you or Bridget." She shook her head. "For Pete's sake, drop it. I'm not going to fret about something this weird. Tell me about Wiley. Isn't that the dog we're going to pick up? He's the German shepherd, isn't he?"

"Yes." He opened the helicopter door for her. "You'll like Wiley. He's not easy. He'll be a challenge for you."

"What do you mean?"

"He's always been a little standoffish. He doesn't trust easily. He was mistreated as a pup before Paco got hold of him." He followed her into the aircraft. "That's why I wanted you to meet him on his home turf with his guardian as a buffer."

"Let's get out of here," Walt said as he started the engine. "Bridget is staring a hole in me. I'm going to hear about tattling to the boss."

"Children tattle," Marrok said. "And I would have been most unhappy if you'd kept quiet."

"That's what I figured." Walt lifted off and headed west. "It was only a case of deciding which one of you I wanted to piss off."

Devon went back to the previous subject. "Who is Wiley's guardian?"

"Sid Cadow," Marrok said. "He's an old rodeo rider. Tough as nails. Sid is almost as much a loner as Wiley. He's in his fifties and had almost all his bones broken at one time or another. He has no family and isn't sociable."

"A strange choice for you to make."

"I don't think so. They suit each other. Neither one of them is great on trust. But Sid loves that dog. It's probably the only thing he does love. I'd hate to be the man who tried to hurt Wiley."

"And you're taking Wiley away from him?"

"He can come back to the ranch with us. It's his decision."

"Where are we going?"

"He has a cabin in the hills in northern Arizona. But when I was a kid he had a place not too far from the reservation where I was born." He added, "As a matter of fact, he used to frequent the bar where I spent most of my time when I was in my teens. That's where I got to know him. He was as much a barroom brawler as I was and used to bust my chops regularly until I learned how he was doing it. Then we came to an understanding."

"So you're friends?"

He shook his head. "He and Wiley are friends. I just pay the bills and receive a certain toleration in return."

"Does he know how special Wiley is?"

"Yes, I told him after he'd had Wiley a year. By that time I knew he wouldn't give up Wiley. I'm not sure he believed me. He does believe that Wiley may be in danger. I think I got that through to him."

"And how is he going to take this move?"

"Not well. I called him and told him why I was coming. He told me to go to hell."

"Not promising."

"No. But we'll have to see, won't we?"

Sid Cadow was standing at the door of his cabin, watching them come up the path. He was a huge man, with a shock of white hair and skin that looked like tanned leather. His expression was forbidding.

"I ain't going to let you take him," he said flatly. "No way."

"He's going, Sid. You can come with him, or you can stay here, but Wiley is going to the ranch," Marrok said. "It's time we put an end to this hiding."

"We're getting along just fine." He looked

at the black-and-tan German shepherd who was streaking around in circles with Ned. "I take good care of him."

"I know you do."

"And if anyone came hunting for him, I'd shoot his nuts off."

"He's going to the ranch," Marrok said. "His life's got to change now. If you're willing to change with him, I'll find a place for you."

Devon could see the hackles rising on both men. Marrok wasn't handling Cadow right, dammit. Would it have hurt him to be a little more diplomatic?

"I don't need anyone finding a place for me. I get along." He turned to Devon. "Who is she?"

"A vet. Devon Brady. She's going to work with the dogs."

"How do you do, Mr. Cadow?" Devon said. "Wiley is a beautiful dog. And very fit. You must exercise him quite a bit."

"We go for long walks in the hills," Cadow said curtly. "It's quiet. We both like quiet." He called to Wiley, "Stop that foolishness. You're acting like a pup."

"That's not bad," Devon said. "He's obviously a very dignified dog. A little fun won't hurt him."

"He remembers Ned from the Paco days," Marrok said. "I've seen them play like that for hours."

"I play with him," Cadow said defensively. "He likes to play fetch with a stick."

"Most German shepherds do," Devon said. "My dog, Tess, used to nag me for hours. She was black and tan, too. She was very, very smart and very loving."

"She couldn't have been as smart as Wiley. I could tell you stories . . ."

"I bet you could," Devon said. He didn't mention how loving Wiley could be. It would have been too personal. He was too prickly to let anyone that close. "Does he swim? Tess could swim like an otter."

"When I let him. The current in the river is pretty strong." He scowled. "Did you really have a German shepherd or are you giving me bull?"

"Yes, I had my Tess. Or maybe she had me. Sometimes I couldn't tell the difference."

"Had? She died?"

"Yes. It broke my heart. I still miss her." She looked him in the eye. "But your Wiley has a chance of living for a long time. Don't be stupid and make him live it without you."

"I won't. He ain't going."

She made a motion as Marrok opened his mouth. "You know better than that."

"Because Marrok thinks Wiley belongs to him? He's my dog now."

"He belongs to both of you. You've invested enough love to ensure that Wiley is at least part yours. But Marrok has a history with him, too. And, he's right, we can't hide him from Danner any longer. Now call him and tell him it's okay for him to go with us. I know he won't leave you unless you do."

"You're damn right he won't." Cadow hesitated. Then he whistled and called. "Wiley."

Wiley skidded to a stop and bounded toward Cadow. He sat down in front of him, his tongue lolling, panting.

"Told you he was smart," Cadow said proudly. "You ain't seen nothing."

"Then come with us and show us what he can do." Devon reached out and let Wiley sniff her hand before she put it gently on his head. He didn't move, but she could sense the caution ingrained in him. "What a lovely boy, you are," she said softly. "Just like my Tess . . ."

"Sid?" Marrok asked.

Cadow hesitated before saying grudgingly. "Maybe I'll let him go for a little while. As long as I'm there to take care of him."

"Good," Marrok said. "Go pack your bag."

"I've got to close up the cabin. I'll follow you down." His hand reached out and caressed Wiley's head. "I'll be with you in a couple hours, pal. Promise."

"Tell him it's okay to go with us," Devon said.

Cadow hesitated again before he said gruffly. "Okay, go along with them, boy. It's all right with me." He turned on his heel and went into the cabin.

Marrok whistled, and Wiley ran to him. "Let's go. Come on, Ned, Wiley." He set off down the path toward the glade where the helicopter waited. "Devon."

"Dogs, first. As usual." She caught up and fell into step. "So here I come trotting at your heels."

He gave a snort. "Trotting at my heels? You're joking. You took over back there."

"You were both being belligerent. I didn't want a fight."

"There wouldn't have been a fight."

"Two alpha males each wanting his own way?"

"I like Cadow."

"But you must have had a lingering competitiveness because of your history with him.

You weren't giving him a chance to defend his family. You had to give him an out, let him make the move."

"I gave him a choice."

She gave him a glance.

"And I didn't need him to tell Wiley to come with me. He would have done it anyway."

"I know." She looked back at the cabin. Had the curtain moved a little? "He's watching us. He had to think that Wiley only came along because he ordered him to do it. Otherwise, it would have hurt him. That dog's the world to him."

"I told you he'd grown to love him."

"You didn't tell me that it would tear him to pieces if we took him. We have to make it as easy for him as possible. Did you mean it when you said you'd find a place for him?"

"I don't lie."

"Good, then I don't have to coerce you. Wiley is that one, the special dog, to him. I know what it's like to be torn away from a dog you love."

"Tess."

"Yes."

"What about your Gracie?"

"I love her. Every dog is special in its own way. There's enough love for every being. Just sometimes a dog reaches out and touches some corner of your heart that no one else can reach. Sarah said something like that about Monty. It's the truth." She glanced back at the cabin. "It wasn't only loneliness that caused him to become attached to Wiley. I could see it. I could see me in him."

"Do you? I see no resemblance at all." He was silent a moment. "And I'd rather look at you. He resembles a beat-up old saddle."

"That has its own worth and beauty," she said. "And you know what I mean."

"Yes. I just thought I'd try to lighten the mood. You . . . touched me."

She looked at him in surprise. "Why on earth?"

"How the hell do I know? You **feel** things." He was silent a moment before continuing awkwardly. "They hurt you. It makes me want to protect you, keep all the bad stuff at bay."

She couldn't take her eyes away from him. He had changed again. A few minutes ago she had wanted to shake him, and now she was melting. He was telling the truth, and that trace of clumsiness was almost endearing. The blending of sexual, slightly wicked, male and puzzled boyishness took her off guard. "I protect myself."

"Not so good. Or you wouldn't be here with me." He suddenly smiled. "But I'm going to try to take your word for it. It will relieve my conscience when we come together."

Heat rippled through her. The boy had vanished, and the male was dominant and on the hunt. "Don't hold your breath."

"No," he said softly. "But it's close. Don't you feel it? It's right there under the surface waiting to happen."

Dammit, she did feel it. She could scarcely breathe, there was a tingling in her wrists, the palms of her hands, her breasts. If he reached out and touched her, she'd go up in flames.

He didn't reach out. "Why not? I wouldn't hurt you. We need it. I wouldn't ask for more than you want to give." He added haltingly, "Though you make me feel like that wild kid I was all those years ago, I'm not him. I can make it good for you. I've learned things . . ."

She swallowed to ease the tightness of her throat. Her heart was beating too hard. "From that madam in Bangkok I suppose?"

"Damn Walt," he said. "Yes, and other places, other times." He looked away from her. "But I promise it wouldn't be like any other experience either of us has ever had. We're . . . different together. You know that."

"I don't want to talk about it anymore."

"Neither do I. I want to do it." He paused. "And so do you." He drew a deep breath. "We're almost at the copter. Stop fighting. I know that I'm not what you want on any permanent basis. I'm not stable, I'm too wild for you. For God's sake, be honest with me. Be honest with yourself. For a one-night stand, I'm exactly what you want."

The heat was flushing her cheeks. "I'm not into one-night—" She stopped as she met his gaze. Be honest, he had said. Heaven knows she was tired of avoiding the truth. "What do you want me to say? You know what I'm feeling. But I made one gigantic mistake, and I'm scared to death of making another one. It wouldn't be a smart or responsible thing to—" She hurried her pace to the helicopter. "And I'm a responsible woman, dammit."

"I see you've got Wiley." Walt had opened the helicopter door for them. "Have any trouble?"

"A little." Marrok gestured, and the dogs jumped into the helicopter. He reached out a hand to help Devon, but she was already climbing into her seat. "Sid will be coming to the ranch later." He got in and fastened his seat belt. "Now there's only Nika to bring in."

"Do we pick her up today?"

"Maybe. I'm going to stop at Paco's cave on the way back, and it depends on how much time it takes there."

Devon's eye's widened. "Why?"

"I told you that I've been meaning to find a way to get Ned to go up to the cave that would ease it for him." He nodded at Wiley. "An old friend to share his memories."

"Will it work?"

"I don't know. I'm going to try." He told Walt. "Give us a few hours."

"Heaven forbid I rush dog therapy," Walt said as he took off. "Even though Danner may be on our heels."

"Don't worry, Bridget would be on the phone drawing me back into the fold at even the hint of that happening." His lips twisted. "Maybe even if there wasn't a hint if she thought she could get away with it."

Fifteen minutes later the helicopter set down on the plateau where Walt had flown the jet once before. Marrok got out of the copter and gestured to the dogs. Wiley jumped to the ground. Ned cringed back against the wall of the aircraft.

"Come on, Ned," Marrok said quietly. "Time to face it."

Ned didn't move.

Wiley gave a low whine, tilting his head as he stared up at the Lab.

Ned stared back at him, then slowly got to his feet and jumped out of the helicopter.

"Good boy," Marrok said. He turned back to Devon and held out his hand. "Are you coming?"

She looked at his hand. Strong hand, beautiful hand. It was the first thing about him that had caused her to notice how magnetic he could be. She hesitated. She could refuse, and he would not insist.

She should probably do that.

Dammit, she was tired of doing only what she should, she thought recklessly. Maybe, as with Ned, it was time to stop hiding her head and face it.

She reached out and took his hand and jumped out of the copter. His grasp was strong, warm, but that was all of which she was aware before he released her and turned away. He started across the plateau. "Two hours, Walt."

"Right."

Devon had to hurry to keep pace with

Marrok as he started up the slope. "Where are we going?"

"The cave. Ned and the other dogs sometimes used to sleep there when Paco was alive." He was watching Ned and Wiley trot up ahead of them. "Ned doesn't want to go. You can see how stiff he is."

"But Wiley doesn't seem to mind."

"I told you, Wiley led a hard life before Paco took him in. He's used to hard knocks. He loved Paco, but he's learned to live with losses."

She smiled. "Good Lord, you sound like a canine psychiatrist."

He shrugged. "I know these dogs. They're all different, with different needs." He glanced at her. "Just as we are."

"What if Ned won't go into the cave?"

"I won't force him. I'm hoping he'll follow Wiley."

"Why do you think it's so important that Ned come to terms with Paco's death?"

"Because I had so much trouble coming to terms with it." His gaze was once more on the opening of the cave at the top of the slope. "I did everything Paco wanted me to do regarding his death. I got the dogs back from Danner and gave them safe havens. Yet I couldn't face going back to the cave for over a year." His lips tightened. "I don't like not being in control. I finally forced myself to go back to the cave, and I stayed there for two weeks. The first few days were hell. Nightmares, memories, guilt, and sorrow. Mostly guilt. It got better. I worked my way through it. By the end of the second week the memories were kinder. The guilt was there, but I'd accepted it. The sorrow never went away."

"Paco wouldn't have expected you to feel guilt, would he? It doesn't sound like him from what you've told me."

"No, but that didn't stop me from feeling it. It should be easier for Ned. He doesn't have all my baggage. All he knows is sorrow and be-wilderment." He was still staring at the cave opening. "You know, I felt as if Paco was with me during that last week. It . . . helped me. Maybe he'll decide to help his old friend, Ned. Pretty crazy, huh? That's probably carrying a bond between dog and human a little far."

She didn't speak for a moment. "No, it isn't. After Tess died I was heartbroken. It was like losing a child or a best friend. But after a little while I began to feel as if she was still with me, that if I turned around, she'd still be there. It brought me comfort. I felt that maybe that's what she wanted. If a creature is so loving and giving in life, why shouldn't that spirit live on? Yes, I believe in bonds that exist after we're separated." She smiled. "So I'm counting on Paco helping out Ned. Why not?"

"Why not, indeed?" he asked gruffly. "You did love your Tess, didn't you?"

"She died too soon. They all die too soon. Even if the spirit lives on, I still wanted her here, with me." She added, "And if I'd had access to Paco's panacea that would have made her one of your dogs of summer, I would have jumped at it. Anyone who has a dog they love would do the same. Even if your **shi'i'go** didn't have the potential to help humans, I'd still throw in my lot to protect it. That's why it's a matter of—" She stopped as she saw that Ned had stopped on the slope and was staring at the cave opening. He was shaking. "Poor boy." Devon covered the distance between them in four strides. She knelt beside the Lab and put her arm around Ned's shoulders. "It's going to be fine," she whispered. "We're all with you."

"Let him go, Devon," Marrok said. "Look at Wiley."

The German shepherd had run up to the cave and had turned and was sitting down, looking at Ned. He was waiting, she realized.

Silent, alert, strangely wise, waiting to help his friend.

Her arms fell from around Ned, and she sat back on her heels.

She was waiting, too.

Ned's gaze was fixed on Wiley as if he were listening.

He finally gave a low whine. He began to climb the slope toward Wiley, his tail tucked between his legs.

"He's afraid," she murmured to Marrok.

Marrok didn't reply.

Ned had reached the top of the slope and was standing there, gazing at Wiley.

Wiley got up and went into the cave.

Ned hesitated, then slowly followed him.

"Remarkable," Devon said. "Did you realize that Wiley would have that powerful an influence on Ned?"

"No, I only hoped," Marrok said. "That's all you can do." He was climbing the slope again. "Now we have to see if it worked."

"Are we going inside?"

"Yes, but not immediately." He stopped at the large flat rock where they'd sat that first time they'd been here. "We'll give Ned a little time."

"And maybe give Paco a little time?"

"I'd never demand help from Paco, dead or alive." He sat down and linked his arms around his knees. "He gave me more than I deserved."

She dropped down beside him. "That's entirely possible. But it doesn't seem to matter. You give what you want to give. And he'd probably approve of everything you've done since he died."

"I didn't kill Danner. Paco believed in revenge." He shrugged. "But it's only a minor delay." He closed his eyes. "The sun feels good, doesn't it?"

"Yes." Her gaze was on his face. "I remember that you said the sun healed you. You don't seem to need much healing. I haven't seen you favor that wound in your shoulder. How is it doing?"

"Good." He didn't open his eyes. "I'll rub a little more of Paco's potion on it when we go inside."

"Why don't you take it with you instead of having to come here to use it?"

"I could be superstitious. Perhaps it wouldn't work anywhere but here."

"That's ridiculous."

He opened his eyes. "Haven't you noticed? I'm not always reasonable. I lived too long with Paco." He stretched. "And I'm not feeling at all reasonable right now. I'm feeling basic and primitive, and I want to feel not think."

She felt tension tighten her muscles. He looked primitive. Lazy and sensual and every muscle catlike basking in the sun. She couldn't take her eyes away from him. It was crazy. One moment she had been thinking of Paco, spirits, and bonding, and now that was all gone.

Feel, not think.

Yes, that was what she was doing. Big-time.

"Thank God." His gaze had shifted back to her face. "I do believe your precious responsibility is about to take a backseat." He got to his knees. "Yes?"

"I'm always responsible," she said unevenly. "It's my nature."

"But we're still going to get what we want, aren't we?" He reached out, and his hand hovered over but did not touch her cheek. "That's why you came."

She remembered that reckless moment in the helicopter when she had taken his hand. If he touched her now, she would probably dissolve. "I'm very much afraid we are."

"Don't be afraid." His brilliant smile lit his dark face. "Never with me. It will be like coming home."

"Somehow I don't think so." Her voice was shaking, and she had to steady it. So was her hand as she reached out to touch him. "I don't feel at all like—"

"Don't touch me." He drew a ragged breath. "Not yet." He jumped up and pulled her to her feet. "Everything else first. I'm not going to want to stop."

"What—" He was pulling her toward the cave. "I won't go there, Marrok. I'm not one of your town girls who—"

"Hush. The dogs."

In the past few minutes, she had almost forgotten Ned and Wiley.

"Just a little while longer," he muttered as he jerked her into the cave. "I just have to check to see—"

Ned and Wiley were lying against the wall of the cave. Ned did not appear relaxed—his eyes were open and his hip was touching Wiley's. "At least, he's staying put," Marrok said. "That's a start. Now it's up to them." He released her to go over to the ice chest. "And we can get the hell out of here." He opened the chest and drew out the stoppered vial of Paco's potion he had rubbed into his wound. "Now."

"What are you doing? Are you hurting?"

"Oh, yes." He took her arm and pulled her

from the cave. "But not my shoulder." He was half pushing, half lifting her up a path past the cave. "It's going to be rough. There's no comfort to be had up here. But with any luck, we won't care."

Her arm was tingling, hot where he was touching her. Her breath was coming short, hard. "Just stop. I don't care where we—"

"I just thought we'd get off the rocks and the shade might—Oh, screw it." He jerked her close and rubbed her body against him. "My God . . ."

Her stomach was clenching, and she was raw, burning . . . "Clothes . . ." she muttered. "Let me go. I have to—"

He was already unbuttoning his shirt and tossing it aside. "I'll help . . ." He unbuttoned three buttons and was jerking her shirt over her head. "Sorry. I'm in a hurry . . ."

So was she. Her clothes were gone in seconds. He was pulling her to the ground. The flat rocks were hot and hard against her back and buttocks as he came over her, in her.

Everything was hot and hard; the rocks, Marrok, the tension that was tearing them apart. . . .

"Good." His voice was guttural, his eyes closed. "Don't move. Let me get used to—"

"Don't move?" She couldn't believe it. She was going crazy. He was holding her still, his thighs pressed against her. She couldn't stand it. "Get used to this." She lunged upward, her nails digging into his back.

Fullness.

Heat.

His back arched, and his lids flew open. "You shouldn't have done that," he said thickly. "I was trying—I want it to last."

"Then use one of your tricks you learned from that prostitute in Bangkok. I can't wait."

"I'm afraid I can't either. Not this time." His hips began moving in a deep, swiveling motion.

She cried out, her fingers closing on his shoulders.

"You like that?"

The sensation was indescribable. "Yes," she whispered.

He plunged deep. "And this?"

She bit her lower lip to keep from screaming. "Stop asking me questions. Just **do** it."

"But I want to ask you questions. I want to know what you like. So I can do it again." He began flexing, moving, plunging rhythmically. "And again. And again."

She had to put an end to this. Or a beginning . . .

She reached down between them. "Do you like this?"

He inhaled sharply, his cheeks flushing. "Oh, yes. But I don't believe I can take much of that."

"I didn't think so. Neither can I, you bastard. Now stop playing and give it to me."

"Whatever you want," he said huskily as he went deep. "As much as you want . . ."

"It would have been better in the cave." Marrok's breath was coming in harsh rasps as he moved off her. "It would have been better anywhere but here. For God's sake, I couldn't even wait to get away from these rocks." He put his arm beneath his head and stared up at the searing blue of the sky. "It's not what I planned. Hell, I didn't have a plan. I just wanted it good for you."

"Well, it wasn't . . . bad." Understatement of the century, she thought dazedly. Primitive, rough, mind-blowing. It was probably the sexual high of her experience. But she wished Marrok would just stop talking and do it again.

Once, a dozen times . . . Good God, that sounded sex-starved. "I like these rocks." She got up on one elbow and gazed down at him. "And I regard it as egotistical of you to take credit or blame in this particular endeavor. I was actively involved."

He frowned. "I seduced you."

"Bullshit. My choice. I wanted you, weighed caution and lust, and tossed caution out the window." She bent her head and brushed her lips across his shoulder. "And I believe I'm going to do it again."

He shuddered. "My, my. Am I the one being seduced?"

"Yes. You're moving too slow."

His hand moved to cup the back of her head. "I'll try to remedy that. I was being careful. I didn't expect you to be this enthusiastic."

She raised her head to look at him. "Why not?" Then she slowly nodded. "Lester?"

"You had a bad marriage."

"Yes."

"Did you like it with him?"

"At first. Then he started to hurt me. Do you really want to talk about this, Marrok?"

"No, I wanted you to tell me that you hated him touching you."

"I did toward the end. But I'm not going to lie to you. I like sex. It was what drew me to Lester in the beginning. He spoiled practically everything else in my life. I wasn't going to let him twist that for me." She made a face. "Though he saw to it that I avoided men like the plague. It wasn't safe for them."

"Good. That cuts down my competition." He bent his head and licked her nipple. "Did I tell you I like your breasts?"

"No, I don't remember our talking much."

"I do." His hand wandered down her body to her belly. "And I like your skin here. It's tight, but there's a sort of voluptuous fullness . . ." He started to stroke her, pet her. "I can see why Enright wanted to get you pregnant. There's something erotic and primitive about thinking of you with my child." He kissed her breast again. "I'm sorry," he whispered. "I didn't use anything. Is it going to be okay?"

"Do you mean did I protect myself? Of course." It was a lie. It hadn't been necessary for her to use contraceptives for a long time. "I'm not worried." And that was the truth. She had made a choice and she was content with it. Whatever happened, she would deal with it. It had been worth it. "And will you quit petting my belly as if I were Ned?"

"There's no resemblance." He bent down and delicately licked her stomach. "Enright will never touch you again," he said thickly. "And you'll never have his child."

"Stop talking about him." Her fingers tangled in his hair. "Why can't you just live in the present and enjoy?"

"I told you I had my brooding moments. This must be one of them."

"Then get out of it." She pushed him back and laid her head on his shoulder. "I'm not going to let you spoil this for me." Her lips moved across his shoulder. The skin was tan, smooth, hot beneath her lips from the sun. She paused as she reached the jagged wound on his shoulder. "This is healing very well. You said you healed quickly. Is it because you're around Ned and the other dogs?"

"Perhaps. I don't know. I've been around them most of my life, so how could I tell the difference?"

She brushed her lips across the wound. "Well, it's very clean. I don't think you need your Paco's medicine."

"Maybe not. But I've had fantasies about you rubbing it into the wound since that first day we came up here. Having your hands on me . . ."

"Have you?" She reached over him, took the vial out of his shirt pocket and opened the stopper. "Pretty weird, Marrok . . ." She put a tiny bit of liquid on her forefinger and gently touched the wound. "You find this erotic?"

He shuddered. "I find everything about you erotic. At the time it was the only way I could think to get you to touch me."

She rubbed a little potion on his nipple. "How does that feel?"

"It stings a little."

"Shall I stop?"

"God, no."

She rubbed some fluid on his other nipple. "Your heart is beating so hard. I can feel it."

"I wonder why."

"I'm wasting this potion."

"It's not a waste. I can make more."

"Oh, good." She moved down. "Then I can rub some right here . . ."

He groaned.

"You **do** like it. But I'll have to get back to that. My hands are shaking."

"Let me do it to you."

"I couldn't stand it. Not right now. But you can do something else for me." She threw the vial aside and moved over him. "Come in, Marrok. Let me **feel** you . . ."

* * *

"Get up," Marrok said. **"We've got** to pick up the dogs and get down to the plateau."

She didn't want to move. "In a minute."

"Now." He kissed her quick, hard. "Walt's going to be here anytime. Open your eyes and get moving."

"I think he'd wait."

"Yes. He'd probably enjoy waiting," he said dryly. "In case you haven't noticed we're naked, out in the open, and that helicopter will come in low. Great visuals."

Her eyes flew open, and she began to laugh. "I didn't think of that."

"I did." He tossed her shirt to her. "I find I don't care for the idea of Walt gaping at you in the altogether."

"Why not? From what Walt said, you two seem to have gone through similar experiences."

"This is different. Get dressed."

She didn't move. "How is it different?"

"How the hell do I know?" He held her shirt out for her. "Put it on."

She slipped her arms into the sleeves. "It wouldn't bother me. I'm not ashamed of my body, and I'm not ashamed of anything I've done."

"I know," he said gruffly. "You're damn incredible. I didn't expect this kind of openness. No inhibitions. No guilt." He started to button her shirt. "When you make up your mind, you go to the max. It's kind of . . . wonderful."

She felt a surge of tenderness. She wanted to go back into his arms and hold him.

No, not now. It had been too good, and she felt warm and languid and vulnerable. She might do something, say something to spoil it. Yet she had to tell him one thing. "You're trying to protect me again, Marrok. You don't have to do that. I know it's only sex, and I did what I wanted to do."

"Shut up." His lips tightened. "I'll do what I please." He got to his feet. "Now finish dressing while I go and round up Wiley and Ned."

She watched him stride down the path before she slowly began to put on her clothes. What a strange man he was. Mature, yet he had that streak of boyishness. Reckless, and yet he was a caretaker. Volatile, and yet she felt oddly steady whenever she was with him.

Don't dwell on Marrok's character or the life that had made him what he was. It would be a mistake. When she had decided to have sex with him, she had abandoned her usual code of conduct. She had wanted him and reached out with no thought of restraint. And, by God, she wasn't sorry that she had accepted him as a ship that passed in the night. But there was a danger if she let herself enjoy anything but the sex. She had known from the moment she met him that they were worlds apart in both temperament and background. Marrok's life had made him diamond hard and incapable of being vulnerable to anyone. And you had to be vulnerable to let yourself be open to any emotional commitment.

So enjoy this brief sensual episode but don't forget that episodes always come to an end.

A ripple of pain went through her and panic followed. See, it was already happening. Veer away. Don't think about Marrok now.

Think about the dogs of summer.

CHAPTER
15

Marrok was standing in the entrance of the cave when Devon came down the path.

"How are they doing?"

"I don't know. They're not in the cave."

She stiffened. "What?"

He held up his hand. "They're fine. Danner didn't come and scoop them up. They're just down on the plateau. They must have gotten bored in the cave." He pointed down the slope. "They're playing together."

Devon watched the two dogs chase, nip, leap, and chase again. "No permanent trauma then."

He chuckled as he whistled for the dogs.

"Now you're the one who sounds like a dog psychiatrist. Very solemn."

She made a face. "Solemn goes with responsible. I told you I was a responsible person. I can't help it."

"At least one of us is responsible. I kind of like that in you. As long as it doesn't keep you from making love to me." He added softly, "I'd have issues with that."

Making love. The phrase sent a thrill of uneasiness through her. It sounded too close to commitment, and she knew that wasn't in the cards. She shook her head. "I don't know why you make this big show of being irresponsible. You may have been that way in the past, but I don't believe anyone could be more responsible than you are now."

His brows lifted. "You're wrong, you know. I pick and choose my moments."

"I don't think so." She looked away from him. "You were very . . . disturbed earlier before you dragged me up that path today."

"Disturbed? I was hot as hell. I was going crazy."

"But you still had to go into the cave and check on Ned. I may be responsible, but I didn't even remember the dogs existed at that moment. You remembered, Marrok."

He frowned. "It was my job." He grimaced. "And I didn't want to have to worry about them. It would have gotten in the way."

"Then perhaps you're not as self-indulgent as you think you are." She stepped forward as Ned came tearing up the slope. "Hello, boy. You seem happy enough." She stroked his black silky head. "Bright eyes . . ."

Wiley was right behind him but keeping his distance. He sat down and stared warily at her. A few minutes later he got up, looked at Ned, and went into the cave.

"What next?" Devon asked.

Ned answered her. He hesitated, then followed Wiley into the cave.

"Do we go in?" Devon asked.

"No, we wait," Marrok said. "I think it's good-bye. If they don't come out in a few minutes, we go in and get them."

In less than two minutes Ned and Wiley came out of the cave. Ned was subdued as he moved to Marrok and rubbed against his legs. "It's okay, buddy," Marrok said quietly. "It will be better next time. Maybe you'll be able to go in alone." He reached down and patted Wiley's head. "Good job. What do you say we get to the ranch and see your friend, Sid?"

Wiley tilted his head and gazed up at him. Grave, knowing, patient.

"I believe he's missing you," Marrok said. "But you're going to have to show him how to adjust just as you did Ned. He may be a little more difficult." Marrok turned to Devon. "I think I hear the helicopter. We'd better get down to the plateau."

Devon listened. "I don't hear it."

"It's coming." He gestured to the dogs. "They hear it, too."

Apparently he was right, Devon realized, as the dogs ears pricked up, and they turned and began to run down the slope. "I'm beginning to feel a little handicapped. Dogs have excellent hearing, but why would you—" She finally heard the rotors in the distance. "SEAL training?"

"No, Paco training. He taught me to block out everything but what I wanted to hear." He held out his hand to help her down the slope. "And you're not handicapped. You see a hell of a lot more than most people."

She took his hand. Her gaze flew to his face as she felt a sensual tingle that she hadn't expected.

"It's not going to go away," he said softly. "It wasn't enough. You know it as well as I do.

Any touch, any word. I wanted you again even when I was walking away from you. Want to do it on a real bed as soon as we get back to the ranch?"

Yes, she did. She was starting to shake at the thought. "I'll have to think about it. It's . . . upsetting." She moistened her lips. "You evidently don't believe in truth in advertising. You said it would be like coming home. No way. Unless home was in the center of a hurricane."

"Okay, I was reassuring you. I wanted it to be like that for you, but I lost control. Maybe we have a chance of that coming later." He frowned. "I'm not perfect."

No, he wasn't. But his faults were like the threads on a piece of granite that gave the stone interest and character. One could never be sure when one of those threads would give way and cause destruction and chaos. Why was she even expecting tameness from him when she had been just as primitive? She pulled her hand away. "You gave me what I wanted. Home is a concept that you'd find boring, and so would I. It's not what we want from each other." She started down the slope. "And I'm not perfect either, Marrok. Let's just work on enjoying the time we have together."

She tried to smile. "Which according to Bridget may not be that long."

Marrok started to curse.

"I'm joking," she said.

"I'm not," he said tersely. "Nothing is going to happen to you."

"There's Walt." She began to hurry as the helicopter set down. "Right on time. Is he usually this prompt?"

"Yes. I mean it, Devon. Bridget is wrong. I'll keep you safe."

He was dead serious and not to be deterred. She tried anyway. "Hey, that's pretty sexist," she said lightly. "It's you Bridget is really worried about. Maybe I should promise to keep you safe." She could feel his gaze on her back as she ran toward the copter. "Come on, Ned, Wiley. Let's go."

Bridget was walking toward the house from the bunkhouse when the helicopter landed. She stood watching as the dogs jumped out and ran toward her. "So this is Wiley . . ." She didn't try to touch him. "Smart boy," she said, gazing into his eyes. "You don't need much help, but I'm here for you if you want me." She turned back to Marrok. "Sid just got here. He was worried about Wiley."

"We stopped at the cave. Ned needed to be there." Marrok helped Devon from the copter. "Any word from Sarah's place?"

She nodded. "There was someone scouting around today. Danner must have broken the code."

"Why didn't you call me?"

"It was obviously reconnaissance. I told them not to do anything in case we wanted to make a move of our own." She turned to Devon. "And we're having trouble with your Janet McDonald. She's decided that she's not needed at Sarah's and wants to come back here."

"She didn't give it long," Marrok said dryly.

"Sarah Logan runs a tight ship. I can see why a woman like Janet would feel useless." Bridget said to Devon, "Your call. But if you tell her to stay, I don't promise you won't have a mutiny on your hands."

"She's safer there."

"If you can keep her from flying the coop."

Devon said wearily, "Bring her back."

Bridget nodded. "Walt, be ready to leave in an hour, okay?" Her gaze shifted to Marrok.

"They'll try to trace us. Do you want me to let them do it?"

Marrok thought about it. "Not yet. We have to bring Nika here first." He started toward the house. "I'll have her brought here tomorrow."

"Do you want me to go after her?" Bridget called after him.

"No, you have enough on your plate." Marrok disappeared into the house.

"And he doesn't trust me," Bridget murmured. She looked down at Wiley. "You know all about distrust, don't you? But I think you trust me. Come on, I'll take you down to the bunkhouse to Sid." She started across the stable yard. "Do you want to go with me to pick up your Janet, Devon? Maybe you can persuade her not to leave Sarah's."

"I doubt it." She hesitated. "Yes, I'll go."

"One hour. But if you tell Marrok you're going, he's going to raise hell. Danner knows about Sarah now. I don't care either way. Do what you like."

"I usually do."

Bridget gazed back at her. "That's not true. You have a keen sense of duty. But you did what you wanted this afternoon, didn't you?"

Devon could hear the heat sting her cheeks. It couldn't be clearer what Bridget meant. She refused to deny it. "Yes, I did. Not that it's any of your business, Bridget."

"It's my business. More than you could dream. You made a mistake. I could tell the minute I saw Marrok get off the helicopter. You're . . . joined. I could see it."

Devon shook her head. "We only had sex. That's crazy."

"You bet it is. You may have ruined everything." She added bitterly, "But I can't do anything about that now. It's too late. I'll just have to try to salvage what I can." Her pace quickened as she looked straight ahead. "Screw him all you please. It doesn't matter now. I'll meet you at the helicopter."

Sarah Logan was waiting at the helicopter pad with Janet McDonald beside her when they landed a few hours later.

"I'm sorry, Devon," Sarah said. "I tried to persuade her to stay."

"I'm not needed here," Janet said. "Nick can stay and watch over those dogs. I have to take care of you."

"Janet . . ." Devon gave up as she studied Janet's expression. "It's safer for you here. But come along if you have to do it."

"I have to do it," she said flatly as she looked at Bridget. "But I'm not sitting next to that viper. I'll sit in front."

"I'm flattered," Walt said. "I think."

"Thanks, Sarah," Devon said as she shut the door. "I'm sorry to bother you."

"I didn't bother her," Janet said as they lifted off. "I tried to help, but she's got so many people, they're stumbling over each other." She glowered at Bridget. "And I knew you didn't realize what a nasty piece of work this one is."

"I'm suspecting," Devon murmured. "But I can handle her."

Bridget snorted. "Not funny."

"I agree. And I wasn't amused at what you said back at the ranch."

"I was honest." She was silent a moment. "I want the best for you. If it doesn't hurt Marrok."

"For God's sake, look at me," she said in exasperation. "I'm a plain Jane. No femme fatale."

"What's this all about?" Janet asked suspiciously.

"Ignore them," Walt said. "It's tactful . . . and safer."

Bridget looked down at the ground below them. "Land at the Monterey airport. We'll change copters. Marrok doesn't want us to lead them back to the ranch."

"Yes, ma'am," Walt said. "Though we'll be lucky if they don't get a fix on that helicopter, too."

"Not in time," Bridget said. "It will be safe enough."

"She's probably lying," Janet said coldly.

Bridget turned to face her. "You're right to suspect me. That's the safest thing to do when you're trying to take care of someone. But you might remember we wouldn't even be in this predicament if you hadn't pulled a tantrum and threatened to bolt. Shut up unless you have something valuable to contribute."

Janet's face flushed with anger. She opened her lips to reply, then closed them again. A moment later she said, "I don't have tantrums."

"What do you call it?"

"Not a tantrum. I did what I thought I should do." She stared Bridget in the eye. "And you'll have to prove to me that you're not a liar."

"I don't have to prove anything," Bridget said. "You're the one who has to prove herself. You're pissed because I put you down. You don't like to lose. But I was only doing my job, and I've done everything I could to make you comfortable and safe. I'm done. Now you can contribute or sulk in the bunkhouse. But don't think I won't work your ass off if you decide to help."

Janet didn't answer for a moment. "I've never been afraid of work. If I decide I want to do it."

Devon stared at Janet in surprise. That was almost a concession on her part, and Janet didn't yield easily. And there was a grudging respect in Janet's voice. Would wonders never cease?

"What would I have to do?" Janet asked.

"Take care of Ned and Wiley. Keep an eye on Devon."

"I could do that," Janet said slowly. "Who's Wiley? Another dog?"

"Yes," Bridget said. "Wiley won't be much trouble. Sid Cadow takes care of him most of the time."

"If it's my job, then I'll be the one to take care of him," she said sourly.

"Talk to Sid," Bridget said. "Work it out between you."

"I don't have to talk to anyone. I do my job."

Good Lord, Devon thought, Bridget had

created a monster situation. Janet and Sid were bound to butt heads if not actually come to blows. Was it a deliberate provocation? It was hard to tell. Bridget's face was completely without expression.

"There's the Monterey airport," Bridget said. "I'll call Marrok and tell him we'll be coming in on a different aircraft." She gave Janet a cool glance. "It's a lot of trouble."

"I'm worth it," Janet muttered. "You'll see."

"I hope that's true," Bridget said skeptically.

Janet muttered something beneath her breath that might have been a curse.

Bridget's gaze shifted to Devon as Janet turned away to look out the window.

There was challenge and cool confidence in her expression. Bridget knew exactly how she had manipulated Janet and was daring Devon to comment.

She was tempted to do it. She didn't like manipulation in any form. Yet Janet now had a goal and a purpose, and Devon couldn't quarrel with that.

Drop it. But keep in mind how easy that manipulation had been for Bridget.

*   *   *

Chad Lincoln was standing on the porch, leaning against a post when they arrived back at the ranch at sunset.

"Well, well, the elusive Sherlock Holmes has returned," Bridget said. "He wasn't the one who I'd thought would be waiting for us. I wonder where Marrok is." She turned to Walt. "You did tell him that Devon was going with me, didn't you?"

"Sure." Walt turned off the engine. "He said that he couldn't expect to keep her from doing what she wanted to do every minute of the day. He told me he'd scalp me if I let anything happen to her. Since he has the historical background to make that happen, I decided I'd be very careful."

"I love the way everyone is deciding what I should and shouldn't be allowed to do." Devon jumped out of the helicopter. "Janet, I'll walk you down to the bunkhouse and introduce you to Wiley and Sid Cadow."

"I'll do it," Bridget said. "My job."

"No, it's my job," Janet said, as she started toward the bunkhouse. "And I don't need anyone to tell me how to do it."

Bridget glanced at Devon and shrugged before strolling after Janet.

Devon only hoped that Bridget would continue to handle Janet with the same deftness she had demonstrated on the helicopter. Which made Bridget a very clever woman. Clever and complicated, with the potential for being extremely dangerous.

"You only brought back your housekeeper," Lincoln called. "I was sure you'd be bringing back one of the superdogs."

"They're not superdogs." Devon turned and walked toward the porch. "That makes them sound like they should be wearing capes and flying over rooftops. Comic book stuff."

"Oh, I agree there's nothing comic about them." He smiled. "But I have a little more experience with them than you do. Marrok and his superdog went on quite a few missions for me, and I'd venture to say the men Ned cured would call him a superdog if they knew he'd done the deed."

"Like that thieving robber chief in Ethiopia?"

His smile faded. "Marrok told you about him? It was a great embarrassment for me. That was the time when I realized on no account should Marrok be permitted to retain control of the dogs."

"I believe he knows how you feel. I'd bet he feels the same about you." She walked up the stairs. "Where is he?"

"He didn't confide in me. He drove out about two hours ago with his dog, Ned. Do you want a guess?"

"I can make my own guesses."

"I'll tell you anyway. I think he's gathering up his pack. The German shepherd, Wiley, is down at the bunkhouse. Now you just came from Sarah Logan's place, so it's not the golden retriever. I'd say he's gone for the mutt. What's her name . . . Nika, that's it."

"And why would he be doing that?" she asked without expression.

"Bait. Use all four dogs as a lure. He wants to rid himself of Danner. I'd have made the same move myself. Only I would have done it much sooner."

"Maybe he didn't want to risk the dogs."

"Or maybe he thought as long as he kept Danner as a threat, he wouldn't have to deal with us. He knows we wouldn't want Danner to get control. It's a standoff."

"Ridiculous."

"Is it? How can you be sure? Marrok is almost a stranger to you." He paused. "Though I'm sure he knows you very well in the biblical sense. It was pretty obvious where you were headed the other evening."

She felt a jarring distaste. "Back off, Lincoln."

"Just commenting. Marrok is a secretive bastard, and he's not above using you."

"You're pretty damn secretive yourself. I've hardly seen anything of you since the first night I got here. Where have you been?"

"I had some errands to run." He gazed out at the setting sun. "And if you ask Marrok, I'm certain he'll be able to fill you in exactly where I've been and what I was doing. I was followed from the minute I left the property. He has someone watching me now." He pointed to the barn. "Three men are there. There are at least a dozen in the bunkhouse. I don't know how many are in the stable. This cozy little ranch is an armed camp paid for by MI6. It's no wonder he wants to draw Danner here."

"And why did you think it necessary to find out how many men he had here? I find that a little . . . odd." She paused. "Perhaps you wanted to feel out the opposition in case you saw an opportunity to gather up the dogs yourself."

He chuckled. "Good thinking." His smile faded. "It's going to happen, Devon Brady. It may not be here and now, but Marrok is going down. If you help me, then I'll see that you don't go down with him. What do you care? He's a half-breed who'd as soon kill you as look at you."

"That's the kind of thing Danner would say about him. I thought you prided yourself on being civilized."

"I recognize the difference. Shall I tell you how many men he's killed?"

"No, I'm not interested. How many men have you killed, Lincoln?"

"There's a difference. I had a duty. He only became a SEAL so that he'd be able to kill without suffering the consequences."

"How do you know?"

"I know." He started down the steps. "I believe I'll go for an evening walk and see what other scum I can flush out of the woodwork. I meant what I said, Devon. You've got Marrok a little off-balance and that's unusual. I might be able to use you. It would be worth your while to consider the offer."

Devon watched him stroll away from her. He looked sleek, dapper, and perfectly groomed. "Snake," she muttered as she opened the screen door. For God's sake, Marrok appeared to be surrounded by people who wanted to take him down. Danner was hovering, Lincoln was waiting for his chance, and even Bridget Reardon was trying to manipulate him.

She glanced over her shoulder at the peaceful scene bathed in golden twilight. **An armed camp,** Lincoln had said. She could see no signs of it. But there had been two guards the first night Marrok had brought her here.

And Marrok would never have risked bringing the dogs here unless he could make sure they were safe.

But for how long would they remain safe? Danner didn't care if the dogs lived or died. He'd proved that on Santa Marina. Did they have the right to use the dogs as bait? And if she decided that Marrok was wrong, how would she stop him?

She would have to think about it.

Marrok arrived back at the ranch two hours later. The dog that jumped out of the car with Ned was a gangly brown animal that had none of the Weimaraner's grace or a boxer's sturdy frame. He had enormous feet, gigantic ears, and startling blue eyes that Devon barely noticed before the dog was on her. His huge tongue licked her face ecstatically.

"Down, Nika." Marrok was pulling the dog down by the collar. "Sorry. We've never been able to teach Nika manners. She gets excited, and everything she learns goes out the window."

Nika's tail was thumping loudly on the wooden porch as she gazed up at Devon in adoration.

"She's wonderful. Is she always this affectionate?"

"Yes. Lousy guard dog. Wonderful friend and companion. She's the best at the hospital visits. But only when Rod can keep her from crawling into bed with the kids."

"Ugly mutt. Never learns." A burly, baldheaded man was getting out of the car. His face was almost unlined, and his powerful build, keen blue eyes, and springy gait belied the hint of age suggested by that bald head. "Come on, Nika. Leave the lady alone."

Nika ignored him as she rubbed her head against Devon's hand.

"She's not bothering me," Devon said. "And she's not ugly. She just has character."

"Rod Zedwick, Dr. Devon Brady," Marrok said. "And don't let Rod fool you. He's crazy about that 'ugly mutt.'"

"To my infinite regret. Otherwise, I'd go out and get a real job." Zedwick smiled. "Glad to meet you, Dr. Brady. Marrok tells me that you've gone through a lot for his dogs of summer. I hope it will be over soon." He looked at Marrok. "The bunkhouse?"

Marrok nodded. "That's where the other dogs are."

Rod sighed. "Nika will go crazy when she sees them. She's never gotten over being a puppy."

"Some dogs never do," Devon said.

He flinched. "Don't tell me that." He was beside Nika and put his hand on her head. She immediately looked up and began to lick his hand. "Stop that," he said gruffly. But his touch was gentle as he rubbed the dog's huge ears. "Let's go. We've got to get settled." He raised his hand, and said to Marrok, "See you."

Nika didn't move.

"Oh, for God's sake." Rod reached into his pocket. "It makes me look bad to have to bribe you." He fed her a treat and started down the steps. "No more until we get to the bunkhouse."

Nika ran after him, her big feet almost tripping her on the steps. She started racing in circles around him, then got bored and streaked down the path.

"A problem child," Devon said, amused.

"And she has him wrapped around her paw. Where did you find him?"

"He was in the SEALs with me. He needed a job, and I needed a guardian for Nika. It worked out fine."

"I can see it did." The man's toughness was as clear as his affection for Nika. "You chose well. Perceptive choices." She shot him a glance. "Responsible choices."

"That word again. You're beginning to remind me of Paco." Marrok turned and held the screen door open for her. "Is your Janet adjusting?"

She nodded. "Once Bridget gave her the job of taking care of the dogs and me. I'm not sure how your other personnel are going to adjust to her."

"It's only short-term. She won't have time to make much trouble."

"Short-term?" She looked at him. "What do you mean?"

He ignored the question. "Is Lincoln still here?"

"Yes, he took a long walk, then came back about an hour ago." She paused. "He said that you had guards watching him all the time."

"I'd be stupid not to."

"He said you knew exactly what he was doing when he took his little trips. Do you?"

"Yes, not such little trips. Las Vegas isn't that close. He went shopping at a men's store there. He had a haircut and a manicure. He made three phone calls. I was able to trace two to London. The third number was routed through three other cell towers, and I'm still working on it."

"Good God, It sounds like you're running your own high-tech spy network."

He smiled. "You can buy most of that stuff off the Internet. But I do have an expert on staff. Larry Farland worked for the NSA for ten years. I thought I might possibly have need of someone with his background. He's pretty good, but he doesn't have satellite. That's a hindrance."

"Why don't you just send Lincoln packing?"

"I may need him. And I definitely need MI6's financial help. I'm safe from his machinations as long as I can keep tabs on him."

Devon wasn't so sure. "He knows why you're bringing the dogs here."

"Of course, he does," Marrok said. "And he's licking his lips, hoping that he can find a way to take them away from me. It suits him just fine."

Just as killing Marrok would suit Lincoln, Devon thought. She had not let herself think of Lincoln's words, but they were suddenly there, chilling her, twisting inside her.

"You're walking a fine line," Devon said. "It could all blow up in your face. Then what would happen to the dogs and the **shi'i'go**?" She moistened her lips. "What would happen to you?"

He chuckled. "I notice you mentioned the dogs first. You clearly have your priorities straight."

Because she hadn't been able to bear to think about anything happening to Marrok. "Why not?" She had to steady her voice. "That seems to be your top priority. Keep the dogs safe and get revenge for Paco. Isn't that the way it goes?"

"Yes, that's the way it goes." He was studying her. "You're upset."

"Dammit, why shouldn't I be upset? I'm not like you. I can't go on for years playing games, killing people, watching people I care about die. It's not—" She jerkily turned away. "Just forget it."

His hand was on her arm, turning her to

face him. "I can't forget it," he said simply. "It hurts me."

It was hurting her, too. Too close. Dear God, she was getting too close to him. "Get over it." She tore away from him and almost ran toward her bedroom door. "Good night, Marrok."

"It's not going to get any better by hiding from it, Devon," he said quietly.

She didn't answer as she shut the door behind her. No, it wasn't any better. The panic was still rising within her. What could she do? Keep calm. This terror didn't have to indicate that she had any special feeling for Marrok. She was a compassionate person, and she would be fearful for the life of anyone she knew. Add to that the fact that she'd had possibly the premier sex experience of her life with him, and it was probably not unusual that she should—

Oh, screw it. Excuses. Hiding away mentally as well as physically just as Marrok had accused her. She'd always tried to be honest with herself as well as others, and she couldn't stop now.

Too close. How close was Marrok to her? Tear down all the lies and protective barriers she'd built and see what was left. She knew what would be left—fear. That terror was what had triggered this panic.

But what else?

She sank down in the easy chair beside the bed and stared into the darkness. Let it come. No more hiding.

What else?

Marrok's door.

Devon drew a deep breath.

She hesitated, then opened the door.

The lamp by the bed was lit and Marrok was sitting up in bed, a sheet flung carelessly over his naked body. "I was going to give you another thirty minutes and come to you." His lips twisted. "Lincoln would be surprised at my control, don't you think? Not what you'd expect from a savage."

"I don't want to talk about Lincoln." Devon closed the door and moved toward the bed. Every time she thought about the danger Chad Lincoln represented, the panic came back. "And anyone who judges someone by race or creed shouldn't matter to you."

"He doesn't."

"The hell he doesn't. You still have a few

hang-ups from your childhood that pop out now and then. That was part of what I was thinking about." She sat down on the bed. "But then so does everyone. Yours just manifest themselves a little more violently."

"That's true." He reached out to her. "Perhaps a good deal more—"

"Don't touch me."

His hand paused, then dropped to the sheet. "I don't like the way this is going."

"No, considering what a lusty bastard you are, I wouldn't think that you would."

He stiffened.

"Oh, I like it." She still wasn't looking at him. "Sexually you're a slam-bang wonder. I can't wait to do it again."

"The conversation is beginning to look more promising."

"But it's not fair to you or myself not to clear a few things up." She moistened her lips. "I feel . . . something for you, Marrok. There's . . . tenderness. I don't know how much, but it might be . . . a lot. And I respect you and admire all you've done and all you are. You're a better man than you think you are. And there's a feeling that might be . . . something else. It scares me."

"Are you done?" he asked hoarsely.

"No, I wanted you to know that none of this makes a difference. It doesn't have to affect you. I just can't pretend it's not here. I have to be honest."

"I've noticed that about you. May I touch you now?"

"Please." She put her head on his chest. "Turn out the light."

"Why? You've scarcely looked at me since you came into the room." But he turned out the light anyway. "I'm glad you didn't. I find I'm not as honest as you are. I have . . . to hide things." He drew her under the sheet. "Otherwise, I might break apart."

"Hush." She pulled her nightshirt over her head and tossed it aside. "You don't have to say anything. That's not why I came."

"Because I'm a slam-bang wonder?"

"Yes." She cuddled closer. "And because I wanted to be close to you. Could we just hold each other for a little while?"

"All night, if that's what you want."

"Your voice sounds . . . funny."

"Imagination." He cleared his throat. "I'm Apache. In the Apache language, emotion is expressed only by words, not tone."

"Interesting. Then I think you're more like your Spanish mother than Apache." His heart was loud, fast beneath her ear. "But I don't want you to hold me like this all night. Just for a little while . . ."

CHAPTER
16

Devon was sleeping, her breath coming steady and deep. She was lying on her side, one arm tucked beneath her head.

Beautiful, Marrok thought, as he watched her. Most people probably wouldn't consider Devon beautiful. Her features were too irregular, her body strong, rather than curvaceous.

But, oh yes, she was beautiful. Her skin glowed with health, and her eyes sparkled with intelligence. The variety of her expressions alone was enough to keep a man fascinated for a lifetime.

My God, what was happening to him?

Eyes and expressions, instead of tits and ass?

And lying here staring at Devon like some young kid with his first crush.

Only he had never had a crush when he was growing up. He had carefully shut sentiment away from him when he realized that could be a weapon to be used against him. How old was he when he'd decided that? He couldn't remember. Maybe when he realized his father didn't care what happened to him when he'd sent him to pick up his drugs from old Nokadano.

But he might have a crush now.

Whatever it was, it felt . . . strange.

He reached out and gently touched her hair. She murmured something beneath her breath but didn't open her eyes.

He took his hand away. He didn't want to wake her yet. He didn't want her to look at him with eyes that were clear and honest and without any hint of guile. She had moved him unbearably earlier tonight. Her frankness had come as a surprise. He had thought she would admit to desire but protect herself from an admission of anything deeper. He should have known better. Devon would never protect herself at the cost of the truth.

And he had always protected himself at any cost.

He carefully moved off the bed and stood up. He hesitated, looking down at her. Dammit, he wanted to stay.

Yeah, do what you want. Stay until she wakes and make sure the bond is so close that she won't want to break free. What difference did it make if that bond could also put her directly in Danner's line of fire and that there was no way he could keep her with him for the long term? There would always be a threat, someone constantly after him. Forget everything and keep her with him. Sure, that would be the thing to do.

The hell it would be. The mere thought of her with Danner made his stomach muscles tighten as panic raced through him. It couldn't happen. It mustn't happen.

He glided toward the bathroom, gathering his clothes as he went.

He wouldn't let it happen.

"What is it, Marrok?" Bridget asked as she came up the porch steps twenty minutes later. "Is there a problem with Lincoln?"

"No more than usual," Marrok said.

"Then why did you phone me in the middle of the night?" She frowned. "Addie?"

"Since she's the only dog not on the premises, I suppose that's a natural conclusion," Marrok said. "Since everyone knows the dogs are my only concern."

"Marrok, dammit."

"If you'll stop guessing, I'll tell you." Marrok went to the edge of the porch. "I want you to get rid of Devon."

She stiffened in shock. "What?"

"Oh, I don't want you to knock her off." His lips lifted sardonically. "Though for a moment I believe you thought I did."

"Don't be an ass. It was just surprise. A few hours ago you would have fought me if I'd tried to take her away. You were in a damn haze. What's changed?"

"I've changed." He shrugged. "Or maybe I haven't changed, and I'm merely getting tired of her. You know what a short attention span I have."

"No, I don't know that, and I'd appreciate your not giving me that bull."

He smiled. "Okay, I find myself feeling a little . . . unsure. I don't like the sensation. It makes me uncomfortable." His smile faded. "And I don't think **uncomfortable** would be the right word for how I'd feel if anything happened to Devon because of this mess I'd dragged her into. **Berserk,** would be a better fit."

Bridget was silent, studying him. It had happened. She had seen it coming, but she'd had no idea it would hit this hard. My God . . .

"So I believe the best course would be for you to take her out of the mix until this is over."

"She won't go. She made her decision to help with the dogs, and I don't mean to hurt your ego, but you're not the sole reason she's here."

"Then find a way to get her away from me. Any way." He turned away and looked out at the fields. "It shouldn't be that difficult. I'm sure you were well schooled in that type of operation by Lincoln and his merry men. Or I could do it myself."

"I wouldn't trust you," she said bluntly. "You have to commit, and you don't want to commit to this. If you did, you wouldn't have called me."

"Clever Bridget." He smiled. "But you're willing to commit, aren't you? You've been wanting to get rid of her since she came."

"It's best." She paused. "Okay, I'll do it. Right away?"

"As soon as possible. I don't know how much time we have before Danner makes his move. Act fast."

"Danner will be cautious. He won't attack without sending someone in to reconnoiter. He'll find out this ranch is a stronghold."

"I know. I've been thinking about it. And when he does attack, it will be with force, and that means more people will be hurt or killed." He paused. "That's why I'm pulling out right after I finish talking to you."

Her eyes widened. "What?"

"I'm going home. I'm taking the dogs and going back where this all began."

"Paco's canyon?"

He nodded. "I know it very well. Every cave, every rock, every cactus, every path." He smiled sardonically. "Don't you think it's fitting that I meet Danner on my own territory? It should bring back memories for the bastard. The last time he was there was when they dumped Paco's dead body on the plateau."

"I think you're crazy. You should stay here, where you're safer." She was studying his face. "But you don't want to be safe. You want to go hunting and howl at the moon."

"I'm good at hunting."

"And what about the dogs?"

"I won't take them there alone. I'll take a team and position them all over the canyon. The guardians will be there to care for the dogs . . . and get them out if anything goes wrong. I told you, I know that area. I can keep them safe."

"So you're going to set up, then let Danner know you're waiting for him?"

"Yes."

"I should be there to help."

"You have your own job to do." He turned away and strode toward the front door. "And if you get Devon hurt, I'll break your neck."

"That's comforting," she murmured, watching the door shut behind him. She hadn't the slightest doubt that Marrok would go lethal if she was clumsy about this. There had been a note in his voice that she had heard before but never to her. She was still reeling with surprise, but she'd better pull herself together and start thinking. Marrok was right, she needed to pull Devon out of the equation, and she should be jumping at the chance.

But she wasn't jumping. There were too many potential hazards. One of them was Devon herself.

She slowly sat down in the swing. Think. Plan. Put all the pieces together.

There could be an opportunity here.

Marrok was gone.

Devon smothered the disappointment that tore through her as she looked at the pillow next to her. It wasn't fair to Marrok to expect him to be here when she woke. She had told him she had no expectations, and yet here she was acting as if he'd betrayed her.

She sat up in bed and glanced at the clock—6:35 A.M. Where was he? It didn't matter. Get up. Get on with her life. She had been more open and vulnerable last night than at any other time of her life, but that didn't mean that she was going to act any different now than she usually did.

She got up and headed for the bathroom. She'd shower, get dressed, and go down to the bunkhouse. Perhaps she'd call Marrok and ask him—No, she'd wait until he contacted her. She'd been aggressive enough.

For Pete's sake, what an immature reaction. This wasn't a game where they took turns. She'd do what she wished and whatever she thought right.

Lord, she wished he'd still been in bed when she'd opened her eyes. She wanted to see his face, talk to him. She felt naked, exposed. She wanted this first confrontation over. Even if it meant hearing words she didn't—

Her cell phone rang.

Marrok?

She eagerly pressed the button.

"Did you think you'd get away from me, bitch?"

Shock jolted through her. She couldn't speak for a moment. "Lester." She drew a deep breath. "I see you managed to get my cell number after all."

"I told you I'd do it. You helped. I'm a cop, and you supplied a good reason for me to use every means to track you down. Everyone wanted to help find poor Devon Brady." He paused. "They didn't know what a slut you are. But I know, don't I?"

"It won't do you any good to know my number. I'm going to throw my phone away as soon as I hang up."

"I wouldn't do that. It's going to make me angry if I want to get in touch with you again. You don't want to make me angry. I might make it harder on that son of a bitch you're screwing. I've decided I'm going to hurt Marrok very badly, Devon. I told you never to fuck another man."

Marrok. Panic soared through her. How had he known about Marrok?

"I hear he's a half-breed. Trust you to pick up a dirty Indian to screw. A rutting animal just like you."

She had to ask it. "How . . . did you know I was with Marrok?"

"I can find out anything I want to find out. You should know that. Didn't I find you every time you ran away? This time you made it easy for me. You brought his dog back from that island. There was a Captain Ramirez who had a report on Marrok. I knew you only went down there to fuck someone and I was right. But now I know your cell number and soon I'll know where you are."

"I'm not with Marrok any longer."

"Yes you are. I can always tell when you're lying," he said softly. "You want to protect him, don't you? You always want to protect them. It's not going to do you any good. It's your fault I have to get rid of them. Do you remember that shyster lawyer, Don Garrett, who went over the cliff in his fancy Porsche?"

His words stunned her. Don Garrett? He'd been the lawyer who had helped her prepare her case all those years ago in Texas. She had heard he'd been killed in an auto accident, but that had only been a short time ago. It seemed impossible that Lester would wait and spin his web of malice all that time before striking.

No, nothing was impossible for Lester.

She felt sick. "You're telling me you did that?"

"I told you not to see anyone. You didn't listen to me."

"You didn't— You never said anything."

"I'm not stupid. I have to protect myself."

"Then why are you telling me now?"

"It doesn't matter anymore. I'm going away. You're coming with me."

"No," she whispered.

"Yes." His voice lowered. "But first I'm going to find Marrok and kill the bastard."

Her heart was pounding with fear. "You won't be able to do that. He's not like Garrett."

"Tough guy? There's always a way. I have contacts. I can pick up the phone and get a hit man to do it for me. I'll wait and watch. When he least expects it, he'll die, Devon."

She closed her eyes as panic raced through her. "What a lot of trouble for nothing. I was going to leave him anyway. He's nothing to me. Just a way to get away from you. I'll be a thousand miles from here by the time you find out where I am."

"Will you? Then maybe he's not that important to me. But I'll still find you and, if he's with you, then I win the jackpot."

The jackpot. To Lester that meant having Devon and killing Marrok.

No!

Her lids flew open as the terrifying thought sank home. He sounded so certain. And what was she doing still talking to him? Maybe he could trace this call. She hung up.

Stop shaking. Start moving. She ran toward the bathroom. Get dressed. Get out of here. Get far away from Marrok. Find a place to hide until she could figure out what to do. How was she going to do it?

As Lester had said, everyone was eager to help a cop find the bad guys. She would be vulnerable on her own. Oh, my God, she had never thought Lester would go so far as to kill. She had never questioned that Garrett's death was an accident. She had known Lester was cruel and malicious, but murder . . .

Stop dithering and accept it. And accept that he would try to kill Marrok if he found her with him.

She wouldn't be with him. Marrok had

enough problems without having to shoulder Devon's. But it might be as difficult to get away from Marrok as it would be to find a safe place.

Or maybe not, he hadn't been with her when she woke this morning. He might be relieved.

She knew someone else who would be relieved to see the last of her.

She pulled out her phone again and called the bunkhouse to talk to Bridget.

"Satisfied?" Enright turned to Danner as he hung up the phone. "Did you get the trace?"

Danner frowned. "No, it was a cell, and she hung up too soon. We may have gotten the nearest tower."

Enright frowned. "That's not my fault. I kept her on the line long enough."

Danner smothered his irritation. He was becoming increasingly annoyed with the arrogant bastard. But Enright might still prove useful. "Yes, you were quite lengthy and vicious. I was impressed. It takes a certain determined mind-set for murder. Were you telling the truth about Garrett?"

Enright didn't answer.

"Ah, I think you were. You're going to get along very well in Nigeria."

"Even if you didn't get the trace, I sent her running. I know her. She might not bolt if it was just her safety involved, but she won't risk other people. And she said she was going to throw the phone away, but she won't do it. If I call her again, maybe we can get a trace and pick her up."

"And then what would you do?"

"Whatever you want me to do."

Danner gave him a shrewd glance. "I'm not sure that's true. You're practically salivating about all the foul acts you want to inflict on the lady."

"She deserves it."

"And I'm perfectly willing for you to have your way. I believe you're the perfect person to persuade her to tell us where Marrok is right now. I'm looking forward to it." It was the truth. He had been imagining Enright with the woman and it would be almost like having his hands on her himself. "I've always found there's something wildly exhilarating about inflicting pain. Male victims are interesting, but women's bodies are so soft, and there so many ways to hurt them. You don't mind if I watch?"

"No." Enright's cheeks were flushed, his

eyes glittering. "I believe I'd like it. Shall I call her?"

It was certainly tempting, but Danner still had another option, and it might be a safer one than the one Enright was offering. Though not nearly as exciting. "Not yet." Danner smiled. "Give her a little time. Anticipation can be so delicious."

"I didn't expect this," Bridget said slowly. "Does Marrok know about this slimeball of a husband of yours?"

"Yes. Didn't you?" Devon asked. "You seem to know everything that goes on around here." Devon fastened her duffel and lifted it off the bed. "You and Lincoln."

"There were a few other things of importance going on. I knew Enright existed. I didn't know he'd cause problems."

"He's causing problems," Devon said flatly. "I have to get away from here. It's what you've been wanting since I came. Now's your big chance to get rid of me. Will you help me leave?"

Bridget didn't answer. "You're afraid of him? He sounds pretty much like scum, but nothing that Marrok couldn't handle."

"He's not going to get the chance. It's my problem. I made a bad mistake when I married Lester, and I know one man has already died because I made that mistake. Marrok's not going to die. And Marrok's not going to kill because of me."

"And he knew about Marrok and Santa Marina. He must have really wanted to find you."

"He's always been able to track me down. He digs until he finds out anything he wants to know. Now are you going to help me or not?"

"I'm thinking about it." Bridget was staring at her. "I'm surprised you trust me."

"I don't trust you. Not worth a damn. But I'm giving you what you want, so there's no reason not to trust you about this. Do you know a place I can stay until I can make plans?"

She nodded. "There's an old vacant winery in the Napa Valley. That should be safe enough for you."

Devon's lips twisted. "According to you, I'm not safe anywhere. No deadly forebodings lately?"

"Mock all you please. I only told you what I felt. But if it makes you feel any better, so far it's only a feeling. No visions. I've never had a vision that didn't come true."

Devon felt that familiar chill. "Then I'm evidently a lucky woman."

"It depends on what you call lucky. If you think talking me into helping you is lucky, then you struck it rich." Bridget turned toward the door. "Let's go. We'll take the jeep."

"We won't run into Marrok? Where is he?"

"He and Walt went to pick up Addie from Sarah Logan's. He said he wants to have all the dogs in one place."

"You already saw him this morning?"

She nodded. "Evidently this was my morning for getting calls to come up to the house."

"Why did he want you?"

She shrugged. "He said he needed me to take over guarding you. I guess that was the gist of it. He was a little reserved."

Reserved. It wasn't a word Devon would ever have connected with Marrok. Yet his response last night hadn't been what she'd expected either. There had been passion close to desperation toward the end, but before that she had sensed a multitude of other emotions so elusive that she had been left bewildered and uncertain.

And he hadn't stayed with her after she had fallen asleep. He had gotten up and called Bridget and told her to take Devon off his hands. Perhaps not that brutally, but that didn't ease the hurt she was feeling.

What was she thinking? she wondered in self-disgust. None of that was important any longer.

Keeping Marrok alive was important.

Making sure Lester never found her was important.

She had to survive and make sure of both. But she'd need one more thing if she was to do that. "Can you get me a gun, Bridget?"

"No problem." Bridget gave her a glance over her shoulder. "I'll give you one before I leave you at the winery."

"The winery has been vacant for the last ten years. It's in pretty bad disrepair." Bridget parked in front of the old Spanish-style hacienda. "And I don't know if there's any food in the pantry. We'll have to see."

"I won't need much food. I'm only going to stay here until I get my head on straight about what's best to do." Devon got out of the car and grabbed her duffel from the backseat. "Is there a town close by where I can rent a car?"

"About fifteen miles west." Bridget got out

of the car "You could probably call and have them bring one out." She strode toward the door. "Come on. I want to get going. I brought you here. Now it's up to you."

"That's fine with me," Devon said. "I don't want you to——"

"God in heaven, I'm sick and tired of all this damn phoniness," Bridget interrupted curtly as she threw open the door. "Dammit, get **out** here," she yelled. "I've served her up to you. Now take her off my hands."

"Don't be impatient, Bridget." Chad Lincoln strolled into the foyer from the back of the house. "That's always been one of your primary faults. Along with monumental arrogance. You were always sure that you were smarter than I was." Almost casually, he took an automatic pistol from his jacket pocket and pointed it at Devon. "But in this case you may have come through with something of value."

Devon stiffened, the breath leaving her body. "What's all this about, Lincoln?"

"Betrayal. Greed. Perhaps, death. The last rather depends on you."

"Stop talking bull, Lincoln." Bridget turned to Devon. "You don't have to be afraid if you do what we say. It could all be over tomorrow if Marrok agrees to terms."

"Losing your nerve?" Lincoln smiled. "She didn't want to be the one actually to threaten you, Devon. It surprised me. She's not usually this soft. She needed me to point the gun, pull the trigger." He gestured with the gun. "Go into the bedroom and relax. I've got it all prepared for you. Windows boarded up and not a hint of a weapon to be found."

Devon didn't move.

"Never doubt I **will** hurt you," Lincoln said. "I prefer to keep you alive since Bridget seems to think we may be able to negotiate for the four dogs. She says Marrok may have a soft spot for you."

"Bridget is mistaken."

"Perhaps. But she's seldom wrong, and if it's not enough of a weakness for negotiation, it may at least give me the pleasure of depriving him of something he wants. I owe him one."

"He would never give up the dogs."

"He might. It's my best chance to date."

Devon turned to Bridget. "You're going to let him do this?"

"I told him to do it," she said coolly. "I've been fighting him for too long. We both knew it was only a matter of time until I came over to his side. Marrok wanted me to put you in storage to keep you safe, and it was my chance. You made it easy for me." She lifted one shoulder in a half shrug. "It's funny how things just seemed to fall into place. Almost as if it was meant to be. I had the opportunity, and I took it."

Devon shook her head incredulously. "You're too smart really to believe Marrok would give up the dogs for me."

"We'll have to see, won't we?" Bridget stared her in the eye. "I have to end this."

"By killing the dogs? You know Lincoln won't guarantee he'll keep them alive. By killing me?"

Bridget flinched. "The dogs have a better chance with Lincoln than Danner. It has to end." She shook her head. "Marrok can't win against the kind of people he's up against. I've known that all along. Now it's all going down, and he can't even see it." Her lips tightened. "And I may as well get my share."

Devon turned back to Lincoln. "She's sold you a bill of goods. Marrok won't bargain for me."

"I tend to believe you. I've not seen anything or anyone that would make Marrok give up what he wanted to keep." He added, "But I could be wrong. I desperately want to be wrong. I've waited too long for a break that would give me the dogs. Bridget was very convincing."

"Why would Marrok give up a fortune to save someone he barely knows?"

Lincoln shrugged. "He's impulsive. Savages are sometimes irrational. And he never really wanted the money the dogs would bring him. He wanted his revenge."

"And to save the dogs."

"Now that would truly be irrational. Even you can see that one doesn't risk everything to save four-footed friends."

"No, I can't see that. The dogs mean more to him than I do."

"You're seeing your own feelings in Marrok." He gestured impatiently with the gun. "And you'd better hope you're wrong. Now shut up and go to the bedroom."

"Do it," Bridget said. "He won't hurt you if you don't resist."

Devon moved slowly toward the bedroom door. What was she going to do? There was no way she was going to let that bastard get away with this. Two more steps and she would be within a yard of where Lincoln stood.

"Devon." Bridget was staring at her expression. "No."

Devon was close enough now. "Go to hell."

She threw her shoulder purse at Lincoln's gun and dove for his knees.

"Shit." Lincoln was on top of her, swinging the butt of the gun viciously at her head.

Pain.

Darkness.

"You weren't supposed to hurt her." Bridget fell to her knees beside Devon. "Bastard."

"I was supposed to do what I had to do to keep the bitch from escaping," Lincoln said as he picked Devon up, carried her into the bedroom, and threw her onto the bed. "Now get out of my way, Bridget. You've done your part."

Bridget slowly got to her feet. "Yes, I've done my part." Smother the anger. It would do no good. "Make sure you keep her safe, or there won't be a deal."

"I won't kill the goose that could lay the golden egg. You'd just better be right about her."

She didn't answer. She couldn't trust herself to speak. She walked out of the house and didn't look back.

* * *

The sun was blinding as Marrok jumped out of the helicopter at Paco's canyon. "Come on, Addie. I'll take you up to visit your old buddies. They're waiting for you."

The golden retriever jumped out of the aircraft and ran ahead.

"Where are you keeping the dogs?" Walt got out of the helicopter. "I don't see anyone."

"You're not supposed to see anyone. I had Larry Farland take a team up on the bluffs first thing this morning. Men are stationed all over the canyon. The dogs are in an enclosure above the cave." Bridget should have called him by now, dammit. It had been hours since they'd left the ranch. What was she doing? "See, Addie knows where they are. She's streaking right up the path toward them."

"I'm surprised Sarah actually let you take Addie. She was definitely hostile."

"I told her I'd bring her back in a few days. If I don't, she'll probably come after her . . . and me."

"You could have left Addie. No one is going to monkey with the property of a man who could be president of the United States in a few years."

"It has to be all four dogs. Danner wants them all."

"And when do you issue the invitation?"

"I don't, you do. We switched aircraft today to throw Danner off, but tomorrow you go back to Sarah's place and pick up Nick Gilroy. No switch of helicopter then. You let Danner's men follow you here. They'll report back to Danner and watch us for a day or two. We'll make sure they see what they want to see. Four dogs. Not too big a force to keep them from taking them."

"It's still a risk."

Did Walt think Marrok didn't know that? "They're at risk every day. I have to get rid of Danner."

Walt didn't speak for a moment. "Where's Bridget taking Devon?"

"Some place in northern California. She said she'd call me when they got there." But she hasn't called yet, he thought again in frustration.

Walt frowned. "I don't like this, Marrok."

He stiffened. "Too bad. Neither do I. But it's done now."

"Bridget is a professional. She could hurt Devon without even meaning to do it if Devon struggles with her."

"She won't hurt her."

"I'm glad one of us is sure of that."

He wasn't sure, Marrok thought. He knew how easily accidents happened in a fight, and Devon would never give up easily. "What the hell was I supposed to do?" he asked harshly. "Let her stick around until Danner came down on us like a ton of bricks?"

"Easy." Walt held up his hand. "I just wanted to make sure you knew what Bridget can be when—"

"I know what Bridget can be," Marrok interrupted. "But she promised she'd take care of Devon. I have to trust her."

"Whatever." Walt's stride lengthened as he reached the cave. "I'm going to go visit the dogs. They're a hell of a lot better-tempered than you."

Walt was right, Marrok thought. His nerves were stretched to the breaking point, and he wanted to reach out and crush something, anything. He glanced at his watch again.

Bridget, dammit, **call** me.

She'd have to call Marrok soon, Bridget thought, as she drove around to the other side of the vineyard. He'd be on edge at not hearing from her that she had Devon settled safely. He'd only wait so long before he'd explode. Marrok was a dangerous proposition at any time, but this situation was too volatile to take risks.

But the call would have to wait. She couldn't trust Lincoln not to try to betray her, and she couldn't predict how he'd do it. She parked the car, got out, and crawled up the slope of the vineyard toward the house.

She had a clear view of the winery from this vantage point and lifted her binoculars to her eyes. The windows were long and wide, and she could see the bedroom door through which Lincoln had taken Devon. But where was Lincoln now?

In the kitchen. She caught a glimpse of him standing in front of one of the counters.

She had taken the time to scout the surrounding buildings after she'd left the house and had not run across anyone else on the property. That didn't mean that Lincoln might not be expecting company. He might be playing straight with her, but she wouldn't count on it.

She pulled out her computer and equipment and pulled up the program and made adjustments. Then she settled down to wait.

Fifteen minutes passed.

Thirty minutes.

Forty-five.

Then the digital number came up on the screen.

Yes.

Bridget closed the computer and tucked it into her bag.

Okay, time to make a move. Lincoln had ended the call and was dialing another number. Marrok. She knew what that call would be about. He would tell Marrok he had Devon and Bridget's part in it. Probably not much more. It would only be a teaser, with the hook coming later.

She needed to get to the winery. Lincoln's last call hadn't really surprised her, but it meant everything was escalated. She had to—

No!

Devon bleeding, her eyes glazing over.

Devon falling.

Bridget buried her face in her arms as chill after chill shook her body.

"No," she whimpered. "No. No."

Pull yourself together. It's not as if it hasn't happened before.

But the picture had never been as clear, the details so precise.

Was that because it was Bridget's fault that Devon would die?

She wanted to throw up.

She drew a deep, shaky breath and forced herself to straighten. She'd call Jordan and talk to him. She **needed** him.

She stopped as she reached for her phone.

No, there was nothing that Jordan could do, and if he sensed she was panicking, he might tell her to drop everything and come back to him. He had done it before.

Not this time, Jordan. I have to work it out for myself.

Maybe it wasn't going to happen yet. Block out that picture of Devon, falling, dying. Ignore the cold that was beginning to freeze her blood.

She began to struggle to her feet, then stopped, her gaze on the house.

A tan car was parked before the front door, and a tall, powerfully built man was getting out of the driver's seat.

"Wake up, bitch."

Stinging pain as a hand cracked against Devon's left cheek. Her lids flew open.

"That's it," Lester said. "I want you wide-awake and feeling everything I do to you." He slapped her again. "Whore."

"May I suggest if you continue in that vein that you'll knock her unconscious again, and she won't feel anything." Lincoln was standing in the doorway. "I don't mean to interfere, but I've been taught to—"

"Lester?" Devon scrambled to sit up and lifted her hand to her head as it swam dizzily.

Chad Lincoln . . . Lester. It had to be a nightmare.

No, Lester was too real, standing before her with eyes shining and his lips curved with malicious pleasure. She had seen him like that too many times through the years.

"Don't hurry. Give her a chance to get her breath, Enright," Lincoln said. "She's not going anywhere."

"Shut up. This is my business."

"True." His glance shifted to Devon. "I really wouldn't argue with anything he wants to do with you. He appears to be very angry."

Lester was always angry, always brutal. "What's he—doing here?"

"Danner sent him. It seems he was dealing with both of us to get what he wanted. When I came through with the prize, he called a few hours ago and told me he was sending Enright down to get you to cooperate in persuading Marrok to step into the trap. He doesn't think trading you for the dogs is too good a bet. He wants Marrok, and he believes Marrok is impulsive enough to come after you."

Keep talking. Her head was clearing now, and she had to gain strength before she could face Lester. "You're double-crossing Bridget. She thinks you want the dogs for yourself."

"Oh, I do. But I don't have the money and power that Danner does. I can be satisfied with a partnership." He smiled at Enright. "And I understand Danner is paying you a pretty penny, too. Something about Nigeria?"

Lester had never taken his gaze from Devon's face. "Get out, Lincoln."

Lincoln straightened. "It seems I'm **de trop**. Though I really think I could do the job better. You have little finesse, Enright." He glanced at Devon. "Give in. Tell him you'll do what Danner wants, and you may survive." He was closing the door. "But then again, you may not."

"You'll survive." Lester took a step closer to her. "You'll survive for a long, long time. I've got it all planned." He jerked open her shirt, and his big hand encircled her left breast. "Danner understands whores like you."

"Danner doesn't even know me." Don't

move. Her strength was beginning to return, and she had to have that strength. "You don't know me."

"I know how weak you are." His hand clenched on her breast with agonizing force, and his face lit up as he saw her arch in pain. "I know how afraid you are of me."

"I was afraid of you." She was panting as she fought through the waves of agony. Not yet. "I was only seventeen, and it's easy to scare a kid. But I got over it."

"No, you didn't. I made you run."

"Not because I was afraid you'd hurt me again. I wasn't afraid for myself."

"Look at you," he said softly. "You're hurting so bad you want to scream."

"Yes." It was almost time. Her head was clear, and strength was flowing back to her. Just endure it for a little longer. "Did I tell you that the first thing I did when I started to run was to learn how to protect myself from you? There are all kinds of ways to handle bullies. I was never going to have to face this kind of punishment again."

His lip curled. "But you are, aren't you? And I'm going to hurt you until you call that half-breed and tell him what I'm doing to you. Then I may stop for a while."

"I'm not calling Marrok." She stared him in the eye. "And I'm done with talking to you."

"The hell you're—"

He screamed as she jabbed her two forefingers into his eyes. His hand loosened, and she rolled away from him and off the bed.

"Bitch!" He was flailing wildly, trying to see her. "I'll **kill** you."

She grabbed the bedside lamp and jerked the cord out of the socket. "No, you won't." She swung the lamp like a mace and it connected with the side of his face. "No more killing, no more pain, no more running."

He staggered back but then kept coming.

She jumped back and did a round kick. Her foot connected with his chin. He grunted but kept coming.

God, he should be down. It had to be pure fury that was keeping him on his feet.

She took two steps to the side and the edge of her hand lifted to come down on the side of his neck.

He countered, grabbing her wrist.

She kneed him between his legs. Then smashed her palm under his nose and up, breaking the bones.

His eyes glazed over, and his knees buckled. He fell to the floor.

She backed away, her breath coming short and hard. Lester was crumpled over, and she couldn't see his face. But he should have been—

"Is he dead?" The door was open, and Lincoln stood in the doorway, a gun in his hand. "I was anticipating screams, but the only scream I heard was from Enright." He was gazing at Lester without expression. "I didn't expect this at all. You always seemed to be such a gentle soul."

"Gentle doesn't necessarily mean helpless." How could she get that gun away from Lincoln?

"No, I'd say that's true." He moved toward Lester. "I repeat, is he dead?"

"I don't know. He should be. The bones of his nose should have shattered and entered his brain. That's what's supposed to happen."

"I know. But I take it that it's only textbook theory for you."

"Of course it is. I'm not a professional killer like you. He could still be alive. I struck him at an awkward angle."

"Well, let's take a look." He knelt beside Enright. "Now how can I check him and still keep my gun handy to deal with you? You're clearly a force to be reckoned with. Oh, I know." He pressed the gun to Lester's heart and pressed the trigger. "Yes, he's definitely dead."

She was staring at him, shocked. "Why did—"

"Danner's orders." Lincoln rose to his feet. "The way he put it was that it's always wise to have more than one arrow to a bow. But when one arrow can do the job, then you should break the other and throw it away. It's much cheaper that way. Evidently Danner decided I was the more efficient arrow."

"So he told you to murder Lester?"

"He would have preferred to do it himself, but he said the idea of giving Enright his last hour with you was appealing. Sort of like a condemned man having a last gourmet dinner."

"And torturing me was to be Lester's final treat?" She shuddered. "What a horrible man Danner must be."

"From what I've heard, he and your ex-husband have similar tastes and characteristics. And there was always the chance that Enright would break you, and he'd get Marrok as a bonus." He smiled. "But you've spoiled that possibility." He gazed down at Enright. "Amazing. Actually, impressive. But now the ball is in my court to get you to make that call to Marrok. I won't be as easy as Enright."

She knew he didn't want to kill her. Danner wanted her alive to lure Marrok. So the gun was a threat but not one that—

"Don't even think about it," Lincoln said. "I could shoot you and make excuses to Danner later."

"It's hard not to think about it," Bridget said from behind him. "When you're such sleazy son of a bitch."

He looked behind him and stiffened when he saw the gun in her hand. "Why, Bridget, is this a double cross?"

"How clever of you to recognize one when you see it. But then you should be very familiar with the concept." She glanced at Enright's body. "He wasn't very smart, was he? Danner just used him and threw him away."

"You heard me talking about Danner? But I was going to tell you about him. Naturally, I was going to bring you in on the deal."

"Not likely. I didn't have to overhear you explaining Danner's nasty modus operandi. I recorded that last call you made to Danner."

He shook his head reprovingly. "What a suspicious bitch you are, Bridget. And what do you intend to do about it?"

"Kill you."

"I do have a gun."

"But mine is pointed at that nicely bar-bered head of yours. Even if you got off a shot, my finger would still pull the trigger."

"Now don't be impulsive. We can come to terms. Naturally I tried to—" He dropped to the floor, firing as he rolled to the side.

Bridget dodged behind the couch, and the bullet plowed into the cushion.

Take your time, Jordan had always told her.

I don't have that much time, Jordan.

Another shot. Closer.

But she saw Lincoln moving across the floor, trying to get behind her.

Draw a bead.

The skull is always best, Jordan had told her.

She pressed the trigger.

CHAPTER
17

"Devon," Bridget called from the other room. "I'm coming in. Don't be afraid. I'm not going to hurt you."

Devon tensed, then instinctively reached down and picked up the lamp with which she had hit Lester.

Bridget appeared in the doorway. Her brows rose as she saw the lamp. "Or maybe I should worry about you hurting me." She put her gun into her jacket pocket. "Does that make you feel better?"

"No. You just killed a man, didn't you?"

"Yes." She glanced at Enright. "But so did you. It's true you might have had a better reason, but then maybe not. It's all how you look at things." She lifted her gaze to Devon's face, then to her open shirt. "Did Enright hurt you?"

"Of course, he hurt me. What did you expect?"

"I didn't expect anything. Enright was the one factor I didn't know about." She smiled faintly. "And I'd say that you managed to hurt Enright more than he did you." She turned. "Put down that lamp and come into the kitchen where I can put a bandage on the cut on your head."

Devon didn't move.

"Look, I know you don't trust me. How could you? You'd be an idiot. But I don't know how I can—Yes, I do." She crossed the room and knelt by Enright's body. She quickly searched him and came up with a shoulder holster. She pulled out the Glock and slid it across the floor to Devon. "Hold on to that. It should make you feel more secure. I'm surprised he didn't try to draw it."

"He probably didn't think of it." Devon touched her breast, which was still throbbing. "He liked to use his hands on me."

"Bastard." Bridget turned away. "Pick up the gun. After all, I did promise you a weapon when you got here."

"A promise you never meant to keep."

"I meant to keep it eventually. I'm doing it now." She disappeared into the other room. "Now come and let me wash that cut before we hit the road. It's not safe here."

Devon bent down and picked up the Glock. "Why should I go with you? Maybe you're going to deliver me to Danner." Yet she still found herself following Bridget into the kitchen. Bridget was right, the gun did make her feel safer. "You set me up. I don't know how much you're lying and how much is truth."

Bridget nodded. "I know. But it's not what you think. It's not good, but I never meant you harm. You were just a way to accomplish an end."

"Stealing the dogs."

"No, getting rid of one of Marrok's enemies. You can accuse me of being ruthless and risking your neck, but I'd never betray Marrok or those dogs." She met Devon's gaze. "And that's the truth." She took down a first-aid kit from the kitchen cabinet over the sink. "You probably don't want me touching you. Will you wash that cut and stick on a bandage so that we can get out of here?"

Devon stared at her for a moment. She might be a fool, but she found herself believing Bridget. She had known from the beginning how fanatical Bridget was about protecting Marrok. She could see her going to any extent to do that. She turned on the water and dabbed at the cut on her hairline. "You killed Lincoln."

"Yes." Bridget handed her a Band-Aid. "It was time to get rid of Lincoln before he had a chance to get rid of me. And it wasn't a falling-out among thieves if that's what you're thinking."

It wasn't what Devon was thinking. She didn't know what to think. "Why? You didn't do it to save me. You're the one who set this up."

"No, I thought you were a risk worth taking. There was a good chance I could control the situation." She put the first-aid kit back on the shelf. "I would have killed Lincoln to keep you safe, but I hoped I could time it so that I could get what I needed before that became an issue."

"What you needed?"

"I knew Lincoln was negotiating with Danner. It was only a matter of time before he made a move on his own. I decided I had to take control before Lincoln brought Danner down on Marrok. But I had to have proof."

"How did you know Lincoln was dealing with Danner?"

"I have a contact in London who managed to trace the calls between Lincoln and Danner. Not easy. The signal bounced back and forth across the Atlantic four times before Jordan was able to focus in on it."

"Jordan?"

"Jordan Radkin. My contact in the U.K." She stepped back. "Will you put that gun away now? Do you think I'm telling the truth?"

"It's difficult to judge. You change like a weathervane."

"Well, judging what you did to Enright, the gun's really not necessary." She added, "Do what you like. It's up to you."

Devon hesitated, then slowly lowered the Glock.

"Progress." Bridget headed for the front door. "Your duffel is over here where you dropped it when you came in. Tuck the gun in it so you can have it handy if you decide you want to shoot me."

Devon followed her to the door. "You still didn't tell me why you needed proof Lincoln was dealing with Danner."

"Because Lincoln is MI6. If I didn't have proof he was going to betray them and take the dogs for himself, then MI6 would come down on Marrok like a ton of bricks. Believe me,

Marrok doesn't need that hassle. So I had to get a tape of a conversation between Lincoln and Danner."

"And you did it?"

"Yes, very satisfactorily incriminating. He was going to double-cross me and MI6 and go into partnership with Danner. It was very clear he was going into business for himself. I'll send the disk to MI6 right away. They don't like traitors. They'll look upon Lincoln's death as a convenient end to a problem." She strode ahead of Devon. "Lincoln down, Danner to go. Now let's hit the road. I don't think Danner will be on his way here since he sent Enright to do his dirty work, but I don't want to take chances." As they reached the porch, Bridget added, "We'll take Lincoln's car. I left mine a couple miles on the other side of the vineyard." She headed for the sedan parked a few yards away. "I took Lincoln's keys before I came in to get you."

"Very efficient. You've obviously been taught well." Devon stopped and turned around to look back. She'd killed a man only a short time before in that house. Or, if she'd not done it herself, she'd meant it to happen, and that was the same thing.

"Regrets?" Bridget's gaze was on her face.

How did she feel? Lester had been a torment and a threat. If he'd not died, then he might have gone on destroying everyone around him. Yet to kill a living person was a terrible thing. "Of course there are regrets. I was forced to take a life." She headed for the car. "But I'd do it again." She got into the car. "Now where do you think you're going to take me?"

"That's up to you." Bridget got in the driver's seat and started the car. "I used you, and I got you hurt. Now you make your own decisions. Not that you wouldn't anyway." She grimaced. "I should have told Marrok that when he wanted you tucked away safe somewhere."

"Screw Marrok," Devon said. "I can't believe he told you to do that to me."

"Yes, you can. You've tapped his protective streak." She looked away. "And a few other reservoirs of feeling that he probably didn't know he had."

"He had no **right.** He's been moving me around to suit himself since the moment I met him."

"Tell that to him." Bridget took out her phone. "And I have to talk to him right away. Lincoln had a chance to make a call to Marrok, and he's probably ready to explode. Lincoln probably didn't tell him about Danner, but I'd bet I figured prominently in that conversation." She dialed the number. "Marrok, don't talk. Devon is fine. I'm going to tell you what happened and why. Then you can vent all you please."

Marrok couldn't believe it. Every word Bridget was saying was stoking the fury that had been burning in him since Lincoln's call.

Fury and a fear that was eating at him until he couldn't think straight.

Vent? He wanted to roar, tear into Bridget and everyone else who stood in his way.

"I may just kill you, Bridget," he said through his teeth.

"You'll do what you have to do," Bridget said. "You handed Devon to me on a golden platter, and I saw a way to use her to rid us of Lincoln."

"Without consulting me."

"You wouldn't have let me do it. Now it's a fait accompli. Lincoln's dead. We evidently got a bonus in getting rid of Lester Enright. And Devon didn't get hurt." She paused. "Well, maybe a little hurt. She's got a cut on her head when Lincoln hit her."

"How bad?"

"Superficial."

"I want to talk to her."

A moment passed before Bridget came back on the phone. "She doesn't want to talk to you. She may be as upset with you as she is with me. Devon, will you please say a few words to him so that he won't think I'm lying about you?"

Devon came on the line. "I'm fine," she said coolly. "As far as I know, everything Bridget said is true."

"What about your head? Is it—"

"Devon handed the phone back to me," Bridget said.

Shit.

"Where are you? I'm coming to get her."

"If she wants to see you, she'll come to you," Bridget said. "She'll make her own decisions. Between us we've done enough manipulating." She hung up.

Marrok muttered a curse as he hung up. Profound relief had been followed by anger and frustration.

"Is Devon okay?" Walt asked.

"I think so. She wouldn't talk to me." He muttered a curse. "Who could blame her? Not only did I let Bridget set Devon up, but I wasn't there when she was cornered by Lester Enright."

"Ugly."

Marrok nodded jerkily. "Bridget killed Lincoln. She was using Devon as bait to trip him up."

"You believe her?"

"Yes," Marrok said grudgingly. "I can see Bridget doing it."

"What do we do now?"

That was the question. He wanted to call Bridget back and tell her to bring Devon to him. He wanted to go after Devon and stay with her and keep her safe. He couldn't do either. He'd burned his bridges, and now he had to pay for it.

"Wait. I want to make sure Devon is safe before we make a move on Danner."

Bridget pulled over to the side of the road after she hung up. "I told Marrok you were going to have to make your own decisions, but it has to be soon."

"Don't try to pressure me, Bridget," Devon said.

"Why not? I'm under pressure. Marrok is under pressure. Everything is going to move fast now. I don't care what you decide to do, but I don't want to have to drop you off without being sure you'll be safe. Do you want to be done with us? Shall I take you to an airport so that you can go back to Denver?" She paused. "Or do I call Walt and tell him to take you to Marrok in Arizona."

Devon stared at her. "Arizona?"

"Paco's canyon. Marrok decided to go to his old stomping grounds to lure Danner."

Devon's lips tightened. "He didn't tell me."

"And that makes you angrier."

"Hell yes."

"Then make a decision."

Devon gazed out the window at the rolling hills. "You want me to go back to Denver."

"I think it's safer for you. I'm done with trying to convince you. Make up your own mind."

Easy to say, Devon thought. She was brimming with resentment at Marrok for treating her like a child who had no will of her own. Yet resentment toward him was only the tip of the iceberg. Devon was silent, letting the memory of what had happened in that hacienda today flow back to her. "I'm mad as hell. Danner sent Lester to torture me just because it amused him. He **liked** the idea. Lincoln said he and Danner were alike, and I believe it. He's a terrible, terrible man." She shook her head in disbelief. "He doesn't even know me, and he did that. I can imagine what he'd do to Marrok and the dogs. I'm not going to let that son of a bitch get near them." Her hands clenched into fists. "I had all kinds of bullshit noble reasons to stay here before. I was going to help save the dogs, help the human race. But I don't feel noble now. I just want to take Danner down and keep him from hurting anyone else. No matter what Marrok did, it's not going to change how I feel about that."

"You're going to go to Marrok."

"He's got the dogs. I'm going to be there when Danner goes after them."

"Then there's something you should know." Bridget looked straight in front of her. "Do you remember I told you that I'd had no vision of your death?"

Devon stiffened. "Yes."

"Well, it happened. A clear picture. You'll be shot in the chest. Blood. I saw you falling to the ground." She paused. "It was night, but I could tell it was desert country, and there were huge red boulders behind you."

Devon felt her stomach twist. "Paco's canyon . . ."

"But if you don't go there, it might not happen."

"And it might happen somewhere else."

Bridget whispered, "You don't believe me."

"I believe you believe that what you thought was a vision will take place."

"But you're still going?"

"I can't hide. There's too much at stake. Lord knows, I don't want to go." She shivered. "You've scared me."

"You're scared? I **saw** it. And I don't know how to stop it. But there has to be a way. I can't go on if there isn't."

Devon had never heard such a depth of despair as in those last words. "It must be terrible for you. You say you've tried to stop it before?"

"Of course I have," she said fiercely. "I've never been able to do it. If I warn someone, they laugh or ignore me. I'm like that Cassandra in mythology, the one whose curse was to have no one believe her prophecies. And if I try to step in myself, it doesn't work. I never know enough. Or there's some element that pops up that keeps me from interceding. Dammit, what good is knowing if I can't prevent it?"

"It's been like that all your life?"

"Since I was seven."

"And your parents knew you had this talent?"

She nodded. "Psychic abilities sometimes

run in families, and it certainly did in mine. So they weren't surprised. But I was just a kid, and they didn't pay any real attention when I told them not to go to Dublin that day. I didn't know why I didn't want them to go. I was just afraid." She looked out the window. "A bridge collapsed, and their car went into the river."

"My God."

Bridget was silent a moment. "So you can see why I have no trouble believing in healing powers or the dogs of summer. I **want** to believe in them. It's the other side of the coin. It's not death, it's life. That's why I came to Marrok when he asked me. I can **do** something. I'm not helpless."

Devon felt a surge of pity mixed with horror. It was no wonder Bridget was sometimes difficult and always complicated. Devon couldn't imagine what she would have been like if she'd been forced to bear that burden. "And you're wonderful with animals. That must be some solace to you." She shook her head. "Sorry. That sounds very Pollyanna."

"Yes, it does." Bridget's gaze shifted back to her, and she smiled faintly. "But you're right. That's yet another side to the coin." She started the car. "I'll take you to the local airport and call Walt."

"Are you going with me?"

"No, Marrok won't want to see me. It's going to take a while for him to forgive me. I'll have to work at Danner from another angle."

"What angle?"

"Enright is dead, and Danner doesn't have a partner now that I got rid of Lincoln. What a pity. Danner's all alone. Maybe I should apply for the job."

"Good God, if you slip up, he'll kill you."

She shrugged. "I used you as bait. Maybe it's time I stepped up to the plate. You should be glad that I'm risking my neck instead of yours."

"You're darned right I'm glad. Maybe I wouldn't have objected to being used as bait if I'd been consulted."

Bridget lips twisted. "Don't say that. I'm not above letting you volunteer if it suits my convenience."

"You don't 'let' me do anything. As you said, my choice."

"I'm sure you'll tell that to Marrok."

"Oh, yes." Devon was beginning to look forward to that confrontation with Marrok. "I have quite a few things I intend to tell Marrok."

* * *

Bridget stood watching as Walt lifted off and turned east. It was almost sundown and would be fully dark by the time Devon reached Paco's canyon. She turned away and strode toward Lincoln's car. She couldn't stand here and think about Devon or Marrok. She had to get a plan together to pull Danner into the trap Marrok was setting.

Her cell phone rang as she got into the car. Jordan. Lord, she didn't want to talk to him now. She would be tempted to lean and, if she did, he'd want to know details so that he could step in. But she couldn't ignore Jordan. One way or another he would get through to her.

"Everything is coming to a head. I killed Lincoln," she said when she picked up the phone. "I'm working on a way to go after Danner."

"That sounds tentative," Jordan said dryly. "I don't like tentative, Bridget."

"Too bad. I'm not Superwoman."

"Almost." His tone had a hint of amusement. "I'd never have sent you there if I hadn't made sure I'd made you into something very special."

"You sound like Dr. Frankenstein. You taught me, you didn't make me into anything."

"I stand corrected. Can you blame me for

wanting to take some credit for you? It's not often that someone as interesting as you comes along." He paused. "And I'm detecting a note of edginess. Did killing Lincoln disturb you?"

"No. Well, maybe a little. I don't like killing. Even bastards like him." He was getting too probing. She had to get away. "I don't have time to talk. Why did you call me?"

"Something disturbed you. It jolted me out of a sound sleep. If it wasn't Lincoln, it was something else."

She should have known Jordan would feel a desperate sense of foreboding. He always knew what was going on with her.

"Tell me what's wrong," he said quietly.

There was no use trying to stall him.

"I don't know if I can keep Devon alive," she whispered. "I saw it happen, Jordan. I saw her shot. I saw her die. I don't know if I can stop it."

"If you can't, you can't. As you said, you're not a superwoman."

"I can't go on like this. I have to find a way to turn it around. If I see it, I've got to find a way to stop it."

"To stop it, you'd have to change the circumstances. Let's look at what you saw. Where did it take place?"

"Paco's canyon. And I've already tried to get her not to go there. She wouldn't listen."

"Then find another piece of the puzzle. One small change that might alter everything. Was anyone with her?"

She thought about it. "No one was standing beside her. If there was anyone else there, I didn't see them."

"Did she have a weapon?"

"No."

"Then change those circumstances."

"And how the hell am I to do that? I've gone through this before. I change one thing, and something happens to change it back."

"Then do you believe it's fate, and you have no say in it?"

"If it were fate, then there would be no reason for me to see it happening. This may be a screwed-up universe, but there has to be some kind of reason and balance. If I could stop it just **once**."

Jordan was silent. "You're sounding desperate, Bridget. Do you need me to come?"

She had let him see the tension, dammit. "No, I can handle it. You're busy setting up the island."

"I can leave it. I can leave everything. You're the only one that's important to me."

"Liar." She had to get off the phone. "I'll call you if I change my mind."

He was silent again. "I'll let you slide away from me now. Not for long, Bridget."

"Good-bye, Jordan." She hung up the phone and drew a deep, shaky breath. Talking to Jordan always sparked a mixture of emotions. He was brilliant and had the experience to cut through all the chaff and shine a light on the darkest corners of her mind. But that ability also made her feel infinitely vulnerable.

Change the circumstances. One little change could alter everything.

She'd think about it. But right now she had to set about getting Danner to Paco's canyon.

The lights of the helicopter speared down through the darkness to reveal Marrok, waiting on the plateau below.

Devon tried to smother the instinctive response that had nothing to do with anger. Dammit, she'd only had to see him to have her body tingle, ready. And not only her body . . .

He was striding toward the copter, jerking open the door. He stood there, looking at her. "I'd offer to help you out, but I don't know if you'd take my hand."

"I don't need help." She got out of the helicopter by herself. "Where's Ned?"

"I left him with the other dogs at a camp in the canyon. I want him to become accustomed to staying there while he's here. He's content with them, and they have guards to protect them."

"From Danner. Bridget says that's why you're here."

His lips tightened. "I'd rather not talk about Bridget."

"You're angry with her. She said you would be."

"Damn straight, she betrayed me. She betrayed you."

"No more than you did. She lied. You lied. She made a prisoner of me. That's what you were planning. Tucking me away somewhere out of your way. At least she released me and sent me on my way." She glanced at Walt. "I wasn't at all sure that Walt didn't have orders this time to take over the job you set Bridget to do."

"Not me," Walt said. "That would be too tough. Marrok can do his own dirty work from now on." He got out of the helicopter. "I'm going to go find Sid Cadow and see if I can drum up a game of poker. Call me if you need me."

Devon started walking toward the canyon. "It sounds as if you've brought everyone from the ranch."

He fell into step with her. "Almost everyone. This canyon is like a labyrinth. There are nooks, ledges, and hiding places all over it. I put the dogs and their guardians in the safest one."

"And I suppose the other nooks and crannies are good for ambushes?"

"Yes."

"How do you intend to get Danner here?"

"I was going to have Walt pick up Nick Gilroy at Sarah's and bring him here. There's no question he'd be followed." He shrugged. "But Nick showed up at the ranch earlier today. He wasn't going to be left out of the action. I had him brought here."

"So now what?"

"I'll find another way. I can concentrate now. I wasn't thinking of much beyond getting you back in one piece."

"Bridget may be able to help. She was going to approach Danner and—"

"No Bridget."

"If she intends to help, then we should let

her. She may be risking her life. She deserves our help."

"I can't trust her."

"If I can trust her after all she put me through, then you shouldn't have a problem."

"It's because of what she put you through that I'll never forgive her. Listen, I don't trust many people, but I trusted her. I'll never do it again. I won't risk you again."

"You don't have anything to say about what happens to me," she said coolly. "And for some reason Bridget is as concerned about you as she is the dogs. You'd be a fool to ignore an asset like that."

He didn't answer.

Stubborn, she thought in exasperation. She hadn't expected anything else. Neither had Bridget. But the more she thought about how alone Bridget was right now, the more she wanted to shake him. But she could tell by his closed expression that he wasn't going to be moved by argument. Maybe later.

She changed the subject. "Where do I sleep?"

"I set up a sleeping bag for you in the cave. Unless you'd rather sleep out in the open."

"I don't care. The cave's fine."

He smiled faintly. "I remember you had

some objections to occupying the cave the last time it was discussed."

She felt heat flush her body. "Was that supposed to be provocative?"

"I hope it was. But it wasn't intentional. I know better than to make a move on you right now. I'm just glad you decided to come home."

"This is your home, not mine."

He shook his head. "It's your home, too. I give it to you." They had reached the cave, and he gestured for her to go inside. "I started a fire for you. It gets chilly after midnight. There's a change of clothes and a toothbrush in that duffel. And there's plenty of bottled water in the icebox."

She remembered that first day, when he'd reached into the box and brought out a bottle of water for her. He'd taken out a vial of Paco's potion and asked her to rub it into his wound.

Too many memories were flooding back. Stop before she remembered how she'd done it after they'd made love on the path. Too late. It was there before her, every move, every touch.

"Good night." She hurried past him into the cave.

He followed her. "I need to see that cut. How bad is it?"

"It's fine," she said quickly. "I don't need any of Paco's potion."

"I have to see it." He gently pushed her hair back from the bandage. He carefully removed it and traced the cut with his forefinger. He said thickly, "Damn Bridget."

She could feel her pulse leap under his touch. She stepped back. "Superficial. Just as she said. I don't even need a bandage now that the bleeding has stopped. It's just a scratch. Leave it alone."

"This is all?" He paused. "Enright didn't hurt you?"

"I don't want to talk about Lester."

His gaze searched her expression, and he opened his lips to speak. Then he turned on his heel. "If that's what you want." He headed for the entrance to the cave. "I'll sleep out here. Call me if you need me."

"I won't need you."

"I'll still be here to guard you."

"I don't need that either."

"I need it." She could see him dropping down on the rock outside, his back to her. "I can't tell you how much I need to guard and protect you. No one is going to hurt or take you away again. That's sheer self-preservation.

It hurt me too much when I thought I might have lost you."

Don't answer. Don't be touched. Keep the anger. Keep the distance.

She took off her shoes and climbed into the sleeping bag in front of the fire. She could feel the warmth from the flames stroking her cheeks. How many years had Marrok slept here before a fire with Paco on the other side? Had they talked, joked? She wished she'd known the old man. Because then she might be able to fathom the enigma that was Marrok.

Close your eyes. Sleep. You're not here to solve puzzles about Marrok. You're here to get Danner. You're here to help save the dogs of summer.

But she couldn't go to sleep. It was hours later, and she was still lying there. Every nerve, every muscle was taut, almost painfully aware of Marrok lying only yards away. She turned over for the hundredth time.

"Are you cold?" Marrok was standing in the opening of the cave. "Do you want me to put more wood on the fire?"

"No."

"I didn't think so." He sank down, sitting tailor fashion near the door. "I was just using it for an excuse. I don't think either one of us is going to sleep. There's too much left unsaid."

"I've said all I want to say."

"Not the words I want to hear. I'm trying to be understanding and sensitive, but it's not working for me."

"It never did."

"Enright. I saw your expression. He hurt you, didn't he?"

She stiffened. "We struggled. Of course, he hurt me."

"How?" he asked hoarsely.

"It doesn't matter. It's not going to happen again."

"How?"

"He grabbed me. He was strong. I bruise easily."

"I don't see any bruises."

"Leave it alone, Marrok."

"I can't. I have to see them. Show me."

"Will you go then?"

He nodded. "Show me."

She unbuttoned her shirt and slipped her bra straps down. "It's over. It doesn't matter."

"My God." He was looking at her swollen

breast, which was livid with red-and-purple bruises. "He did that to you?"

"Bruises heal." She started to pull her bra straps up.

"No." He was suddenly beside her. "Not yet." His head was pressed against her breast. "I'm sorry I wasn't there for you." His voice was muffled. "I'm sorry I let him do that to you."

"You didn't let Lester do anything. He did it all himself." She forced herself to keep her arms at her sides and not slide them around him. "And not for long. Only until I was ready to fight him."

"You should have told me about him. You should have let me take care of him for you."

"I told you once before. I take care of my own problems."

"I can't let you do that. Not anymore."

"I think you'd better leave now, Marrok." She kept her voice steady with an effort. "You've got what you came for."

"No, I haven't." He lifted his head. His dark eyes were glittering in his taut face, and his lips were tight with pain. "I want to look at you for a minute. I want to remember what he did to you."

"Why on earth?"

"It's important." He bent his head and his lips gently brushed her breast. His cheek was warm, hard, and faintly rough against her flesh as he rubbed it back and forth. "Because every now and then it will come back to me and remind me that I have to make sure that nothing like that can ever happen to you again."

She felt a melting deep inside her. "Leave, Marrok. You said you'd go."

He didn't move for a moment, his cheek still pressed against her breast. "Okay." He sat back on his heels, pulled her bra straps up, and buttoned her shirt. "I won't touch you again." He stood up and went back to his former place near the door. "I just had to know. It was driving me crazy. Just let me stay for a little while longer." He leaned back against the rock wall and stared into the fire. "I've been thinking. I'm angry at Bridget, but I'm the one to blame for all of this."

"Yes, you are."

He smiled crookedly. "I can always count on you for honesty, can't I? But you see, I didn't realize what a bastard I was being. Did I want you to be safe? With all my heart. But there was another reason I asked Bridget to get you away from me." He paused. "I told you that I couldn't be as honest with you as you were with

me. I had to push you away. You frightened
me. I'd never felt like that before. It was like
part of me was . . ." He stopped searching for
words. "Flowing out, and I knew I might never
get it back." He shrugged. "I'd been alone all
my life. That's the way I wanted it. I don't
know how to handle feeling like this."

"No one asked you to handle it," she said
unevenly. "I told you I didn't intend to back
you into a corner."

"But I have to learn." His gaze shifted from
the fire to her face. "I have to convince you to
stay with me. Because now I know I'm more
frightened of having to go on without you."
He rose to his feet. "That's all. I just had to say
it. Go to sleep. I won't bother you anymore tonight."

He was gone. Devon saw him once more
settling outside the cave.

Go to sleep? How was she going to do that
when she was aching for him, with him? She
was unbearably touched. For God's sake, don't
lose your grip because of a few words.

But those words had been spoken with raw
simplicity and truth.

And there was the slightest trace of mois-
ture on her breast where his cheek had rested.

Why did that sign of vulnerability shake

her to the core? He would never admit to it. She shouldn't let go of anger. He had behaved with his usual arrogance and ignored her independence and self-will.

You'll be shot in the chest. Blood. You'll fall to the ground.

Bridget's words came out of nowhere, bringing the same chill as the first time she had heard them.

Death. Life.

My God, cling to anger when there might not be time for anything else? She didn't know if she believed Bridget's prediction, but life was too short to take chances.

A moment later she'd struggled out of the sleeping bag and was out of the cave.

"Marrok, dammit." She dropped to her knees beside him. "You were **wrong** to do what you did, to ask Bridget to move me around like a puppet. I can't believe how wrong you were."

He sat up, and said soberly, "I can. One way or another I've been wrong all my life."

"You can't just shift me around on a whim."

"It wasn't a whim. It was the farthest thing from a whim that you can imagine."

"Then it's time you shaped up. I'm not going to have to worry about you doing something like that again."

He went still. "Does that mean that I'm going to get the chance to do it?"

"What a way to put it," she said shakily. "You step out of line again, and I'll strangle you."

He reached out, his hands hovering over her shoulders. "Is touching you out of line?"

"No." She went into his arms. He felt strong, good, solid, closing out the night. Closing out Bridget's words. "You do that very well. It's when you start to think that I have problems. You should never have gotten out of bed and left me alone to wonder and fret. That's where all the trouble started."

"It won't happen again." He was stroking the back of her hair. "I didn't expect you to forgive me this easily. I was prepared for a fight. Why?"

Shot in the chest. Blood . . .

"You got lucky. It occurred to me that few things are worth letting anger twist and poison your life. I know what being a victim is, and I'll never be one again. I can handle anything you can hand out. I can handle you, Marrok." She nestled closer. "And you told me it's going to be a cold night. I don't like sleeping bags."

"Neither do I. But it's going to be colder out here."

"Then let's go inside." She saw his expression. "We're past that, Marrok. I'm not afraid of competition from women you screwed years ago. I've got an edge." She got to her feet and held out her hand to him. "You're nuts about me. And heaven help me, I feel the same. We've got a long way to go, but that's a start."

"One hell of a start." He jumped to his feet, and his arm encircled her waist, whisking her into the cave. All signs of hesitancy and awkwardness were gone. He was Marrok again, bold, dynamic, with that hint of reckless energy. And he was definitely impatient. "And we'll worry about everything else later. I don't care how long a way we have to go. Let's just enjoy the journey."

The shadow of the flames was leaping on the walls of the cave, playing over the hollow of his high cheekbones and the sensual curve of his mouth. Beautiful, she thought hazily. Everything about him was powerful and sensual and full of fire.

"But that journey's got to start soon," he murmured. His fingers unbuttoning her shirt were deft but shaking, and his breathing was beginning to quicken. "I'm about to go up in—" He froze, his fingers on the buttons halting. "I'm being selfish again. You've gone through too much today, and I'm ready to pull you into bed. Why don't you sock me?"

She looked at him, surprised. "Good Lord, I think you're being sensitive."

He scowled. "Not willingly."

"And at the wrong time."

"Does that mean I don't have to be sensitive?"

She shook her head as she recalled the faint trace of liquid on her breast after he'd left her. Not the time to mention it. She'd probably never mention it.

"It means that making love is wonderful and healing, and that's all the sensitivity I want from you tonight." She kissed him long and hard. "Understand?"

"Whatever you say." He was stripping her with the speed of light. "Whatever you want."

Whatever she wanted.

This was what she wanted. **He** was what she wanted. She had a sudden memory of how earlier tonight she'd been thinking of Marrok and Paco together in the cave. She'd wished she'd known him, that she could have seen them together.

Are you here, Paco?

He's going to be okay. You took good care

of him all those years ago. I promise I'll take care of him from now on.

"Hey." Marrok was looking down at her, smiling. "Why do I feel you're not paying attention to me?"

I'll take care of him, Paco.

Her arms slid around him and pulled him down to her. "I'm paying attention," she whispered. "I couldn't be paying more attention to you, Marrok."

CHAPTER
18

"**Wake up.**" **Marrok gave her a** lingering kiss. "I'm not going to make the mistake of going off and leaving you with no word. That got me in bad trouble. But I have to get up and make my rounds."

He was already dressed, she noticed. She pulled him down for another kiss before releasing him. "Rounds?"

"Check on the dogs and sentries."

"I'll go with you."

He shook his head. "I'm moving fast. I have men spread all over the canyon. I've called Nick Gilroy and asked him to come down and take you to the dogs. He should be here in about twenty minutes. I'll meet you there in an hour and we'll have breakfast."

"Couldn't you call them and check?"

"I could. I won't. I don't believe in remote command, and I don't trust phones in guerilla conditions. I want to see my men and have them see me." He stood up and moved toward the cave opening. "I suppose it's my Indian blood speaking. I'm sure Geronimo wouldn't have taken to those newfangled gadgets either. See you later."

Devon was smiling as she shook her head. As usual, Marrok was wired and restless. In this case it was probably justified because of the threat he and his men were facing. Her smile faded as the magnitude of the threat hit home. She'd been able to ignore the danger during last night's passion, but it was now here again before her.

Dammit, why wouldn't Marrok listen when she'd asked him to cooperate with Bridget? He had been absolutely implacable.

And there was nothing she could do about it. Maybe Bridget wouldn't even come up with a plan to end this nightmare Marrok had lived with all these years. It might be up to Marrok and Devon to do it.

In the meantime she'd better start moving

and get dressed. Nick would be here soon, and she didn't want to keep him waiting. She threw back the blanket and got up.

"The dogs seem to be settling in pretty well," Devon said to Nick as she watched the four dogs lolling lazily on the rust-colored rocks. It was quite an encampment; not only the guardians but several other men were moving around the area. Sid Cadow was cooking bacon and eggs on a Coleman camp stove, and for once he appeared relaxed and in his element. "No problems?"

Nick shook his head.

"Marrok made sure all the guardians were here except Addie's Sarah. And I understand Addie has always been very adaptable. Sid is taking care of her."

She smiled. "And what are you doing, Nick?"

"Right now, I'm guarding you." He grinned. "Can't you tell?"

"Is that what Marrok told you to do?"

"He made me aware that he'd be very upset if I weren't extremely careful of you," Nick said. "Actually, it made me feel a sense of purpose. A man of my age appreciates being thought competent in that area. I was even given a gun. And I was beginning to think my warrior days were over."

Devon's smile faded. "You have other talents. You don't need to be using a gun."

"I told you, I like it. My blood is stirring, and I feel alive again." He added, "And I like your Marrok. So do his other men here."

"He's not my—" She stopped in the middle of the denial. Marrok did belong to her if he could belong to anyone. Just as she belonged to him. It was still tentative and uncertain, but the bond was there. "You can trust him, Nick."

"We're going to have to trust him," Nick said soberly. "Walt said that Danner's men may be all over this canyon before everything's said and done. I spoiled his plan to draw Danner here when I showed up at the ranch. Walt said that Marrok's toying with the idea of luring him here himself."

Her gaze flew to his face. "What? That would be crazy. They might just decide to kill him and get the dogs later. He's been a target for years."

"I'm only repeating what Walt told me," Nick said. "Maybe it was only a passing thought on Marrok's part."

"And maybe it wasn't." Panic mixed with rage was tearing through her. "It's just the kind of thing he'd do." He'd gone after that man following them from her clinic without a second thought, she remembered. She could still recall his expression: intent with a hint of underlying excitement. "He likes it. He grew up battling everything and everyone around him. Most of the time alone."

"Don't blame the messenger. Take it up with Marrok."

Much good that would do her. She hadn't been able to stop him from doing anything he really wanted to do since she'd met him. They might be closer now, but Marrok was Marrok. He'd be as stubborn as he'd been when she'd broached letting Bridget help them.

"That bacon sure smells good. Do you want me to get you a plate? Marrok must have gotten tied up."

Nick obviously wanted to escape her obvious disturbance. Poor guy, it wasn't his fault. "Yes, please." She watched him go over to the campfire. There was something different about Nick, a spring in his step, a lightness and camaraderie with everyone around him . . . and a trace of the excitement she'd seen in Marrok. He was so damn happy about the coming confrontation with Danner that she wanted to shake him.

Men.

This was no game. Nick could be killed. All these people who cared so much for the dogs could be killed.

Marrok could be killed.

Nick was pointing to the biscuits in a pan and looking at her inquiringly.

She nodded. She didn't care whether she had them or not, but Nick was—

Her cell phone rang. She stiffened.

London?

"Can you talk?" Bridget asked when she answered.

"Yes."

"I don't have much time. I routed this call through the U.K. so that Danner wouldn't know I was calling you. Danner's man, Caswell, is keeping a friendly eye on me, and he's going to be less than friendly if he manages to get close enough to hear the conversation."

"Friendly? With Danner?"

"Like a good partner. Of course, Danner is planning on cutting my throat as soon as he gets what he wants from me. That goes without saying."

"What does he want?"

"Marrok." She paused. "You. Lincoln did a great job of convincing him you might be the way to get Marrok to surface. He's even willing for me to step in as substitute for Lincoln. He understood perfectly my shooting the bastard's head off." She added, "So I offered to trade you for a percentage."

"I hope it was a good one," she said dryly. "I'd hate to be thought cheap."

"Thirty percent. That's all I could talk him into since you're not a sure thing," she said. "But it's a way I can lead him to Paco's canyon."

She went still. "What?"

"Danner didn't question that I had to move you after I killed Lincoln. It would have been stupid to stick around when Danner knew where we'd been holding you. So I chose Paco's canyon."

"Isn't that a little coincidental? Paco's canyon is Marrok's territory. Danner knows that."

"Maybe. I'm not even sure Danner believes me. He went along a little too easily. I don't care as long as I can position him for Marrok. Tell Marrok Danner may have something up his sleeve." She was speaking quickly now. "Caswell is coming toward me. It's going to be tonight. Right after dark. We're coming by car from Tucson. You can't see the road from the canyon that way. You're supposed to be bound and gagged in the foothills on the other side of the canyon from the cave. There's a cluster of boulders beside the gully that runs up the canyon to the top. Marrok will know where it is. He can wait there and pick Danner off."

"Yes, he could do that."

"You sound . . ." Bridget said. "You can get Marrok there?"

"I'll get him there."

"Not you. Marrok has to be alone. Or have him take Walt as backup. Any sign of any significant show of force, and I'm a dead woman. He can take two, maybe three people if they know what they're doing. But not you. You shouldn't be anywhere near that place. Do you understand?"

"I understand."

Bridget hung up.

Devon slowly put her phone back in her pocket. The chances of her getting Marrok to go anywhere that Bridget told him to go were nil. He'd made it clear that he'd never trust Bridget again. And if he did decide to go, it would be by his rules, his plans.

And that meant Bridget could be killed.

She had run a high risk and didn't deserve to have that risk made even more critical.

"Here it is"—Nick was beside her with two plates of food—"enough chow to keep a lumberjack happy. Though we may have four dogs over here asking for—What's wrong?"

"Nothing." Devon took the plate. "Good heavens, you're right. This should last me all day if I manage to get it down."

"What's wrong?" he repeated.

She shook her head. "It will be okay. Just something I have to work out."

"I'm here," Nick said quietly. "We've worked out quite a few things between us over the years."

"And I may let you help with this," Devon said. "I just have to figure out what to do." God knows, she had no idea right now. She saw Marrok coming down the path and tried to gather herself together. Don't be as transparent with him as she had with Nick. It shouldn't be too difficult. Marrok was busy keeping this armed camp in shape. Just avoid him as much as possible and don't let him see how terrified she felt.

She waved. "It's about time you got here. Come over here and help me eat this mountain of food."

* * *

"Three days," Marrok said to Sarah on his cell. "It shouldn't be more than that before I'll try to return Addie to you."

"It had better not be longer than that. You gave me Addie as my responsibility, and I take it seriously."

"I know you do. So do I."

Silence. "I believe you. Is there anything John and I can do?"

"I'll let you know." He hung up and stared thoughtfully at the sun beginning to set in the west. It might not be bad to call on John Logan's resources. His security people were top-notch, and he might need—

"I need to talk to you." Nick Gilroy was coming toward him down the path. "Devon sent me with a message."

"Why didn't she come herself? I haven't seen her all afternoon."

"You're not going to like it," Nick said.

Marrok stiffened. "I already don't like the sound of this."

"She wants you to meet her at the gully on the other side of the canyon. Well, not at the gully, somewhere above the gully in the rocks on the path up the canyon."

He stiffened. "And why won't I like it?"

"Danner. Bridget's bringing him to the canyon." He held up his hand as he saw Marrok's expression. "She told him that's where she had stashed Devon. She called Devon and told her to make sure you were somewhere in those rocks to pick him off."

Marrok began to curse. "Bridget. And Devon's going to go and meet her?"

"No, Devon will wait for you on the path leading to the top of the canyon. She just wanted to ensure that you'll be there waiting. She was worried about Bridget. The only way she could be sure that you wouldn't stage some kind of full-scale attack that might get Bridget killed was to go herself. She knew you'd follow her."

"You're damn right I will." He started at a trot down the path. He had to stop at the cave and get his rifle and more ammunition. "How much time do I have?"

"Not long. Just after dark." He was running beside Marrok. "Devon told me to get Walt and Rod Zedwick to go with you. They both have SEAL experience, and she thought you'd want them. They're waiting at the bottom of the path."

"All very neatly planned." Marrok gazed at

the setting sun. His stomach was twisting with fear. "Devon always wants everyone safe and happy. Me, Bridget. Only this time she may get herself killed. **Damn** Bridget. I may pick her off at the same time I nail Danner."

"Bridget told Devon not to go herself."

"It didn't help, did it? She's going to be there." He saw Walt and Rod and speeded up his pace. His heart was already pounding with terror and dread.

Not much time. Stay up in those rocks, Devon. For God's sake, stay away from that gully.

The rays of the sun were slanting blue-red, paler, longer. Soon they would be gone entirely.

Just after dark.

"This brings back memories, Bridget." Danner was gazing at the wall of the canyon as they parked the car near the gully. His expression was wistful. "I spent many happy hours with Marrok and Paco here in this canyon. Do you know, I'm basically a simple man. Marrok thinks I was pretending, but a part of me truly wanted all to go well for that old man."

"I can see why Marrok might have a few

doubts," Bridget said. "You did beat Paco to death."

"Sometimes violence becomes necessary." He smiled at Bridget. "You understand. After all, you blew off poor Lincoln's head."

"I'm not criticizing you." Bridget opened the car door and got out. It wasn't quite dark, but the rocks were giant, looming shadows above them. She hoped to hell Marrok was up there somewhere ready to take Danner out. The trip from Tucson had been very uncomfortable. Danner had been entirely too affable, too slick.

Cat and mouse?

Danner gestured to the two men in the backseat. "Gentleman, suppose you take a look around? One can't be too careful." He turned to Bridget as his men spread out over the terrain and disappeared in the labyrinth of boulders. "Now where is this lady Lincoln was so convinced would move Marrok to cooperate?"

"Farther up the gully." Bridget started up the incline.

"Do you know, Devon Brady has been wielding an astonishing amount of influence over the men around her. Enright was obsessed with her, and Marrok evidently must feel something for her. She must be very stimulating. Enright quite whetted my appetite with all his plans for her. I think I may decide to toy with her myself."

Bridget didn't answer.

Danner said softly. "And you really shouldn't have left her alone out in the wilds. There are all kinds of critters out here in the desert."

Definitely cat and mouse.

Draw her gun now or wait for Marrok's shot?

But Danner was standing half behind one of the boulders by the side of the path. Marrok wouldn't be able to get a clear shot.

Danner suddenly laughed, his gaze on the path. "And I believe we have a critter right here. I was wondering where you were, Caswell." He shined his flashlight. "Our vet?"

"A bitch," Caswell said as he pushed Devon ahead of him down the trail. "She damn well hearty made a eunuch of me."

Shit.

Horror tore through Bridget.

It was Devon, bruised, lip bleeding.

"Devon Brady," Danner said. "What a surprise. And I actually didn't believe you, Bridget. Of course, you said she was tied up and ready for serving. Wasn't it lucky I sent Caswell up here ahead of us to pave the way? We might have missed her."

She could see the glint of the gun in Danner's hand.

Devon shot in the chest. Blood. Devon falling to the ground.

Oh, God, it was going to happen.

Change the circumstances, Jordan had said.

How?

"She must have gotten loose." Bridget started up the incline toward Devon.

Devon had been alone. Stand next to her.

Devon had not been armed. Give her a gun.

"I told you she was here, didn't I?" Bridget had almost reached Devon and Caswell. "Now everything can go through just as we planned, Danner."

Marrok, where the hell are you?

"Stand where you are, Bridget," Danner said. "The game's over. I think you knew I wasn't the fool you were trying to play me. But I had the chance to turn Marrok's trap against him. Let's see if Marrok does care anything about her." He raised his voice. "Are you out there, Marrok? I'm going to have Caswell do a little selective shooting. He's very angry at your lady. The left kneecap first, I think. That's very painful. However, we could negotiate . . .”

Marrok steadied the rifle, sighting down the infrared scope.

The shot had to be absolutely accurate.

There wouldn't be any interference from the other men who had been in the canyon. Walt and Rod had taken them out minutes after they had hit the trail.

He couldn't get a clear shot at Danner, but Caswell was standing in the middle of the path.

Two shots, quick succession.

Then **move.**

The first shot shattered the hand in which Caswell was holding the gun.

He screamed and dropped the gun.

“Down!” Bridget pushed Devon to the ground and rolled with her to the side of the path.

The second shot entered Caswell's temple.

“Dammit, I told you to stay away, Devon,”

Bridget muttered. "You weren't supposed to be here."

"I didn't want to be here," Devon said. "Do you think I wanted to be in the way? I stayed up in the canyon. Caswell was on me before I even saw him." Her gaze searched the rocks from where the shot had come. "Was it Marrok? But where did he—"

"Danner!" Bridget was looking back at where Danner had been standing. "Marrok went around in back of him after he made the shot at Caswell. He's **got** him."

Devon hoped that was true. She could see Marrok and Danner struggling, but she couldn't tell what was happening. "What are we doing staying here when we could be helping him?" She jumped to her feet. "You have a gun, don't you?"

"Yes, but it may not be—I think—" She stood up and then said, "**Yes.** Danner's down."

CHAPTER
19

Marrok's hand sliced down on Danner's arm, and his gun went flying a few feet away. His next blow sent Danner to his knees.

"You caught me by surprise." Danner stared up into the barrel of the Glock Marrok was pointing at him. "I don't care that you shot Caswell, but I'm angry at myself that I didn't foresee your climbing around those rocks and pouncing. It was an Indian tactic, and you know this canyon so well. I thought I remembered everything about you, but I suppose I always wanted to forget you were a half-breed. I wanted to be a father to you and that would have spoiled everything."

"Bullshit." Marrok hand tightened on the

gun. "Make a move, Danner. Stop talking and make a move, so I can blow you to hell."

"Marrok?" Devon called.

"Stay where you are." Marrok's eyes never left Danner.

"Ah, the Brady woman," Danner said. "You really do care something for her. I might have been able to bargain for the dogs after all. Oh well, I really prefer to confront you on even ground."

"In case you haven't noticed, you've lost, Danner. I'll give you one minute to go for that gun on the ground beside you. Then I'll put a bullet between your eyes anyway."

"You're giving me a chance. Considering your background, it's unusual that it bothers you to kill in cold blood."

"My blood isn't cold right now."

"Then it must be our past history together. You haven't won," Danner said softly. "It's only a matter of time until I get my hands on those dogs. I just have to be a little more patient. But I'm very angry with you, Marrok. I'm going to have to punish you."

"Then it will have to be from hell."

"No, I'm not that patient. Do you know, at times I really did wish you were my own son? I was proud of you."

"Liar."

"No, it's true. At first, I only meant to use you, but I found you were almost as strong as I was." He shook his head. "But then I realized that you had streaks of weakness. Paco was one of them." His gaze shifted to Devon. "That bitch is another."

"Shut up about her, Danner."

"You see, she must mean something to you. What a sense of power that gives me. I took your Paco away from you. Shall I take her away, too?"

"Your minute is up." He aimed the gun.

"You're angry. You don't want her to die. Remind me to tell you how that old Indian howled when we—" He suddenly rolled toward Marrok away from the gun on the ground, reaching into his pocket and drawing out a Beretta. He shot upward, and the bullet skimmed Marrok's side even as he dodged. He staggered, then recovered.

But Danner was on his feet and moving in and out of the rocks, keeping off the path. Marrok was after him, gaining on him.

Then he saw the gleam of the moonlight on the barrel of Danner's gun as he lifted it.

Marrok instinctively dove to the ground

and got off a quick shot as he rolled behind a boulder.

But Danner's bullet wasn't aimed at him.

"Devon!" Bridget's voice.

Devon.

Oh, God. Marrok lifted his head and stared in agony at Devon and Bridget.

It was like a slow-motion montage in a horror film.

Bridget diving between Devon and Danner's bullet.

Bridget's back arching as the bullet struck her.

"Bridget!" Devon fell to her knees beside the other woman. "Dear God, her chest . . ." Devon was dragging Bridget behind a boulder. "I've got her, Marrok. I'll take care of her. Get that son of a bitch."

Marrok was already on his feet and darting after Danner.

She had to stop the bleeding, Devon thought desperately.

The bullet that had struck Bridget had entered her chest and had to be lodged somewhere near her lungs or heart.

Blood. So much blood.

Devon took off her shirt, tore it into strips, and tried to find a place for a pressure point near the wound.

"Devon . . ." Bridget's eyes were open. "I don't want to die."

"You're not going to die," Devon said shakily. "I'm a great vet. I can handle this wound until we can get you help. But, dammit, you shouldn't have pushed in front of me."

"It was the only way," she whispered. "I had to . . . change it. You would have died. I knew it. But I have . . . a chance."

"A good chance. Now stop talking."

"Marrok . . . tell him he owes me. Tell him I want him to stay with me."

"We'll all stay with you."

"Tell Marrok . . ." Her eyes closed. "It was the only way . . ."

Devon froze. Was she dead? No, she was still breathing. She was only unconscious.

She reached for her cell phone. First, call 911 and ask them to send help for Bridget. Then call Walt and get him to bring down the dogs and stay with her.

Then go after Marrok and hope to hell she didn't find him dead.

*　*　*

"You're falling behind, Marrok." Danner was near the top of the canyon. "Come and get me."

"You've reached the end of the path," Marrok said. "And the plateau is two hundred feet below. Where do you think you're going to go from here?"

"Down the way I came," Danner said. "After I kill you, of course."

"You're not going to kill me. This is the end for you, Danner." Marrok moved off the path and into the shadow of the boulders. The moonlight was too bright, and he was a clear target on the path. So was Danner. But he didn't want to shoot the bastard. That would be too easy. He wanted his hands on him, dammit. He wanted to bruise and tear him apart as Danner had killed Paco.

A werewolf would tear him apart.

Why had he thought of Paco's words from so long ago? Because the moon was bright, and he felt as savage as that boy he had been.

"I don't see you, Marrok. Are you trying to sneak behind and ambush me again?"

"I'd have to have wings," Marrok said. "You've run yourself into a blind alley. All I have to do is come and gather you up."

"No, you'll have to wait for your chance. I

know how you hate to wait. On the other hand, as I told you, I'm very patient. You'll make a mistake, and I'll take you out."

"You're wrong. I can wait."

Danner chuckled. "But you're thinking about Paco and the Brady woman I killed."

"You didn't kill Devon. You shot Bridget Reardon."

"Did I? What a pity. I'll have to take your word for it. I couldn't stay around to make sure. But no real harm done. There's always tomorrow. Bridget Reardon was an annoyance to me, too."

Marrok could tell Danner had reached the top of the path. He stopped, his gaze searching the area around the boulders at the top. No, Danner must be hiding on the far side of that bank of boulders near the edge of the cliff. Marrok would have a hell of a hard time working his way around so that he could get a clear shot. Maybe if he swung off the cliff below and climbed up that way . . .

"Give me the dogs, Marrok," Danner coaxed. "It's not too late. I'll share with you. It's what I always wanted to do. Paco just got in the way. He was such a disappointment. Destroying the panacea, then only leaving the dogs for me to use. For a while I wasn't even sure he'd tell me about the dogs. We had to beat him for hours to get him to tell us where he'd hidden the formula."

"Shut up, Danner."

"And then he finally broke down and told us he'd destroyed the formula, and the only thing left of the panacea was in the dogs. It was too weird. Naturally, we had to be sure. We couldn't stop the questioning."

"No, you wouldn't stop."

"It's hurting you, isn't it?"

"It will stop when I kill you. You're on the rocks behind the boulder, aren't you?"

"How did you know that?"

"I have very good hearing. The sound of your voice is different because you're by the cliff edge. And I used to come up there all the time. Do you see all the crevasses between the rocks?"

"Yes."

"Do you hear anything?"

"What are you getting at?"

"A family of rattlesnakes used to live there. The rocks were hot and slick, and they'd lie basking in the sun all afternoon. One time I saw five there."

Silence. "You're lying."

"Why would I try to frighten you?"

"To make me come around the boulder so that you can pick me off."

"That's a possibility."

"It won't work. You'll be picked off yourself. I'm calling my men to come up and get me."

"Go ahead. I believe they're probably being kept a little busy at the moment." He paused. "Did you hear that?"

"What?"

"It's like peas being shaken in a tin cup."

"You're bluffing. I don't hear anything."

Marrok had been bluffing. But there was an edgy note in Danner's voice that convinced him to push it a little harder "Strange. You're so much closer to them."

"I don't hear anything but that damn coyote howling. The same one that's been yapping for the last five minutes."

Coyote. What was he talking about? Marrok didn't hear any howling.

And then he heard the rattle.

"Shit," Danner said.

Marrok heard one shot, two.

He started up the path, keeping low, darting from side to side.

Another shot, ricocheting off the boulders at the top of the cliff.

A howling behind him.

Not a coyote. A dog.

No, two dogs.

Ned and Wiley tore into view and bounded up the path, almost knocking Marrok aside as they passed him.

They were heading for the top of the cliff.

"No!" Marrok yelled. He took off after them at a dead run. "Heel, Ned. Dammit, stop."

Ned ignored him. He and Wiley had already reached the boulders at the top and were running behind them.

More shots.

Oh, God. The son of a bitch had shot them.

He tore around the boulder.

Danner was on the ground, and both dogs were on top of him. Ned was ripping at the arm holding the gun, and Wiley had his teeth in the man's throat.

Danner screamed. He was trying to lift the gun. "Get them off me!"

"Sorry. They don't seem to be paying any attention to me." Marrok carefully aimed to avoid hitting the dogs and put a bullet in Danner's forearm.

Danner screeched, and the gun fell to the ground as the bone shattered.

Marrok felt a fierce surge of satisfaction. "It

hurt, didn't it? How many of Paco's bones did you break, Danner?"

Danner was still trying to ward off Ned and Wiley. "Get these dogs off me!"

"They don't like you. Do you think they remember you caging them after you killed Paco?" He walked toward him. "They hate cages."

Suddenly, both dogs were backing off Danner, looking at Marrok.

"I'll kill you all." Danner was raving. "Damn dogs, damn snakes . . . I'll kill you all." He managed to roll to the side, and his other hand closed on the gun. "And you, Marrok. I'll kill—"

"Good-bye, Danner."

Marrok's bullet shattered his skull.

Dead.

Marrok crossed the distance between them and stood looking down at Danner.

"I'm sorry it took a long time, Paco," he whispered. "I've killed the bastard. Now you send him to hell, okay?"

Ned and Wiley were not even staring at the man they'd been savaging only minutes before. The rage and ferocity were suddenly gone from their demeanor. They sat down beside Marrok and looked up at him as if asking for instructions.

"It's over. It's okay now," Marrok said.

"You did well." Though how and why they had suddenly appeared he had no idea. He'd worry about that later. "Let's go down and see about Bridget."

He met Devon when he was halfway down the canyon.

She stopped on the path and drew a deep breath as Ned and Wiley ran to greet her. "Thank God. I heard the shots. Danner?"

"Dead. How is Bridget?"

"Bad. Still alive—911 sent an air ambulance to pick her up. They should be here any minute. I left Walt with her." She looked down at the dogs. "He was worried about Ned and Wiley. Sid said they broke away from the other dogs and took off. He was going after them when I called him. Sid said it was weird. They both had their heads cocked as if they were listening to something. Then they bolted."

I don't hear anything but that damn coyote howling, Danner had said.

The phantom coyote that Marrok had not been able to hear.

The rattlesnakes that had distracted Danner enough to keep him from killing the attacking dogs.

Marrok had thought he'd heard a rattle, but he'd seen no sign of the snakes Danner had been muttering about before his death. Could they have slid back into the crevices? Or had it all been Danner's imagination, aided by the thought Marrok's words had planted? He didn't find the latter possibility viable. Danner was too cool to be drawn, and the bastard's voice had been genuinely terrified.

Paco?

He took Devon's hand and started striding quickly down the hill. "Who knows? Maybe they were listening to something."

The air ambulance was landing when they reached the plateau.

Walt was standing by Bridget's stretcher with Nika and Addie by his side. He looked up at Devon soberly. "She's not going to make it. They're taking her to the hospital in Tucson, but she'll be lucky if she's not DOA when she gets there."

Devon's heart plummeted. "No, I promised her she'd live. She's **got** to live. For God's sake, I'd be dead if it wasn't for her."

Marrok's comforting hand was on her arm.

"She'll live," he said. "We're going to do everything we can, Devon."

"She said she didn't want to die," Devon said jerkily. "She said to tell you to stay with her, that you owed her."

"She didn't have to remind me of that." His hand tightened on Devon's arm. "I know how much I owe her. And you're damn right I'll stay with her. I'll bring Ned and Wiley with me. If I need them, I'll send for Nika and Addie, too."

"You may have a few problems getting the hospital to let you do that," Walt said. "They have rules."

"That can be broken. Get Sarah Logan on the phone and have her start pulling strings. I want clearance by the time we reach the hospital." He started for the plane that had just landed. "And I'll take care of getting the pilot to accept them myself right now. They have to be on the plane, close to her."

Devon watched him stride across the plateau with Wiley at his heels. She began to feel the faintest flicker of hope. Marrok had said Bridget would live and he had been with Ned on many missions when the Lab had managed to cure the incurable.

Walt was dialing his cell. "Don't get your hopes up," he said gently. "She's bad, Devon."

"I know that." She looked down at Bridget. She had known her for such a short time, and their togetherness had been fraught with such a multitude of emotions—suspicion, anger, admiration, amazement. They had not really had a chance to become friends. Yet this woman may have given her life for Devon. "But she said she had a chance. We've got to see that she gets it." She took Bridget's hand. Lord, it was cold and limp. "We're here, Bridget," she whispered. "I don't know how it works, but we'll stay with you. We'll bring you through this."

No response.

Ned was whimpering in distress. He moved close to Bridget, his nose gently pushing against her cheek as if trying to wake her.

"That's right, try to help her, Ned," Devon said unevenly.

But Sarah Logan had said that not all the patients had gotten better after the hospital visits with the dogs of summer. Two had still died.

She couldn't think about that now. She had to hold on to this slim hope.

Marrok and two white-coated men were

coming toward them, and her hand instinctively tightened on Bridget's. "Here we go. Hold on, Bridget. That's all you have to do. Hold on . . ."

Darkness.

Was this death? Bridget wondered. Wasn't there supposed to be a tunnel and some kind of light? There was no light, only this thick darkness.

She should be dead. She had felt herself slipping away, but someone had brought her back. But she wasn't sure that she could stay . . .

"Don't be stupid. Of course, you can stay. That's what this is all about."

Jordan.

She must be alive. Jordan wasn't dead.

"You're bloody right I'm not. Can you see me?"

No, she could only hear him. The darkness was too intense.

"I'm on my way to you. But you have help there. They kept their promise. You made it through the operation. All you have to do is keep fighting. You've never had trouble doing that." He paused. "Why the hell did you jump out in front of her?"

Make a difference. What's the use of being able to see it unless you can make a difference?

"The difference could have been your death instead of hers."

Make a difference.

"When this is over, we're going to have a little discussion. I never sent you there to be a human sacrifice."

You sent me here because it was important, because it could make the biggest difference of all. You were right to send me.

"Not if you die on me," Jordan said. "So that's not going to happen. Get your butt in gear and keep fighting."

Stop ordering me around. I'll do it for myself, not so that you won't feel guilty.

Silence. "Guilty? I never feel guilty."

Go away. I don't want to argue with you. I have to concentrate on keeping alive.

"I'll be there soon."

She could feel him fading away. Yes, come soon, Jordan. She always felt safer when Jordan was with her. From the time she was a teenager, nothing was quite as bad if Jordan was there.

In the distance beyond the darkness, she could hear a dog whimpering. Ned?

And someone was holding her hand. It was a strong, masculine, firm grip.

Marrok.

Yes, they were keeping their promise.

Fight.

"How is she?"

Devon looked up to see Janet standing in the doorway of the waiting room. "I don't know. They managed to get the bullet out without too much damage to her vital organs. But that doesn't mean she'll make it. The doctors say she shouldn't have lived this long. Why are you here? Bridget isn't one of your favorite people."

"No." Janet frowned. "But I don't want her to die. Maybe she's not as bad as I thought. Walt said she took that bullet for you."

"Yes, she did."

"Then she's probably . . . okay." Janet put the overnight case she was carrying on a chair by the door. "I brought some of your clothes and stuff. Walt didn't think you'd be coming back to the ranch for a while."

"Are you back at the ranch?"

Janet nodded. "Marrok sent word that everyone should go home. Didn't he tell you?"

"No, he's been pretty busy. We've been with Bridget since she got out of surgery." She nodded at the coffee machine. "I just came out to get coffee."

"Is there anything I can do?"

Devon shook her head. "Thank you. Just go back to the ranch and make sure the other dogs are safe."

"Well, that's kinda what I wanted to talk to you about," she said awkwardly. "Sid wants to know if Wiley's okay."

"He's fine. He and Ned have been camped out in Bridget's room." She studied Janet's expression. "Did Sid tell you about the **shi'i'go**?"

"Yeah, sounds pretty nuts to me." She moistened her lips. "But Sid ain't stupid. So maybe there's something to it."

"There's something to it," Devon said. "And I hope we'll have some concrete proof soon." She rubbed the back of her neck. Lord, she was tired. "Tell Sid we'll bring Wiley back to the ranch as soon as we can."

"That's what I told him. I said you'd take good care of Wiley, but he's crazy about that mutt."

"It sounds like you're getting along pretty well with Sid."

"He's not a bad guy. He just had to be put in his place at first. We understand each other."

Yes, Devon could see how they would come

to an understanding. They were two loners, each of whose rough, hard pasts would strike an answering note in the other. "And how is Gracie?"

"Fine. Follows me around, getting in my way. Sid's been taking her for walks. She puts up with him, but she likes me better."

"I'm sure she does," Devon said gently. "She's always loved you, Janet."

"Yeah, I guess so." She shifted uneasily. "I'll stay if you need me. You know that."

"I know." She walked across the room and put her arms around Janet. The other woman stiffened but didn't step back. So prickly, so afraid to show emotion. "I'll need you more when we get Bridget straightened out." She released her. "Good-bye, Janet."

A flush turned Janet's cheeks ruddy. "You don't have to get all mushy." She turned away. "Me and Sid will take care of things. Don't you worry."

Devon watched her walk down the hall before she turned back to the coffee machine.

Not worry? Maybe not about the ranch or the other dogs, but Bridget was an unending anxiety. It was over twelve hours since they had arrived at the hospital, and she couldn't see any difference in her condition. What frightened her was that the medical staff couldn't either. They were astonished that she was still alive and refused to encourage hope.

But Bridget had survived this long. She wouldn't give up, dammit.

Devon took the two cups of coffee and headed back toward Bridget's room.

As Devon entered the room, Wiley's tail thumped the floor from where he was curled up in the corner.

Marrok looked up from where he was sitting in the visitor's chair by Bridget's bed. "You were gone a long time."

"Janet came by. I talked to her for a while." She crossed the room and handed him his coffee, her gaze on Bridget's face. "Does she have a little more color, or is that my imagination?"

Marrok shrugged. "I don't know. I can't tell the difference." His hand reached down to pat Ned's head. "I'm not going to lie to you. I told you that I thought she'd make it. But sometimes it doesn't happen right away. She was too close to death, and because it was violent, there's trauma that's difficult to overcome. It's easier if it's only an illness that doesn't throw the body into shock."

"Sarah Logan told me that Addie couldn't cure everyone."

Marrok nodded. "All I can say is that I've never taken Ned on any mission where he's failed. Does that help?"

"Yes." She glanced back at Bridget. "And there **is** more color. I won't believe anything else."

He smiled. "And if there isn't, you'll will it to happen." He reached out and squeezed Bridget's hand. "Do you hear that, Bridget? Now do what she tells you." His smile faded, and his gaze narrowed on Bridget's face. "I think I felt her hand move."

Devon inhaled sharply. "Should I call someone?"

"No, it's gone now. But it was there—" His phone rang, and he picked up. "Marrok." He listened for a moment. "No, I don't care who you are. She's not in a condition to receive visitors. Call tomorrow and we'll—" He frowned. "Arrogant bastard. He hung up on me."

"Who hung up?"

"Some friend of Bridget's. Jordan Radkin. He said he was coming to see her."

"Where was he?"

"Downstairs. He said he'd just flown in from London. Well, he can just turn his tail around and fly back. I won't have him bothering her."

Devon was puzzled. "How did this Radkin even know she was hurt?"

"How do I know? I'll ask the son of a bitch when I see him."

"Before or after you kick him out?" His attitude reminded her of that first confrontation between Marrok and Sid Cadow. Evidently, this Jordan Radkin had stirred the same male antagonism. "Let me talk to him."

Marrok slanted her a glance. "Are you trying to save me from myself?"

"I'm curious, and I don't want you rude to someone Bridget may care about. She didn't impress me as having that many people close to her."

"Quite right."

They turned to see a tall, broad-shouldered man standing in the doorway. "I'm Jordan Radkin." He came toward the bed. "And since Bridget has limited support on the personal front, I have to make up for it in determination." He looked down at Bridget. "She almost bought it, didn't she?"

His voice was cool, Devon thought. Everything about him was cool and contained. He was somewhere in his thirties with a dark complexion, chestnut-colored hair, and gray eyes that glittered with alertness and intelligence. "You don't seem upset. She could still die."

He shook his head. "You have no idea how upset I was when it first happened. But my being upset would do her no good right now. Emotion gets in the way."

"Tomorrow would be a better day for a visit," Marrok said tersely. "I believe I mentioned that."

"I believe you did. But Bridget will be better off with me to help her. Besides being distant relations, we've been together a long time."

"Not for the last three years," Marrok said coolly.

Radkin smiled faintly. "Yes, even the last three years, Marrok." He turned to Devon. "And I appreciate your trying to keep the peace between me and Marrok, but it's time we came face-to-face." He took Bridget's hand and said to her softly, "Rest time is over. Time to come back to us now."

"That's not going to do any good. She's been unconscious for—"

But Bridget was opening her eyes!

"That's a good girl," Radkin said. "Now don't try to talk. That might be too—"

"Screw you," Bridget whispered.

Radkin chuckled. "I thought you'd object to that hint of condescension. Have I told you how much I missed that scalding tongue of yours?"

"I've got to call the nurse and tell them you're awake," Devon said as she headed for the call button. "He's right, don't talk, Bridget."

"No hurry now," Radkin said. "Marrok's **shi'i'go** has done its work. She'll recover very quickly now. I just had to be here and jar her a bit. Sometimes she actually pays attention to me. Oh, for the old days when she looked upon me as a god."

Bridget snorted.

Radkin's brows rose. "I believe that disgusting sound might take more effort than words." He squeezed Bridget's hand. "So I'll leave and let you pamper yourself. I'll be back tomorrow. I have a few things to do." He turned to Marrok. "It wouldn't hurt for you to stay with her for the rest of the day. It's not necessary, but it may help a little."

"I wasn't planning on leaving her. If I were, I wouldn't give a damn what you think."

Radkin smiled. "You're just as Bridget described you. Only she said that you'd made progress and were ready. I'm not at all sure she's right. She has a tendency to become involved and lose her perspective." He turned away and wheeled to face Marrok. "By the way, you won't have any problem with Danner's death. I called on a few friends with MI6, and they sent a team out to do cleanup. The body will be found in an alley behind a Las Vegas casino. An obvious theft and assault."

"Why would you do that?" Marrok asked.

"We'll discuss it tomorrow." He headed for the door, then stopped as he saw Wiley sitting in the corner. "Well, what have we here?" He squatted before the German shepherd. Wiley tensed and gazed at him warily. He bared his teeth. "Shh, it doesn't have to be this way. Let it go, Wiley." He put his hand out and gently touched the dog's head. "Let it all go . . ."

Wiley froze, his eyes closing. Then he slowly sank to the floor, the tension leaving his big body.

"Good," Radkin said. "Now remember . . ." He got to his feet. "I'll see you tomorrow, Bridget." He left the room.

Devon was staring at Wiley, who was still lying in the same position and appeared mellower than she had ever seen him. "What the hell did he do to him?"

"Wiley . . . difficult," Bridget whispered. "Jordan likes . . . difficult."

"I've seen you have that effect on animals." Marrok was staring after Radkin. "But not that—"

"Powerful," Bridget said. "I'm not that powerful. I never wanted to be. Not like him. And I was right about you, Marrok. He knows I am. It's time . . ." The nurse was hurrying into the room, and she made a face. "Stay close. They may kill me trying to find out why I'm getting well."

Marrok reached down and touched Ned's head. "We won't leave you. You told Devon I owed you. You couldn't be more right." He stood up. "But I'll move out into the hall for a few minutes." He paused. "Just who is Radkin to you?"

She smiled. "All kinds of things. He's right; I was dazzled by him when he first came to me. It took a while for me to get over that. Since then he's been teacher, cousin, friend, thorn in my side, bane of my existence." She paused. "And it was Jordan who sent me to you, Marrok."

He frowned. "No, it was Chad Lincoln. I came after you after he recommended you."

"As Jordan said, he has friends at MI6. He pulled strings, and they told Lincoln what to do."

"What's all this about? I don't—"

"You'll have to leave, Mr. Marrok," the nurse said. "The doctor will be here any minute, and I have tests to make before he gets here."

"I told you," Bridget murmured. "Stay close, Marrok."

CHAPTER
20

Devon stared into the darkness of Bridget's hospital room. The atmosphere was so different than it had been only hours ago. Then fear, dread, and guilt had been present every minute. Now there was only infinite gratitude and relief.

"You're smiling." Bridget had opened her eyes. "I'm glad someone is happy. Why didn't you or Marrok keep those doctors from giving me a shot? I didn't want to go to sleep."

"They did it before they let us back in." Devon handed her a cup of crushed ice with a straw. "And a little more sleep didn't hurt you."

"Turn on the light." She took a sip. "How much sleep?"

"About six hours."

"Where's Marrok?"

"He was with you until about fifteen minutes ago. He had to take the dogs for a walk. He should be back soon." She tilted her head. "I can't believe you're looking this well. It's incredible."

Bridget shook her head. "I told you I had a chance. I just had to have help."

Devon was silent a moment. "There's no way to thank you. But I'm going to say it anyway."

"I didn't do it for you. I did it for me. I had to prove that I could change what was going to happen, that I could make a difference. But everything seemed to be going wrong. I was going to give you a gun. I stood beside you so that would be different, too. But in the last minute I knew that there was only one way to stop it from happening."

"You were very brave. And I don't believe you did it entirely for yourself."

"Well, maybe I did it a little bit for you." She paused. "And for Marrok. If Danner had killed you, it would have destroyed everything I've tried to do here. He would have gone berserk."

"Berserk is a strong word."

"He used the word first," Bridget said. "But it's okay now that Danner's dead. No, not okay. There are still so many problems. But we can work it out." She closed her eyes. "Let me rest for a few minutes. When Jordan gets here, I'm going to have to run interference between him and Marrok. It may be a strain, and I'm not in as good shape as I'd like to be. I thought I'd bounce back quicker."

"You're recovering at an amazing rate. And your friend Jordan isn't going to come back until morning."

"He'll be here soon. He knows I want him."

"You're that . . . close?"

"Are you asking if he can read my mind? Sometimes. Probably more than he lets me know."

Would Radkin come? Devon wondered. It wouldn't surprise her. Mind reading, visions, things that went bump in the night. She'd become exposed to all of them lately.

"He's coming." Bridget's lids opened. "He just got off the elevator."

A moment later Jordan Radkin came into the room. "Really, Bridget, you're most impatient."

"We have to take care of Marrok and the dogs."

"Danner is out of the picture. We have a little time."

"We have to move."

His smile suddenly lit his face with surprising warmth. "This is upsetting you. Very well, I'll take care of it. You're a very stubborn—"

"What are you doing here?" Marrok had walked into the room with Ned and Wiley. His gaze went to Bridget. "You're awake. How do you feel?"

"I'll feel better after we finish with this," Bridget said. "What do you intend to do with the dogs now, Marrok?"

"I've made emergency arrangements. I have a place to take them to in Montana until I can work out a better way to protect them. I'm going to tap Sarah Logan and her husband and see if they can find a safe way to work out the problems." He glanced at Radkin. "And he has no need to know anything more about any plans I have."

"Jordan probably knows the exact location of your hideaway and how much you paid for it," Bridget said. "And we have a better idea. Tell him, Jordan."

"Bridget and I could see this day coming, and we made some advance preparations," Radkin said. "I purchased a large piece of property for you on an island in the Caribbean. It will be a perfect place for the dogs . . ." He glanced at Devon. "And there's a small town on the north end of the island that would make living there not totally uncivilized. You could work. I know that's important to you. It will give you both time to catch your breath, and I'll make sure the property is well guarded."

Marrok's gaze narrowed on his face. "Why would you do all that?"

"It's our turn." Radkin smiled. "We've been waiting since you made your deal with MI6 to step in. You weren't ready for us. Bridget says you are now."

"And where is the money coming from?"

"Bridget and I belong to a very old family that has acquired a substantial number of assets over the years. We occasionally invest in projects we consider worthwhile. Your dogs of summer have the potential of meeting that criterion."

"And have enough mystique and hocus-pocus connected to them to make the public friendlier to people like you who aren't exactly normal?" Devon asked.

"Actually, they generally refer to us as freaks when we come to public attention. That's why we try to keep our people beneath the radar."

"I can see that would be more comfortable," Marrok said. "Your offer is a little too generous. What do you want out of this?"

"There's a hospital on Antigua that's only a few hours away. Naturally I'd expect visits there several times a week."

Marrok's lips twisted. "And nothing else?"

"Dammit, we don't want to use you like Lincoln did," Bridget said. "No scumbag missions. We just have to get you far away from here. It's only a matter of time until MI6 is going to rally and send someone else to try to replace Lincoln. And Danner's men knew about the dogs. Someone else may try to make a move. The more people that know, the more dangerous it is."

"And you're doing this out of the goodness of your heart?"

Bridget's hands tightened on the sheet. "No, not me. Purely selfish. I found out that you were making a difference with the dogs. There's not much worthwhile in the world, but that is. I wanted to share in it. I still want to do that. Will you go?"

"Probably not." Marrok looked at Radkin. "I don't like the idea of being your guest."

Devon had heard enough. "Let's get out of here, Marrok. They're going to keep on pushing, and you're going to keep on finding reasons not to do it because you're wary of not being totally in control." She stood up. "You should have known better than to handle it like this, Bridget."

Bridget blinked, then smiled. "Can't you see? I'm in a hospital. I'm sick and not myself."

"We'll talk to you later." Devon headed for the door. "Marrok?"

"Coming." He snapped his fingers for the dogs to come. "At least you didn't snap your fingers for me."

"I got tired of listening to all you high-powered people arguing with each other," she said, as they walked down the hall. "It's all up to you, and no argument is going to make you do something you don't want to do. Where can we go to talk?"

"The park across the street. Ned and Wiley are beginning to think of it as home." He entered the elevator and pressed the button. "And you don't consider yourself high-powered?"

"Maybe. But I'm the only one who doesn't think that they know what's best. I don't know what the heck is right or wrong. I just want you and the dogs to be safe." They were at the front entrance and, a moment later, started across the street. "For the first time since Paco died, you have a chance for a fresh start. But it shouldn't be Bridget's way or Jordan's way, or even Sarah's way. It should be your way."

He smiled faintly. "You seem to be very passionate about this."

"I am passionate. About you, for you. I can't be any other way."

"And I thank God for it." His voice was soft as he took her hand. "Every day, every minute."

"What do you expect? I told you once that I couldn't choose anyone more suitable to take care of the **shi'i'go.** You gave up years of your life, you risked death, you cared for those dogs with love. You're pretty damn perfect for the job. So no one is going to tell you what to do." She sat down on a park bench beneath a street-light. "You tell us."

"You don't have to be so fierce. I wasn't being intimidated by Bridget and Radkin."

"But they were talking about how good it would be for me. I don't enter into this, Marrok."

"You enter into it. You tend to dominate it." He sat down beside her and Ned and Wiley curled up at his feet. He bent down and stroked Ned's head. "But you'd tar and feather me if I made the wrong decision for these guys."

"You're damn right I would." She leaned back on the bench. "So don't think of a cozy little town in the Caribbean for me. Think what would be best."

"I've been thinking since you whisked me out of that hospital room."

"Is it that you don't trust Bridget and Radkin?"

"I have to trust Bridget. She almost gave her life for you. I'm a little suspicious of this family business that's feeling so generous to me." He shrugged. "Radkin? Why should I trust him? But I dealt with Lincoln for years and didn't trust him."

"And rightly so. Then it's a possible lack of control?"

"Yes. But I could probably get around that. The first thing I'd do would be to jettison Radkin's guards and bring my own people."

She smiled. "And build a stockade as strong as the ranch."

"Stronger. And if it's an island, there would have to be sea and air escape routes."

He was already planning, thinking, working out the details. "What about Montana? How does that compare?"

"Closer. Familiar. I'm better able to negotiate the system. But I'd have to either let MI6 in again for funding or seek other help. But I could probably still keep the dogs safe."

"Then make your decision."

"What a pushy broad you are." He gazed at her. "It really doesn't matter to you, does it?"

"I'll go with you anywhere, anytime." She smiled. "I like the snow. I like the sun. Wherever you decide, we'll make it good."

"What a remarkably lucky man I am." He cupped her face in his two hands. "Have I told you that I love you?"

"No, but I knew it. You talked around it a lot, and I knew it was hard for you to come right out and say it." She gave him a quick kiss. "More of that later. Now you have to concentrate on more important things."

"There's nothing more important, just more urgent." He kissed her again and pulled her to her feet. "Come on, let's get back to Bridget. I wouldn't want her to have a relapse."

She fell into step with him. "She's still strong enough to nag you."

"But you'll be there to ward them both off and protect me. You can't imagine how secure that makes me feel."

"Sarcastic bastard." She punched him in the arm. "You don't deserve me."

"I know," he said soberly. "That's why I have to joke about it."

She could feel her throat tighten with emotion. She reached down and patted Wiley's head. "And do you have something to tell Bridget?"

"Yes."

"Which is it? Snow or sun?"

"I grew up in the desert." He smiled. "What do you suppose? It has to be the sun."

CHAPTER 21

Six months later

An island in the Caribbean

"I believe I'm jealous, Devon," Bridget said as she got off the helicopter at the pad a short distance from the white plantation house. "I just got back from Dublin, and the weather was less than balmy."

"That's Marrok's main complaint." Devon smiled as she gave Bridget a hug. "He says the weather is too perfect. When he talks about sun, he wants hot and searing to the bone."

"Where is he?"

"At the cottages. He's trying to negotiate a treaty between Janet and Sid. They don't agree on anything but Wiley. He said he'd meet us at the garden." She studied her. "You look very fit."

Bridget made a face. "It took forever to get back on my feet. Tell Marrok that his **shi'i'go** hocus-pocus is pretty slow going."

"What do you expect? You were at death's door. Maybe beyond it. Are you going to stay the night?"

Bridget shook her head. "No, the helicopter is supposed to pick me up in an hour. I have to get back to Dublin. Jordan wants me to go to Paris."

"So naturally you'll do it," Devon said.

"It's my job." She started across the stretch of lush green grass toward the house. "Just as Marrok was my job. How is he?"

"Starting to get bored and restless. It was fine while he was busy setting up his stockade here. But you know Marrok, he needs a challenge."

"How about you?"

"Between taking care of the dogs, starting a new practice in town, and dealing with Marrok, I'm not lacking in challenges."

Bridget studied her. "You don't seem too harried. I've never seen anyone look so mellow."

"No?" Devon smiled. "I'm not ready to settle down either. But this period has been good for both of us. Why did you come? Just to check on your family's investment?"

"Partly. Partly to close unfinished business." She gestured to the envelope she was carrying. "And to give this to Marrok."

Devon gestured. "Well, there he is." Marrok was standing on the patio talking to Nick Gilroy and gesturing at the dogs running on the grounds a short distance away. "Marrok likes to alter the exercise regimes for the dogs every other day. It may be good for them, but it's driving Nick crazy."

"I can see Marrok has too much time on his hands," Bridget murmured. "I think we may have to save him from himself."

Marrok turned to face them as Nick strolled down the steps and moved toward the dogs. "Bridget." He took her hands. "You look well. Why are you here?"

"Nothing like being abrupt." Bridget's gaze was on the dogs. "That's quite a pack. Gracie is running with them. And there are several other dogs."

"Why not?" Marrok said. "We wanted to see if the **shi'i'go** dogs had the same effect on other dogs as they did on Sarah Logan's Monty."

"And have they?"

"Only time will tell, but Devon said their checkups show an astonishing increase in strength and vitality."

"I'm surprised Sarah let you bring Addie with you."

Marrok smiled. "I told her that we had to test her dogs sometime. If Monty and the others showed any sign of a decline when I took Addie away, I promised her I'd bring Addie back to her. Monty and Maggie have remained as strong as ever."

"Then the effect is permanent."

"Again, only time will tell. The outlook is leaning toward positive."

"Good heavens, you sound like a scientist."

"I feel like one." Marrok grimaced. "All I need is a clipboard and horn-rimmed glasses."

"Sit down," Devon said. "Have a glass of iced tea."

Bridget sat down at the table shaded by a turquoise umbrella. "Thanks. I'm thirsty, and I have a lot of talking to do."

Devon poured her a glass of tea. "Catching up? We've been doing most of the talking."

"What are Sarah and John Logan doing to legally protect the dogs?"

"Mostly exploratory work so far," Marrok said as he dropped into a chair. "John says that he has to have the right people in place before he even starts to leak any information about the **shi'i'go.**"

"That's smart," Bridget said. "Particularly since he doesn't have all the information himself."

"He does." Marrok's gaze flew to her face. "I told Sarah and John everything. I couldn't expect cooperation unless I gave it."

"My, my, how you've changed," Bridget said. "Your influence, Devon?"

"More tea?" Devon asked.

"You're being diplomatic." Bridget grinned. "And I do think that it's your influence." She leaned back in her chair and gazed out at the mountains. "Or maybe it's this place. Everything seems . . . easy here. Soft breezes, sun, blue sky . . ."

"Why did you come?" Marrok interrupted. "I know you, Bridget. You never do anything without a reason."

"Maybe I want to hit you up for a job."

He shook his head. "I'd give it to you. But I don't think that's why you came."

"No." She made a face. "I came because Jordan said that it's up to me to tell you a story."

"What story?"

"One that you're probably not going to believe, not at first." She was silent. "So let's play the suppose game." She kept her eyes on the green mountains. "Suppose that your mother, Catrin Munoz, was a member of our family. Not close. She belonged to a distant but very important branch. She was shallow, unstable, and wild as a hawk, but other members of her immediate family were more responsible. When she came back to Madrid after deserting you, her brother, Rico, decided it would be wise to keep an eye on you."

"I'm already tired of your game," Marrok said harshly. "It's a lie. She left me, and there was no kindly uncle, Rico, watching over me."

"I never said Rico was kindly. He was only a cut above your mother in character. But he did know that there was danger in Catrin's casting her seed about indiscriminately. So he hired someone to keep an eye on you to make sure there was no fallout from Catrin's promiscuity. His orders were not to interfere unless you became a problem."

"A problem?" Devon echoed. "He didn't consider having his nephew being brought up by a dope addict a problem? What kind of scumbag was he?"

"I told you, not a nice guy," Bridget said. "He didn't care about Marrok as long as the kid didn't interfere with his lifestyle. What he didn't want was having the core family angry enough to cut him off from funds when he needed them."

"I could hardly have interfered with someone half a world away," Marrok said sarcastically. "Though if I'd known what an ass he was, I might have tried."

"Those were the reports Rico was getting about you, violent, erratic, unstable. Even as a child you were reckless and striking out at all comers. Nothing to upset Rico or make him uncomfortable. That wasn't what he was worried about." She paused. "But then he received another report. A local shaman, Paco, had taken you in and was training you. That disturbed him."

"You mean that for the first time in his life someone had been kind to Marrok?" Devon asked tartly.

"No, he was afraid Paco might have seen something in him. After all, Paco was a mystic. It was possible. Rico felt that he was out of his depth and sent a report to London to our people there telling them about Catrin's indiscretion. They took it very seriously and sent a man to Arizona, Edmund Gillem, to see Paco. He had to be warned. But your Paco had already seen the danger in you and still wanted to keep you with him. You'd been with him two years and still not shown any signs, so Edmund Gillem told Paco to call on him if there was a problem. Paco seemed to be handling you as well as anyone could, considering your temperament. We didn't hear from Paco again, but we still kept a close eye on you."

"This is bull, Bridget," Marrok said impatiently. "Peddle your story somewhere else. Paco would have told me about this so-called visit."

"Would he? He was terribly excited. Paco was curious; he loved to explore the unknown. You've always told me that. Now he had something interesting to experiment with. He probably told himself he had seen it in you all along."

"Seen what?"

Bridget smiled. "Haven't you guessed? **Shi'i'go.** Summer."

Devon inhaled sharply. "What are you talking about?"

"Catrin Munoz's bloodline had a history of producing individuals with a very rare talent. Not every generation, perhaps only one, or two in the four hundred years we've been documenting her family. None in the last two centuries."

"**Shi'i'go**," Devon repeated. "Get to the bottom line, Bridget."

"Healers. Extraordinarily powerful. And everyone close to them seemed to have glowing health and vitality. Probably one of the reasons the members of the family flourished and lived very long lives in a time when that wasn't common." Bridget took a sip of her tea. "Though the two men who possessed the talent both died violent deaths. The Munoz men were not the tamest offspring our family has produced. You wonder if they would still be around now if their lives had not been cut short."

"Wait a minute." Devon was trying to make sense of this. "You're saying that the dogs have no ability to heal?"

"No, the dogs can heal. That's been proved by those visits to the hospital. It just didn't start with a panacea created by Paco. There was never a panacea. It was always Marrok."

Marrok shook his head. "Paco had me feed the dogs the panacea."

"No panacea," Bridget said quietly. "You fed them, but you also petted them, you touched them, you lived with them. You gave them your strength. Just as they later gave it to those patients in the hospital. **Shi'i'go**."

"Bullshit."

"I didn't think you'd accept it easily. The transfer doesn't seem to happen with people. It must be because there's an inherent healing ability in dogs anyway. Some people call it psychological, but it does exist. Ask nurses and doctors in any hospital. The dogs are strong but not nearly as strong as you. It's diluted in them. Why else did Paco make you come with him when he took Ned to visit a dying patient? He knew that he'd need you. It was a gamble with the dogs but not with you. And when Lincoln sent you on the missions with Ned, weren't you near them, touching every patient? I think Paco must have first noticed your effect on the dogs. They weren't aging, they were growing in strength. Then he started experimenting." She looked him in the eyes. "It's true, Marrok."

"What you believe is truth. Paco **told** Danner it was the dogs." His hand clenched into a fist on the table. "He was being beaten to death, and he told him it was the dogs."

"To protect you. He loved you. So he sacrificed the dogs. But he loved the dogs, too, and wanted to make it right. He told you that you had to protect them, didn't he?"

"Yes."

"And you did, Marrok," she said softly. "All

these years, you did. You put aside everything, you grew, you worked and became a very special human being that had nothing to do with **shi'i'go**." She got to her feet. "I've got to get back to the helicopter pad. It's almost time."

Marrok stood up. "I don't believe any of this, you know."

"You believe some of it. After it sinks in you'll believe more." She handed him the envelope. "It's the family tree of the Munoz family. I had it copied. I thought you might want it."

"Why didn't you tell him before?" Devon asked. "Why wait until now?"

"Do you know how much power a healer has? It's staggering. Misused, it could create chaos, sway the fate of countries as Lincoln was having you do. It would inspire worship or hatred depending on what side of the fence you are on. When Marrok was a boy, he hated the whole world. If he'd had power then, it would have been a disaster. Later, as he matured, it became better, but there was still that streak of bitterness and violence. He had to work his way through it." She started across the patio. "I think I hear the rotors of the helicopter. Are they close, Marrok?"

"Yes, five minutes to the south," he said absently. "And I don't like the idea of you and your precious family treating me as if I couldn't make decisions for myself."

"We just wanted to make sure they were the right decisions. You had a fondness for death and mayhem." She smiled. "And it's your family, too . . . cousin."

He thought about it. Then he smiled faintly. "As long as I can pick and choose. You wouldn't be too bad as a relation."

"Don't turn your back on Jordan and the others. You may need all the help you can get. Devon said she thought you needed a challenge. I just handed you a king-size one. The dogs may be safer because there was no panacea, but you're going to be faced with monumental decisions. You can't heal everyone, and there will be people who will hate you for not being able to do it."

He scowled. "If I even believe a tenth of what you're telling me."

"But you'll have to experiment, you'll have to find out what's truth and what's not. That's your nature." She started across the stretch of lawn, then stopped and turned around. "I've only run into one other healer, but if you need help, call me, and I'll put you in touch with him. I hear he wasn't any happier than you about discovering that talent." She smiled. "Good-bye. Next time I come, I promise it will be a social occasion." She turned and walked rapidly toward the descending helicopter.

"I'm . . . stunned," Devon said as she watched her. "It's plausible, but I'm still having to turn my thinking around."

"Don't be too quick. I haven't seen any proof."

And he didn't want it to be true, Devon thought. Who could blame him? The responsibility would be staggering, and there was still too much of the wild, reckless Marrok in him to accept it calmly.

Calm? No way. Not Marrok.

"And this may not be proof either. May I?" She took the envelope from him and opened it. She studied the paper and handed it to him. "Only a family tree as Bridget said. Very carefully documented for the Munoz branch of a Devanez family. Your name is on it."

His lips lifted in a crooked smile. "You mean the bad penny was actually acknowledged at last?"

"Acknowledged? If Bridget is right, you may well be the superstar."

"Disgusting." He grimaced. "I don't want to be a superstar. I want to be left alone."

"Then ignore everything Bridget told you." She turned and started walking toward where the dogs were playing. "Look how beautiful they are. Gracie's coat is shinier than I've ever seen it. She's very happy here."

"You're changing the subject."

"Yes. I'm going to start accepting search and rescue missions again next month. Bridget says Gracie gets upset on the missions. May I take Ned?"

"Of course. I may go with you."

She shook her head. "You'll be too busy." She stooped and patted Ned, who had run up to her. "Because you're not going to be able to ignore what Bridget said. You'll be reaching out, searching, experimenting, just as your Paco did. Bridget says it's your nature, but I think Paco gave it to you as a gift." She picked up a large twig and threw it with all her strength. Ned took off, and the other dogs raced after him. "Just as he gave you his dogs. He may have wanted you to save them, but he wanted them to help you, too. He wanted them to give you something he thought you needed."

Marrok watched the dogs running joyously, muscles flexing, tails pluming in the bright sunlight.

He took Devon's hand. "**Shi'i'go?**"

She nodded. "In the very best sense." Her grasp tightened on his. "Summer."

LIKE WHAT YOU'VE SEEN?

If you enjoyed this large print edition of
DARK SUMMER, here are a few of Iris Johansen's
latest bestsellers also available in large print.

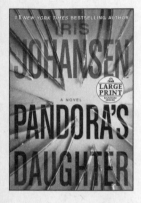

PANDORA'S DAUGHTER
(paperback)
978-0-7393-2753-1 • 0-7393-2753-4
$25.95/$34.00C

STALEMATE
(hardcover)
978-0-7393-2596-4 • 0-7393-2596-5
$28.95/$35.95C

KILLER DREAMS
(hardcover)
978-0-7393-2595-7 • 0-7393-2595-7
$28.00/$37.00C

ON THE RUN
(hardcover)
978-0-7393-2594-0 • 0-7393-2594-9
$28.00/$40.00C

Large print books are available wherever books
are sold and at many local libraries.

All prices are subject to change. Check with your
local retailer for current pricing and availability.
For more information on these and other large print titles,
visit www.randomhouse.com/largeprint.